THE MONTAGUE TWINS

THE WITCH'S HAND

NATHAN PAGE AND DREW SHANNON

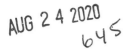

ALFRED A. KNOPF
NEW YORK

THIS IS A BORZOI BOOK PUBLISHED BY ALFRED A. KNOPF

Library of Congress Cataloging-in-Publication Data
Names: Page, Nathan, author. | Shannon, Drew, illustrator.
Title: The witch's hand / Nathan Page and Drew Shannon.
Description: First edition. | New York : Alfred A. Knopf, 2020. | Series: The Montague Twins ; volume #1 | Summary: Orphaned teens Pete and Al Montague and their adopted sister, Charlie, already known for solving mysteries in their small New England town, begin studying magic as they investigate a disappearance connected to a seventeenth-century witch.
Identifiers: LCCN 2018048652| ISBN 978-0-525-64676-1 (hardcover) | ISBN 978-0-525-64677-8 (pbk.) | ISBN 978-0-525-64679-2 (ebook)
Subjects: LCSH: Graphic novels. | CYAC: Graphic novels. | Brothers and sisters—Fiction. | Twins—Fiction. | Supernatural—Fiction. | Magic—Fiction. | Mystery and detective stories.
Classification: LCC PZ7.1.P33 Cur 2020 | DDC [Fic]—dc23

The artwork for *The Montague Twins* was created with traditional and digital drawing techniques.

MANUFACTURED IN CHINA
July 2020
10 9 8 7 6 5 4 3 2 1

First Edition

We would like to dedicate this book to our families.

—NATHAN AND DREW

CHAPTER 1

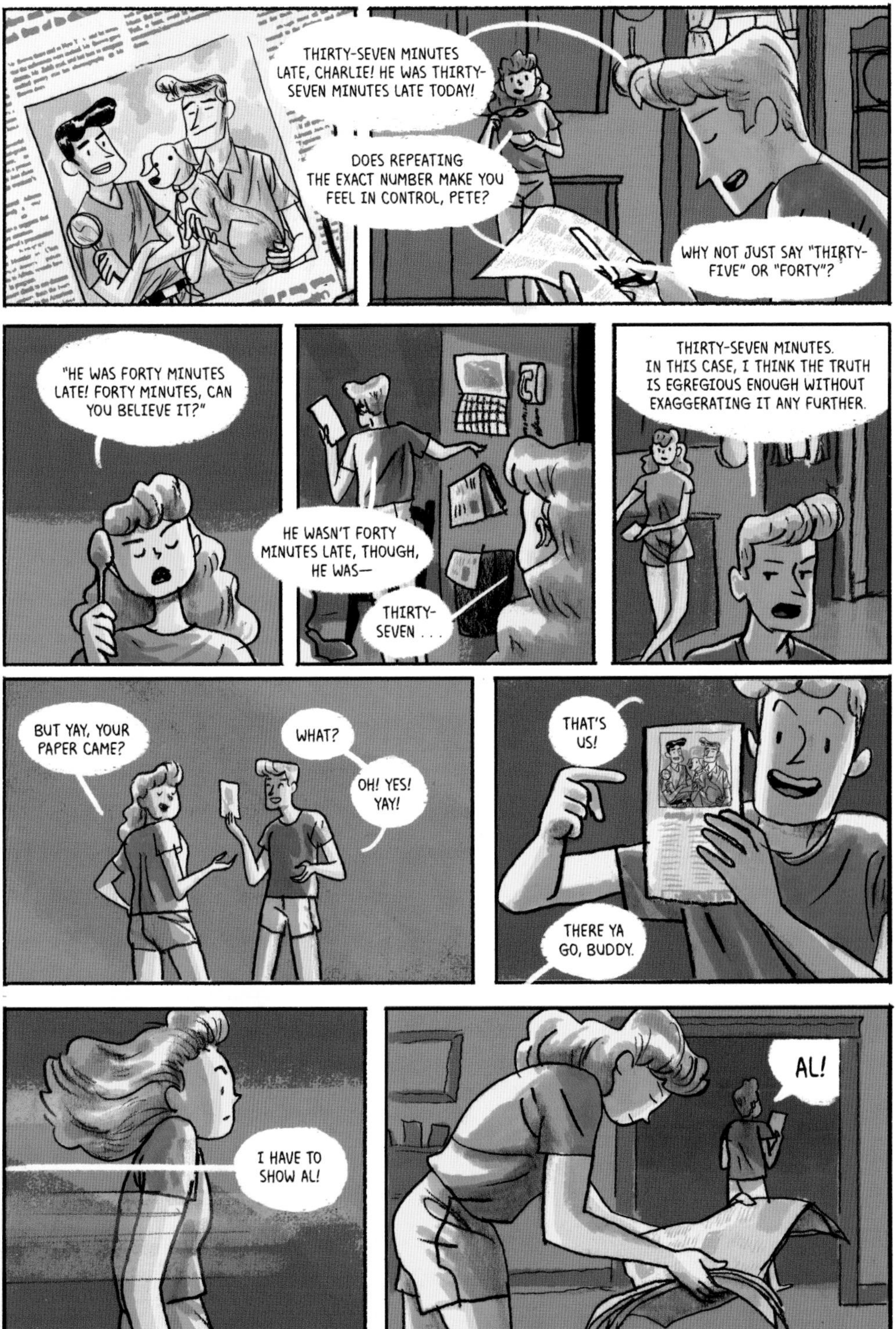
THIRTY-SEVEN MINUTES LATE, CHARLIE! HE WAS THIRTY-SEVEN MINUTES LATE TODAY!
DOES REPEATING THE EXACT NUMBER MAKE YOU FEEL IN CONTROL, PETE?
WHY NOT JUST SAY "THIRTY-FIVE" OR "FORTY"?
"HE WAS FORTY MINUTES LATE! FORTY MINUTES, CAN YOU BELIEVE IT?"
HE WASN'T FORTY MINUTES LATE, THOUGH, HE WAS—
THIRTY-SEVEN . . .
THIRTY-SEVEN MINUTES. IN THIS CASE, I THINK THE TRUTH IS EGREGIOUS ENOUGH WITHOUT EXAGGERATING IT ANY FURTHER.
BUT YAY, YOUR PAPER CAME?
WHAT?
OH! YES! YAY!
THAT'S US!
THERE YA GO, BUDDY.
I HAVE TO SHOW AL!
AL!

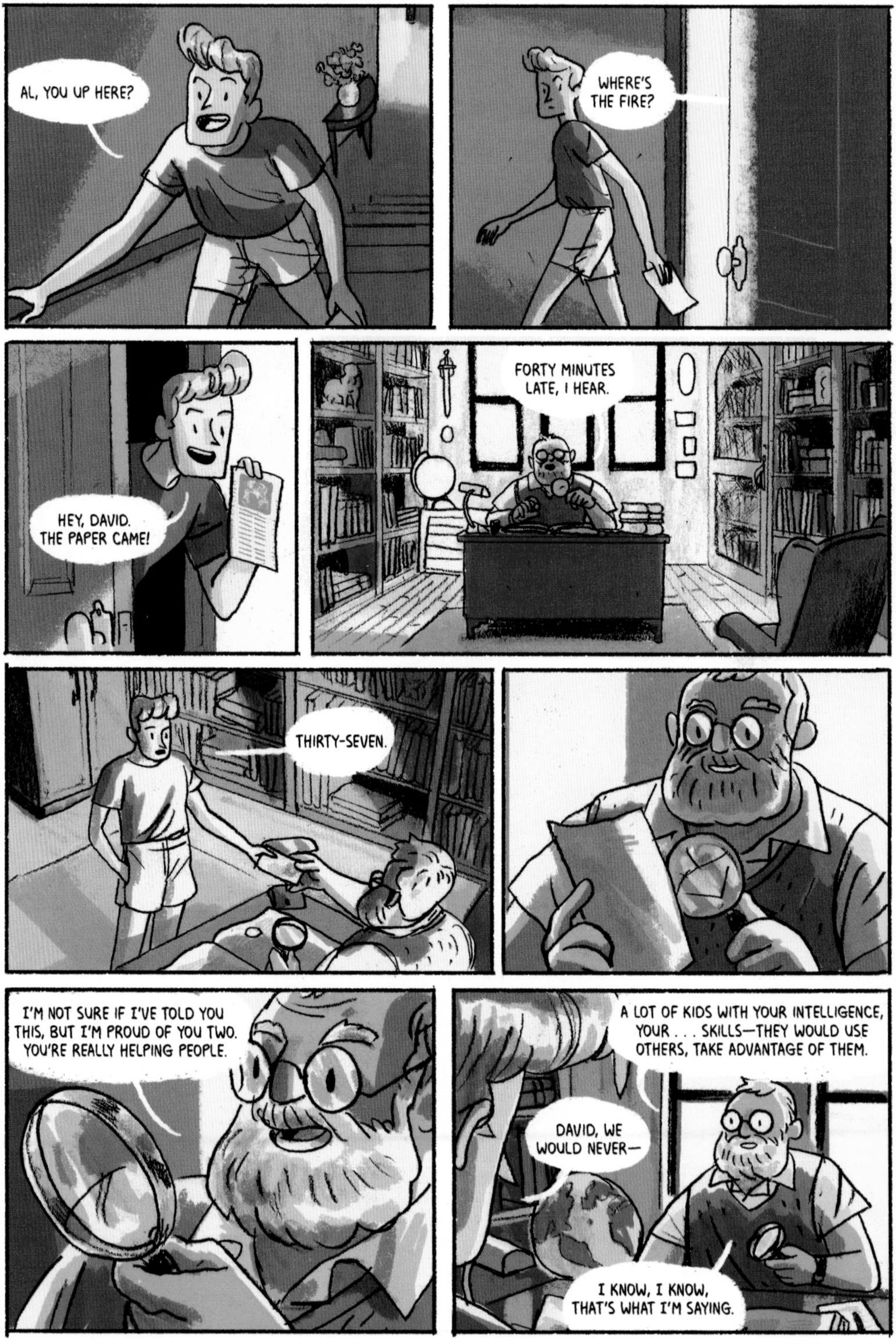
AL, YOU UP HERE?
WHERE'S THE FIRE?
HEY, DAVID. THE PAPER CAME!
FORTY MINUTES LATE, I HEAR.
THIRTY-SEVEN.
I'M NOT SURE IF I'VE TOLD YOU THIS, BUT I'M PROUD OF YOU TWO. YOU'RE REALLY HELPING PEOPLE.
A LOT OF KIDS WITH YOUR INTELLIGENCE, YOUR . . . SKILLS—THEY WOULD USE OTHERS, TAKE ADVANTAGE OF THEM.
DAVID, WE WOULD NEVER—
I KNOW, I KNOW, THAT'S WHAT I'M SAYING.

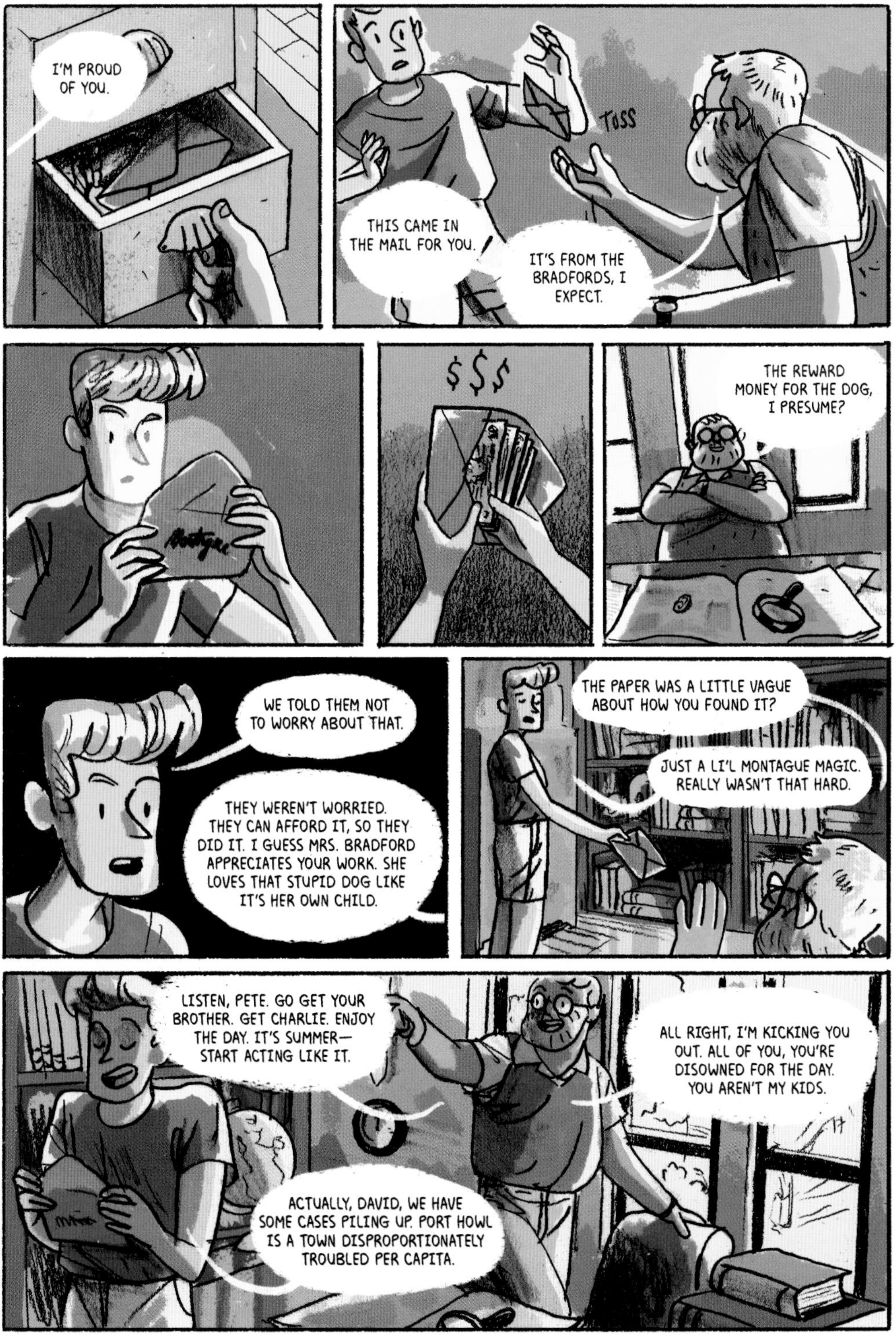
I'M PROUD OF YOU.
THIS CAME IN THE MAIL FOR YOU.
TOSS
IT'S FROM THE BRADFORDS, I EXPECT.
$$$
THE REWARD MONEY FOR THE DOG, I PRESUME?
WE TOLD THEM NOT TO WORRY ABOUT THAT.
THEY WEREN'T WORRIED. THEY CAN AFFORD IT, SO THEY DID IT. I GUESS MRS. BRADFORD APPRECIATES YOUR WORK. SHE LOVES THAT STUPID DOG LIKE IT'S HER OWN CHILD.
THE PAPER WAS A LITTLE VAGUE ABOUT HOW YOU FOUND IT?
JUST A LI'L MONTAGUE MAGIC. REALLY WASN'T THAT HARD.
LISTEN, PETE. GO GET YOUR BROTHER. GET CHARLIE. ENJOY THE DAY. IT'S SUMMER—START ACTING LIKE IT.
ALL RIGHT, I'M KICKING YOU OUT. ALL OF YOU, YOU'RE DISOWNED FOR THE DAY. YOU AREN'T MY KIDS.
ACTUALLY, DAVID, WE HAVE SOME CASES PILING UP. PORT HOWL IS A TOWN DISPROPORTIONATELY TROUBLED PER CAPITA.

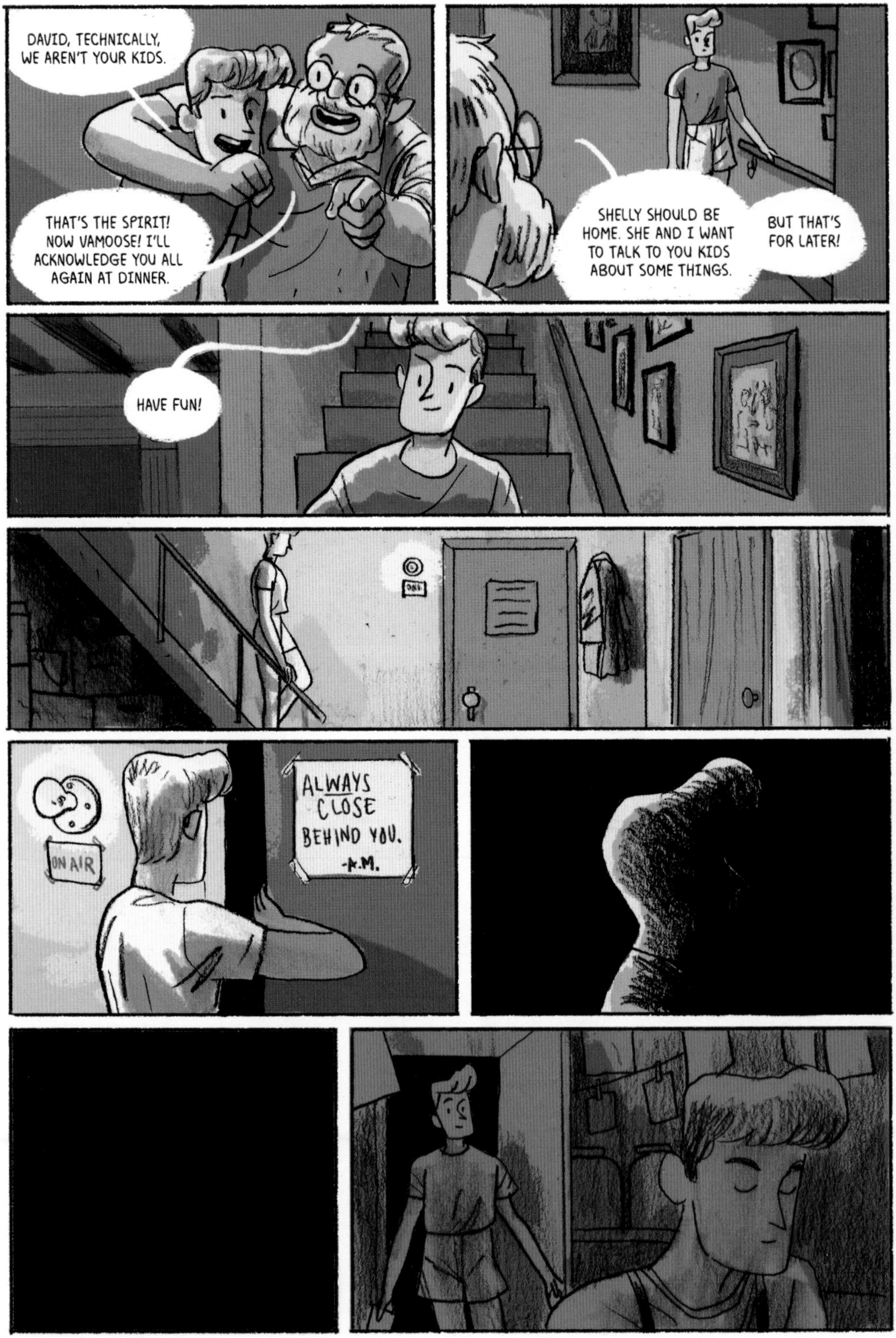
DAVID, TECHNICALLY, WE AREN'T YOUR KIDS.
THAT'S THE SPIRIT! NOW VAMOOSE! I'LL ACKNOWLEDGE YOU ALL AGAIN AT DINNER.
SHELLY SHOULD BE HOME. SHE AND I WANT TO TALK TO YOU KIDS ABOUT SOME THINGS.
BUT THAT'S FOR LATER!
HAVE FUN!
ON AIR
ALWAYS CLOSE BEHIND YOU. -A.M.

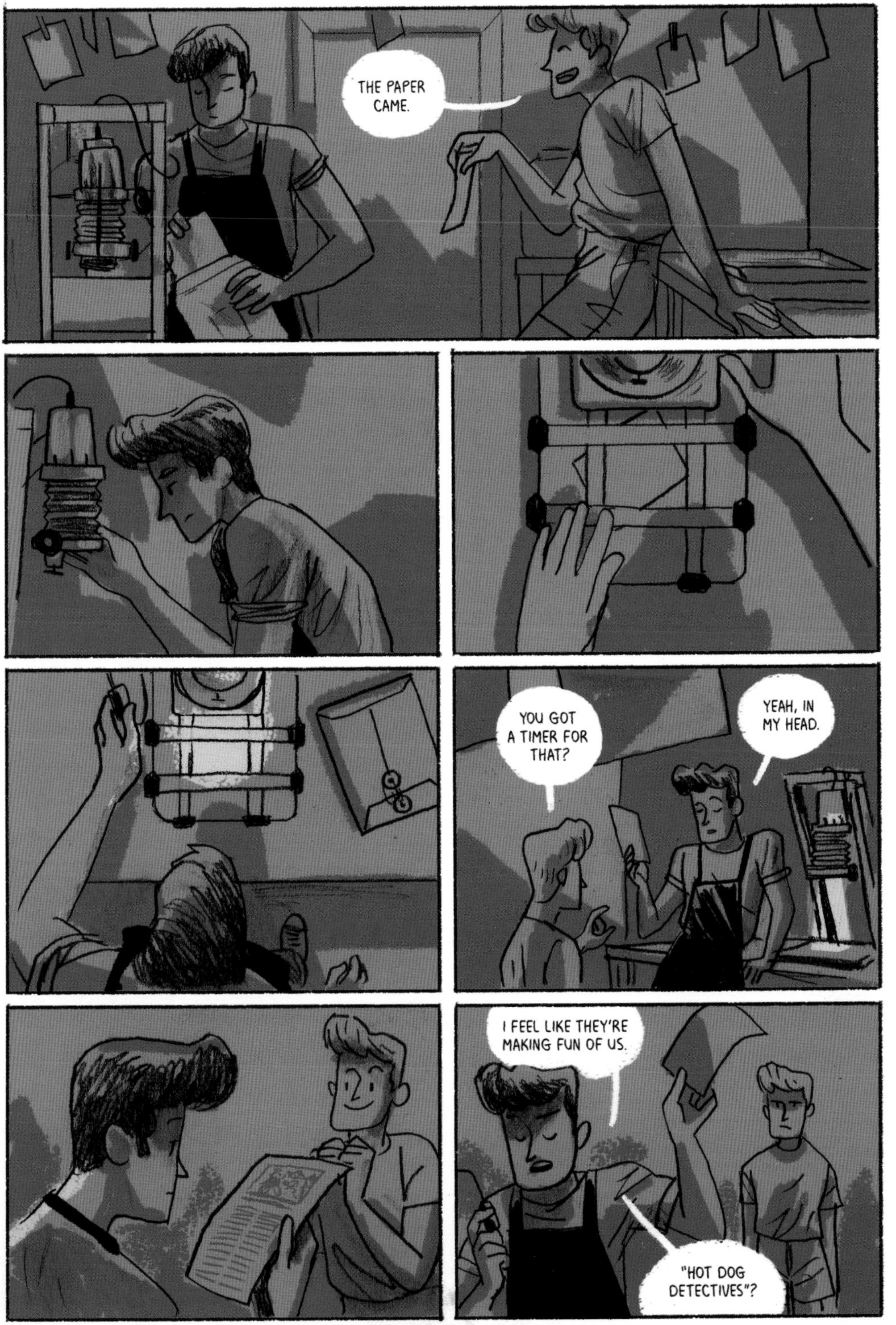
THE PAPER CAME.
YOU GOT A TIMER FOR THAT?
YEAH, IN MY HEAD.
I FEEL LIKE THEY'RE MAKING FUN OF US.
"HOT DOG DETECTIVES"?

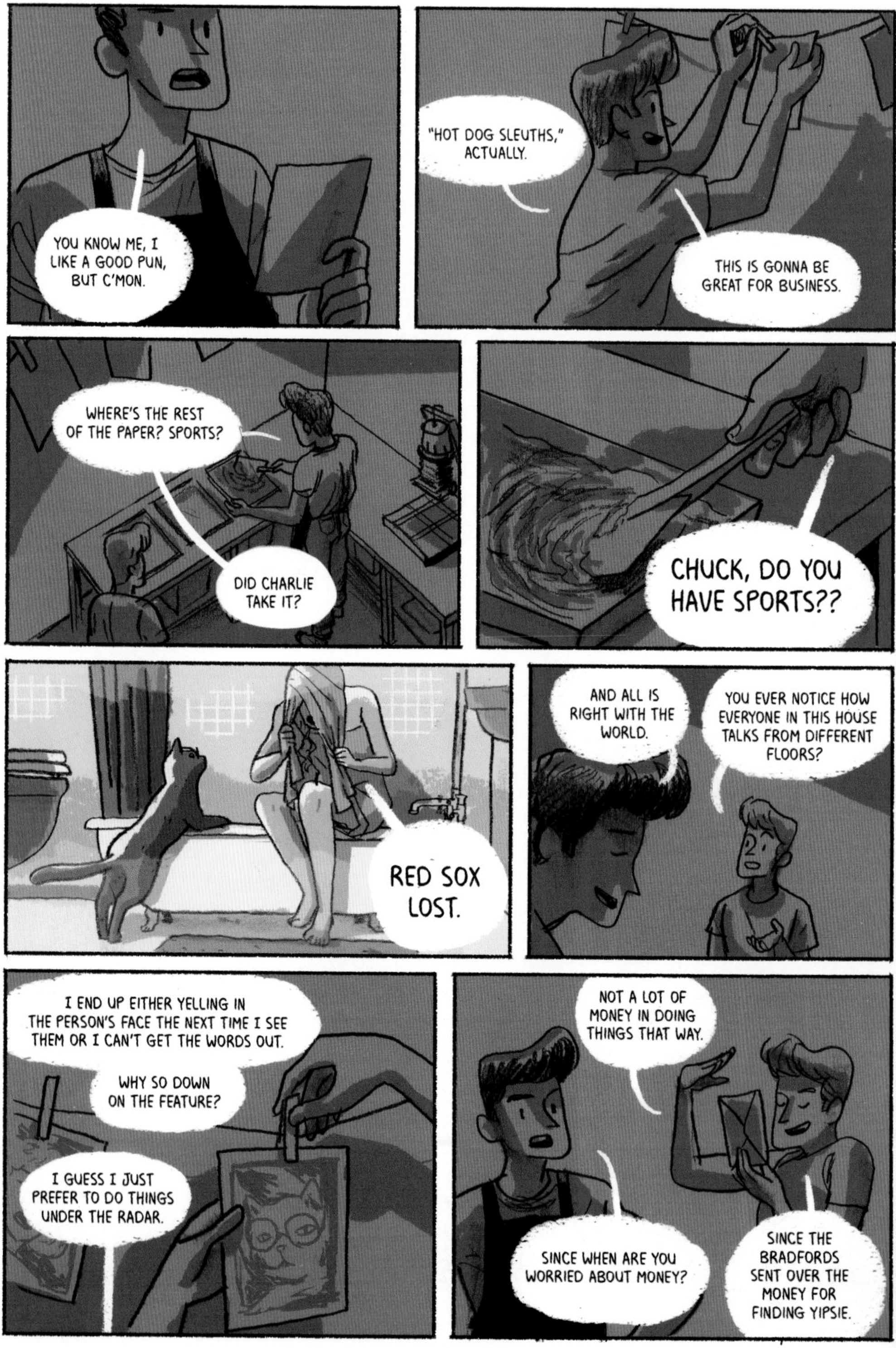
YOU KNOW ME, I LIKE A GOOD PUN, BUT C'MON.
"HOT DOG SLEUTHS," ACTUALLY.
THIS IS GONNA BE GREAT FOR BUSINESS.
WHERE'S THE REST OF THE PAPER? SPORTS?
DID CHARLIE TAKE IT?
CHUCK, DO YOU HAVE SPORTS??
RED SOX LOST.
AND ALL IS RIGHT WITH THE WORLD.
YOU EVER NOTICE HOW EVERYONE IN THIS HOUSE TALKS FROM DIFFERENT FLOORS?
I END UP EITHER YELLING IN THE PERSON'S FACE THE NEXT TIME I SEE THEM OR I CAN'T GET THE WORDS OUT.
WHY SO DOWN ON THE FEATURE?
I GUESS I JUST PREFER TO DO THINGS UNDER THE RADAR.
NOT A LOT OF MONEY IN DOING THINGS THAT WAY.
SINCE WHEN ARE YOU WORRIED ABOUT MONEY?
SINCE THE BRADFORDS SENT OVER THE MONEY FOR FINDING YIPSIE.

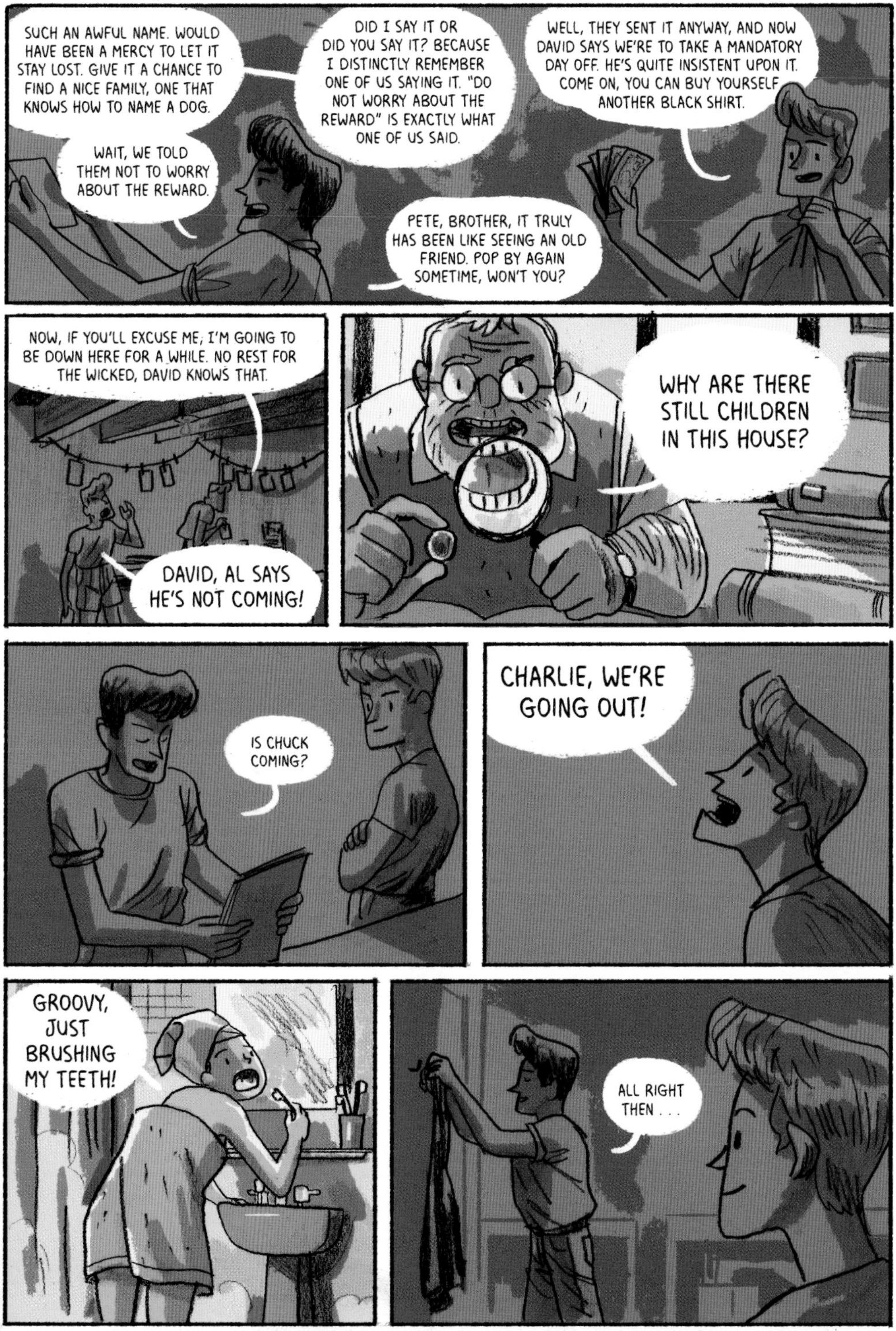
SUCH AN AWFUL NAME. WOULD HAVE BEEN A MERCY TO LET IT STAY LOST. GIVE IT A CHANCE TO FIND A NICE FAMILY, ONE THAT KNOWS HOW TO NAME A DOG.
WAIT, WE TOLD THEM NOT TO WORRY ABOUT THE REWARD.
DID I SAY IT OR DID YOU SAY IT? BECAUSE I DISTINCTLY REMEMBER ONE OF US SAYING IT. "DO NOT WORRY ABOUT THE REWARD" IS EXACTLY WHAT ONE OF US SAID.
PETE, BROTHER, IT TRULY HAS BEEN LIKE SEEING AN OLD FRIEND. POP BY AGAIN SOMETIME, WON'T YOU?
WELL, THEY SENT IT ANYWAY, AND NOW DAVID SAYS WE'RE TO TAKE A MANDATORY DAY OFF. HE'S QUITE INSISTENT UPON IT. COME ON, YOU CAN BUY YOURSELF ANOTHER BLACK SHIRT.
NOW, IF YOU'LL EXCUSE ME, I'M GOING TO BE DOWN HERE FOR A WHILE. NO REST FOR THE WICKED, DAVID KNOWS THAT.
DAVID, AL SAYS HE'S NOT COMING!
WHY ARE THERE STILL CHILDREN IN THIS HOUSE?
IS CHUCK COMING?
CHARLIE, WE'RE GOING OUT!
GROOVY, JUST BRUSHING MY TEETH!
ALL RIGHT THEN . . .

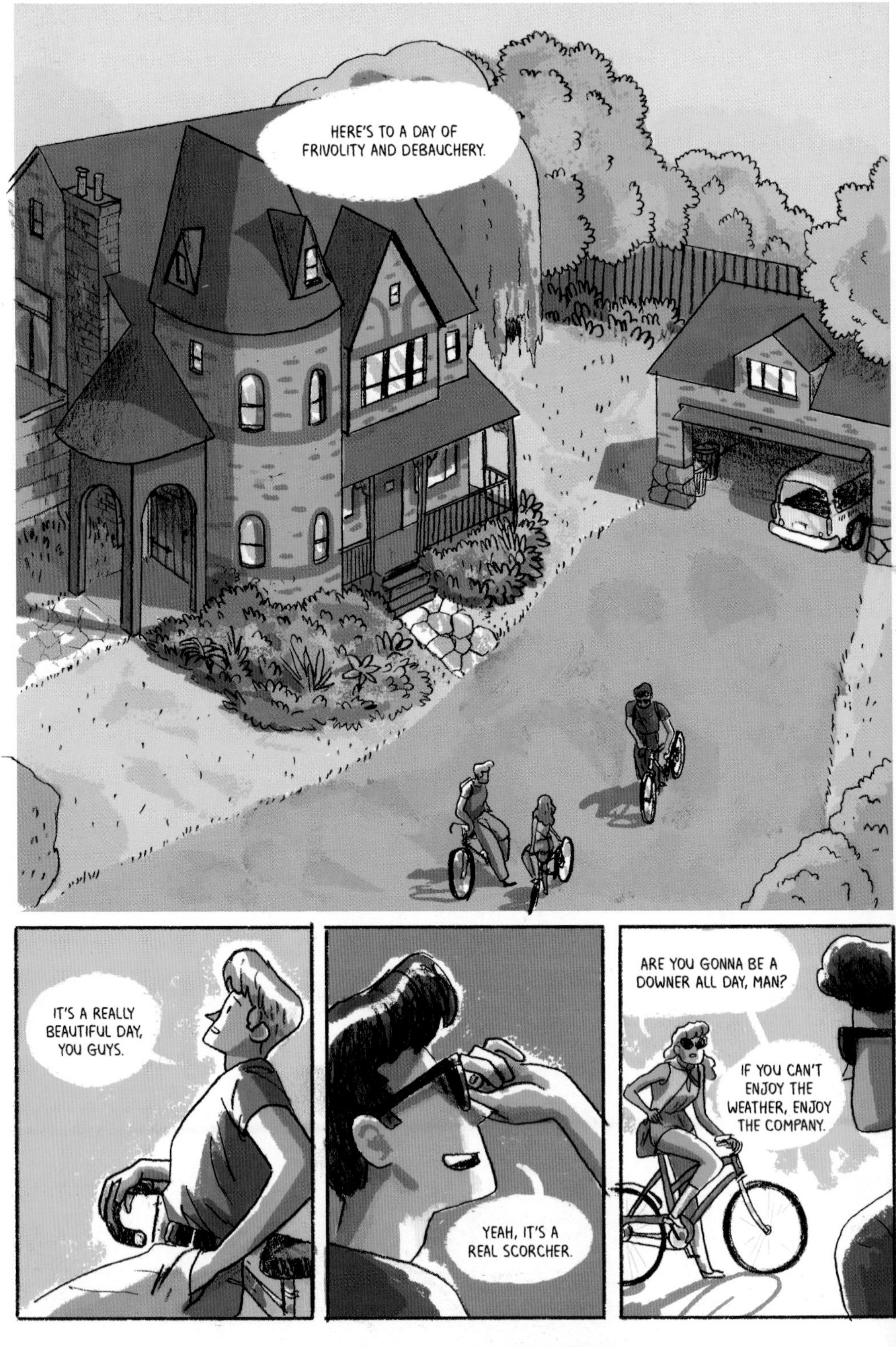
HERE'S TO A DAY OF FRIVOLITY AND DEBAUCHERY.
IT'S A REALLY BEAUTIFUL DAY, YOU GUYS.
YEAH, IT'S A REAL SCORCHER.
ARE YOU GONNA BE A DOWNER ALL DAY, MAN?
IF YOU CAN'T ENJOY THE WEATHER, ENJOY THE COMPANY.

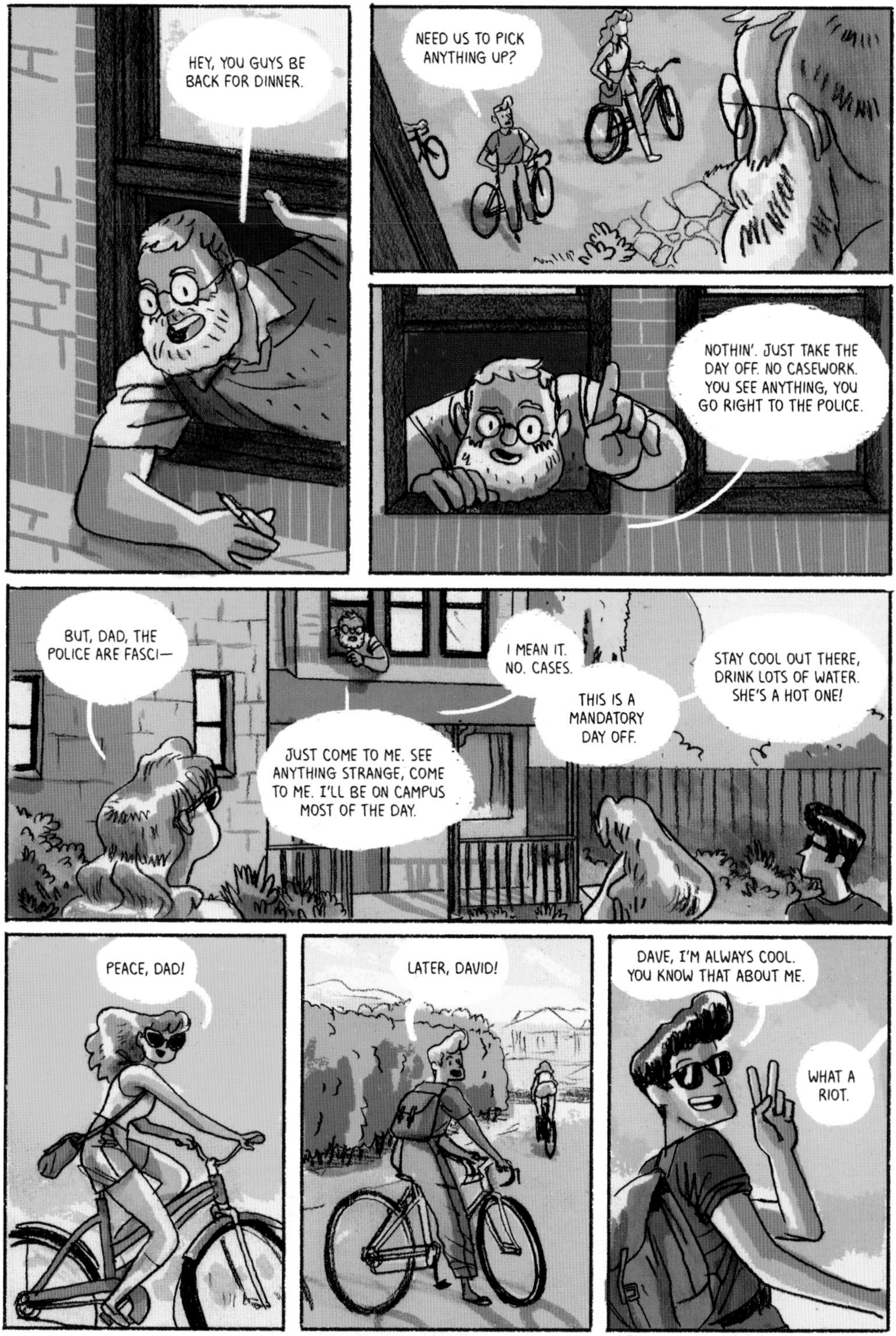
HEY, YOU GUYS BE BACK FOR DINNER.
NEED US TO PICK ANYTHING UP?
NOTHIN'. JUST TAKE THE DAY OFF. NO CASEWORK. YOU SEE ANYTHING, YOU GO RIGHT TO THE POLICE.
BUT, DAD, THE POLICE ARE FASCI—
JUST COME TO ME. SEE ANYTHING STRANGE, COME TO ME. I'LL BE ON CAMPUS MOST OF THE DAY.
I MEAN IT. NO. CASES.
THIS IS A MANDATORY DAY OFF.
STAY COOL OUT THERE, DRINK LOTS OF WATER. SHE'S A HOT ONE!
PEACE, DAD!
LATER, DAVID!
DAVE, I'M ALWAYS COOL. YOU KNOW THAT ABOUT ME.
WHAT A RIOT.

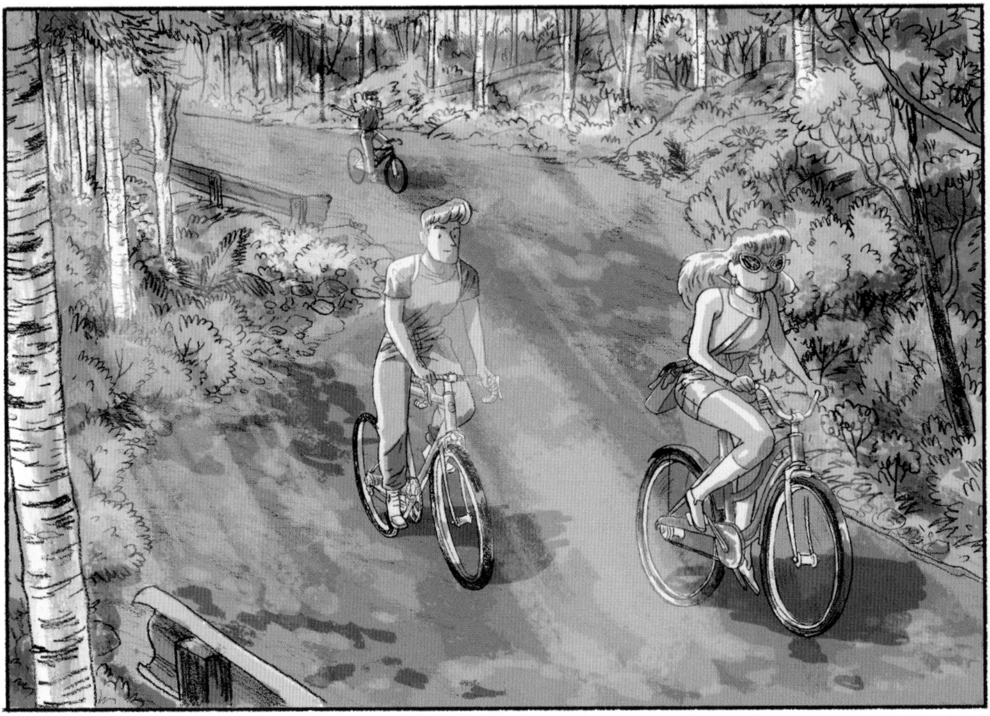

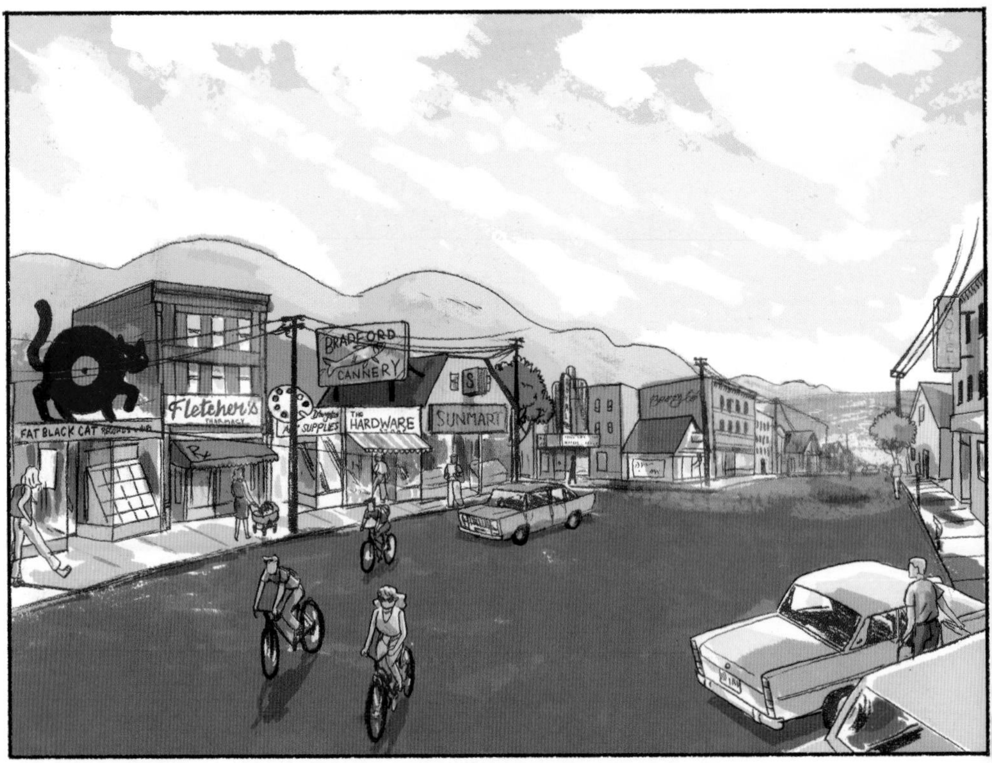
BRADFORD
CANNERY
Fletcher's
FAT BLACK CAT
SUPPLIES
THE
HARDWARE
SUNMART

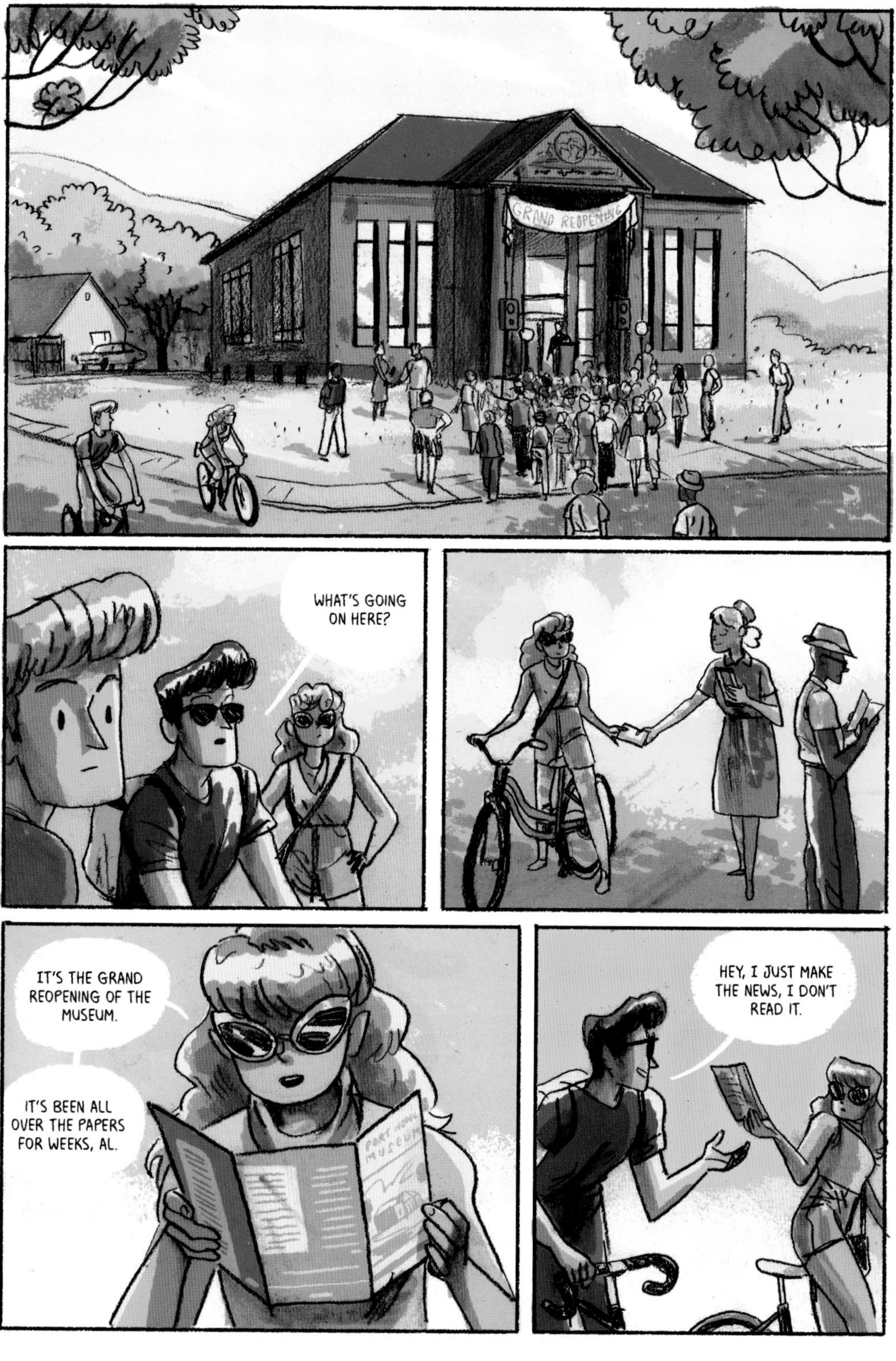
GRAND REOPENING
WHAT'S GOING ON HERE?
IT'S THE GRAND REOPENING OF THE MUSEUM.
IT'S BEEN ALL OVER THE PAPERS FOR WEEKS, AL.
HEY, I JUST MAKE THE NEWS, I DON'T READ IT.

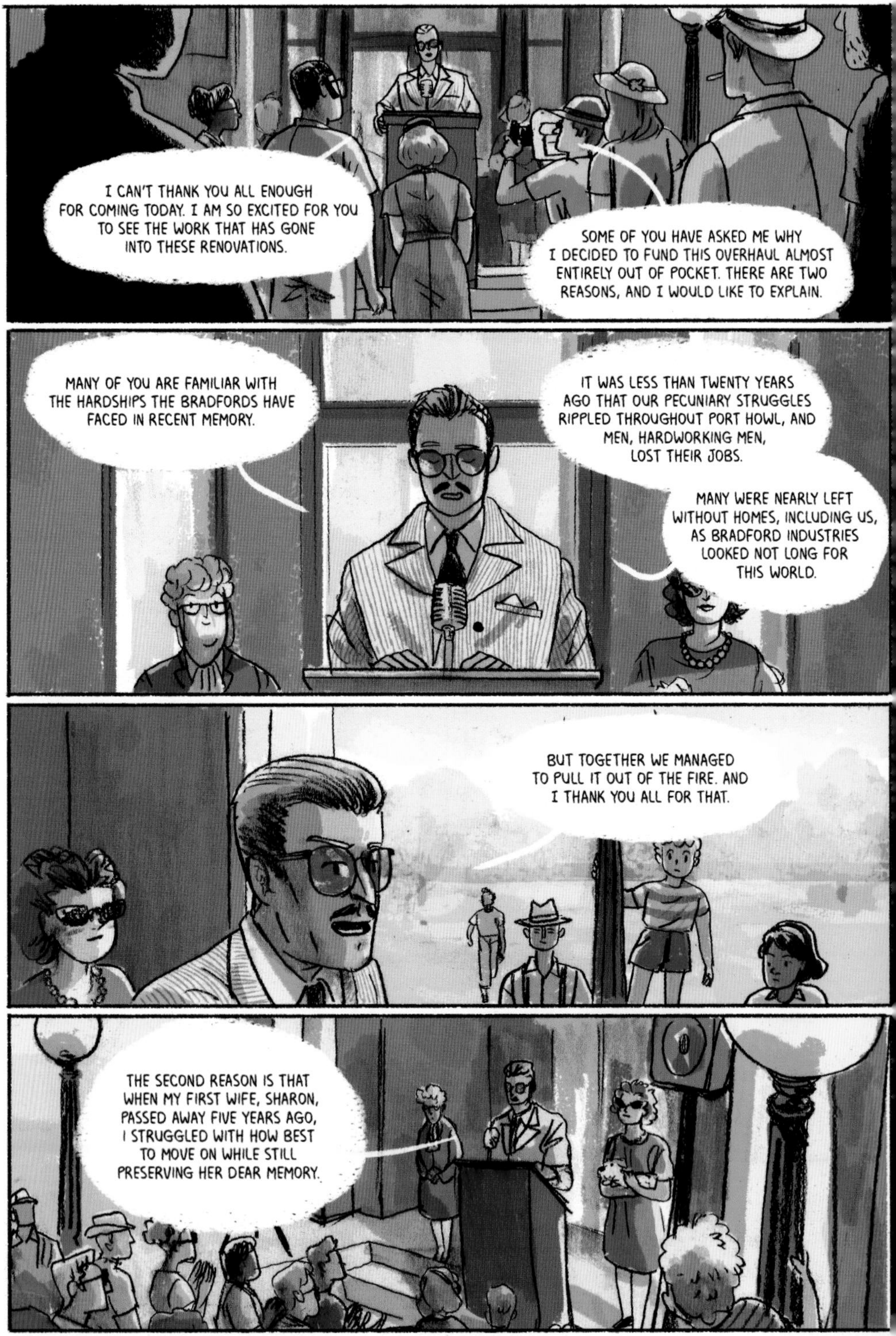
I CAN'T THANK YOU ALL ENOUGH FOR COMING TODAY. I AM SO EXCITED FOR YOU TO SEE THE WORK THAT HAS GONE INTO THESE RENOVATIONS.
SOME OF YOU HAVE ASKED ME WHY I DECIDED TO FUND THIS OVERHAUL ALMOST ENTIRELY OUT OF POCKET. THERE ARE TWO REASONS, AND I WOULD LIKE TO EXPLAIN.
MANY OF YOU ARE FAMILIAR WITH THE HARDSHIPS THE BRADFORDS HAVE FACED IN RECENT MEMORY.
IT WAS LESS THAN TWENTY YEARS AGO THAT OUR PECUNIARY STRUGGLES RIPPLED THROUGHOUT PORT HOWL, AND MEN, HARDWORKING MEN, LOST THEIR JOBS.
MANY WERE NEARLY LEFT WITHOUT HOMES, INCLUDING US, AS BRADFORD INDUSTRIES LOOKED NOT LONG FOR THIS WORLD.
BUT TOGETHER WE MANAGED TO PULL IT OUT OF THE FIRE. AND I THANK YOU ALL FOR THAT.
THE SECOND REASON IS THAT WHEN MY FIRST WIFE, SHARON, PASSED AWAY FIVE YEARS AGO, I STRUGGLED WITH HOW BEST TO MOVE ON WHILE STILL PRESERVING HER DEAR MEMORY.

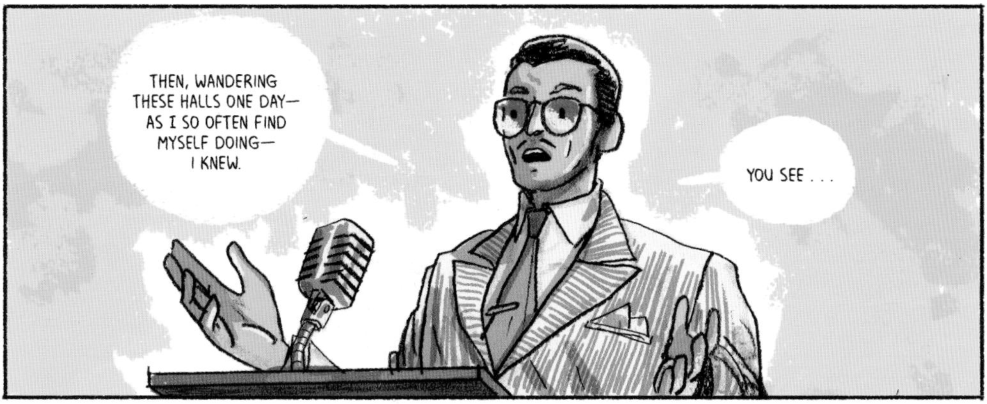
THEN, WANDERING THESE HALLS ONE DAY— AS I SO OFTEN FIND MYSELF DOING— I KNEW.
YOU SEE . . .

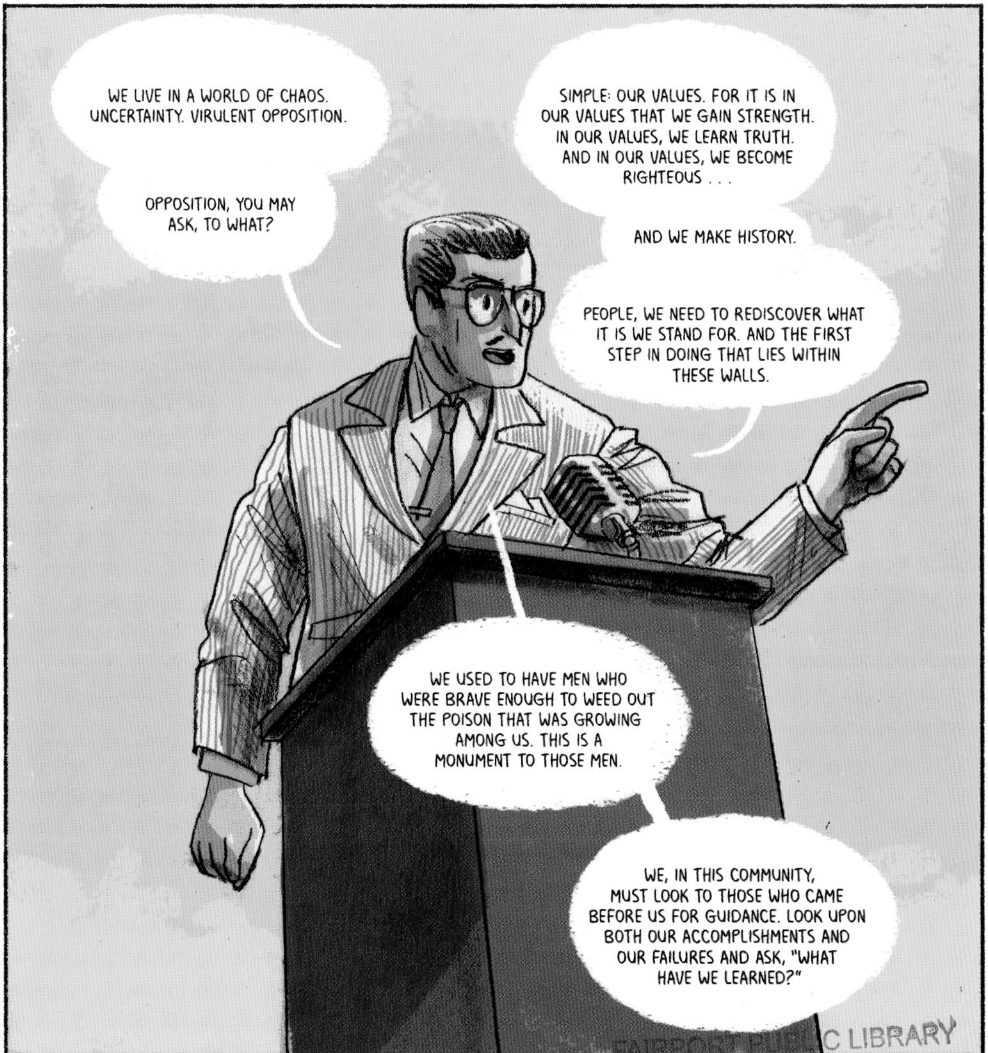
WE LIVE IN A WORLD OF CHAOS. UNCERTAINTY. VIRULENT OPPOSITION.
OPPOSITION, YOU MAY ASK, TO WHAT?
SIMPLE: OUR VALUES. FOR IT IS IN OUR VALUES THAT WE GAIN STRENGTH. IN OUR VALUES, WE LEARN TRUTH. AND IN OUR VALUES, WE BECOME RIGHTEOUS . . .
AND WE MAKE HISTORY.
PEOPLE, WE NEED TO REDISCOVER WHAT IT IS WE STAND FOR. AND THE FIRST STEP IN DOING THAT LIES WITHIN THESE WALLS.
WE USED TO HAVE MEN WHO WERE BRAVE ENOUGH TO WEED OUT THE POISON THAT WAS GROWING AMONG US. THIS IS A MONUMENT TO THOSE MEN.
WE, IN THIS COMMUNITY, MUST LOOK TO THOSE WHO CAME BEFORE US FOR GUIDANCE. LOOK UPON BOTH OUR ACCOMPLISHMENTS AND OUR FAILURES AND ASK, "WHAT HAVE WE LEARNED?"

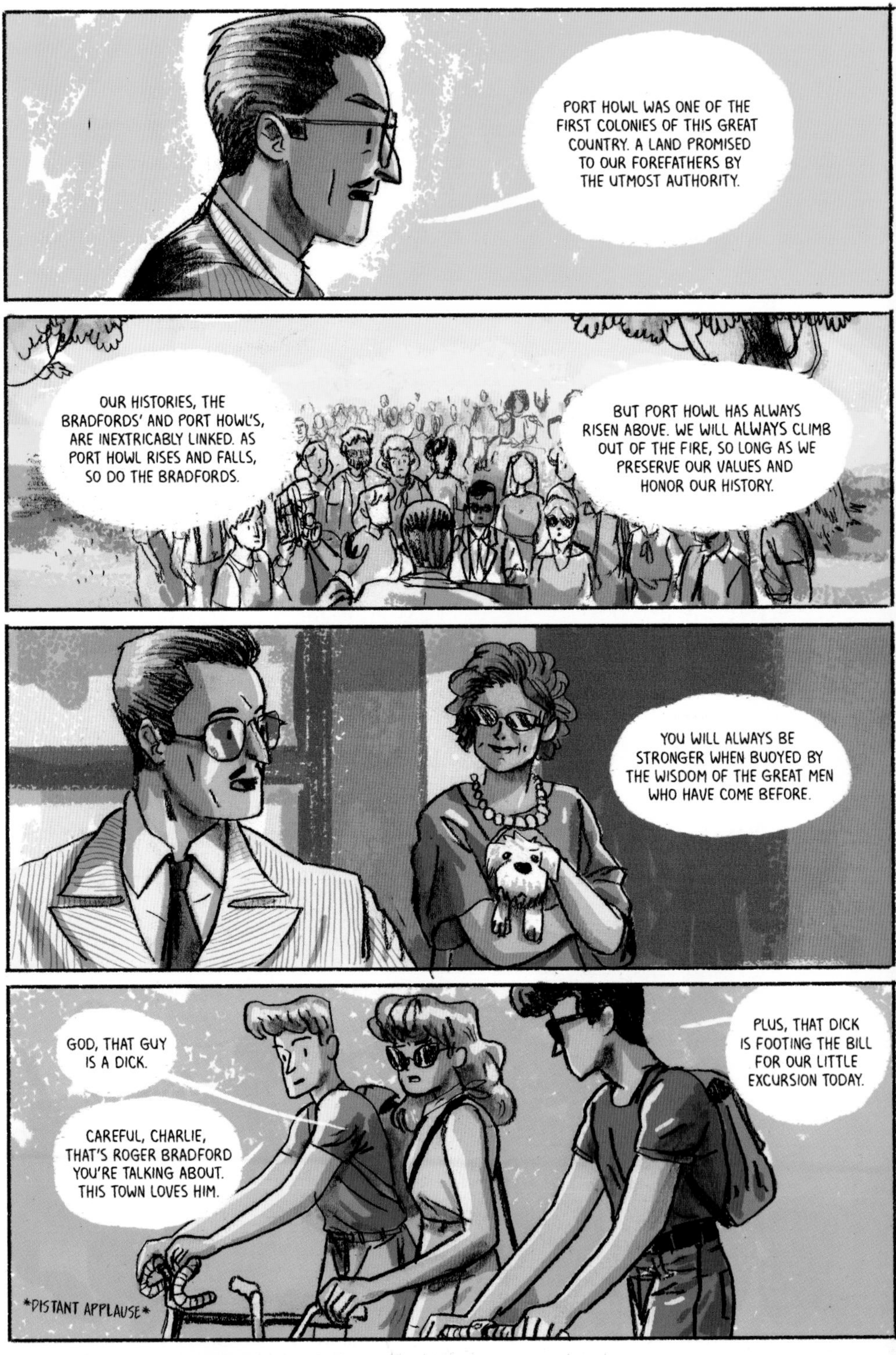
PORT HOWL WAS ONE OF THE FIRST COLONIES OF THIS GREAT COUNTRY. A LAND PROMISED TO OUR FOREFATHERS BY THE UTMOST AUTHORITY.
OUR HISTORIES, THE BRADFORDS' AND PORT HOWL'S, ARE INEXTRICABLY LINKED. AS PORT HOWL RISES AND FALLS, SO DO THE BRADFORDS.
BUT PORT HOWL HAS ALWAYS RISEN ABOVE. WE WILL ALWAYS CLIMB OUT OF THE FIRE, SO LONG AS WE PRESERVE OUR VALUES AND HONOR OUR HISTORY.
YOU WILL ALWAYS BE STRONGER WHEN BUOYED BY THE WISDOM OF THE GREAT MEN WHO HAVE COME BEFORE.
GOD, THAT GUY IS A DICK.
CAREFUL, CHARLIE, THAT'S ROGER BRADFORD YOU'RE TALKING ABOUT. THIS TOWN LOVES HIM.
PLUS, THAT DICK IS FOOTING THE BILL FOR OUR LITTLE EXCURSION TODAY.
DISTANT APPLAUSE

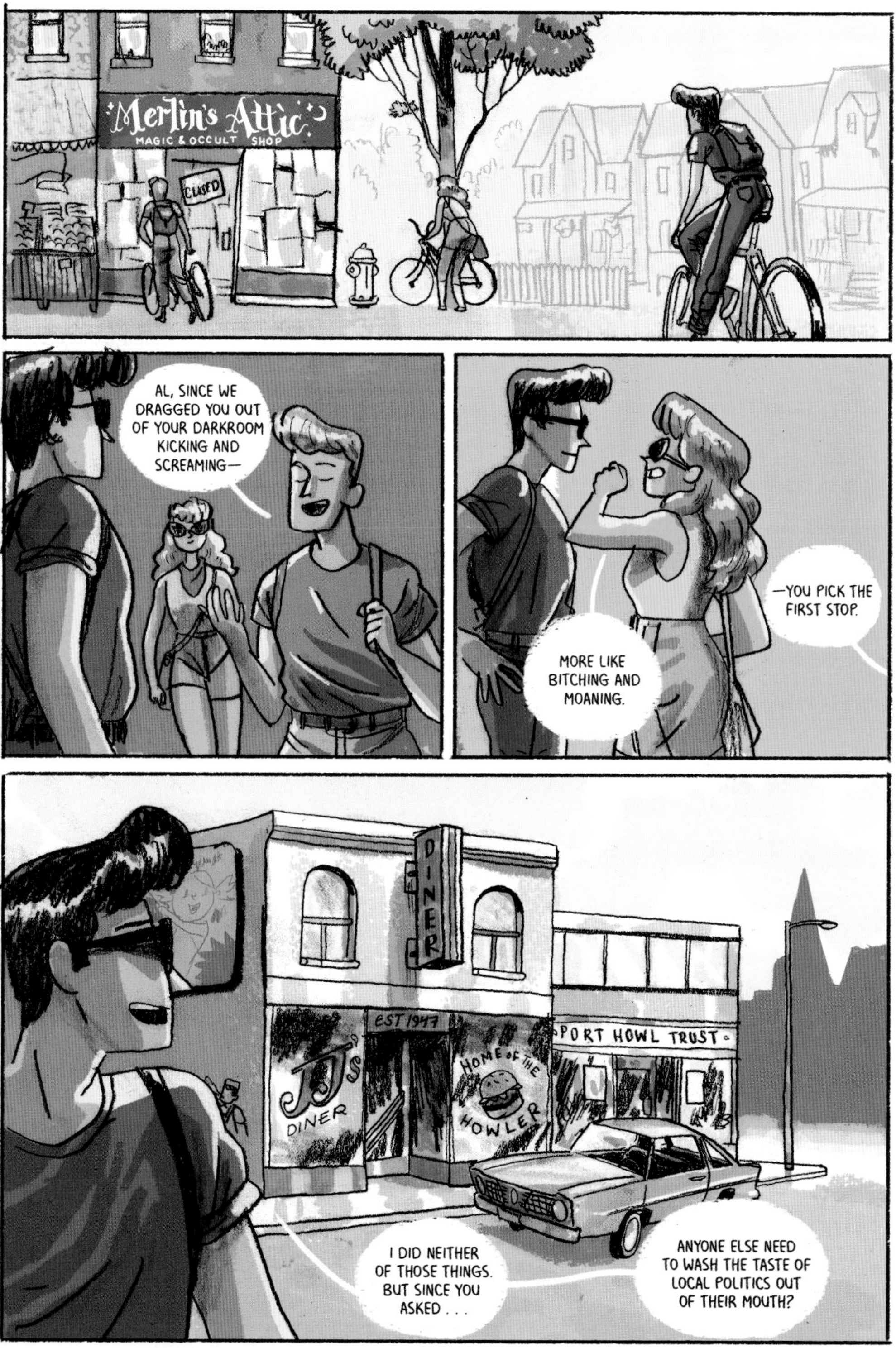
Merlin's Attic
MAGIC & OCCULT SHOP
CLOSED
AL, SINCE WE DRAGGED YOU OUT OF YOUR DARKROOM KICKING AND SCREAMING—
—YOU PICK THE FIRST STOP.
MORE LIKE BITCHING AND MOANING.
DINER
EST 1947
JJ's DINER
HOME OF THE HOWLER
PORT HOWL TRUST
I DID NEITHER OF THOSE THINGS. BUT SINCE YOU ASKED . . .
ANYONE ELSE NEED TO WASH THE TASTE OF LOCAL POLITICS OUT OF THEIR MOUTH?

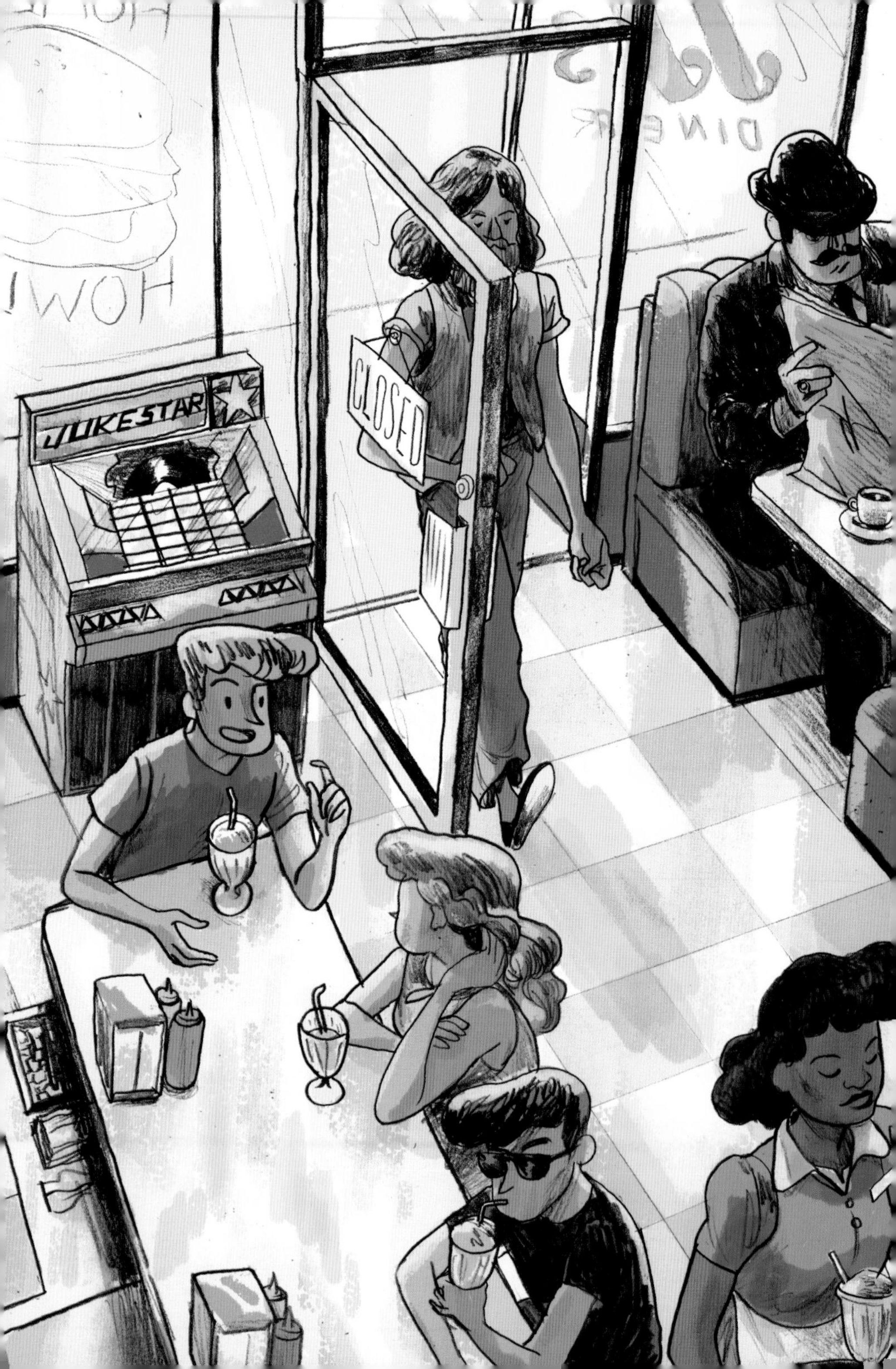
JUKESTAR
CLOSED

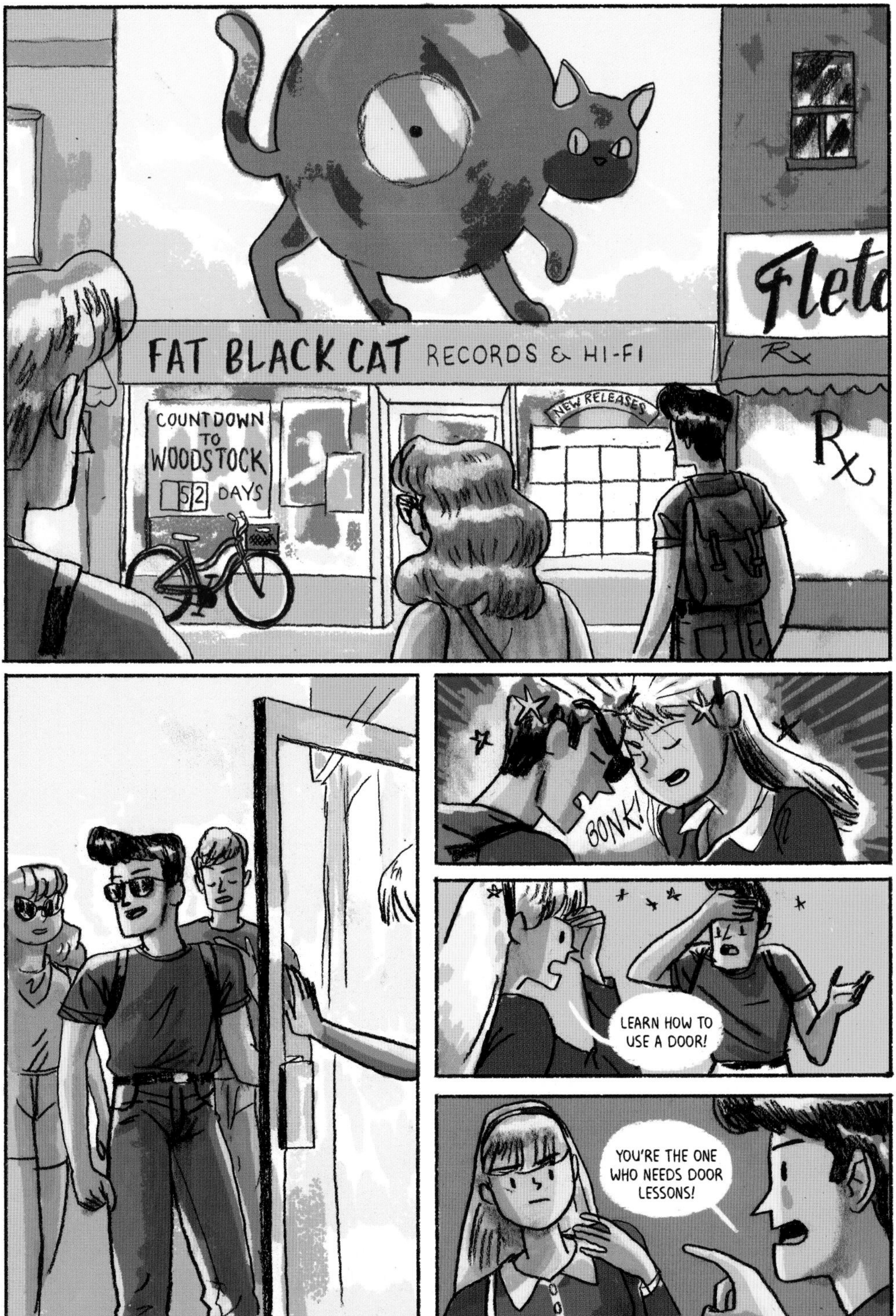
FAT BLACK CAT RECORDS & HI-FI
COUNTDOWN TO WOODSTOCK 52 DAYS
NEW RELEASES
Fletc
Rx
Rx
BONK!
LEARN HOW TO USE A DOOR!
YOU'RE THE ONE WHO NEEDS DOOR LESSONS!

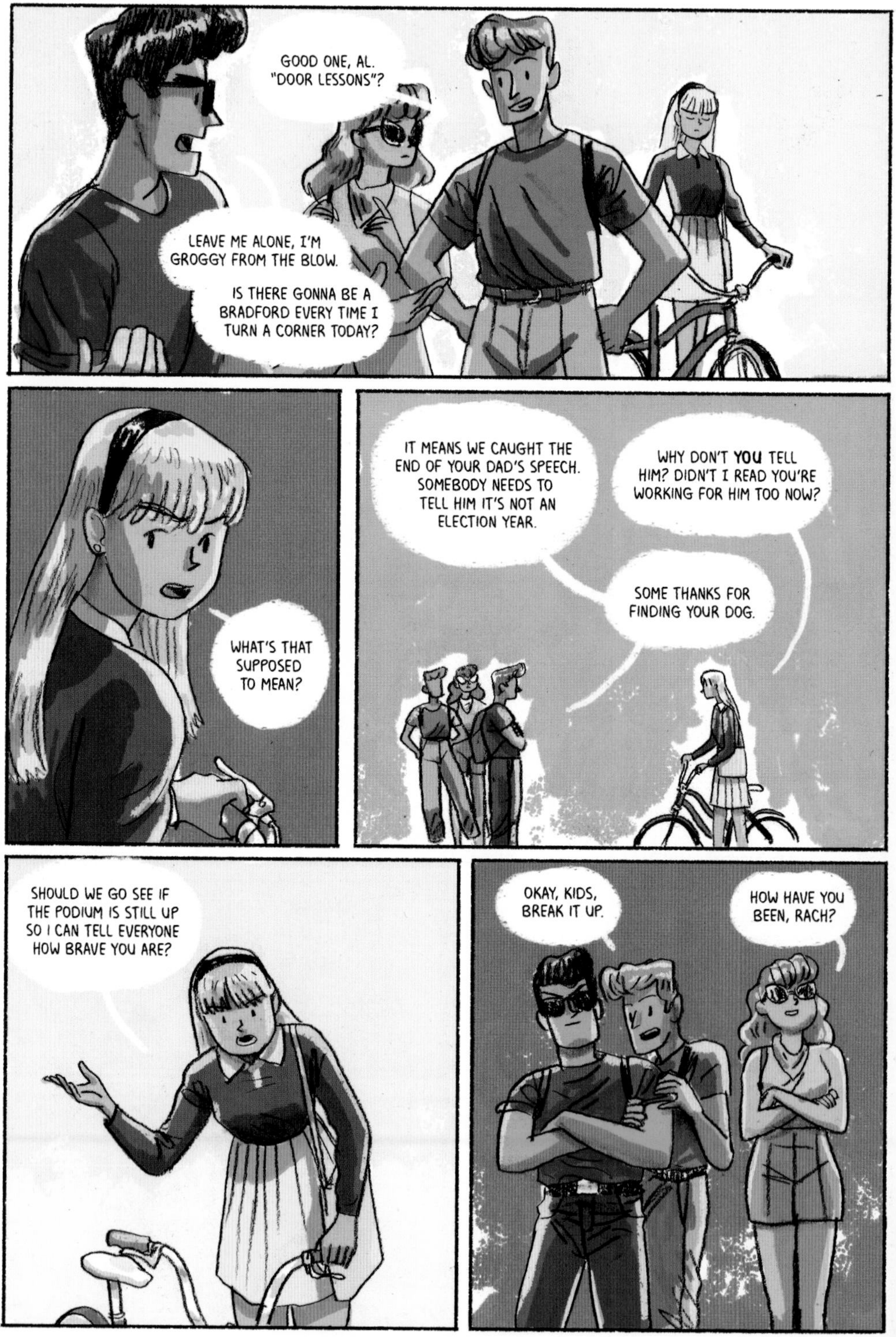
GOOD ONE, AL. "DOOR LESSONS"?
LEAVE ME ALONE, I'M GROGGY FROM THE BLOW.
IS THERE GONNA BE A BRADFORD EVERY TIME I TURN A CORNER TODAY?
WHAT'S THAT SUPPOSED TO MEAN?
IT MEANS WE CAUGHT THE END OF YOUR DAD'S SPEECH. SOMEBODY NEEDS TO TELL HIM IT'S NOT AN ELECTION YEAR.
WHY DON'T **YOU** TELL HIM? DIDN'T I READ YOU'RE WORKING FOR HIM TOO NOW?
SOME THANKS FOR FINDING YOUR DOG.
SHOULD WE GO SEE IF THE PODIUM IS STILL UP SO I CAN TELL EVERYONE HOW BRAVE YOU ARE?
OKAY, KIDS, BREAK IT UP.
HOW HAVE YOU BEEN, RACH?

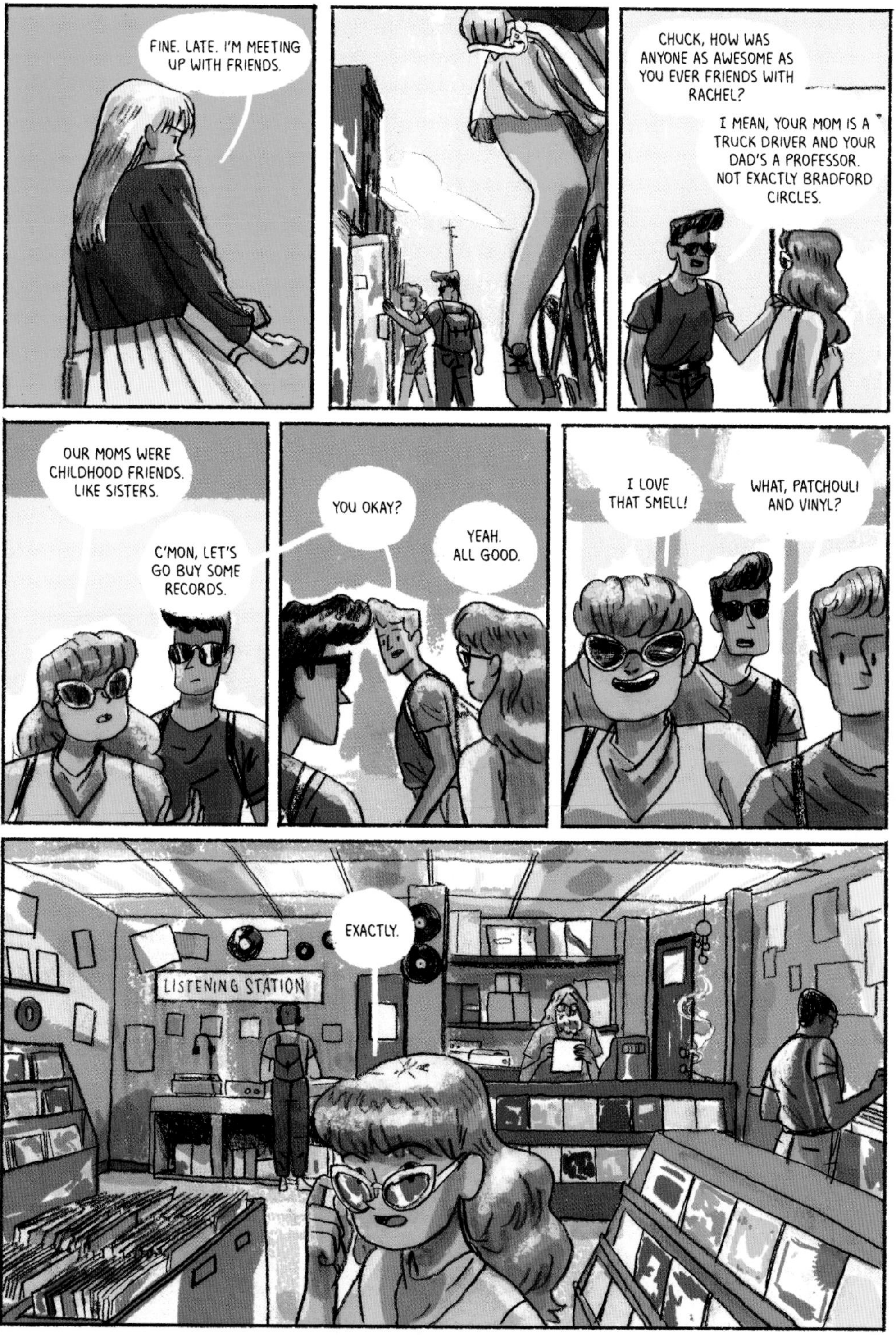
FINE. LATE. I'M MEETING UP WITH FRIENDS.
CHUCK, HOW WAS ANYONE AS AWESOME AS YOU EVER FRIENDS WITH RACHEL?
I MEAN, YOUR MOM IS A TRUCK DRIVER AND YOUR DAD'S A PROFESSOR. NOT EXACTLY BRADFORD CIRCLES.
OUR MOMS WERE CHILDHOOD FRIENDS. LIKE SISTERS.
C'MON, LET'S GO BUY SOME RECORDS.
YOU OKAY?
YEAH. ALL GOOD.
I LOVE THAT SMELL!
WHAT, PATCHOULI AND VINYL?
EXACTLY.
LISTENING STATION

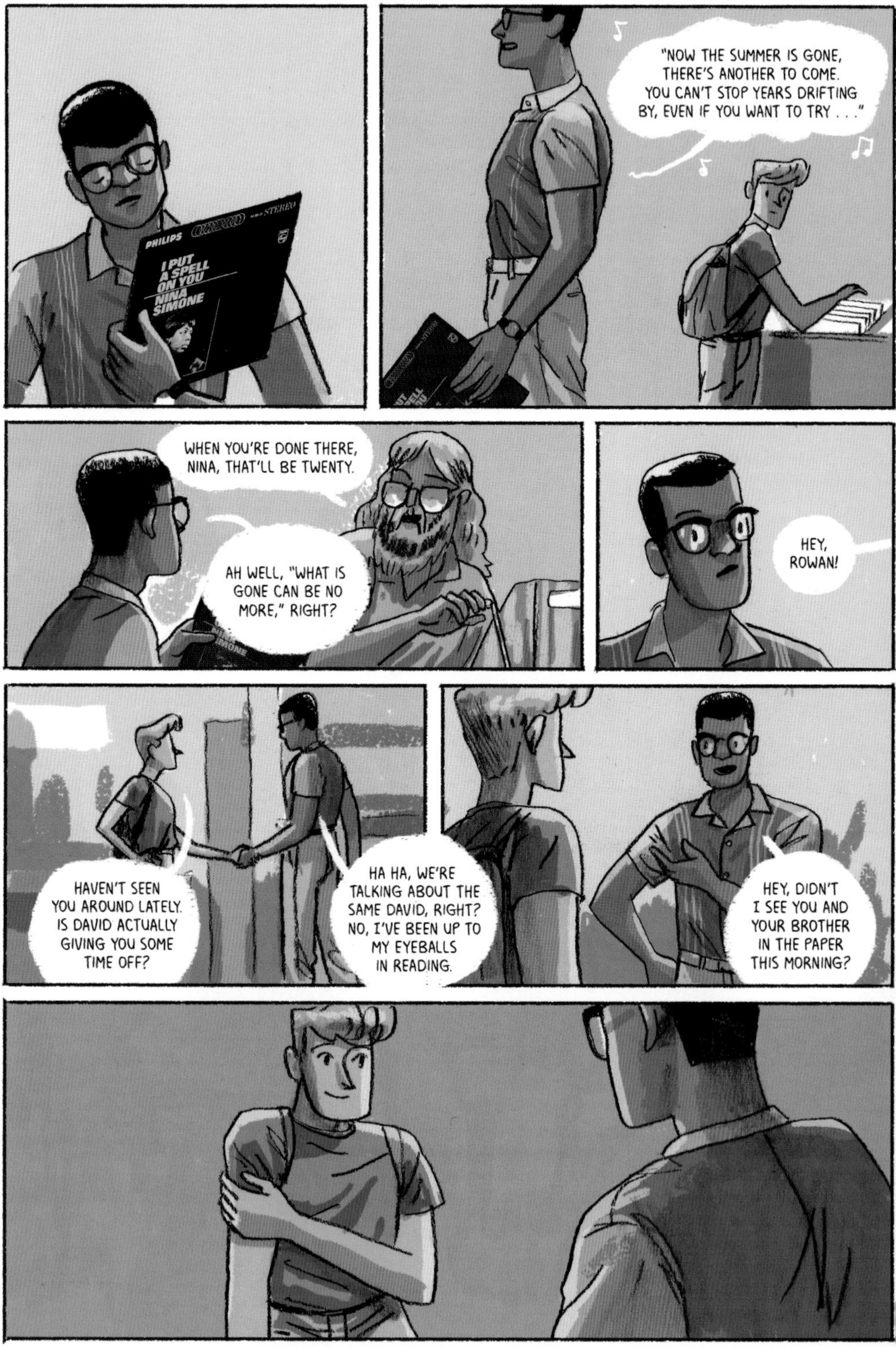
PHILIPS
STEREO
I PUT A SPELL ON YOU
NINA SIMONE
"NOW THE SUMMER IS GONE, THERE'S ANOTHER TO COME. YOU CAN'T STOP YEARS DRIFTING BY, EVEN IF YOU WANT TO TRY . . ."
WHEN YOU'RE DONE THERE, NINA, THAT'LL BE TWENTY.
AH WELL, "WHAT IS GONE CAN BE NO MORE," RIGHT?
HEY, ROWAN!
HAVEN'T SEEN YOU AROUND LATELY. IS DAVID ACTUALLY GIVING YOU SOME TIME OFF?
HA HA, WE'RE TALKING ABOUT THE SAME DAVID, RIGHT? NO, I'VE BEEN UP TO MY EYEBALLS IN READING.
HEY, DIDN'T I SEE YOU AND YOUR BROTHER IN THE PAPER THIS MORNING?

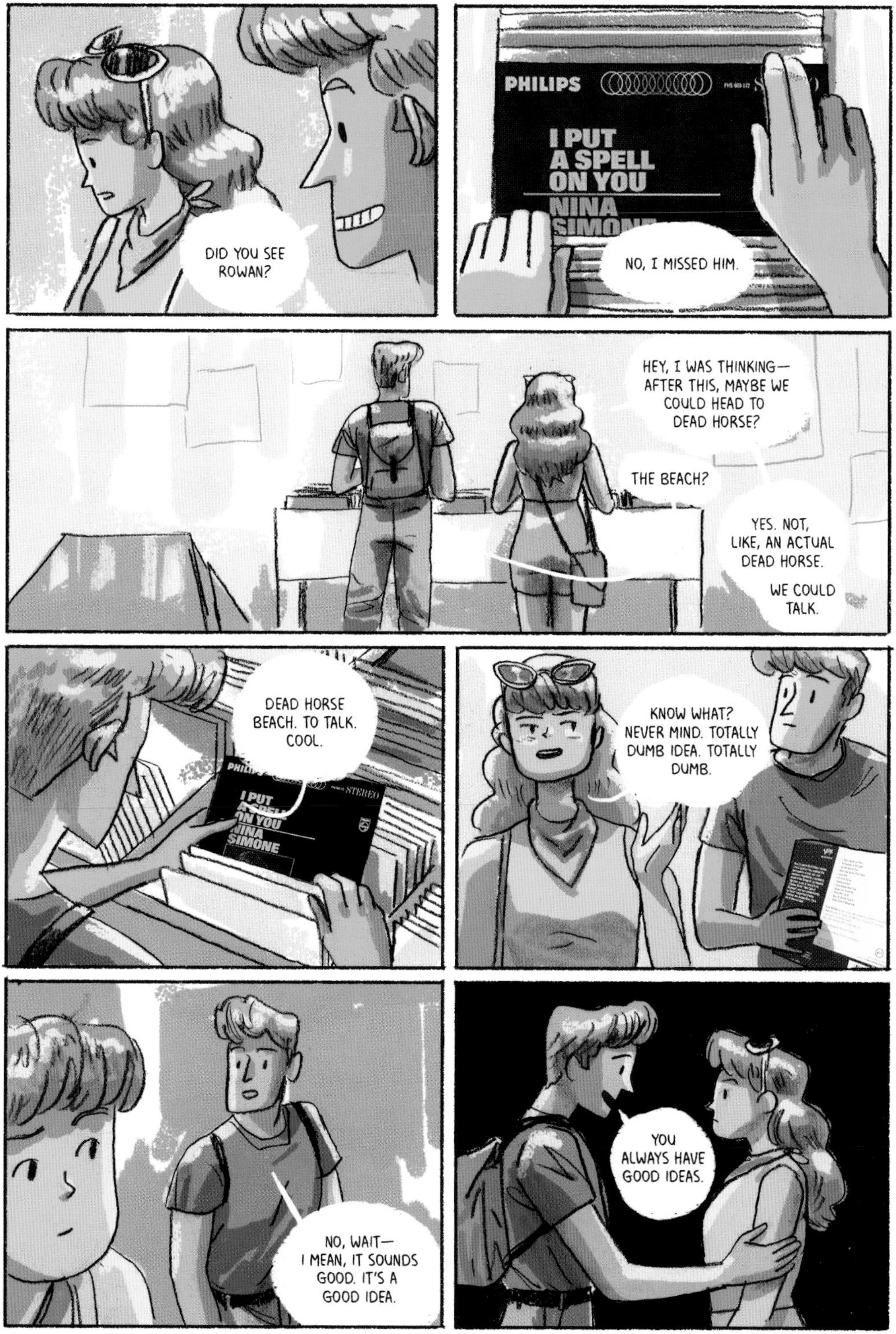
DID YOU SEE ROWAN?
PHILIPS
I PUT A SPELL ON YOU
NINA SIMONE
NO, I MISSED HIM.
HEY, I WAS THINKING— AFTER THIS, MAYBE WE COULD HEAD TO DEAD HORSE?
THE BEACH?
YES. NOT, LIKE, AN ACTUAL DEAD HORSE.
WE COULD TALK.
DEAD HORSE BEACH. TO TALK. COOL.
KNOW WHAT? NEVER MIND. TOTALLY DUMB IDEA. TOTALLY DUMB.
NO, WAIT— I MEAN, IT SOUNDS GOOD. IT'S A GOOD IDEA.
YOU ALWAYS HAVE GOOD IDEAS.

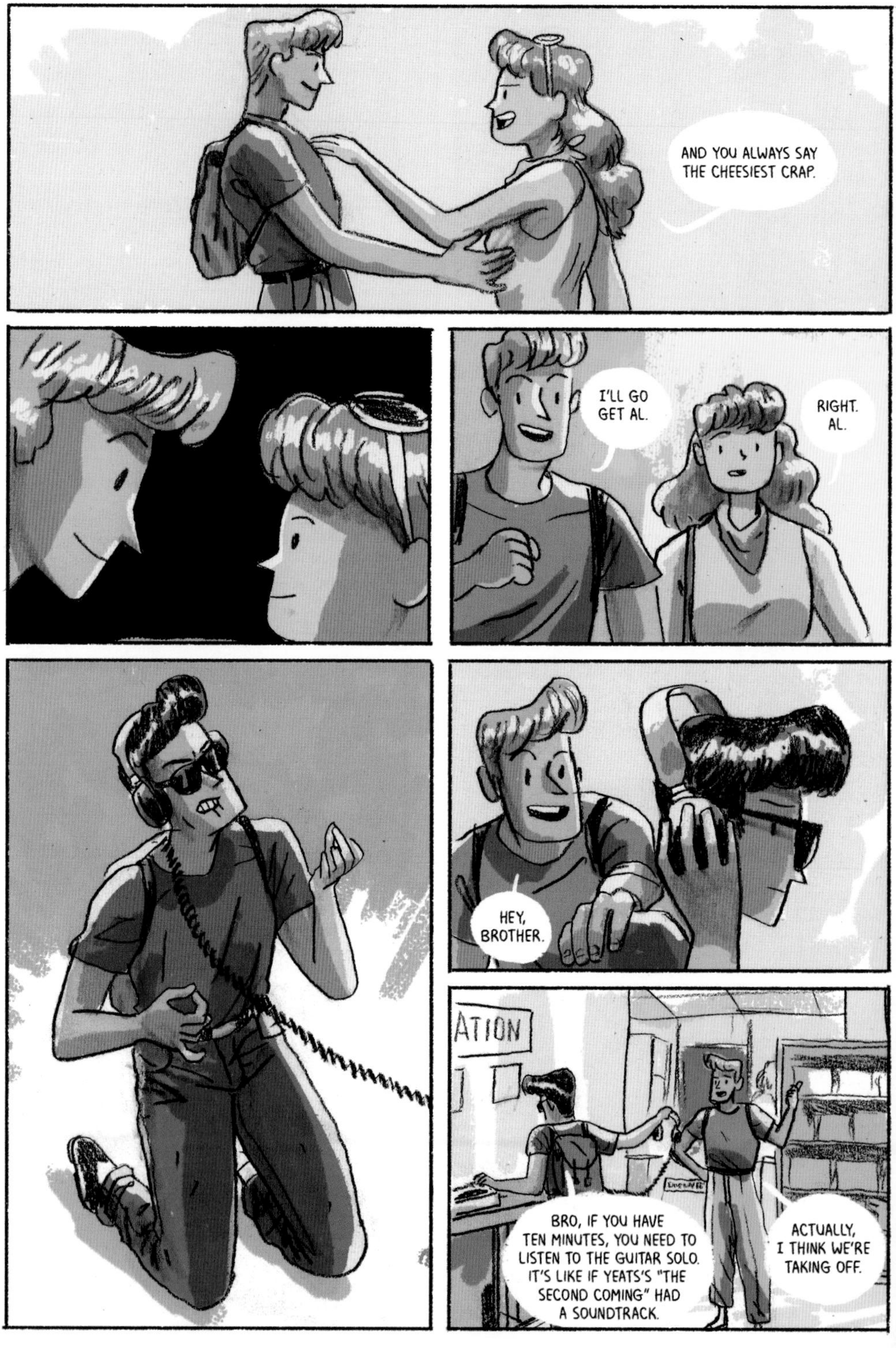
AND YOU ALWAYS SAY THE CHEESIEST CRAP.
I'LL GO GET AL.
RIGHT. AL.
HEY, BROTHER.
ATION
BRO, IF YOU HAVE TEN MINUTES, YOU NEED TO LISTEN TO THE GUITAR SOLO. IT'S LIKE IF YEATS'S "THE SECOND COMING" HAD A SOUNDTRACK.
ACTUALLY, I THINK WE'RE TAKING OFF.

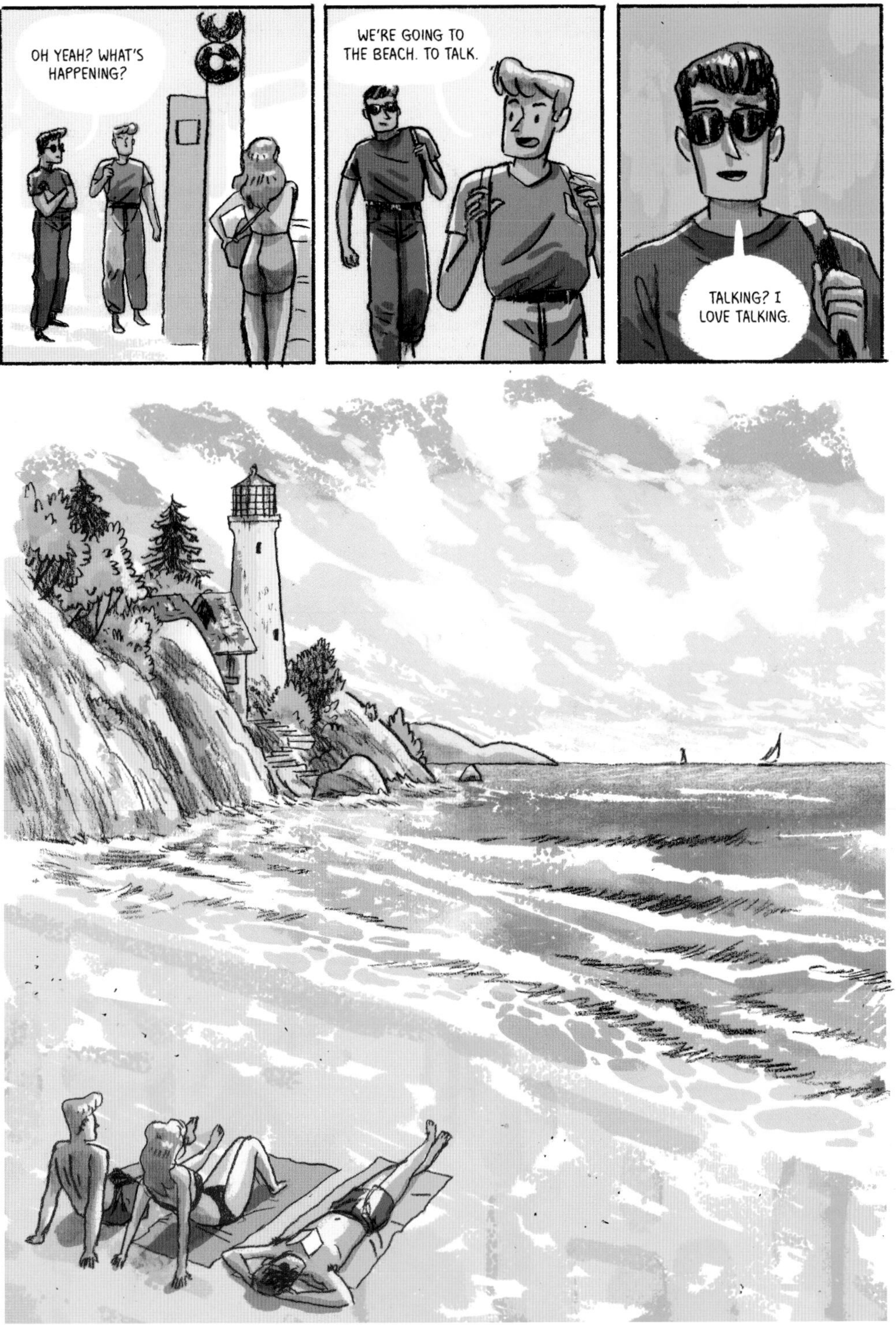
OH YEAH? WHAT'S HAPPENING?
WE'RE GOING TO THE BEACH. TO TALK.
TALKING? I LOVE TALKING.

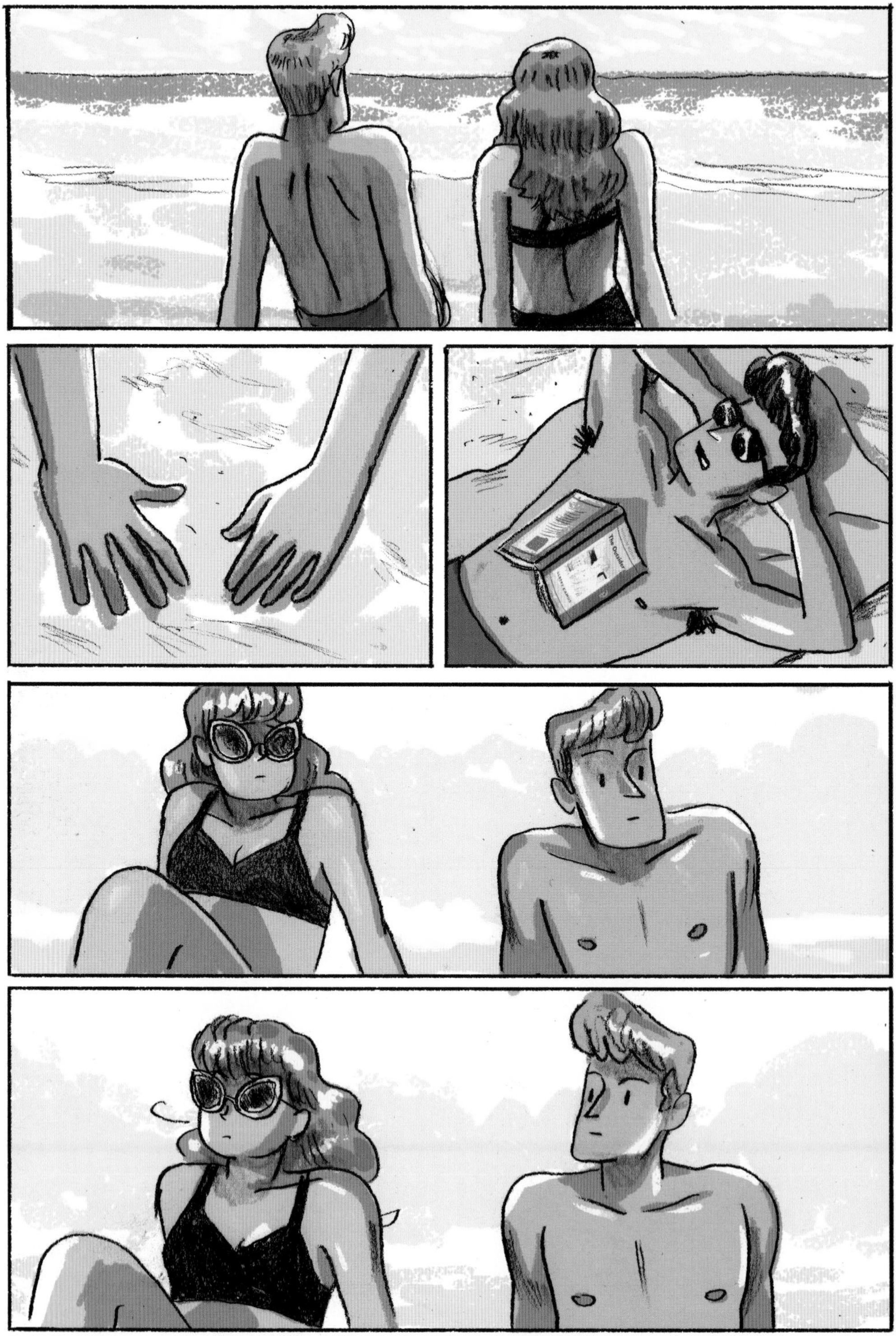
The Outsider

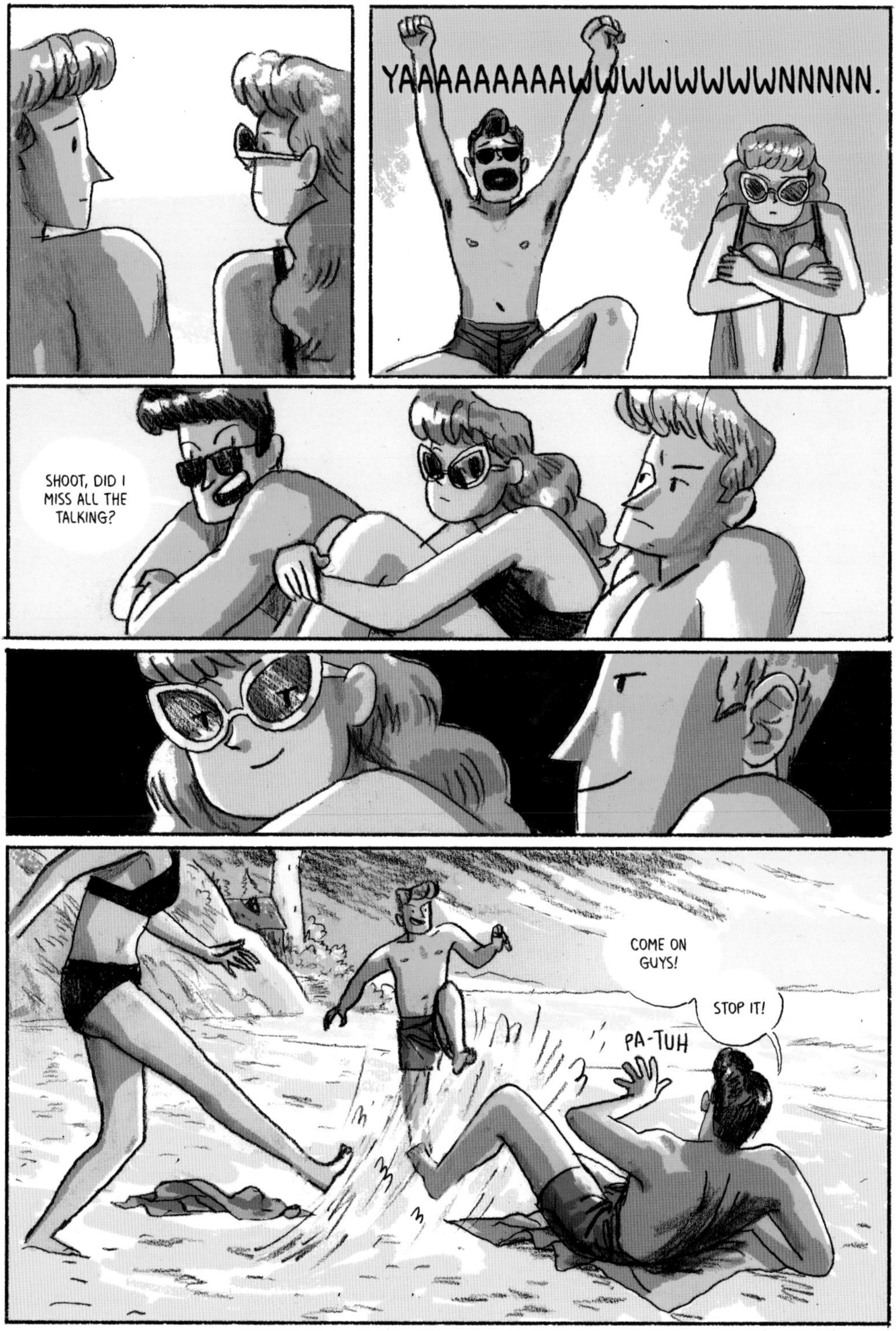
YAAAAAAAAWWWWWWWWNNNNN.
SHOOT, DID I MISS ALL THE TALKING?
COME ON GUYS!
STOP IT!
PA-TUH

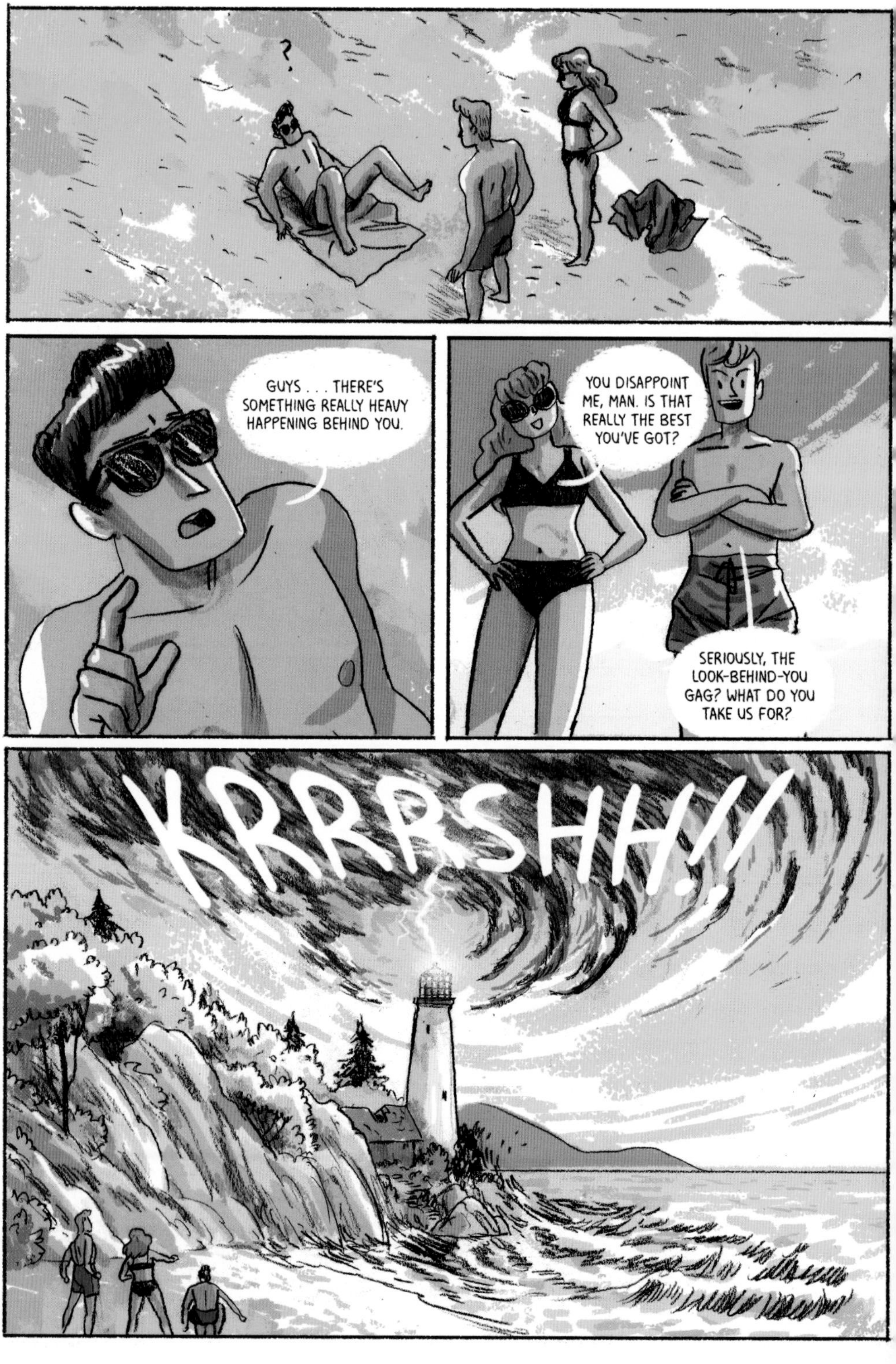
?
GUYS . . . THERE'S SOMETHING REALLY HEAVY HAPPENING BEHIND YOU.
YOU DISAPPOINT ME, MAN. IS THAT REALLY THE BEST YOU'VE GOT?
SERIOUSLY, THE LOOK-BEHIND-YOU GAG? WHAT DO YOU TAKE US FOR?
KRRRSHH!!

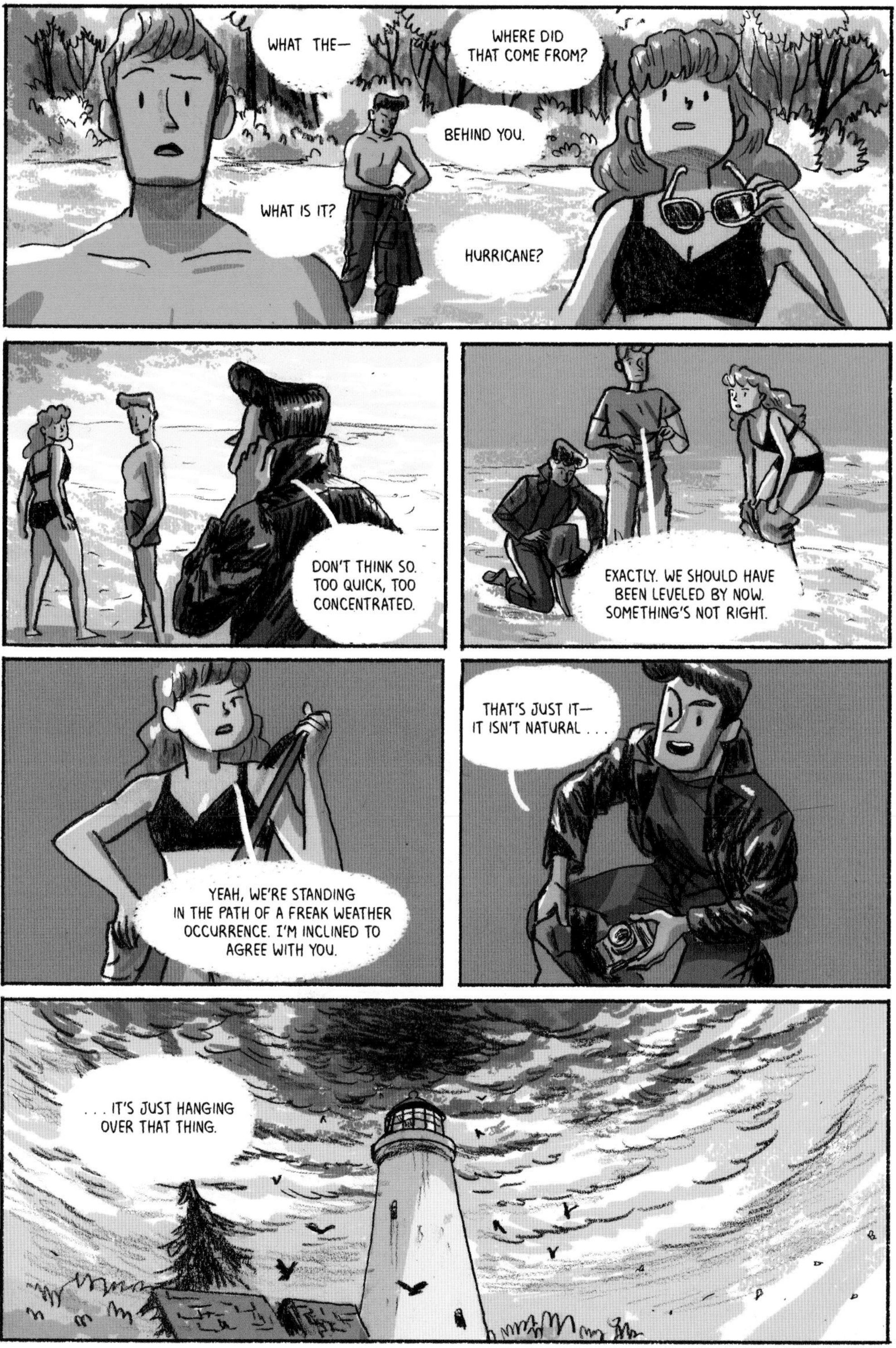
WHAT THE—
WHERE DID THAT COME FROM?
BEHIND YOU.
WHAT IS IT?
HURRICANE?
DON'T THINK SO. TOO QUICK, TOO CONCENTRATED.
EXACTLY. WE SHOULD HAVE BEEN LEVELED BY NOW. SOMETHING'S NOT RIGHT.
YEAH, WE'RE STANDING IN THE PATH OF A FREAK WEATHER OCCURRENCE. I'M INCLINED TO AGREE WITH YOU.
THAT'S JUST IT— IT ISN'T NATURAL . . .
. . . IT'S JUST HANGING OVER THAT THING.

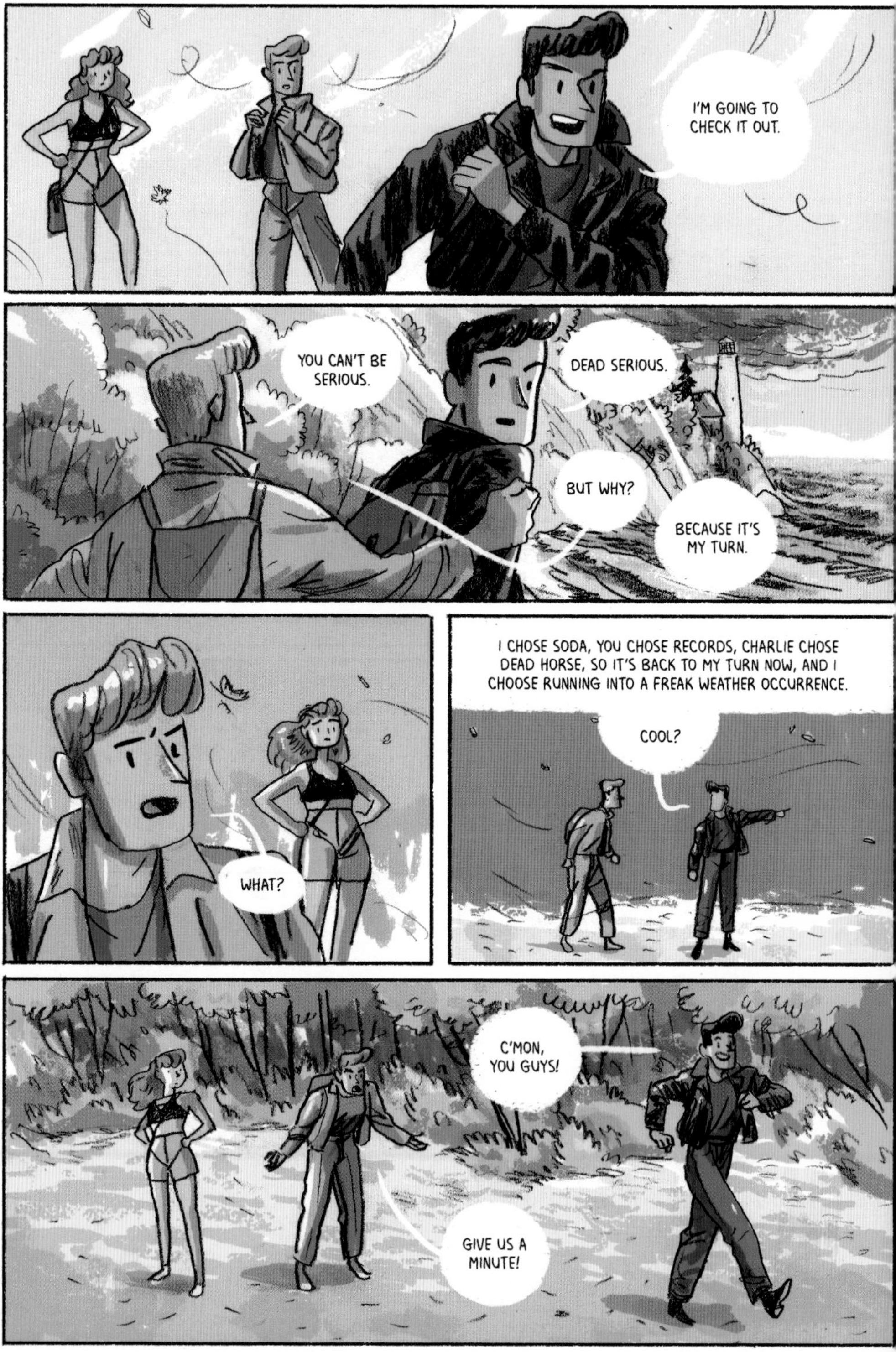
I'M GOING TO CHECK IT OUT.
YOU CAN'T BE SERIOUS.
DEAD SERIOUS.
BUT WHY?
BECAUSE IT'S MY TURN.
WHAT?
I CHOSE SODA, YOU CHOSE RECORDS, CHARLIE CHOSE DEAD HORSE, SO IT'S BACK TO MY TURN NOW, AND I CHOOSE RUNNING INTO A FREAK WEATHER OCCURRENCE.
COOL?
C'MON, YOU GUYS!
GIVE US A MINUTE!

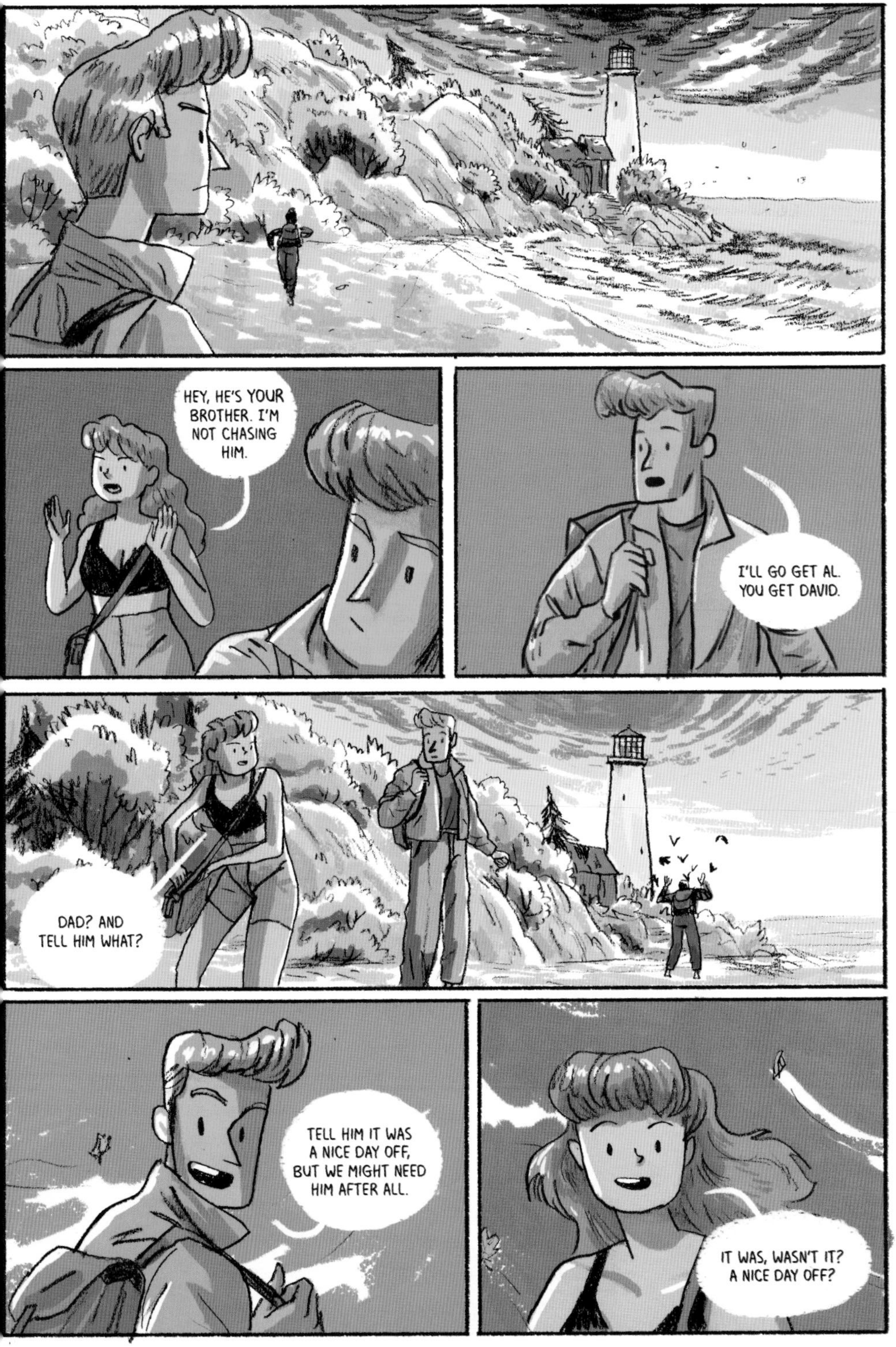
HEY, HE'S YOUR BROTHER. I'M NOT CHASING HIM.
I'LL GO GET AL. YOU GET DAVID.
DAD? AND TELL HIM WHAT?
TELL HIM IT WAS A NICE DAY OFF, BUT WE MIGHT NEED HIM AFTER ALL.
IT WAS, WASN'T IT? A NICE DAY OFF?

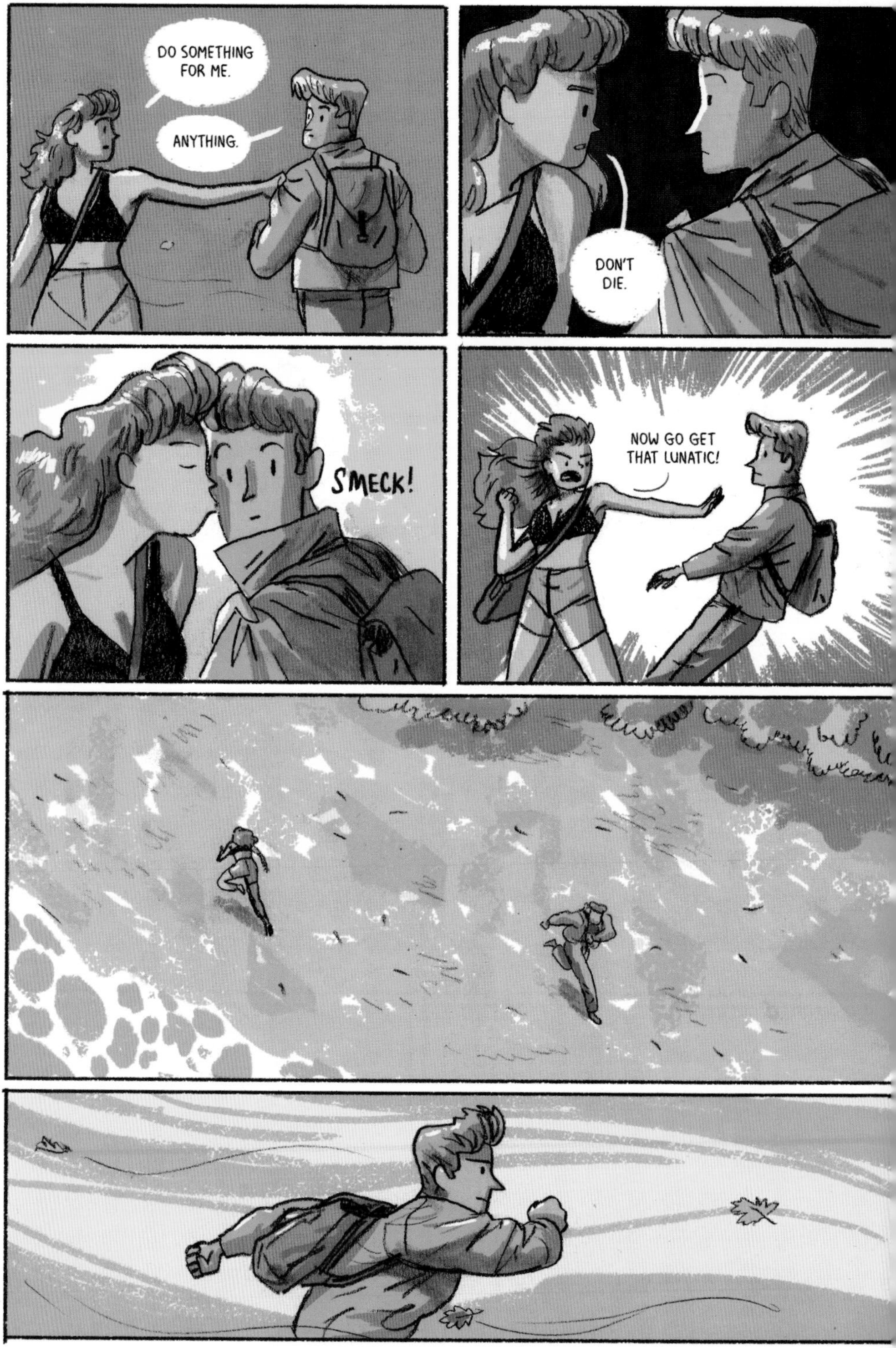
DO SOMETHING FOR ME.
ANYTHING.
DON'T DIE.
SMECK!
NOW GO GET THAT LUNATIC!

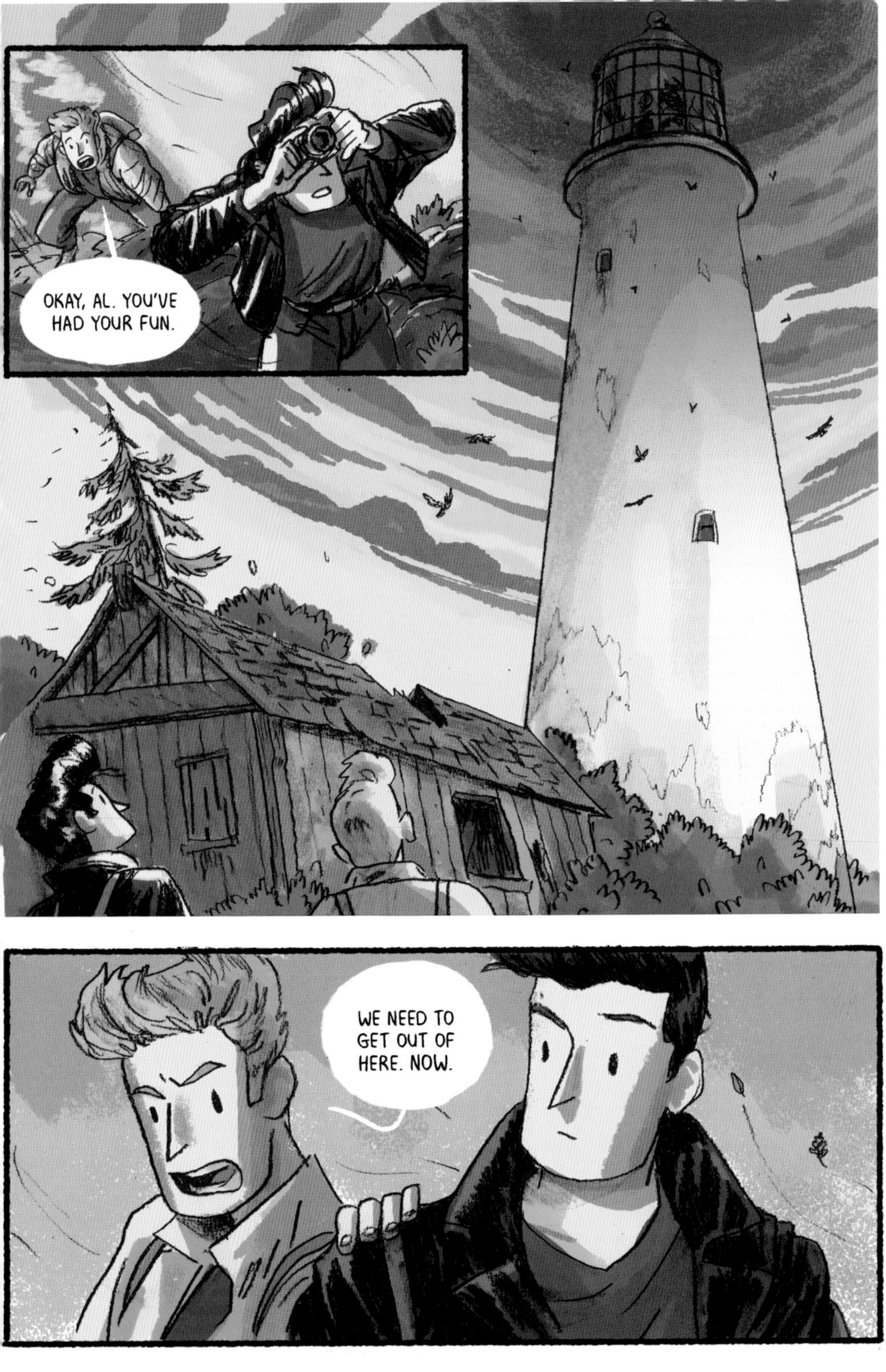
OKAY, AL. YOU'VE HAD YOUR FUN.
WE NEED TO GET OUT OF HERE. NOW.

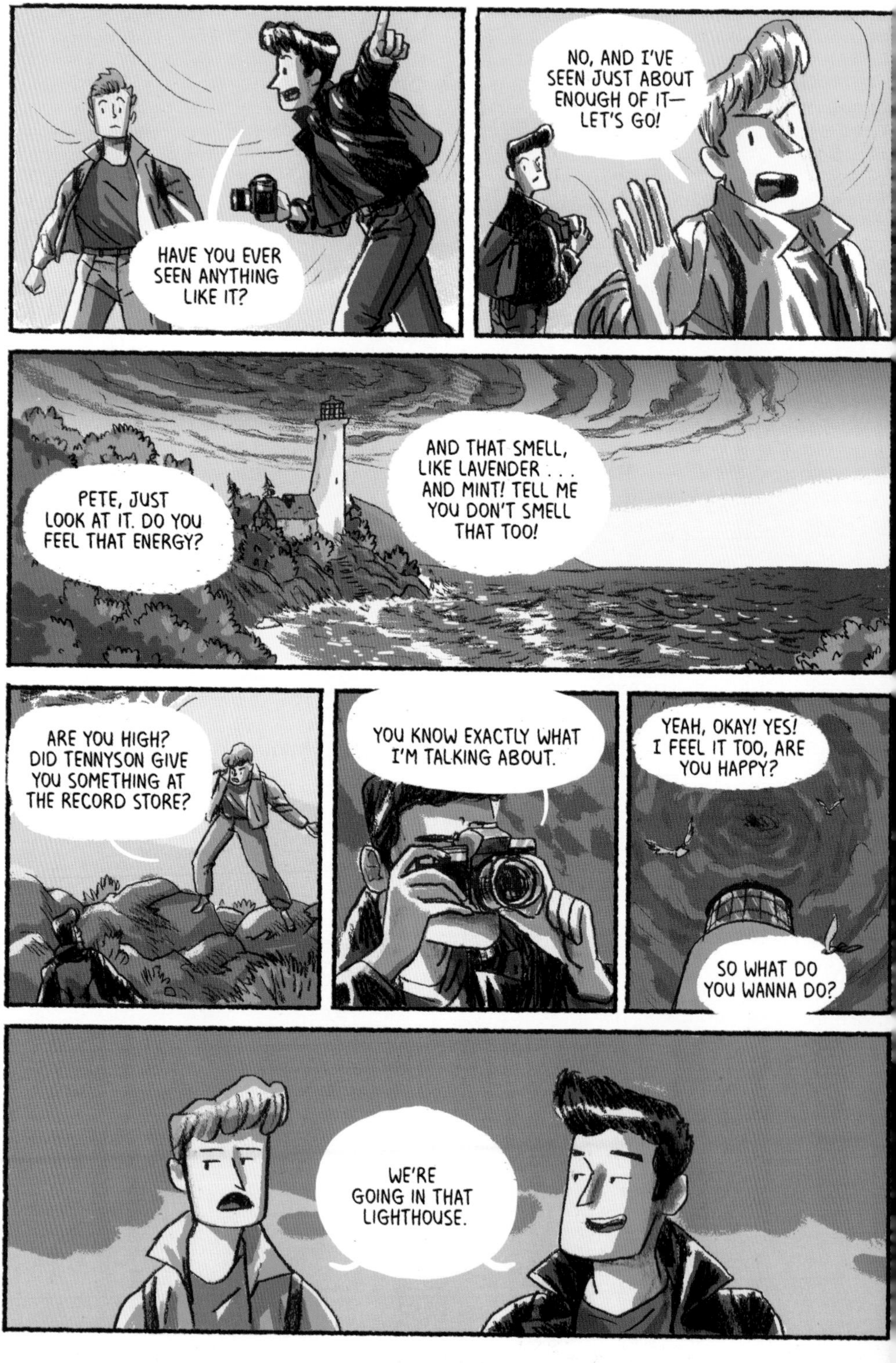
HAVE YOU EVER SEEN ANYTHING LIKE IT?
NO, AND I'VE SEEN JUST ABOUT ENOUGH OF IT—LET'S GO!
PETE, JUST LOOK AT IT. DO YOU FEEL THAT ENERGY?
AND THAT SMELL, LIKE LAVENDER . . . AND MINT! TELL ME YOU DON'T SMELL THAT TOO!
ARE YOU HIGH? DID TENNYSON GIVE YOU SOMETHING AT THE RECORD STORE?
YOU KNOW EXACTLY WHAT I'M TALKING ABOUT.
YEAH, OKAY! YES! I FEEL IT TOO, ARE YOU HAPPY?
SO WHAT DO YOU WANNA DO?
WE'RE GOING IN THAT LIGHTHOUSE.

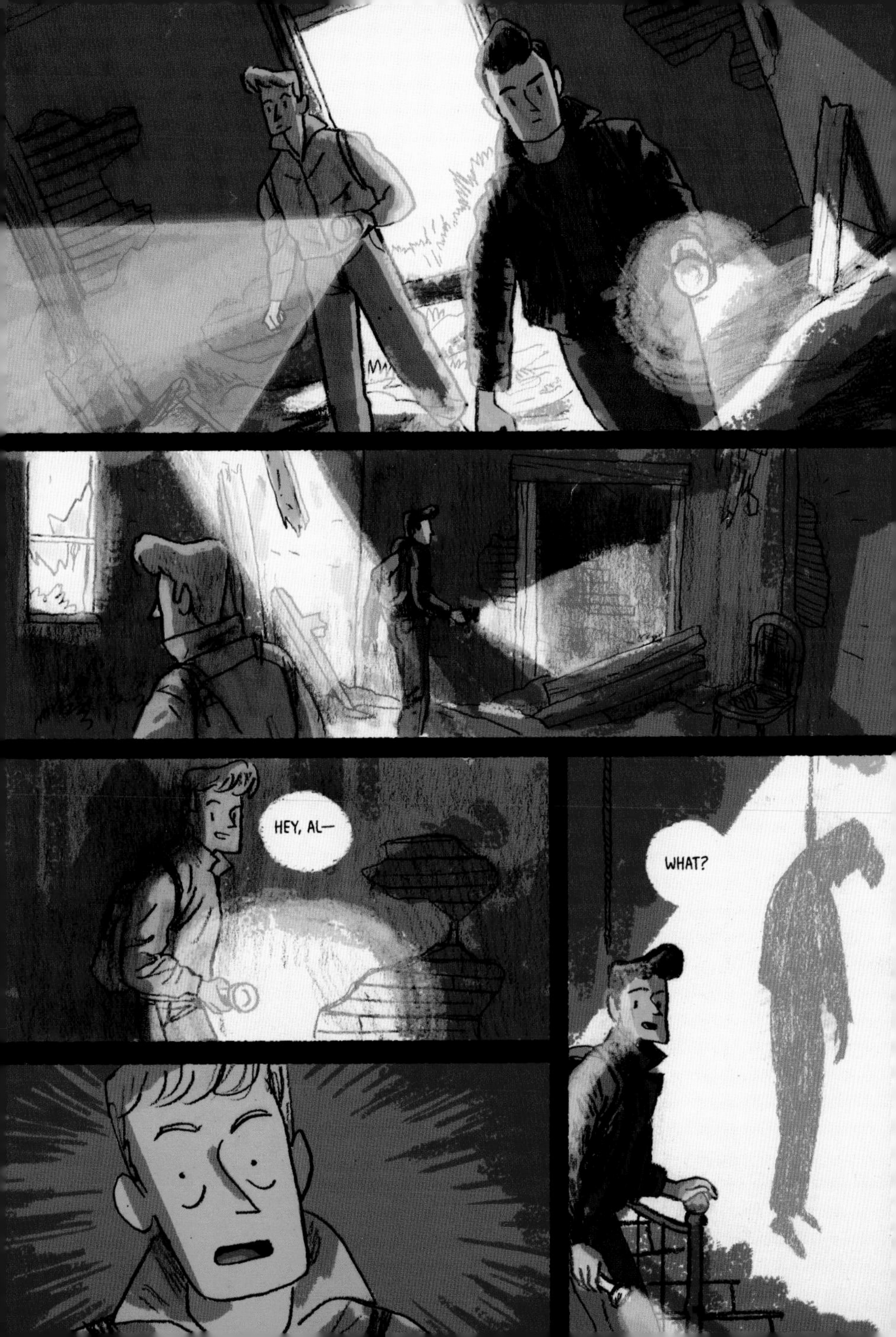
HEY, AL—
WHAT?

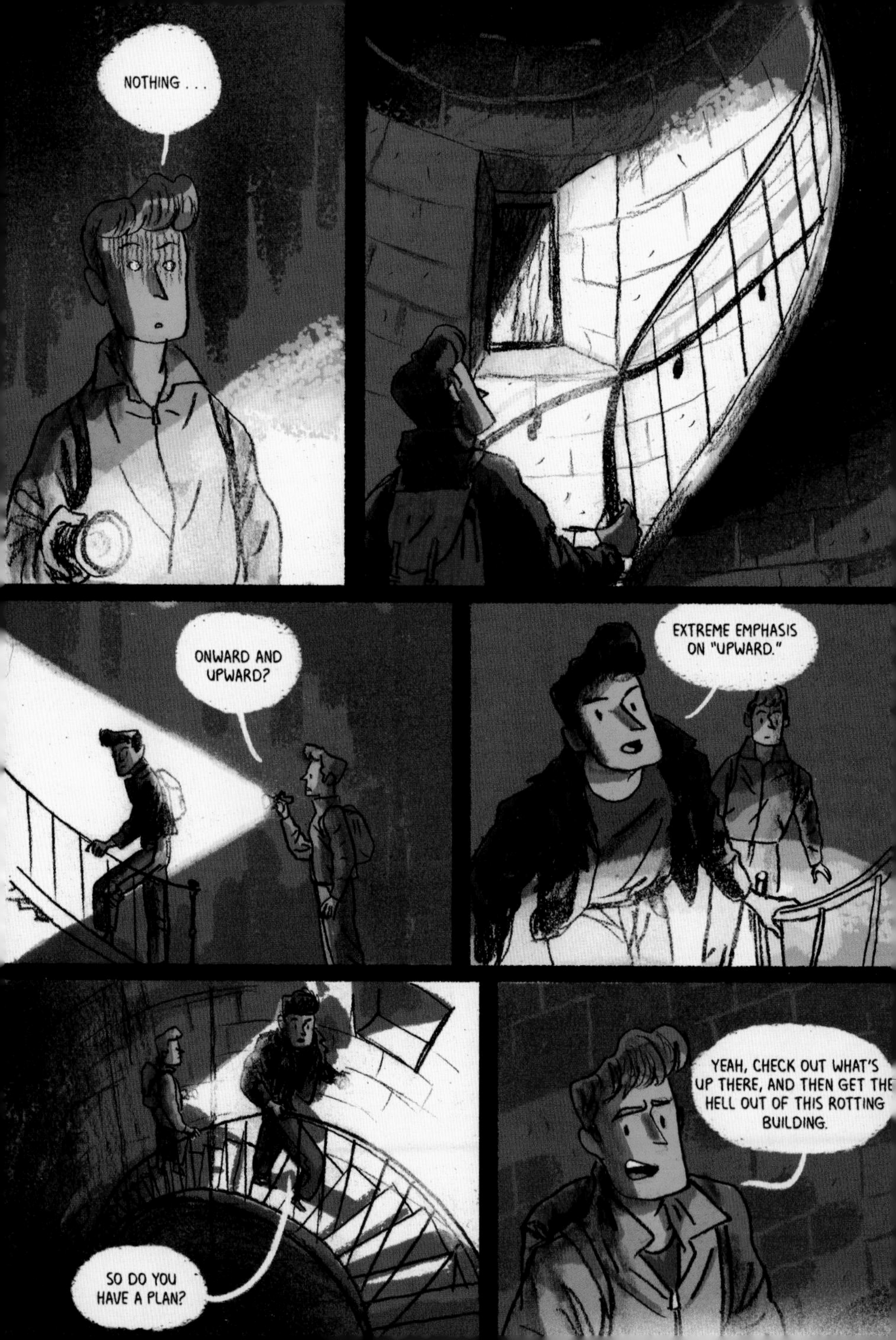
NOTHING . . .
ONWARD AND UPWARD?
EXTREME EMPHASIS ON "UPWARD."
SO DO YOU HAVE A PLAN?
YEAH, CHECK OUT WHAT'S UP THERE, AND THEN GET THE HELL OUT OF THIS ROTTING BUILDING.

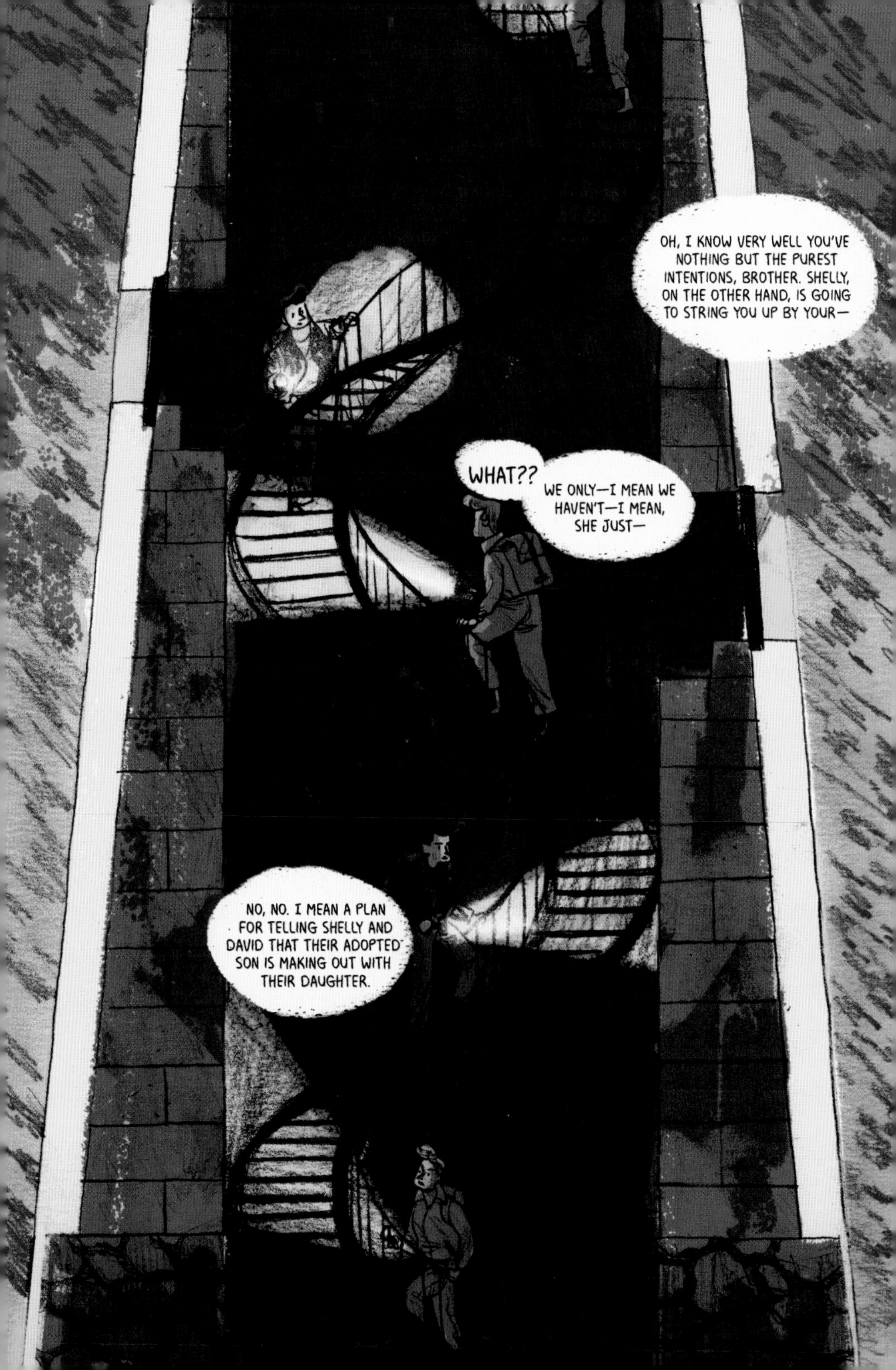
OH, I KNOW VERY WELL YOU'VE NOTHING BUT THE PUREST INTENTIONS, BROTHER. SHELLY, ON THE OTHER HAND, IS GOING TO STRING YOU UP BY YOUR—
WHAT??
WE ONLY—I MEAN WE HAVEN'T—I MEAN, SHE JUST—
NO, NO. I MEAN A PLAN FOR TELLING SHELLY AND DAVID THAT THEIR ADOPTED SON IS MAKING OUT WITH THEIR DAUGHTER.

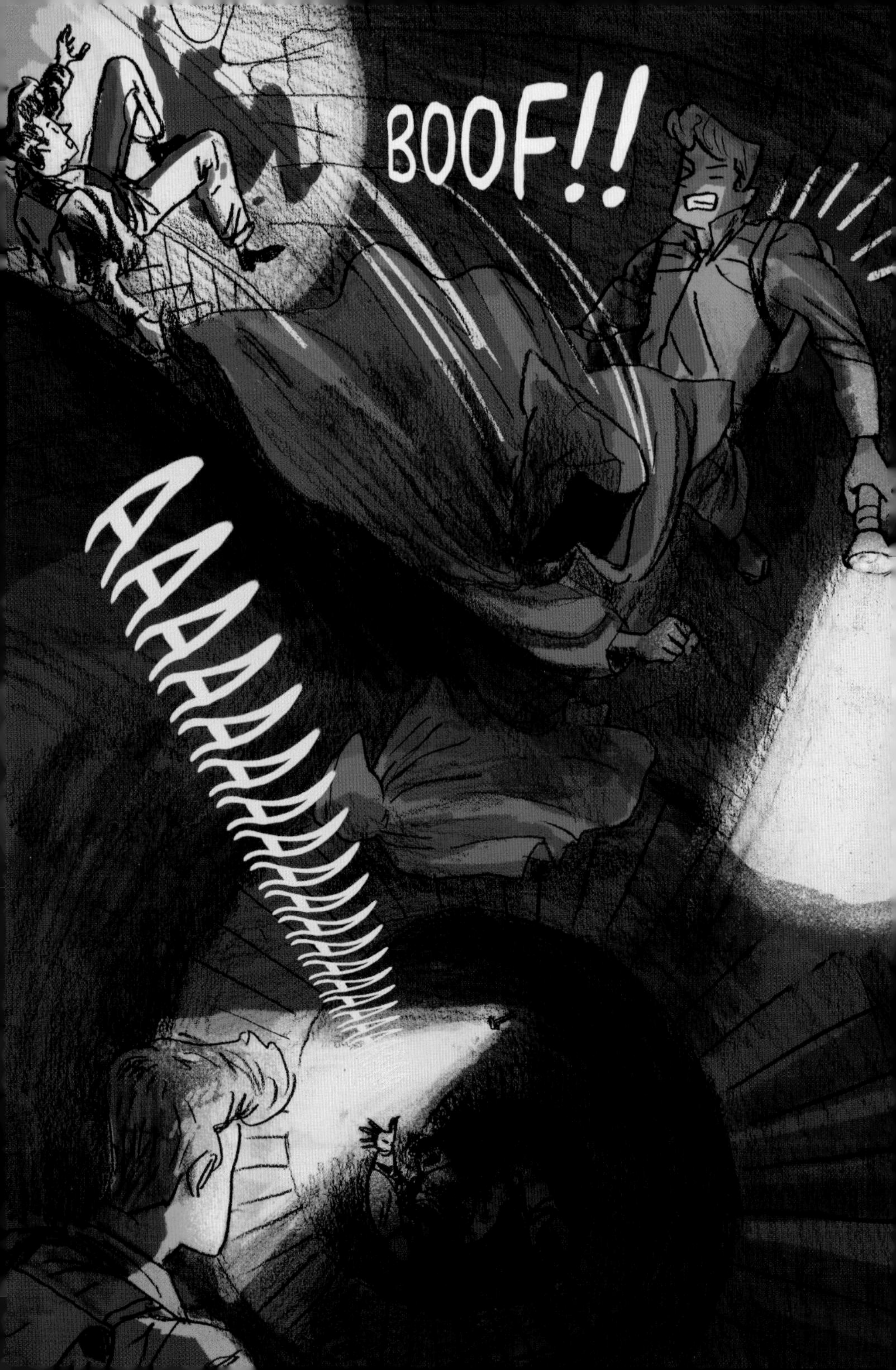
BOOF!!
AAAAAAAAAAAAAAAAAAAAA

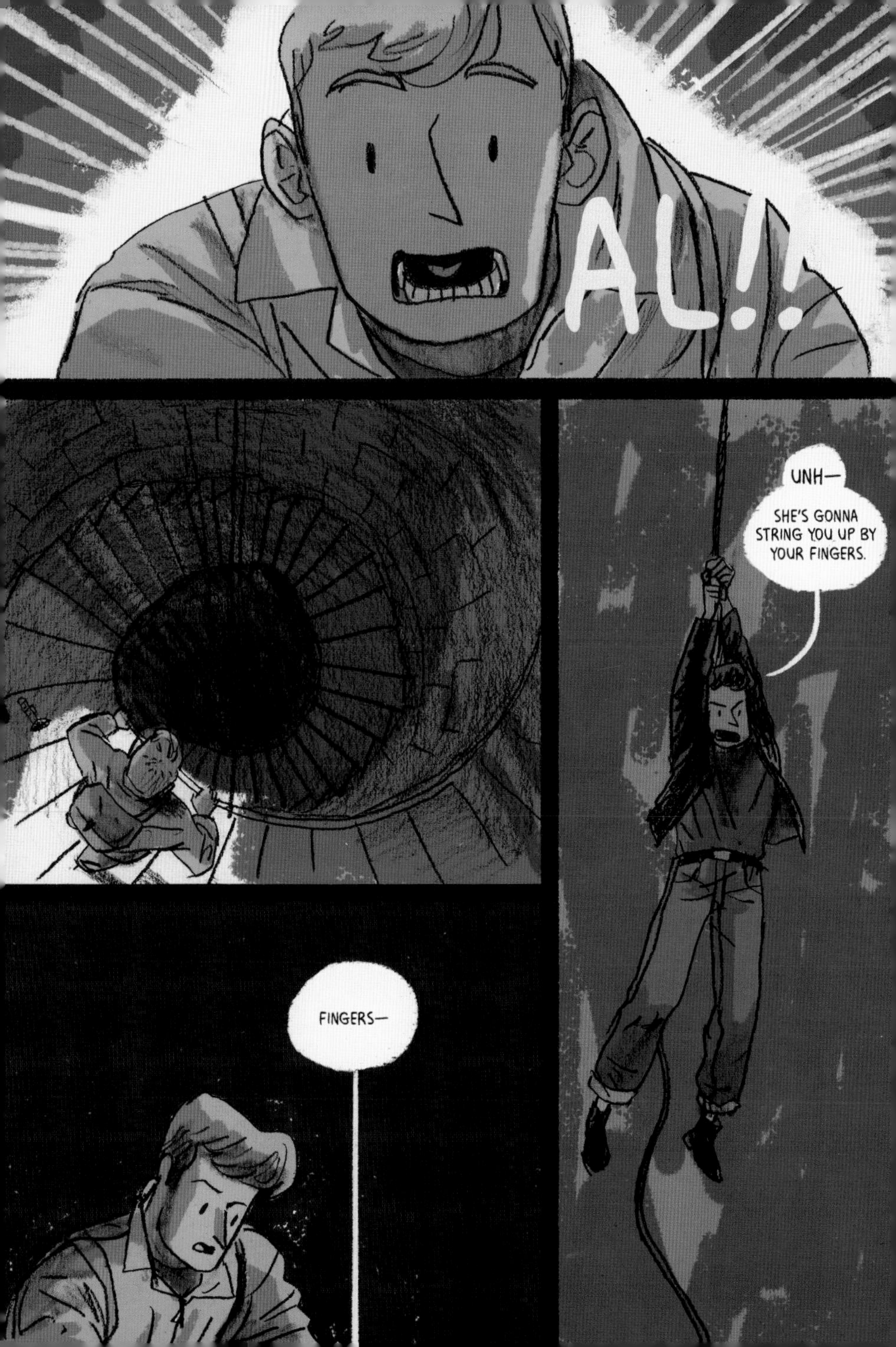
AL!!
UNH—
SHE'S GONNA STRING YOU UP BY YOUR FINGERS.
FINGERS—

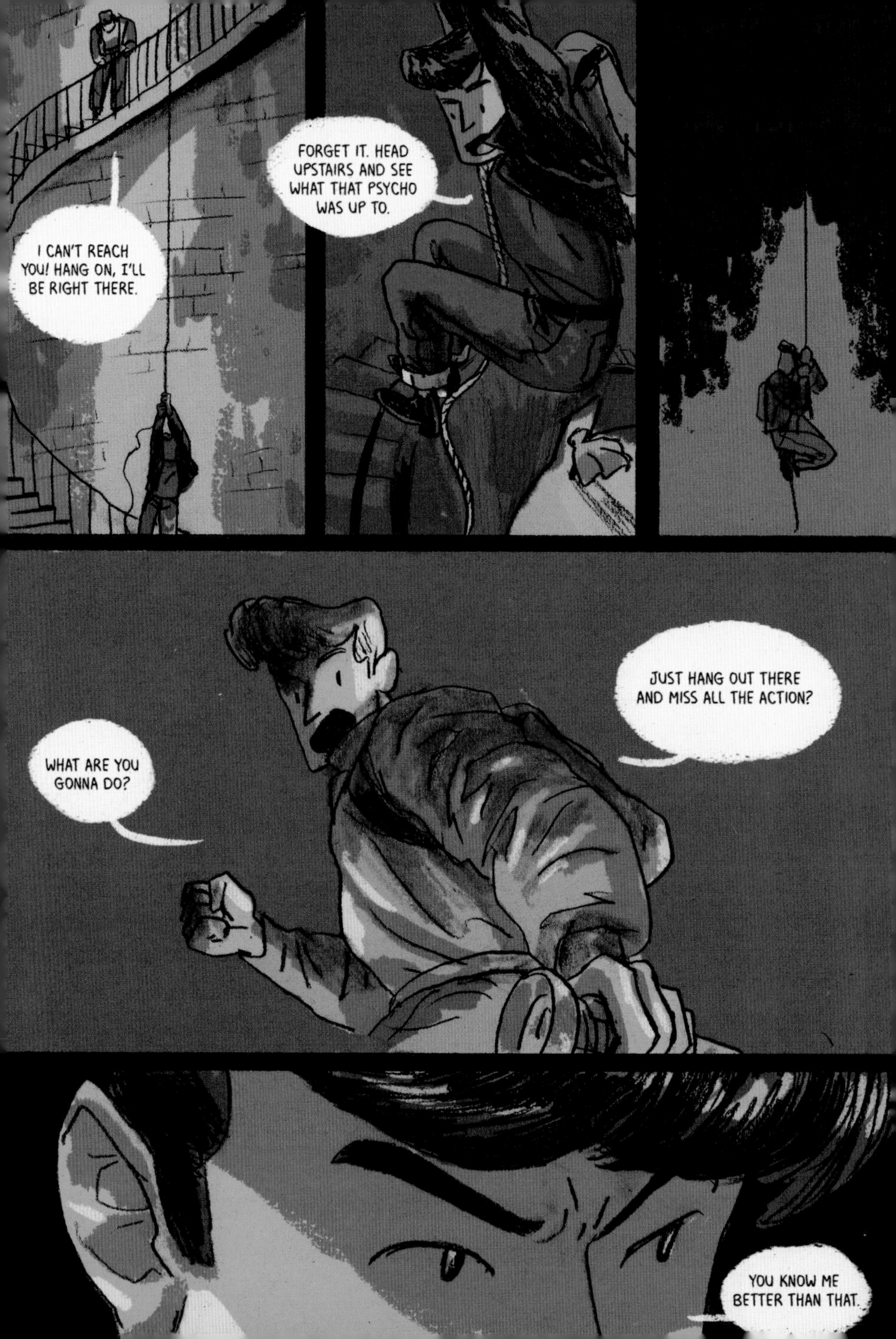
I CAN'T REACH YOU! HANG ON, I'LL BE RIGHT THERE.
FORGET IT. HEAD UPSTAIRS AND SEE WHAT THAT PSYCHO WAS UP TO.
WHAT ARE YOU GONNA DO?
JUST HANG OUT THERE AND MISS ALL THE ACTION?
YOU KNOW ME BETTER THAN THAT.

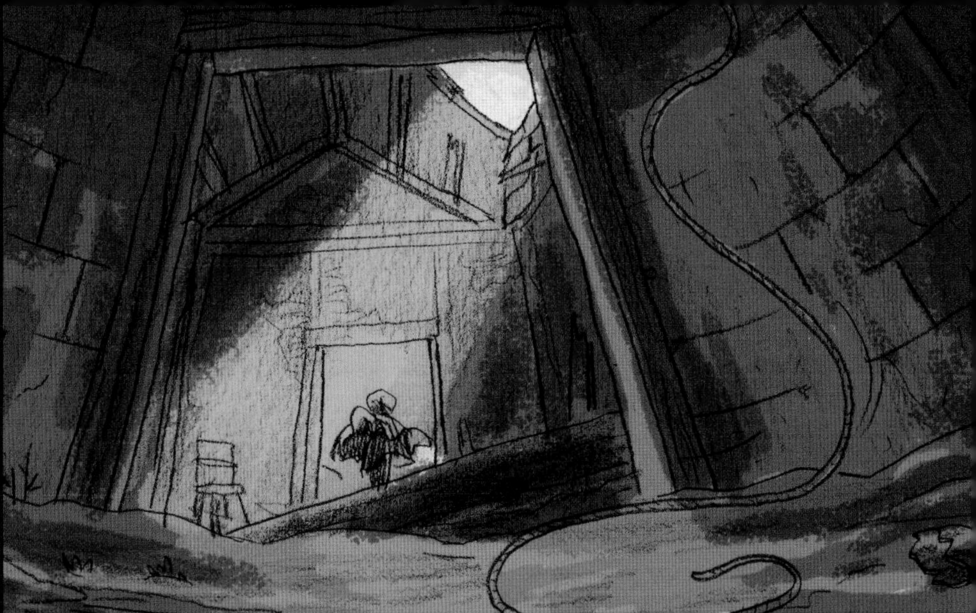
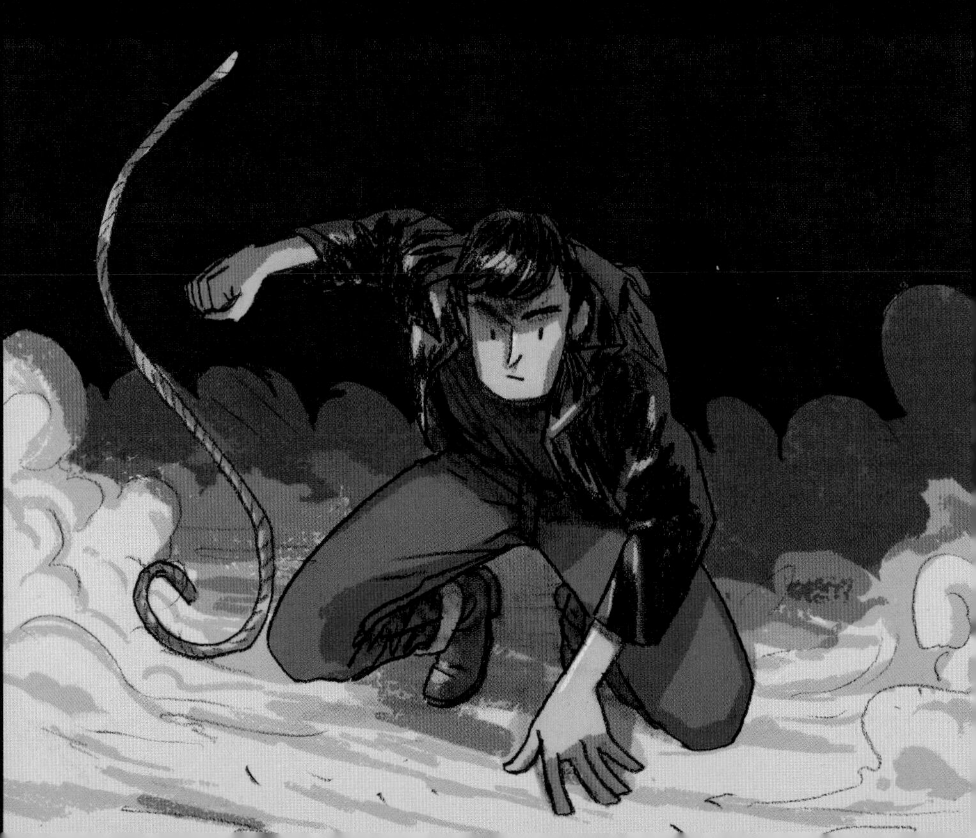

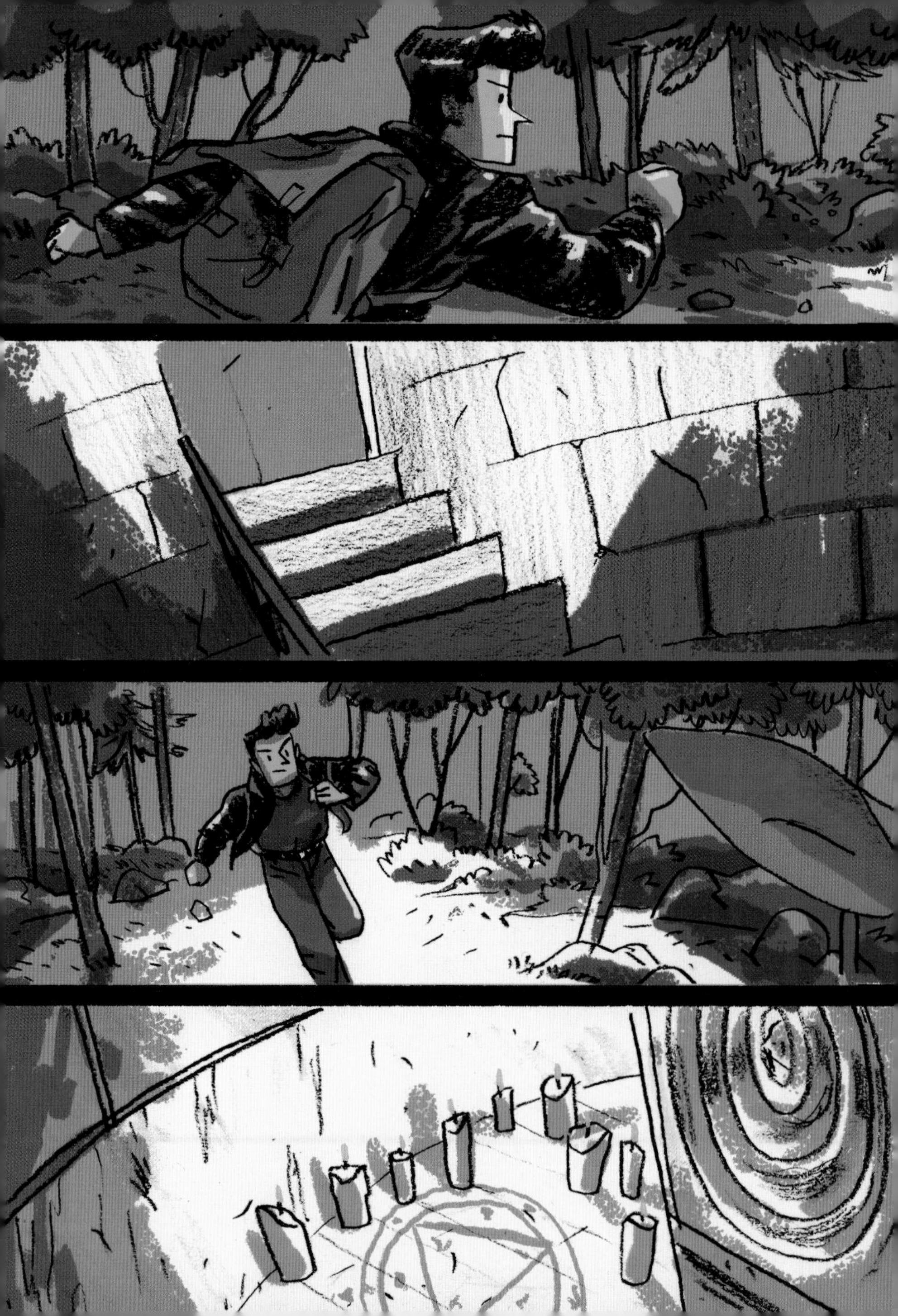

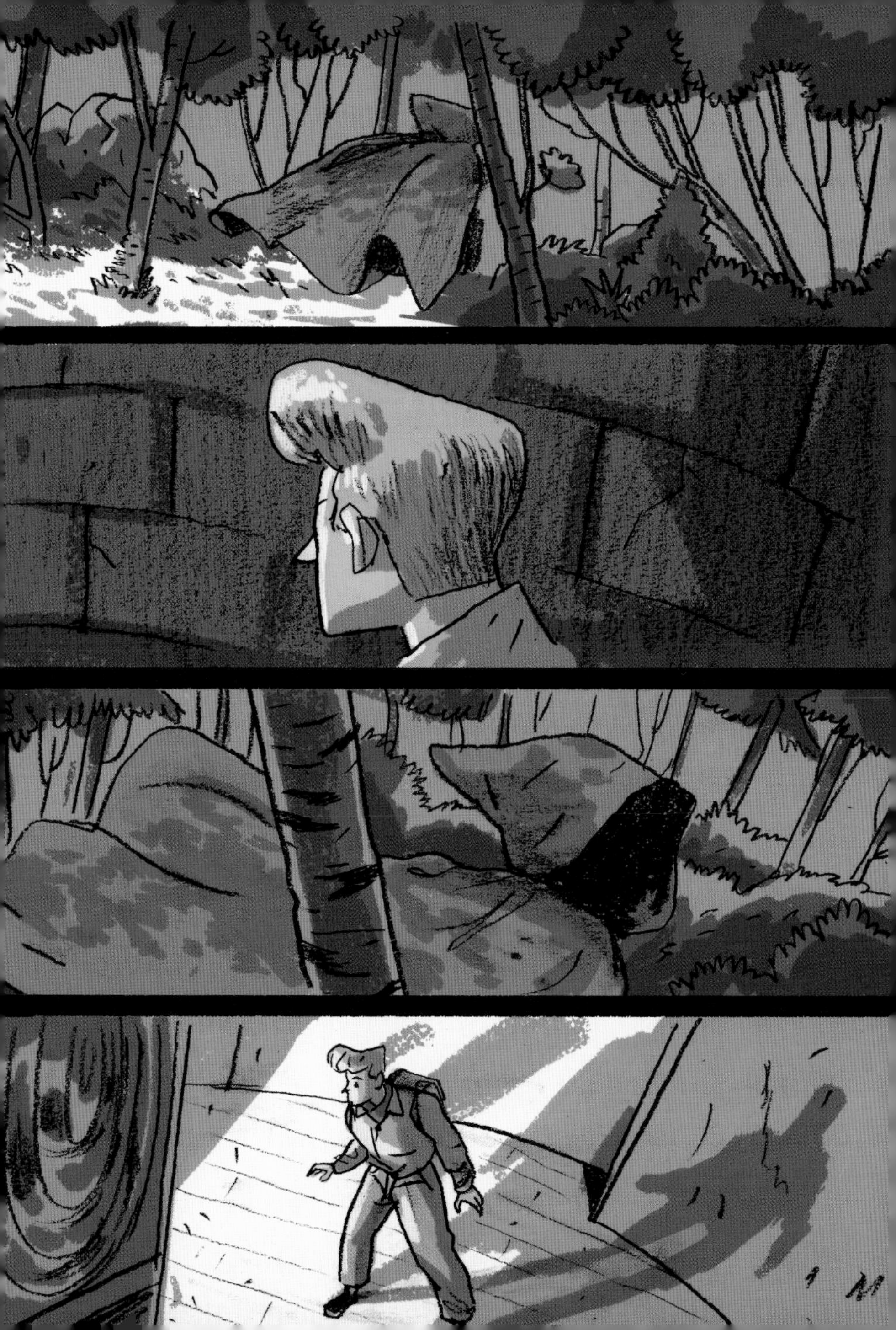

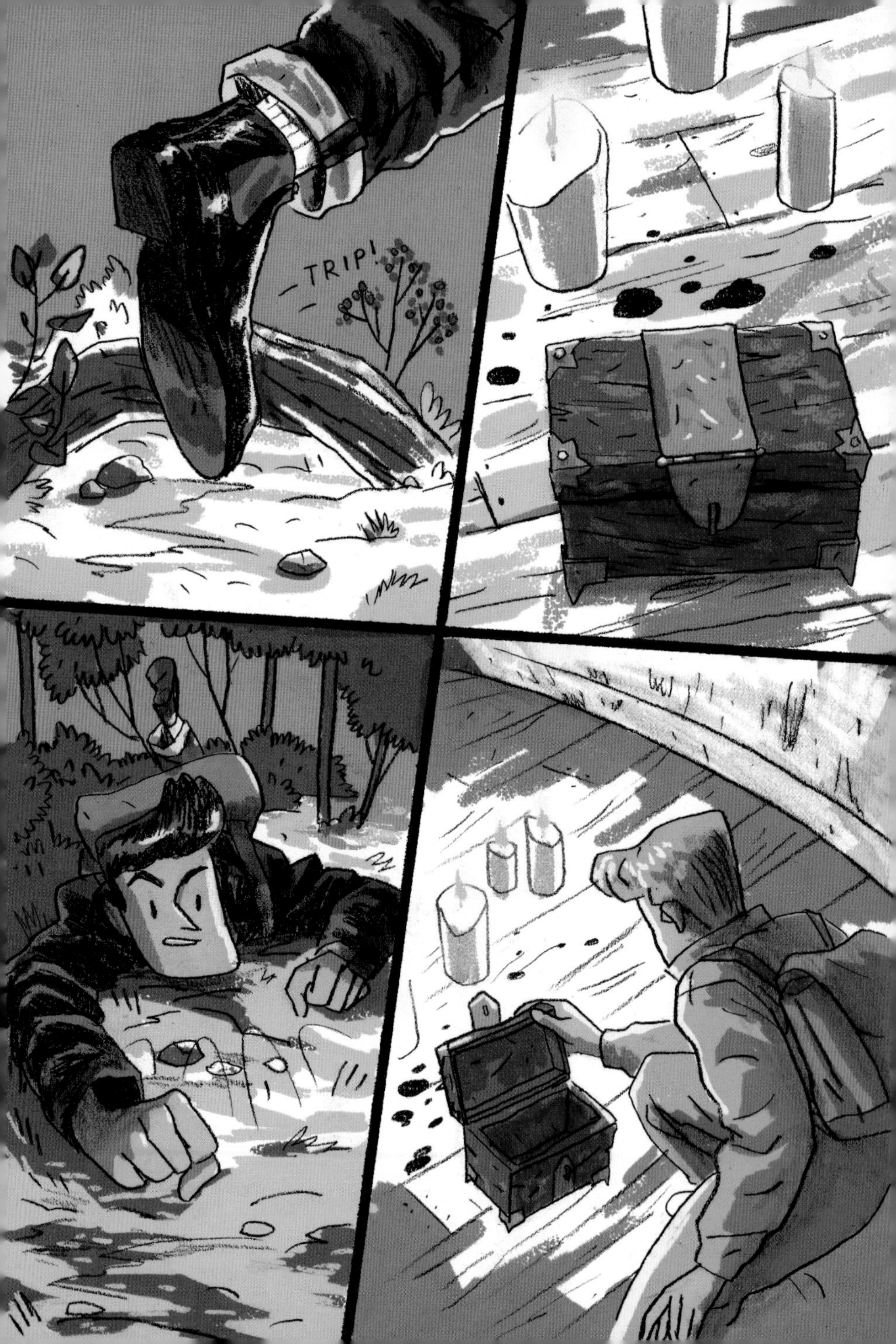
TRIP!

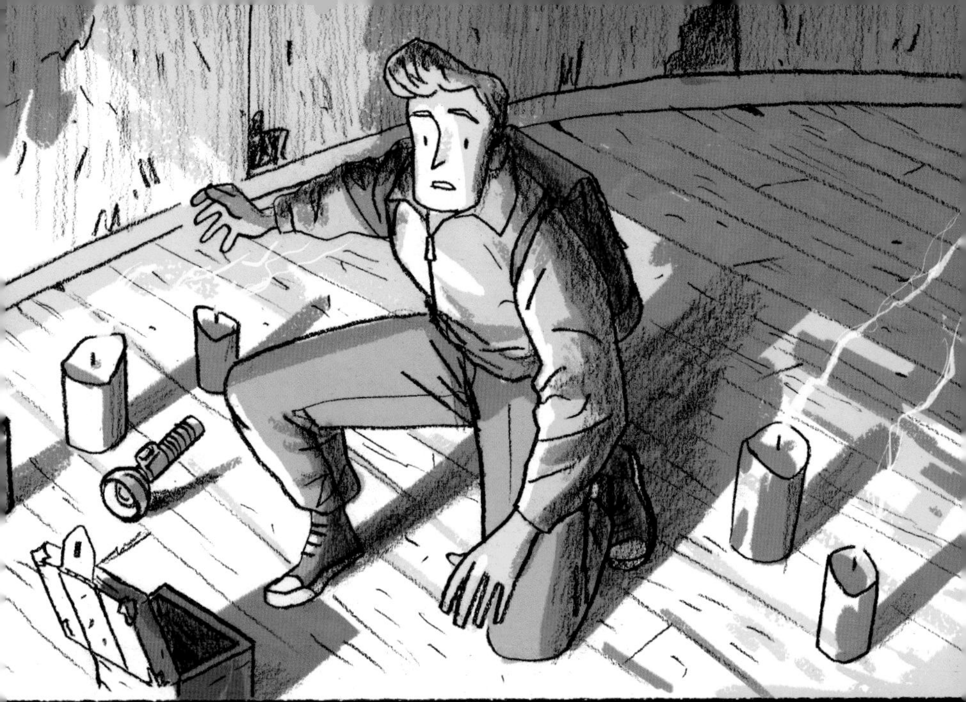

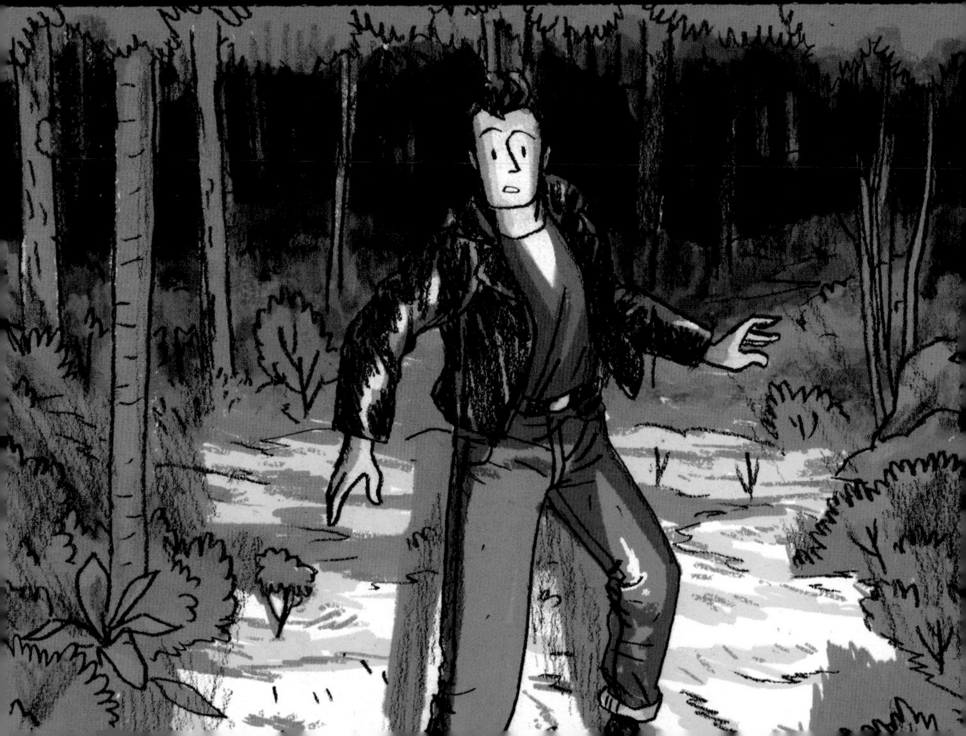

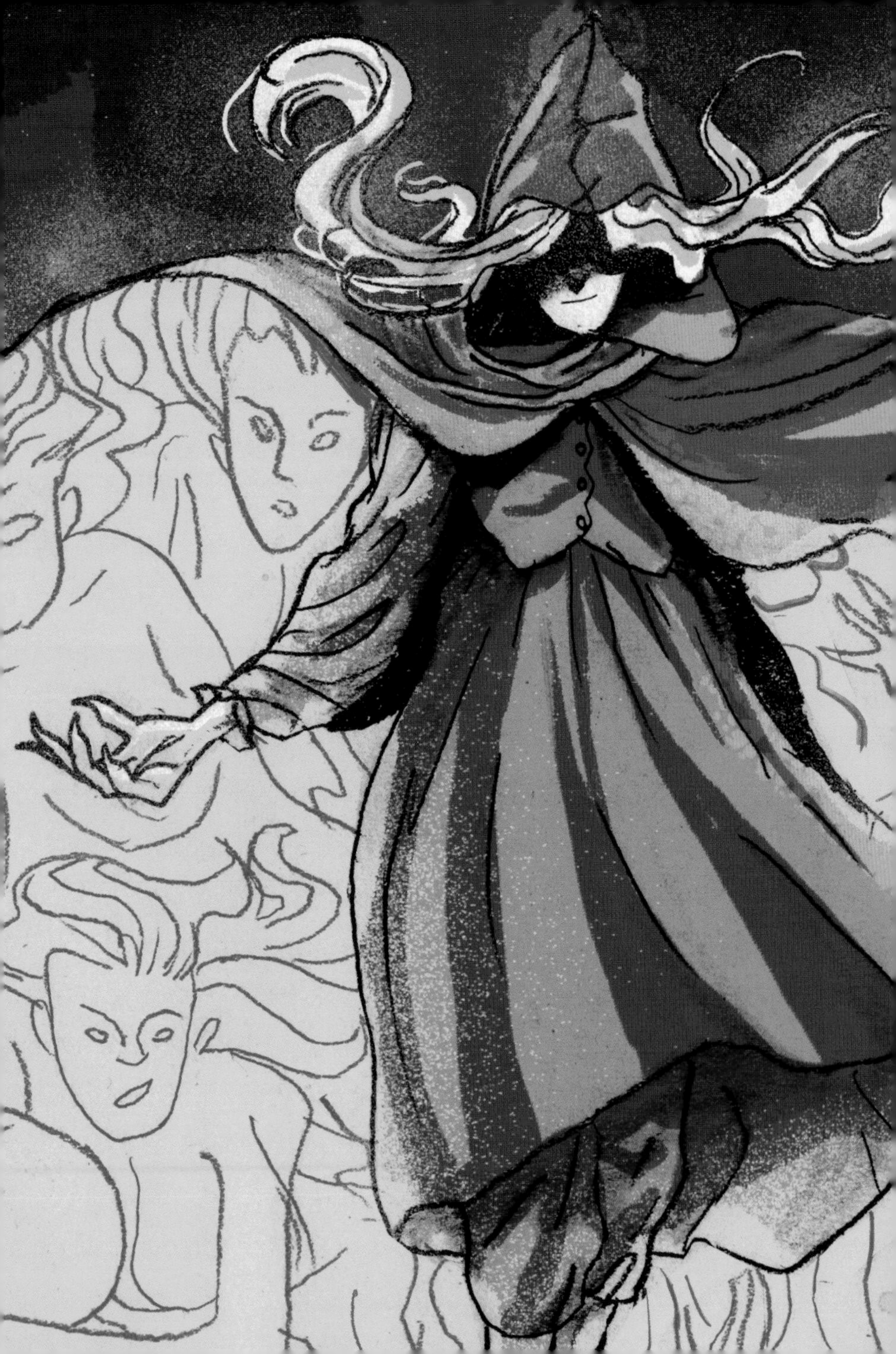

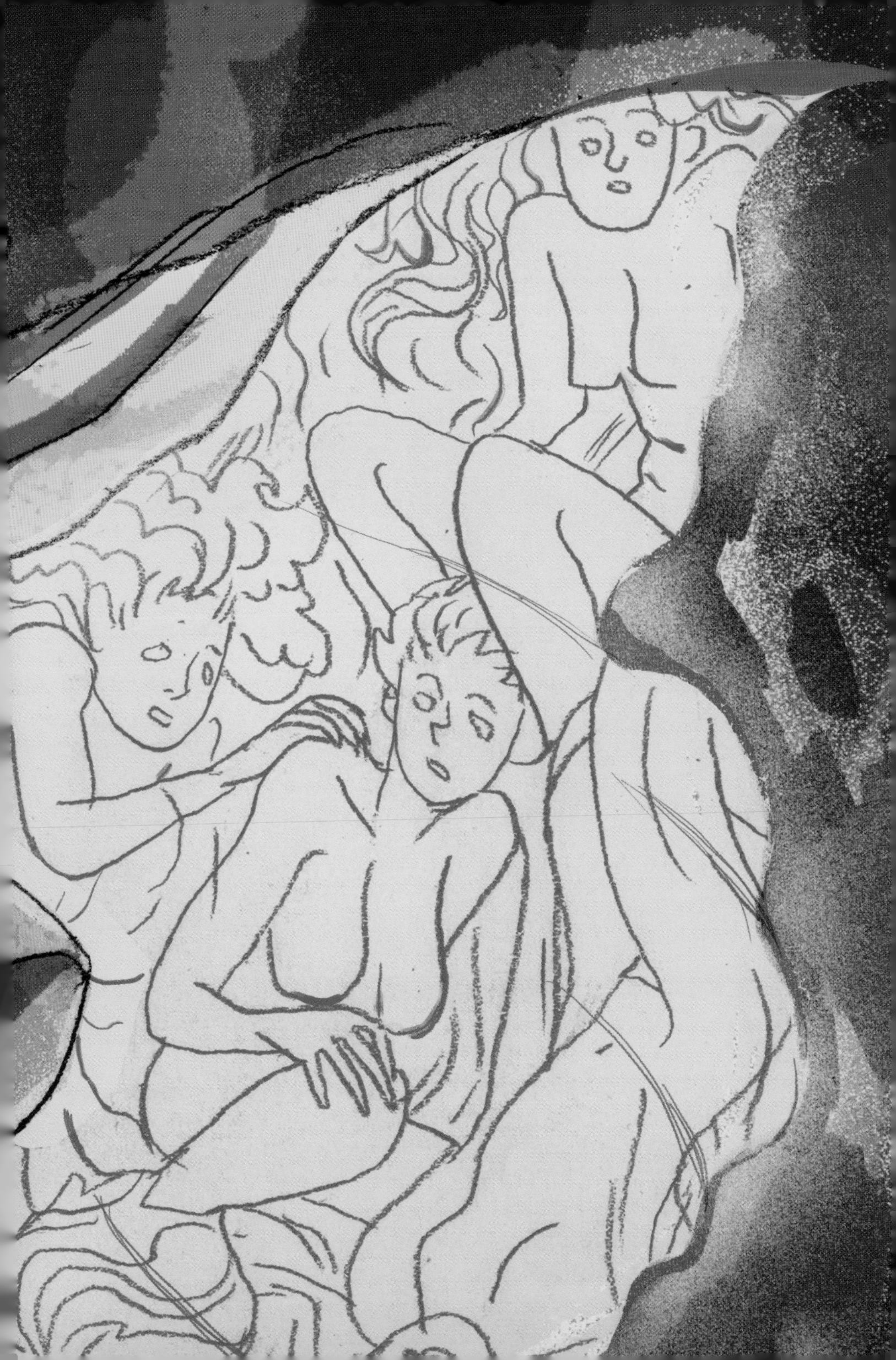

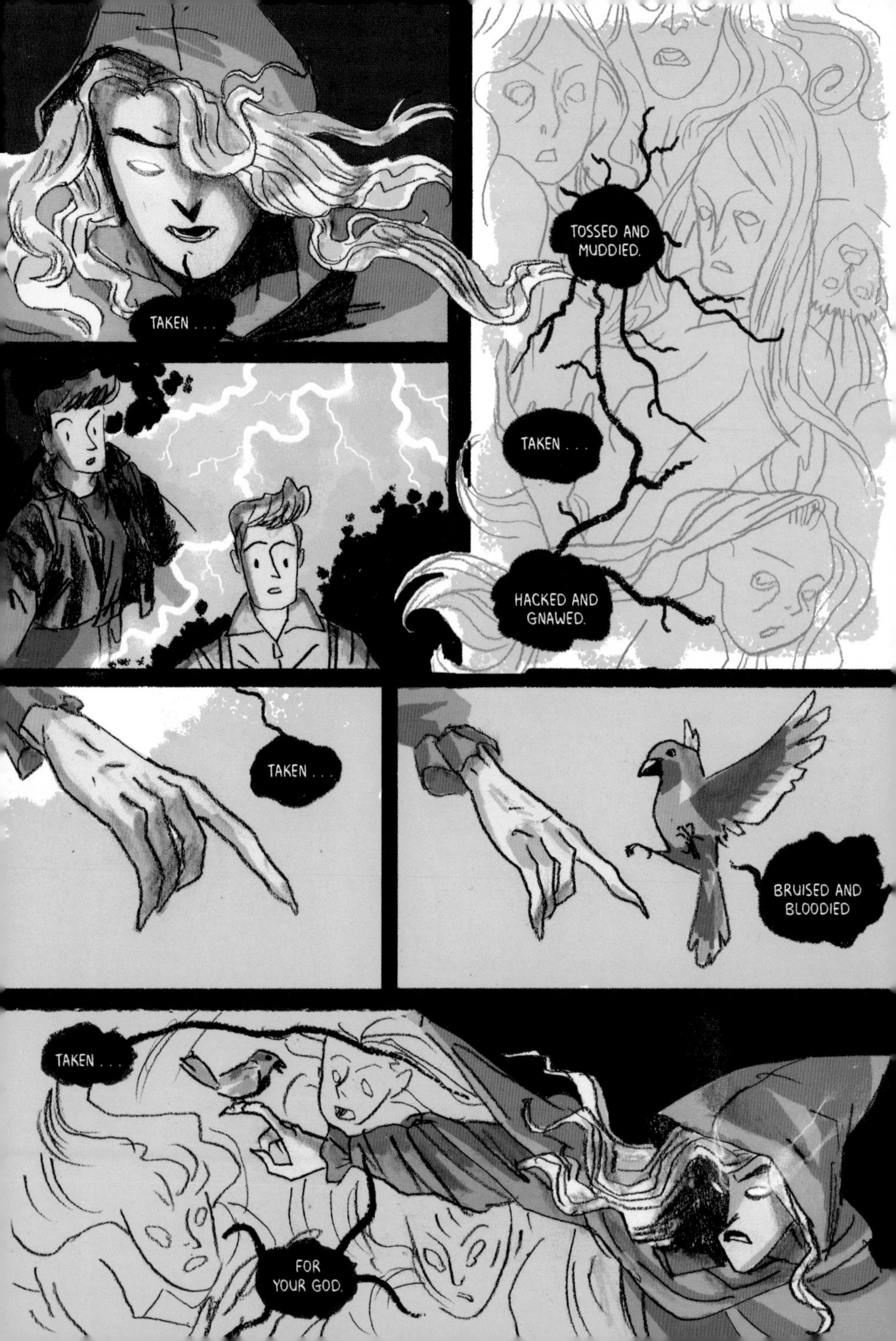
TAKEN . . .
TOSSED AND MUDDIED.
TAKEN . . .
HACKED AND GNAWED.
TAKEN . . .
BRUISED AND BLOODIED
TAKEN . . .
FOR YOUR GOD.

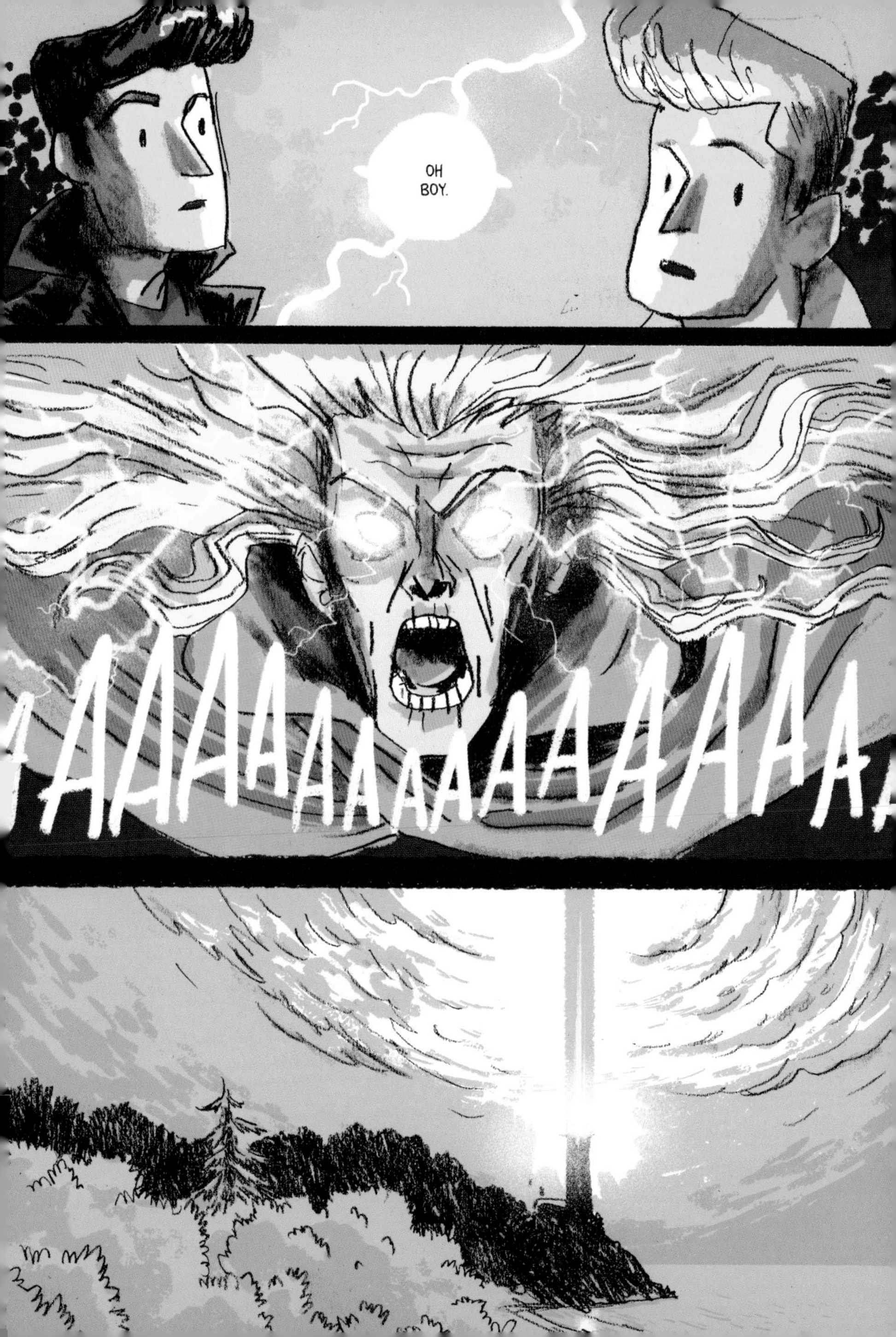
OH BOY.
AAAAAAAAAAAAAAAAAA

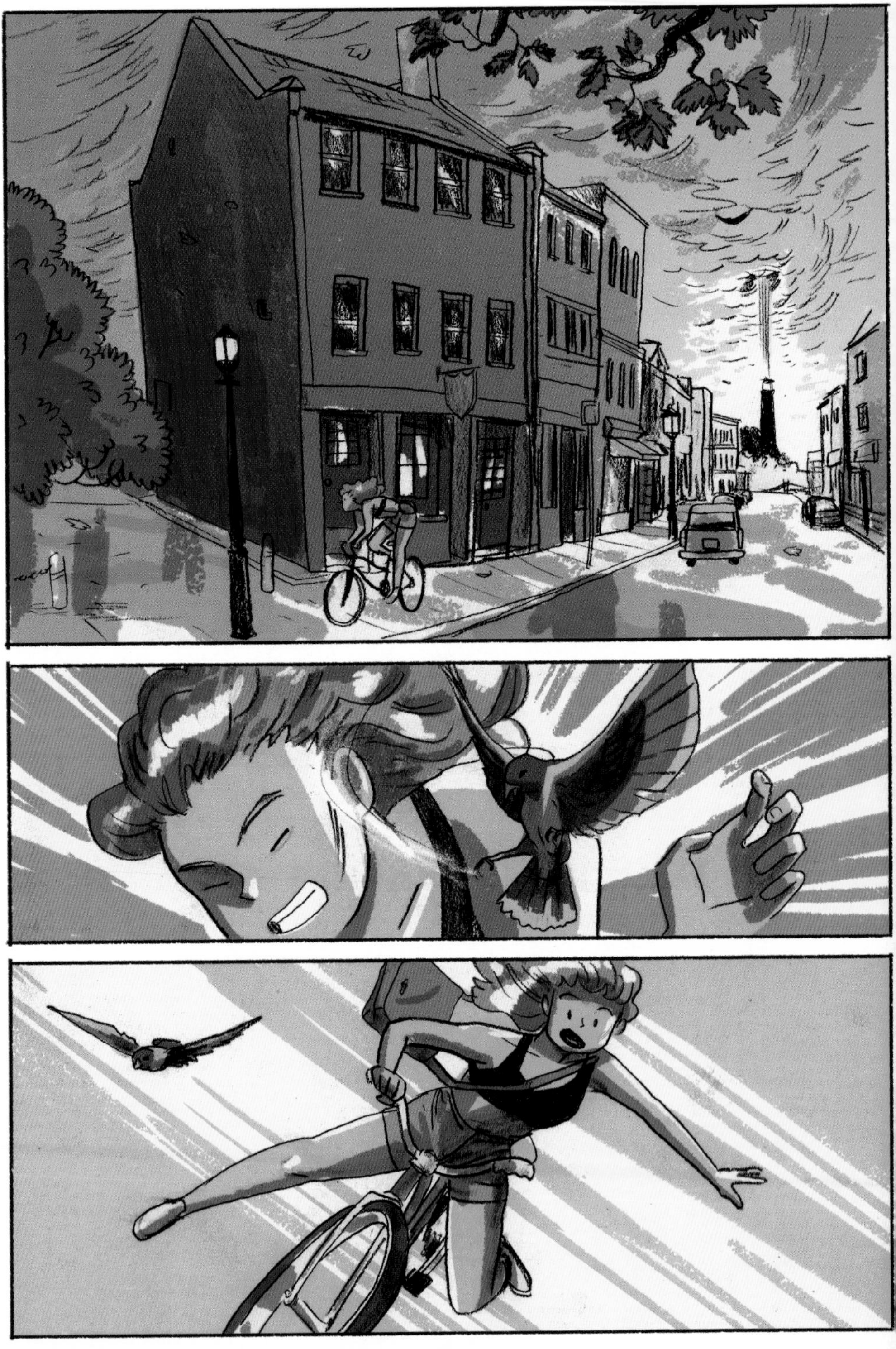

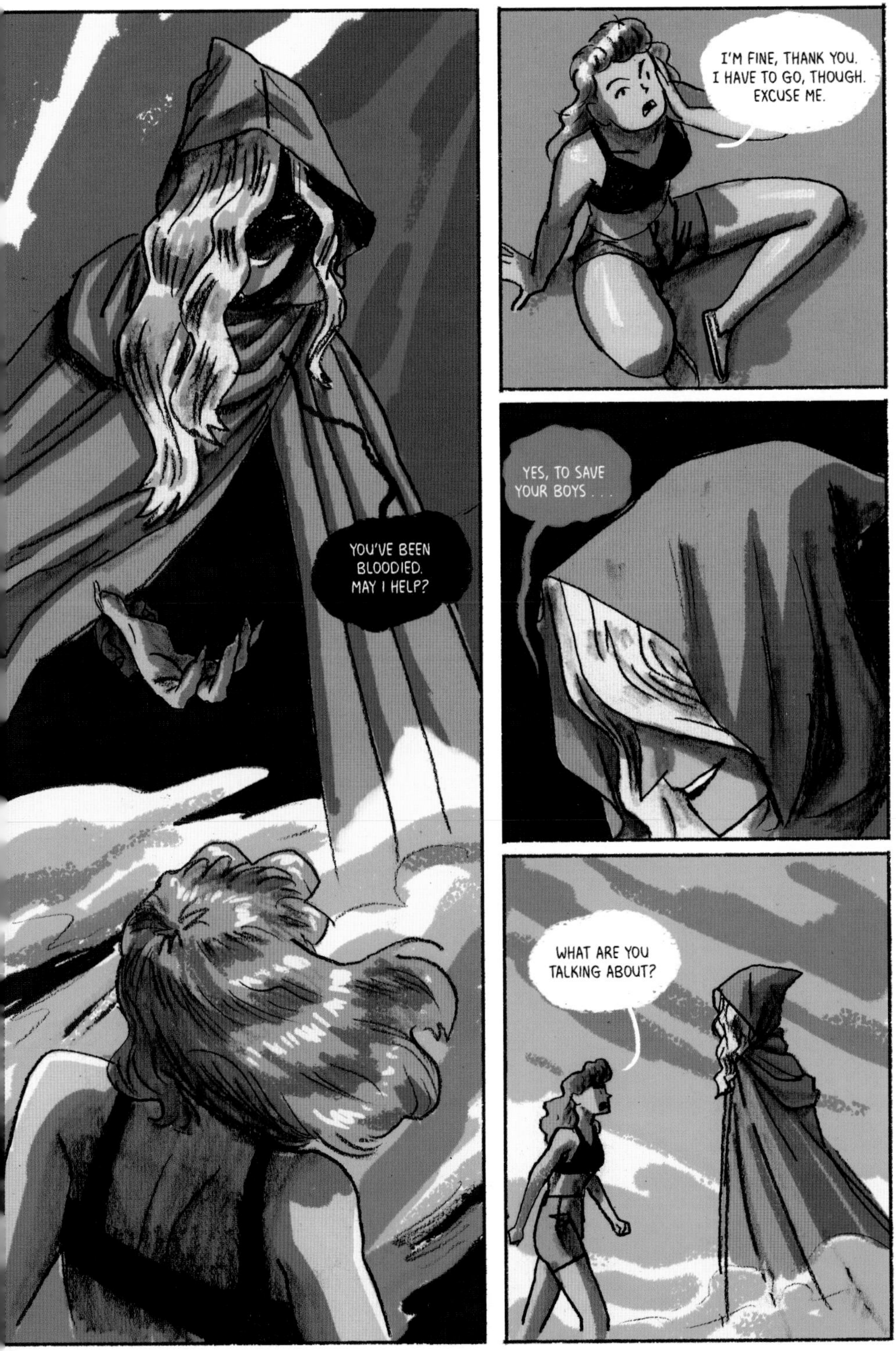
YOU'VE BEEN BLOODIED. MAY I HELP?
I'M FINE, THANK YOU. I HAVE TO GO, THOUGH. EXCUSE ME.
YES, TO SAVE YOUR BOYS . . .
WHAT ARE YOU TALKING ABOUT?

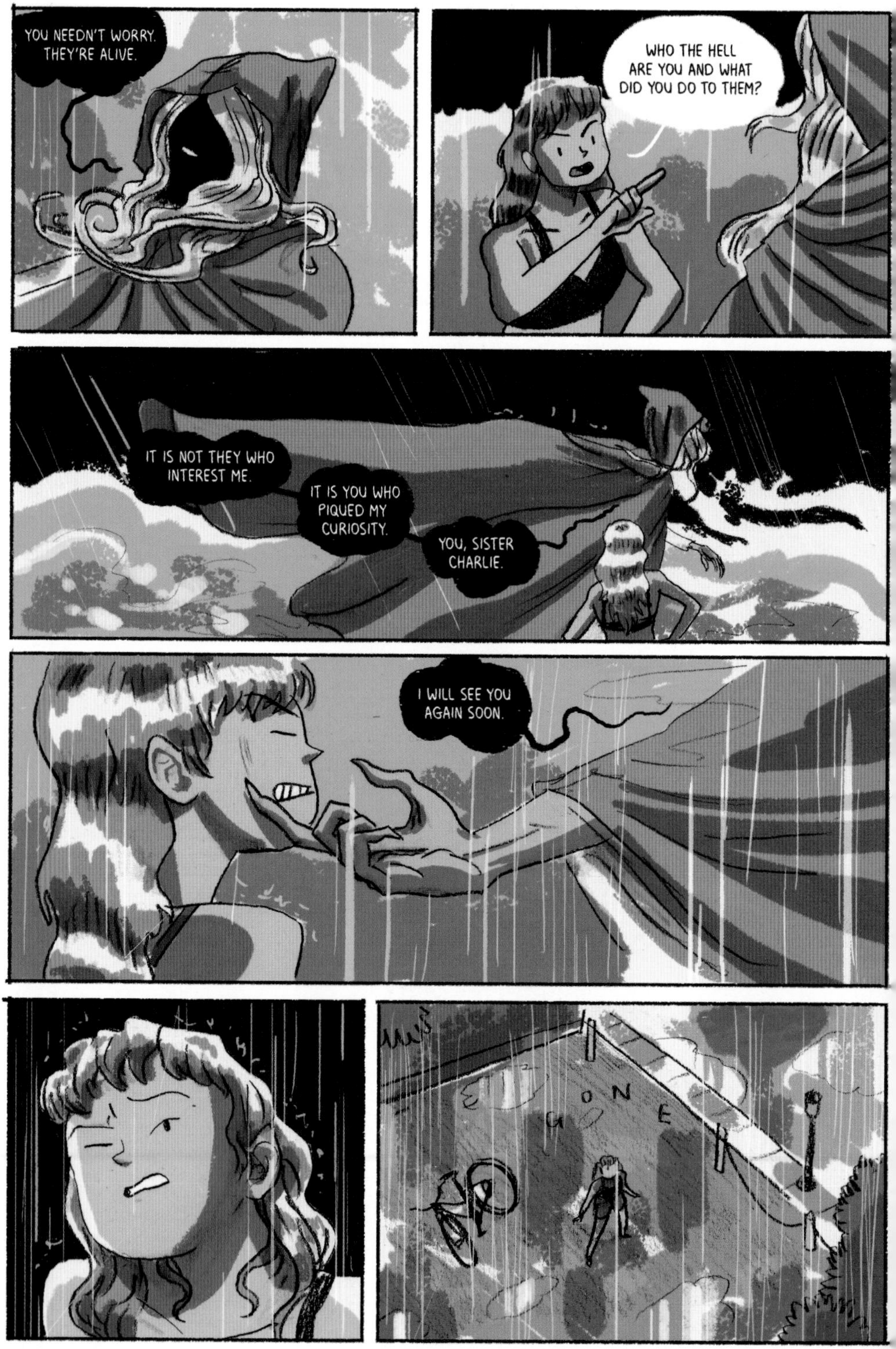
YOU NEEDN'T WORRY. THEY'RE ALIVE.
WHO THE HELL ARE YOU AND WHAT DID YOU DO TO THEM?
IT IS NOT THEY WHO INTEREST ME.
IT IS YOU WHO PIQUED MY CURIOSITY.
YOU, SISTER CHARLIE.
I WILL SEE YOU AGAIN SOON.
G O N E

CHAPTER 2

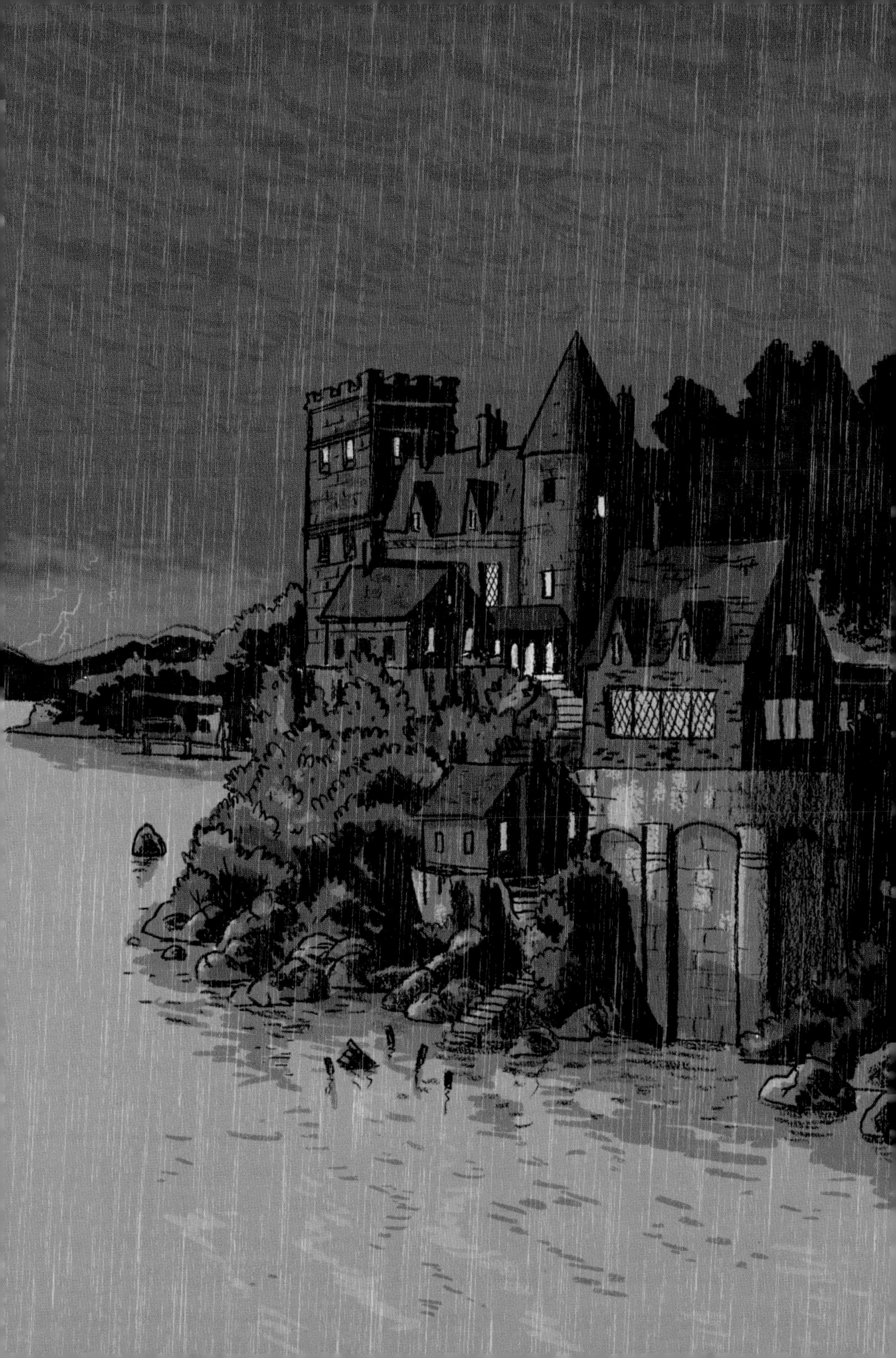

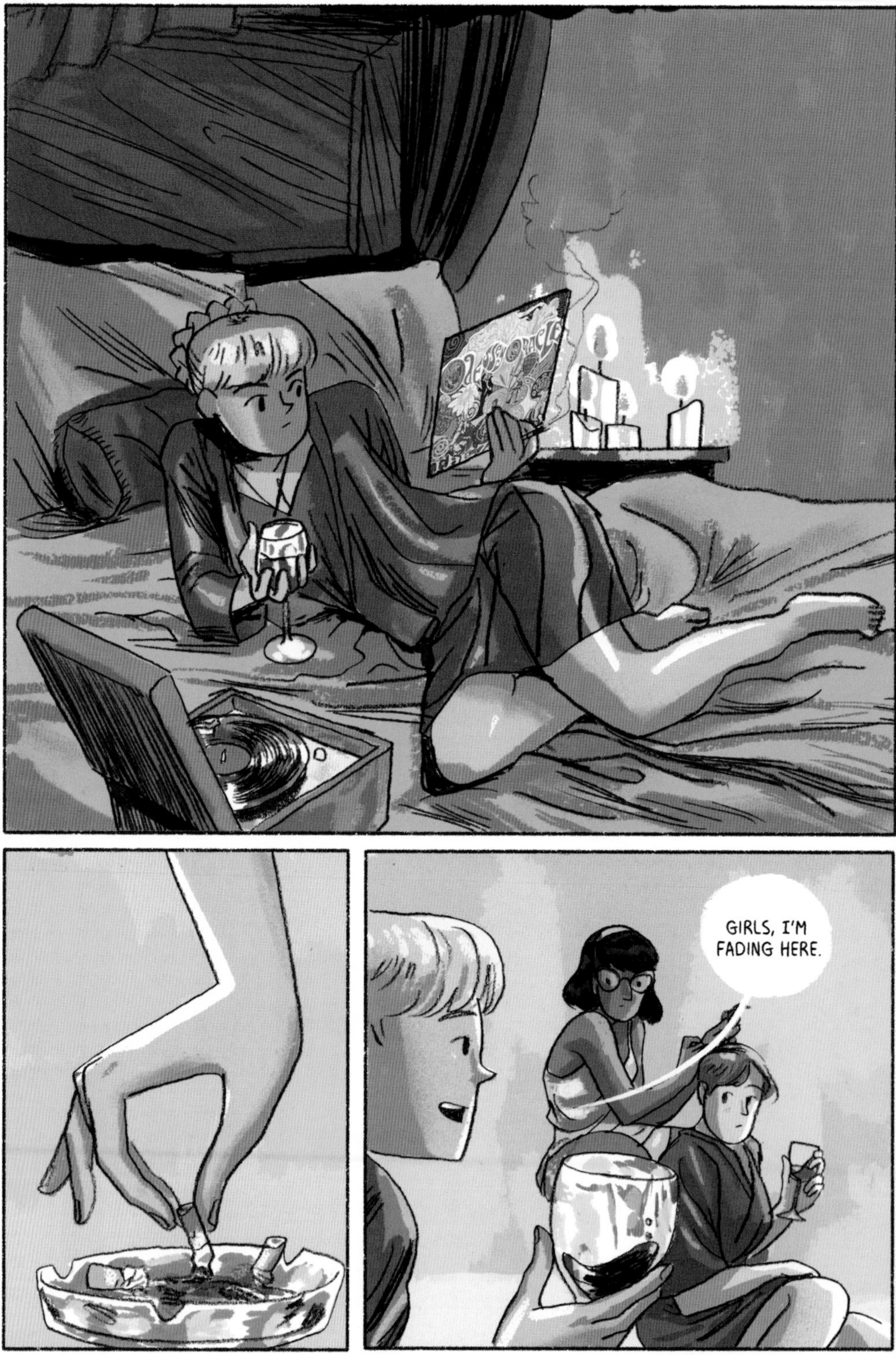
GIRLS, I'M
FADING HERE.

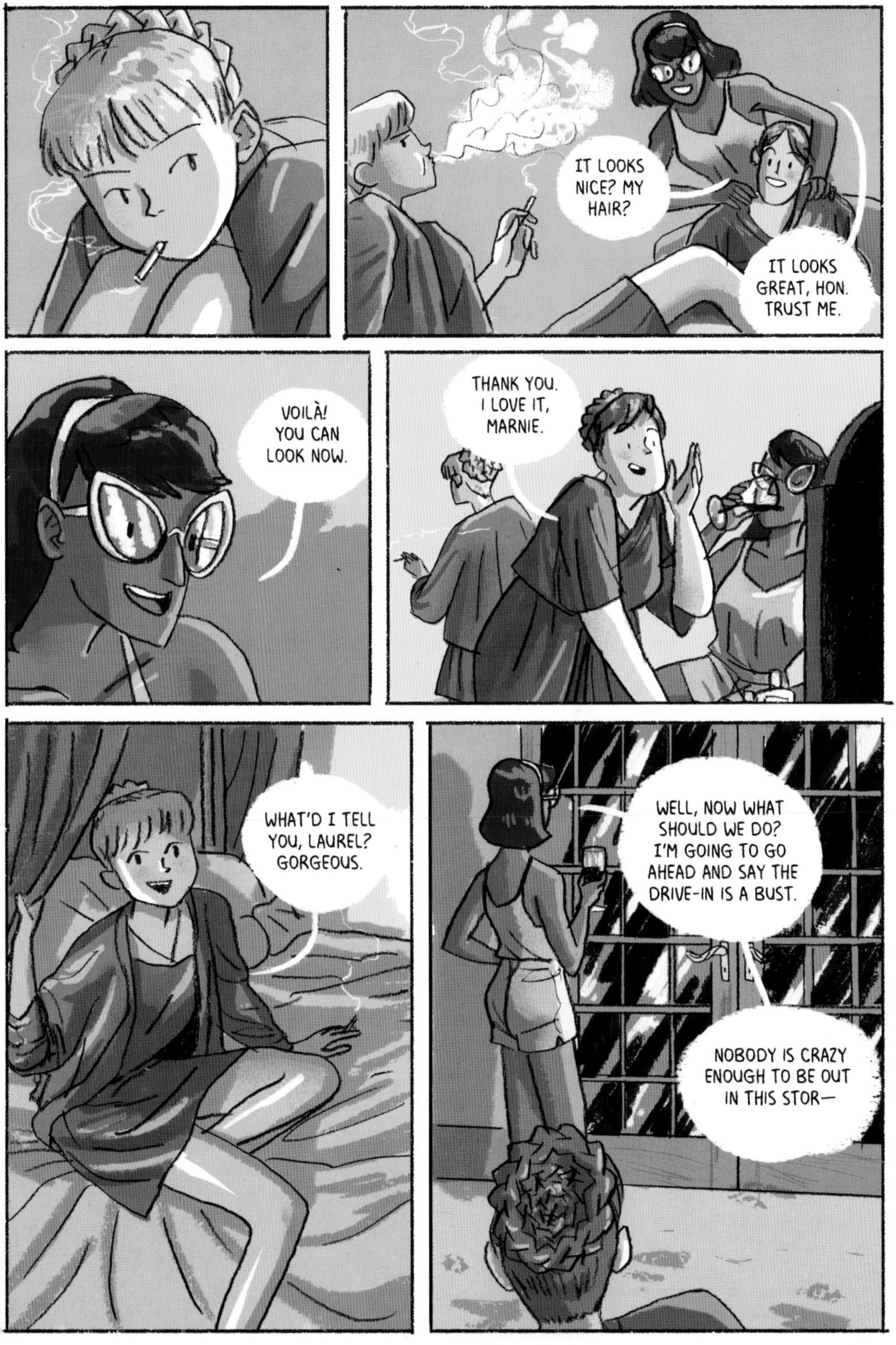
IT LOOKS NICE? MY HAIR?
IT LOOKS GREAT, HON. TRUST ME.
VOILÀ! YOU CAN LOOK NOW.
THANK YOU. I LOVE IT, MARNIE.
WHAT'D I TELL YOU, LAUREL? GORGEOUS.
WELL, NOW WHAT SHOULD WE DO? I'M GOING TO GO AHEAD AND SAY THE DRIVE-IN IS A BUST.
NOBODY IS CRAZY ENOUGH TO BE OUT IN THIS STOR—

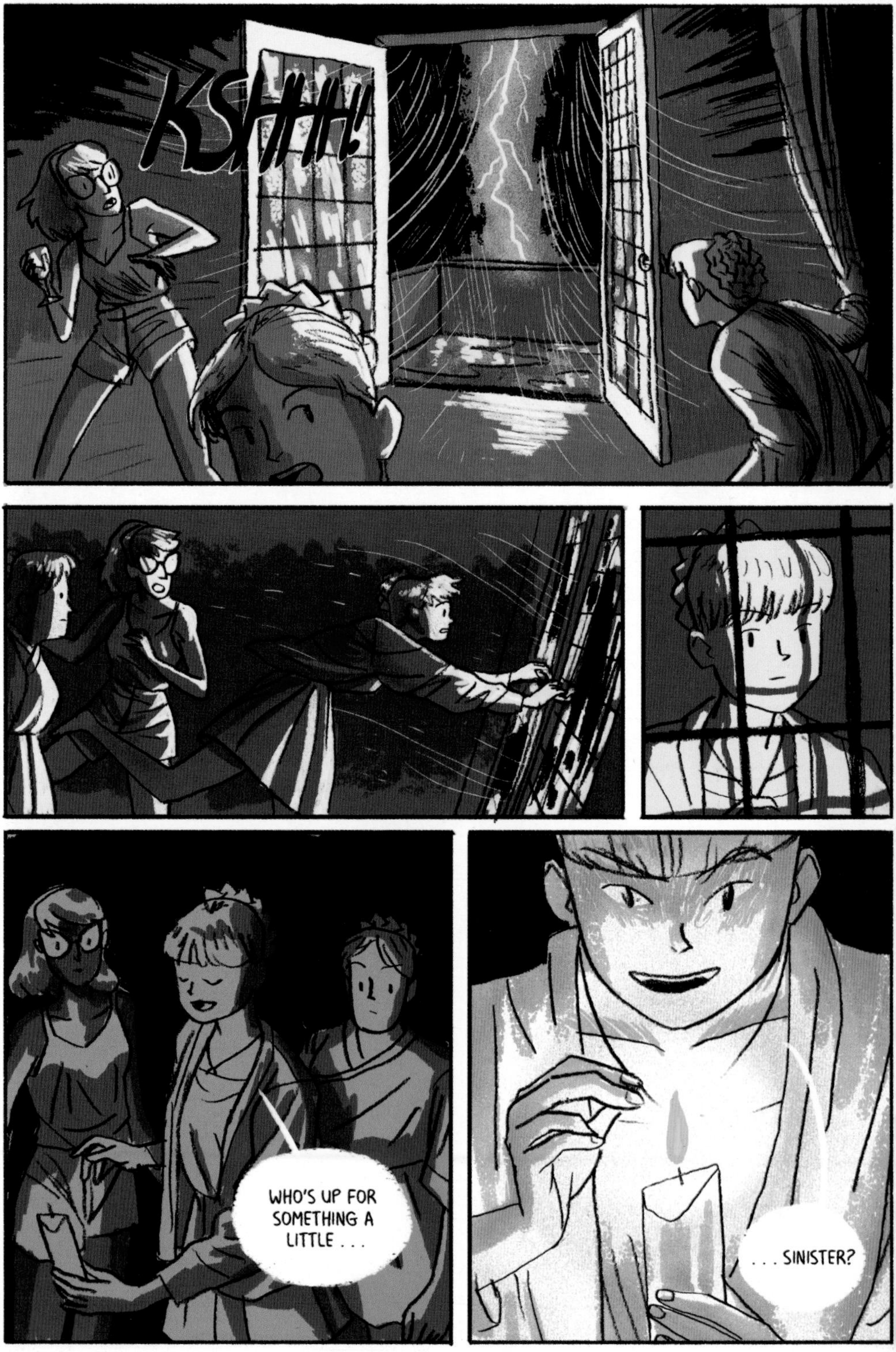
KSHHH!
WHO'S UP FOR SOMETHING A LITTLE . . .
. . . SINISTER?

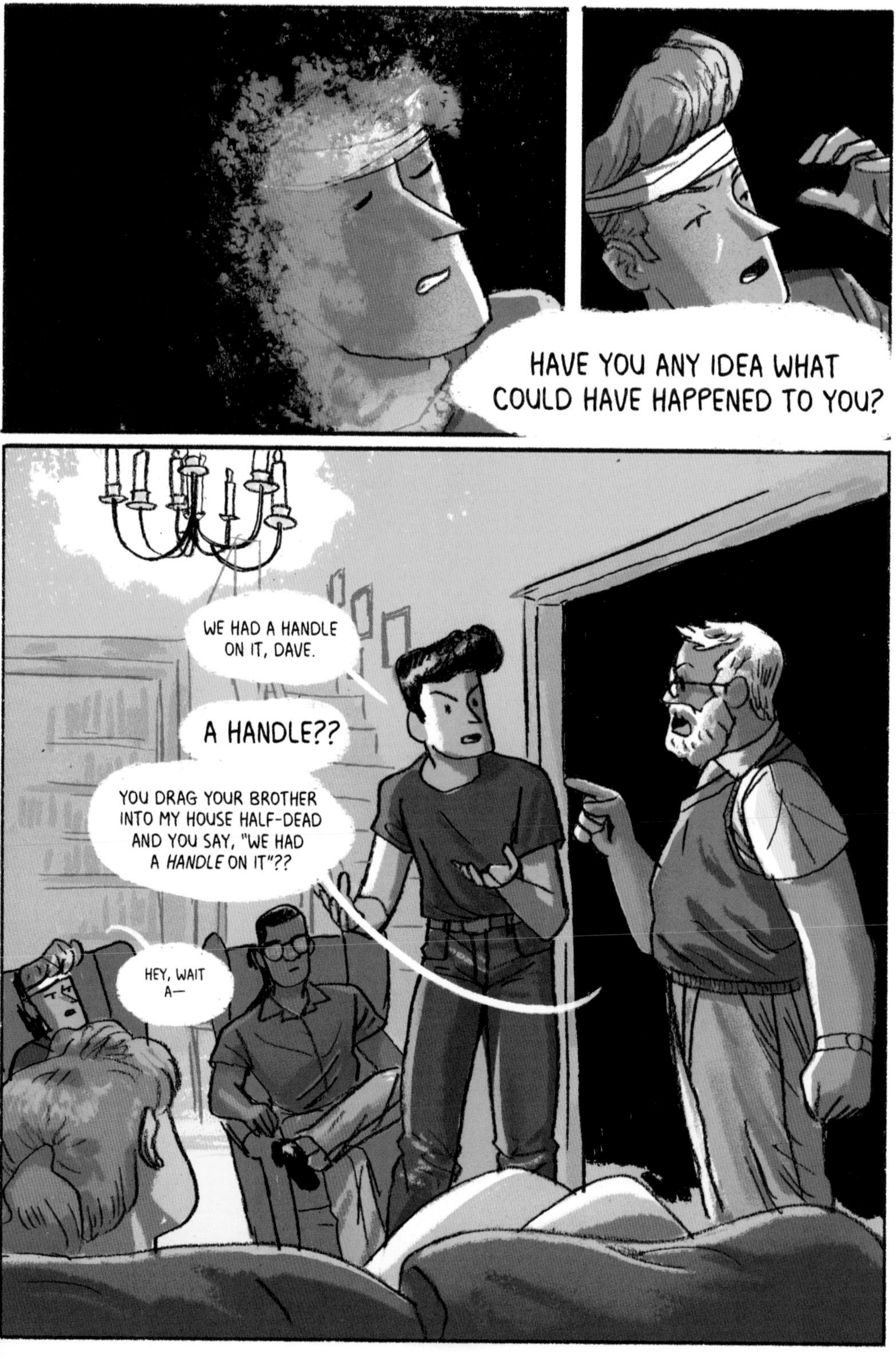
HAVE YOU ANY IDEA WHAT COULD HAVE HAPPENED TO YOU?
WE HAD A HANDLE ON IT, DAVE.
A HANDLE??
YOU DRAG YOUR BROTHER INTO MY HOUSE HALF-DEAD AND YOU SAY, "WE HAD A *HANDLE* ON IT"??
HEY, WAIT A—

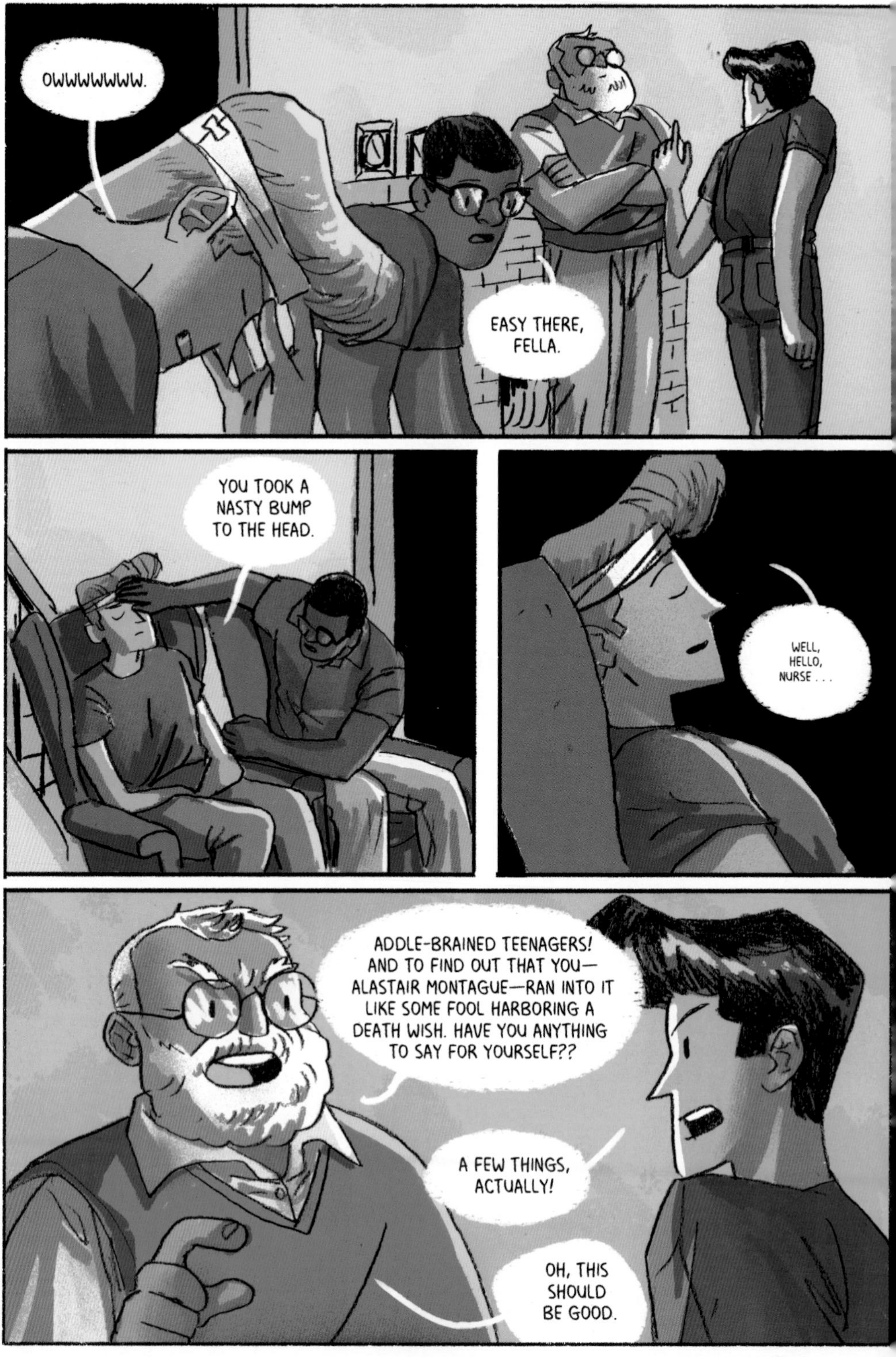
OWWWWWWW.
EASY THERE, FELLA.
YOU TOOK A NASTY BUMP TO THE HEAD.
WELL, HELLO, NURSE . . .
ADDLE-BRAINED TEENAGERS! AND TO FIND OUT THAT YOU—ALASTAIR MONTAGUE—RAN INTO IT LIKE SOME FOOL HARBORING A DEATH WISH. HAVE YOU ANYTHING TO SAY FOR YOURSELF??
A FEW THINGS, ACTUALLY!
OH, THIS SHOULD BE GOOD.

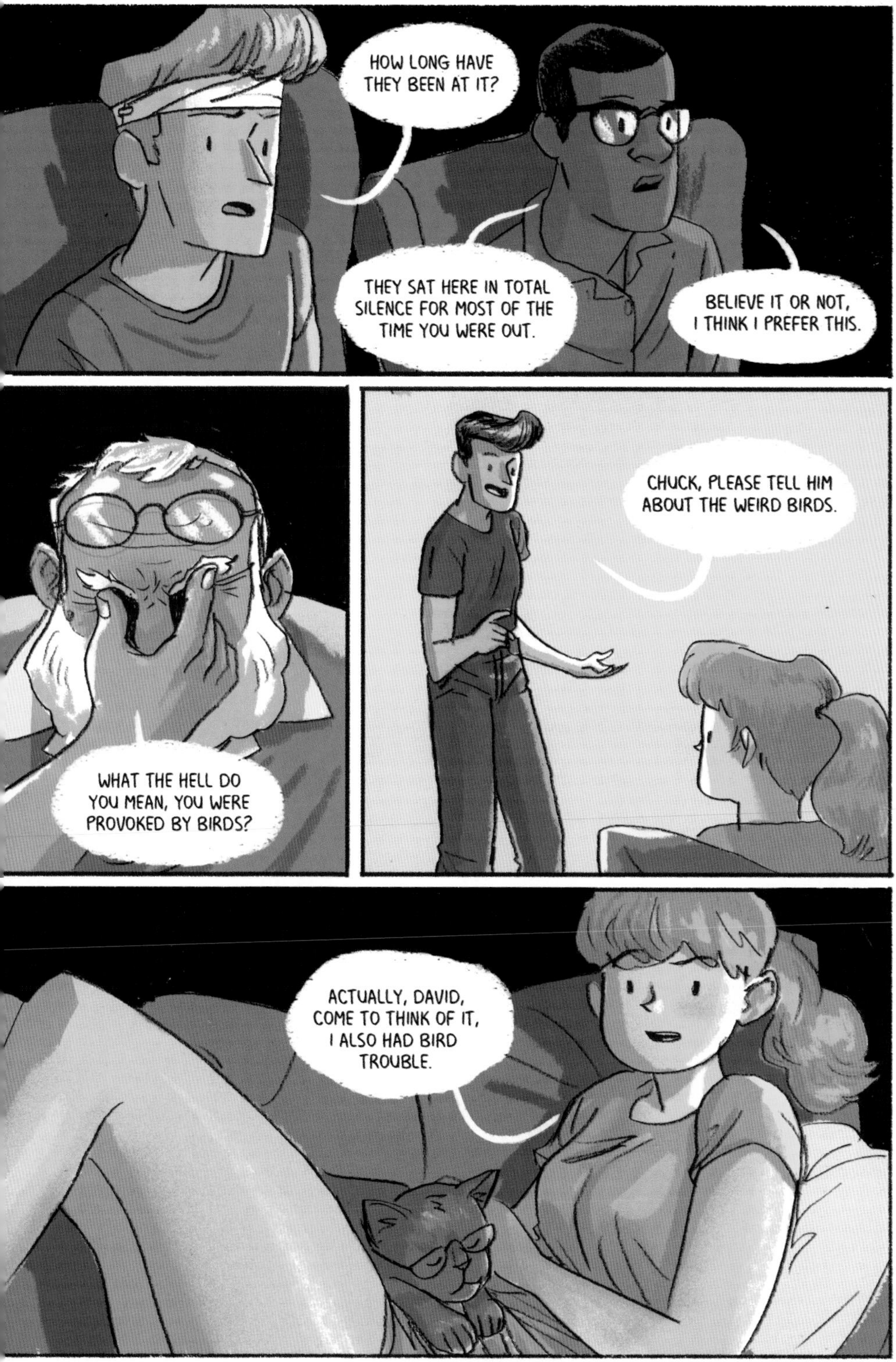
HOW LONG HAVE THEY BEEN AT IT?
THEY SAT HERE IN TOTAL SILENCE FOR MOST OF THE TIME YOU WERE OUT.
BELIEVE IT OR NOT, I THINK I PREFER THIS.
WHAT THE HELL DO YOU MEAN, YOU WERE PROVOKED BY BIRDS?
CHUCK, PLEASE TELL HIM ABOUT THE WEIRD BIRDS.
ACTUALLY, DAVID, COME TO THINK OF IT, I ALSO HAD BIRD TROUBLE.

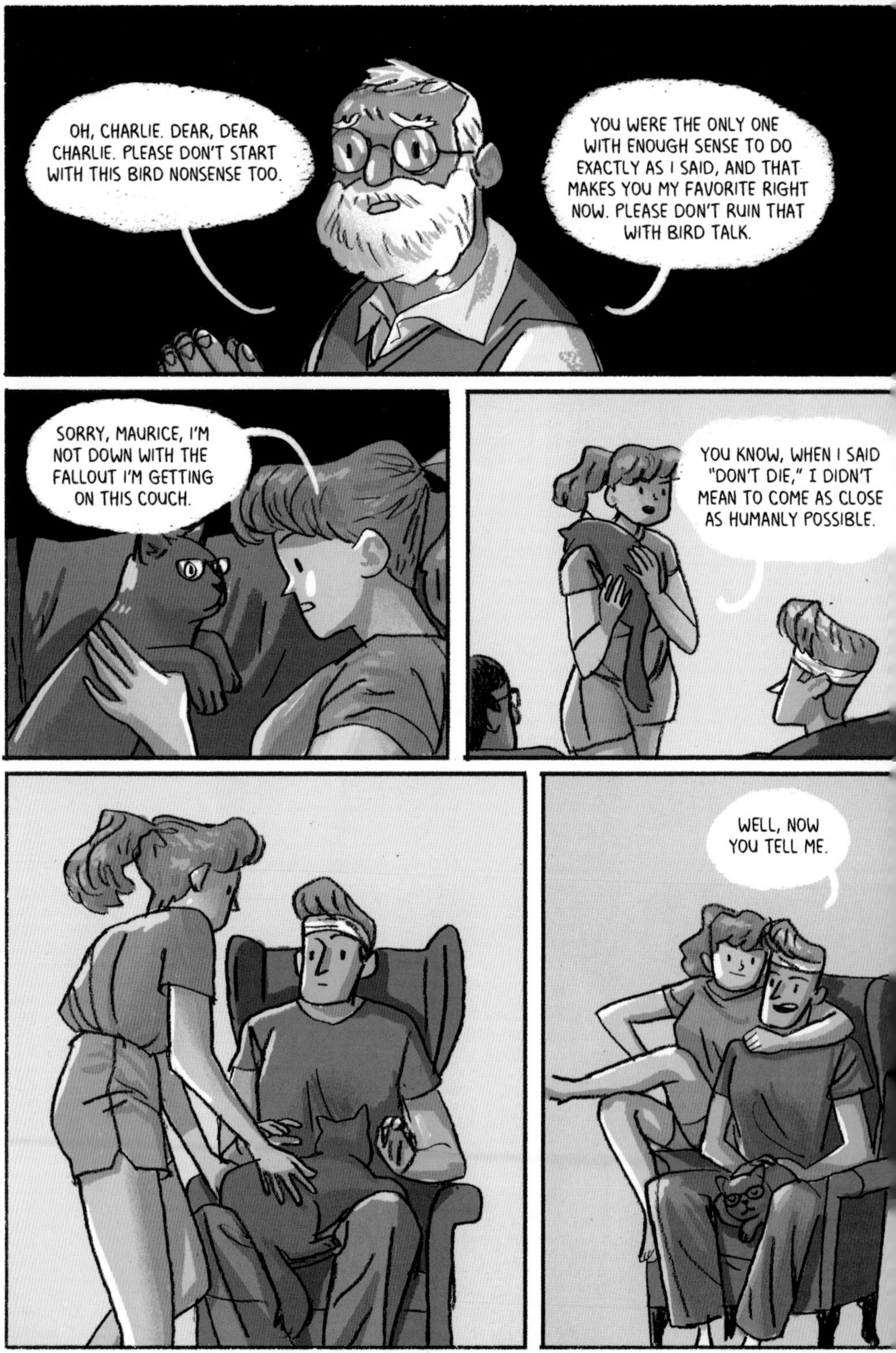
OH, CHARLIE. DEAR, DEAR CHARLIE. PLEASE DON'T START WITH THIS BIRD NONSENSE TOO.
YOU WERE THE ONLY ONE WITH ENOUGH SENSE TO DO EXACTLY AS I SAID, AND THAT MAKES YOU MY FAVORITE RIGHT NOW. PLEASE DON'T RUIN THAT WITH BIRD TALK.
SORRY, MAURICE, I'M NOT DOWN WITH THE FALLOUT I'M GETTING ON THIS COUCH.
YOU KNOW, WHEN I SAID "DON'T DIE," I DIDN'T MEAN TO COME AS CLOSE AS HUMANLY POSSIBLE.
WELL, NOW YOU TELL ME.

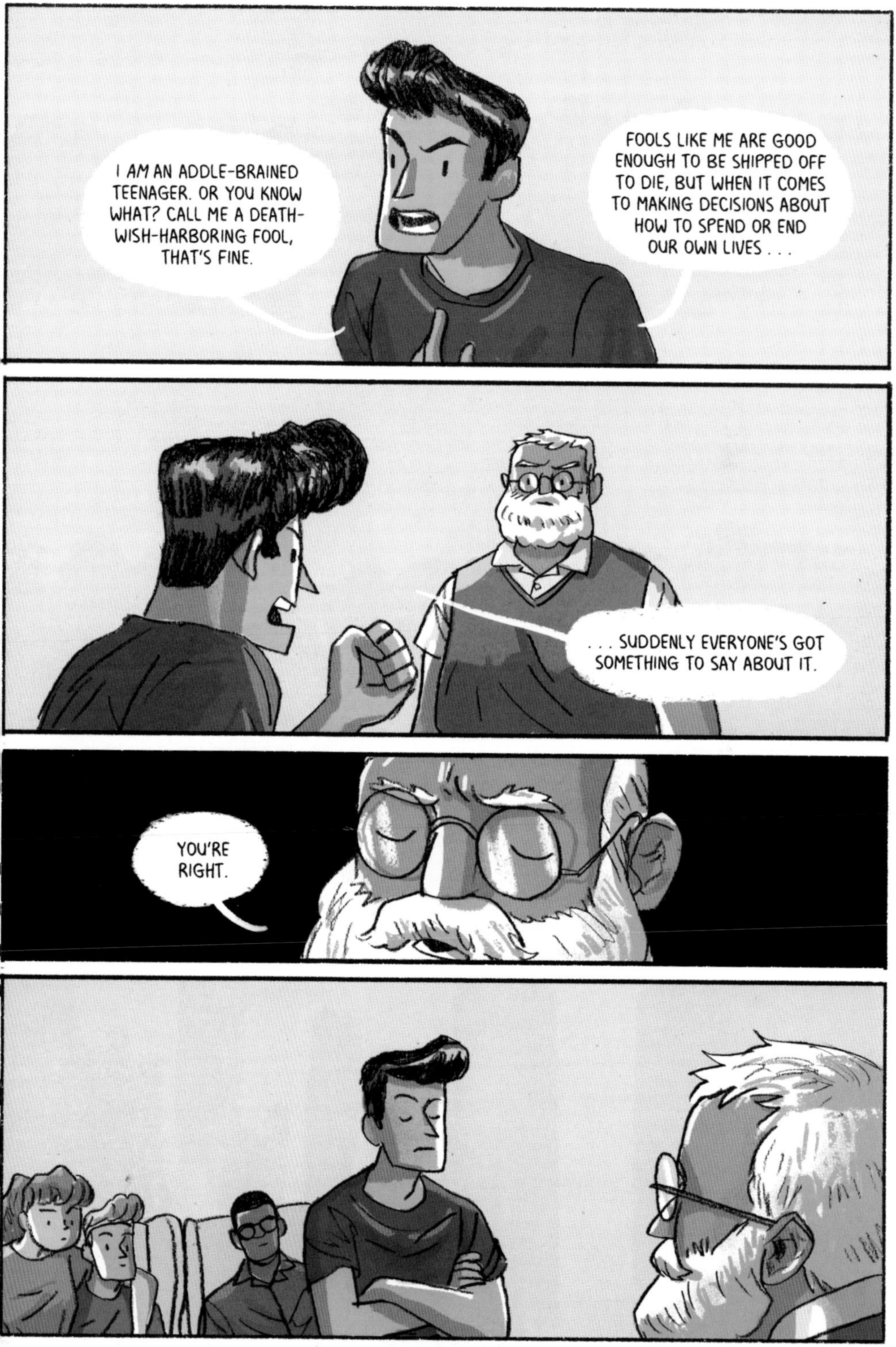
I *AM* AN ADDLE-BRAINED TEENAGER. OR YOU KNOW WHAT? CALL ME A DEATH-WISH-HARBORING FOOL, THAT'S FINE.
FOOLS LIKE ME ARE GOOD ENOUGH TO BE SHIPPED OFF TO DIE, BUT WHEN IT COMES TO MAKING DECISIONS ABOUT HOW TO SPEND OR END OUR OWN LIVES . . .
. . . SUDDENLY EVERYONE'S GOT SOMETHING TO SAY ABOUT IT.
YOU'RE RIGHT.

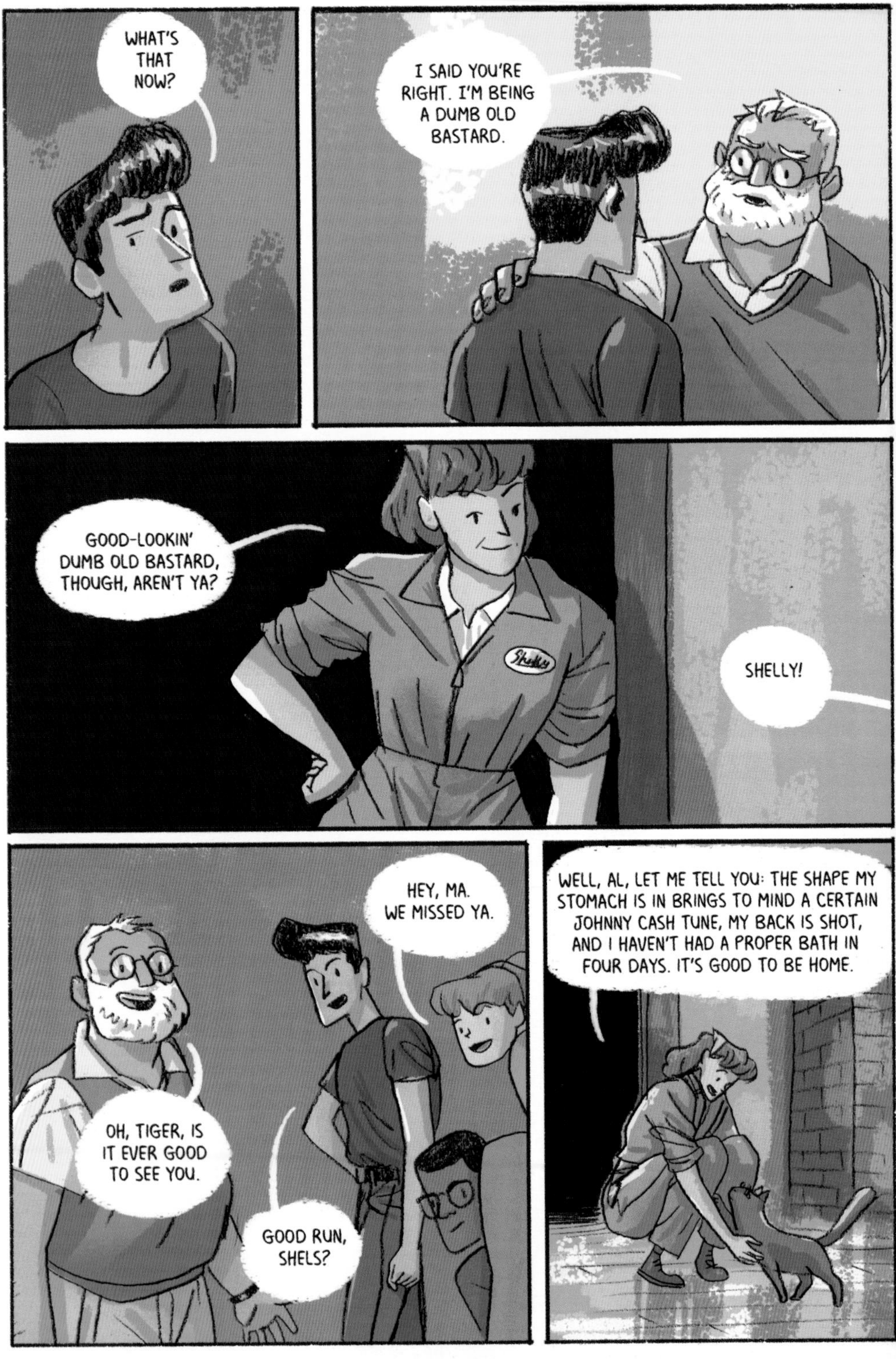
WHAT'S THAT NOW?
I SAID YOU'RE RIGHT. I'M BEING A DUMB OLD BASTARD.
GOOD-LOOKIN' DUMB OLD BASTARD, THOUGH, AREN'T YA?
SHELLY!
HEY, MA. WE MISSED YA.
OH, TIGER, IS IT EVER GOOD TO SEE YOU.
GOOD RUN, SHELS?
WELL, AL, LET ME TELL YOU: THE SHAPE MY STOMACH IS IN BRINGS TO MIND A CERTAIN JOHNNY CASH TUNE, MY BACK IS SHOT, AND I HAVEN'T HAD A PROPER BATH IN FOUR DAYS. IT'S GOOD TO BE HOME.

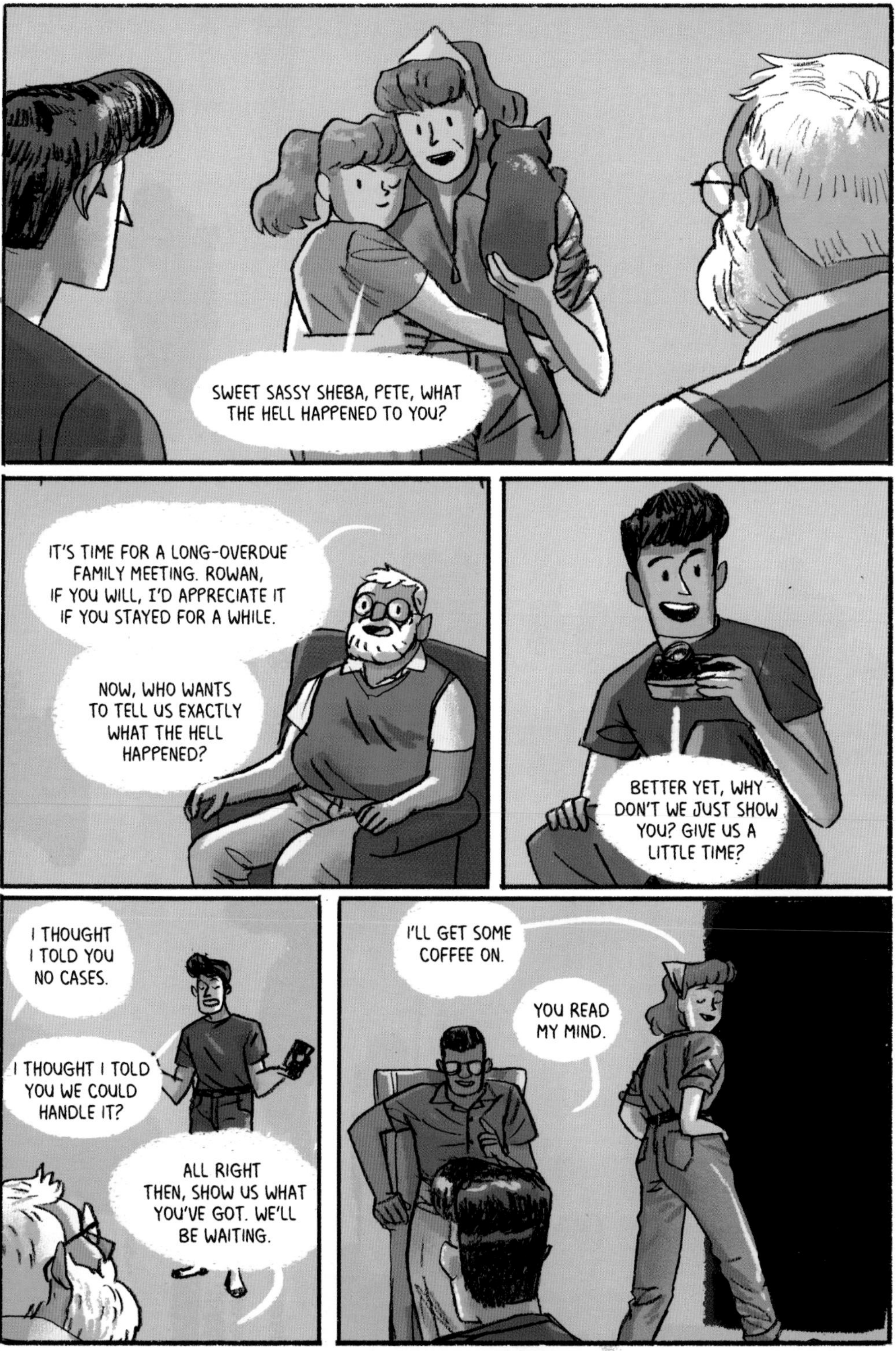
SWEET SASSY SHEBA, PETE, WHAT THE HELL HAPPENED TO YOU?
IT'S TIME FOR A LONG-OVERDUE FAMILY MEETING. ROWAN, IF YOU WILL, I'D APPRECIATE IT IF YOU STAYED FOR A WHILE.
NOW, WHO WANTS TO TELL US EXACTLY WHAT THE HELL HAPPENED?
BETTER YET, WHY DON'T WE JUST SHOW YOU? GIVE US A LITTLE TIME?
I THOUGHT I TOLD YOU NO CASES.
I THOUGHT I TOLD YOU WE COULD HANDLE IT?
ALL RIGHT THEN, SHOW US WHAT YOU'VE GOT. WE'LL BE WAITING.
I'LL GET SOME COFFEE ON.
YOU READ MY MIND.

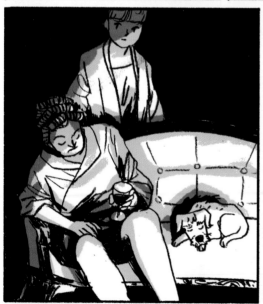

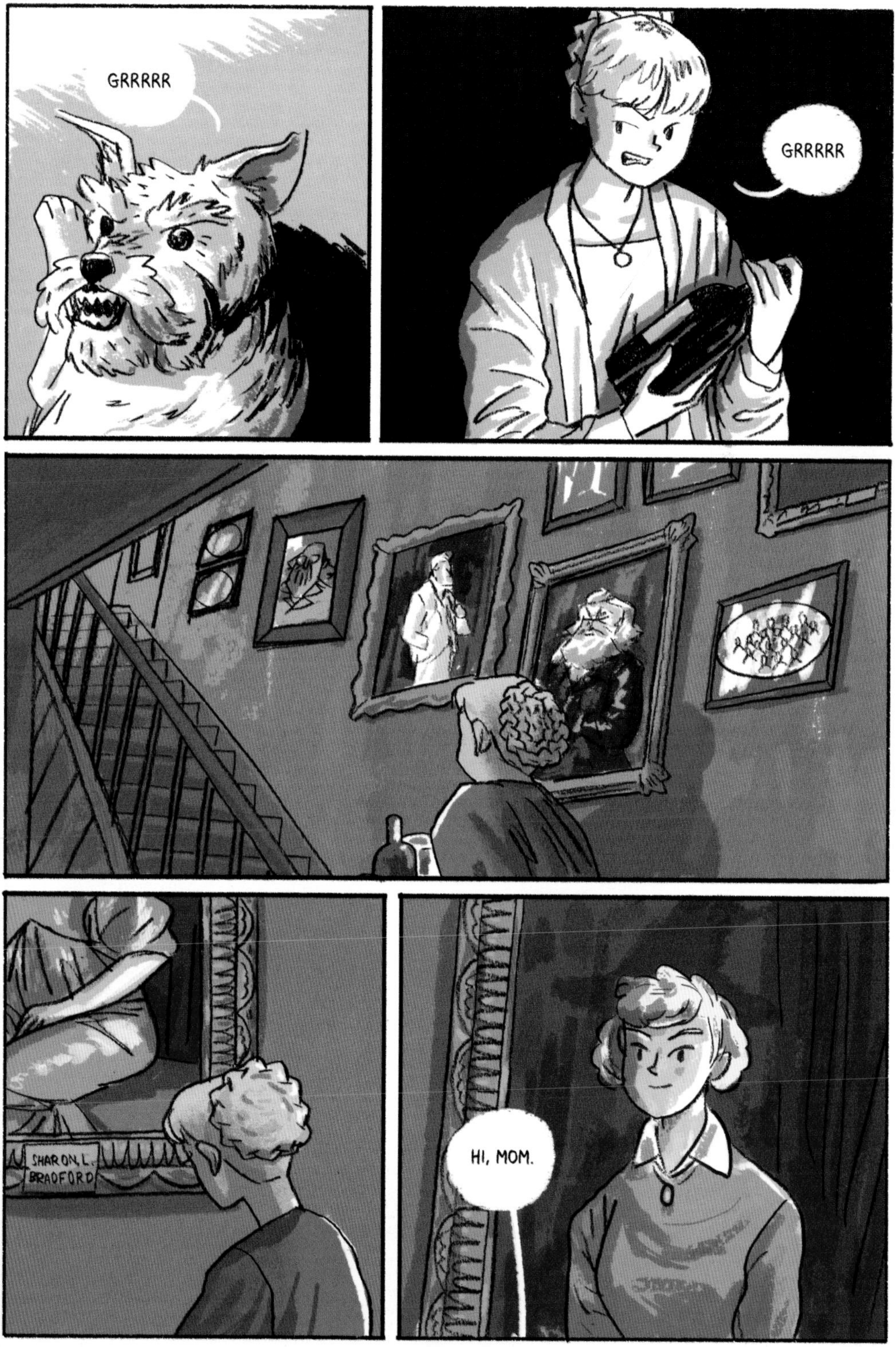
GRRRRR
GRRRRR
SHARON L. BRADFORD
HI, MOM.

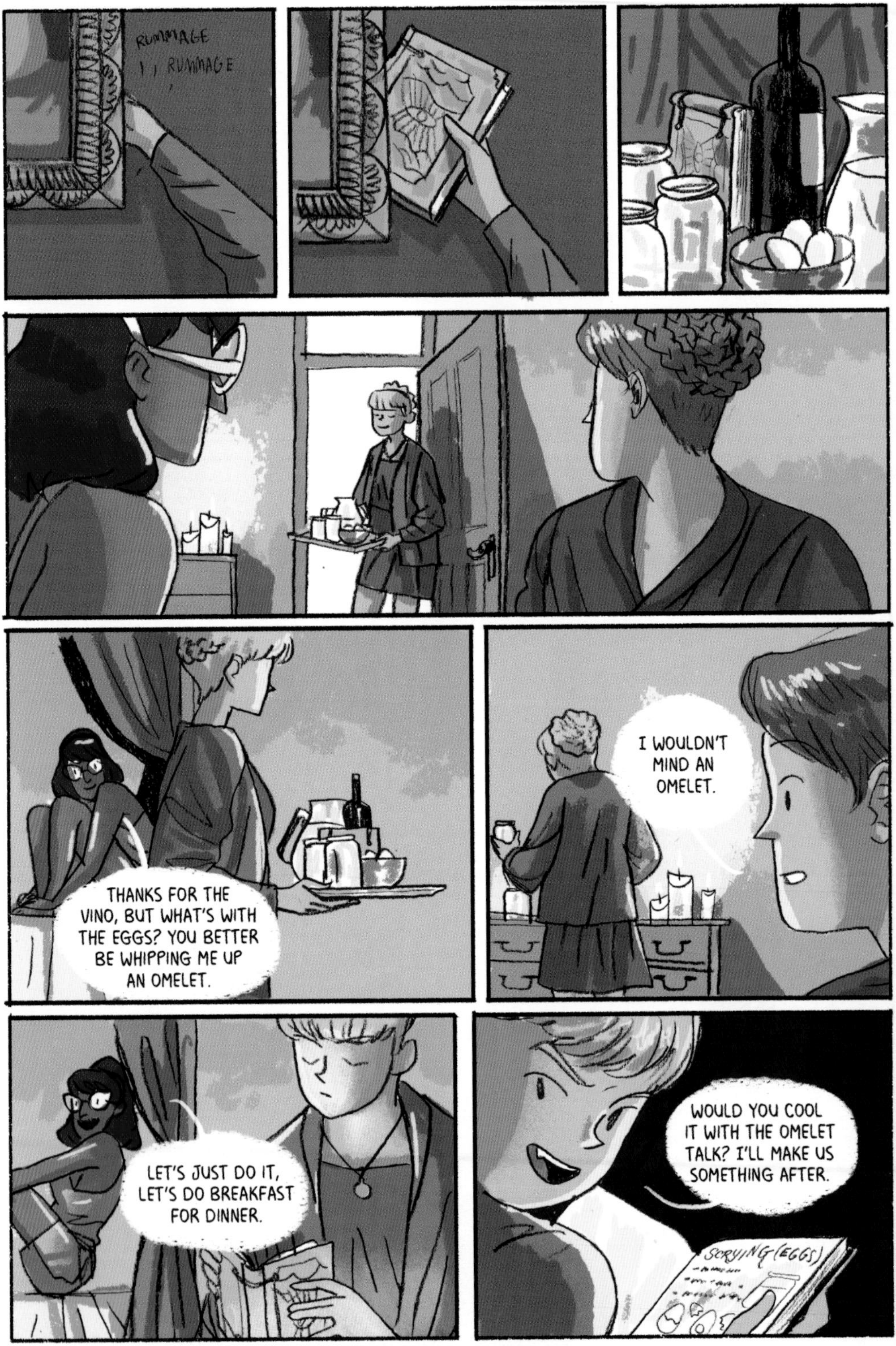
RUMMAGE
RUMMAGE
THANKS FOR THE VINO, BUT WHAT'S WITH THE EGGS? YOU BETTER BE WHIPPING ME UP AN OMELET.
I WOULDN'T MIND AN OMELET.
LET'S JUST DO IT, LET'S DO BREAKFAST FOR DINNER.
WOULD YOU COOL IT WITH THE OMELET TALK? I'LL MAKE US SOMETHING AFTER.
SCRYING (EGGS)

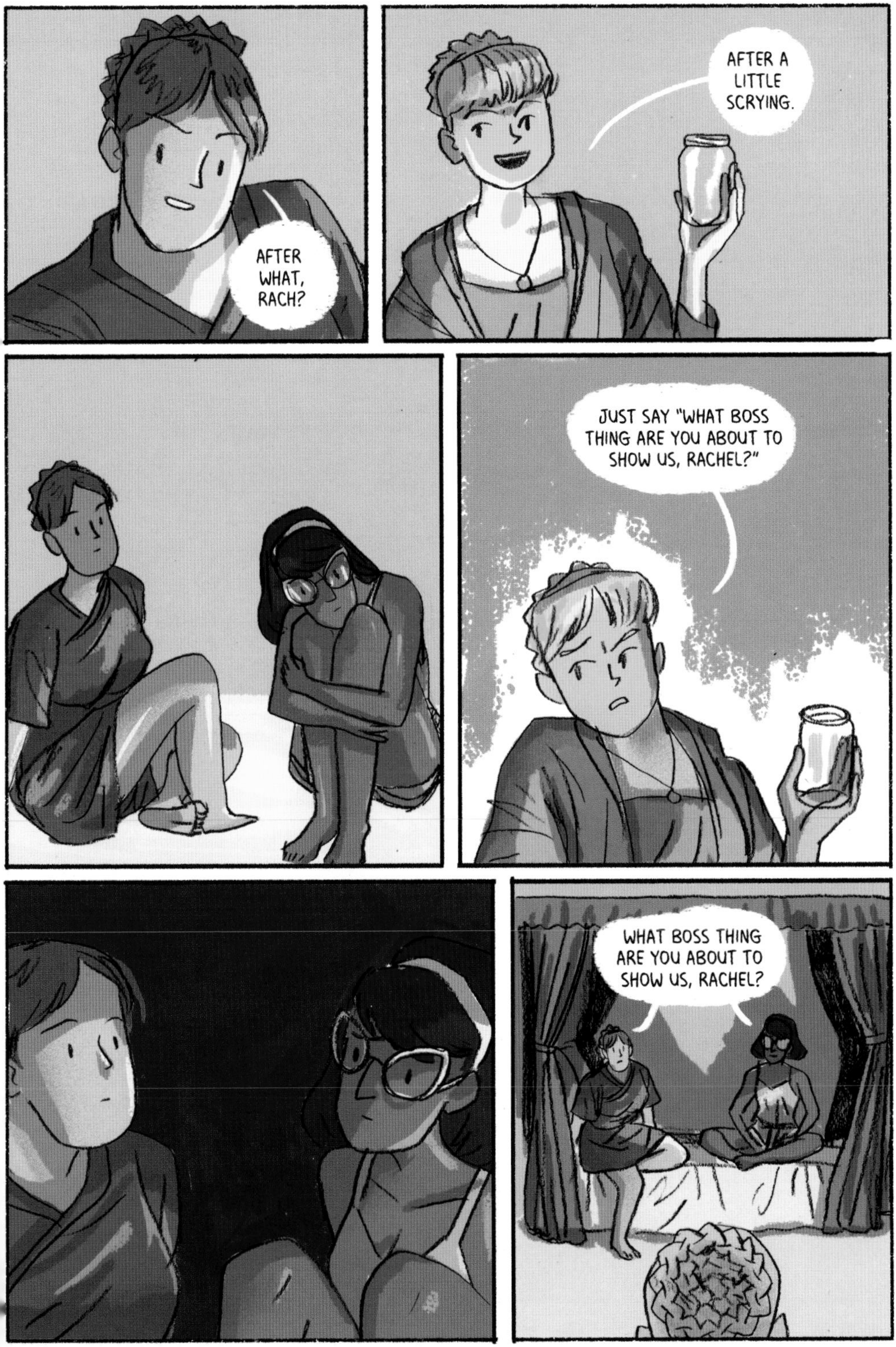
AFTER WHAT, RACH?
AFTER A LITTLE SCRYING.
JUST SAY "WHAT BOSS THING ARE YOU ABOUT TO SHOW US, RACHEL?"
WHAT BOSS THING ARE YOU ABOUT TO SHOW US, RACHEL?

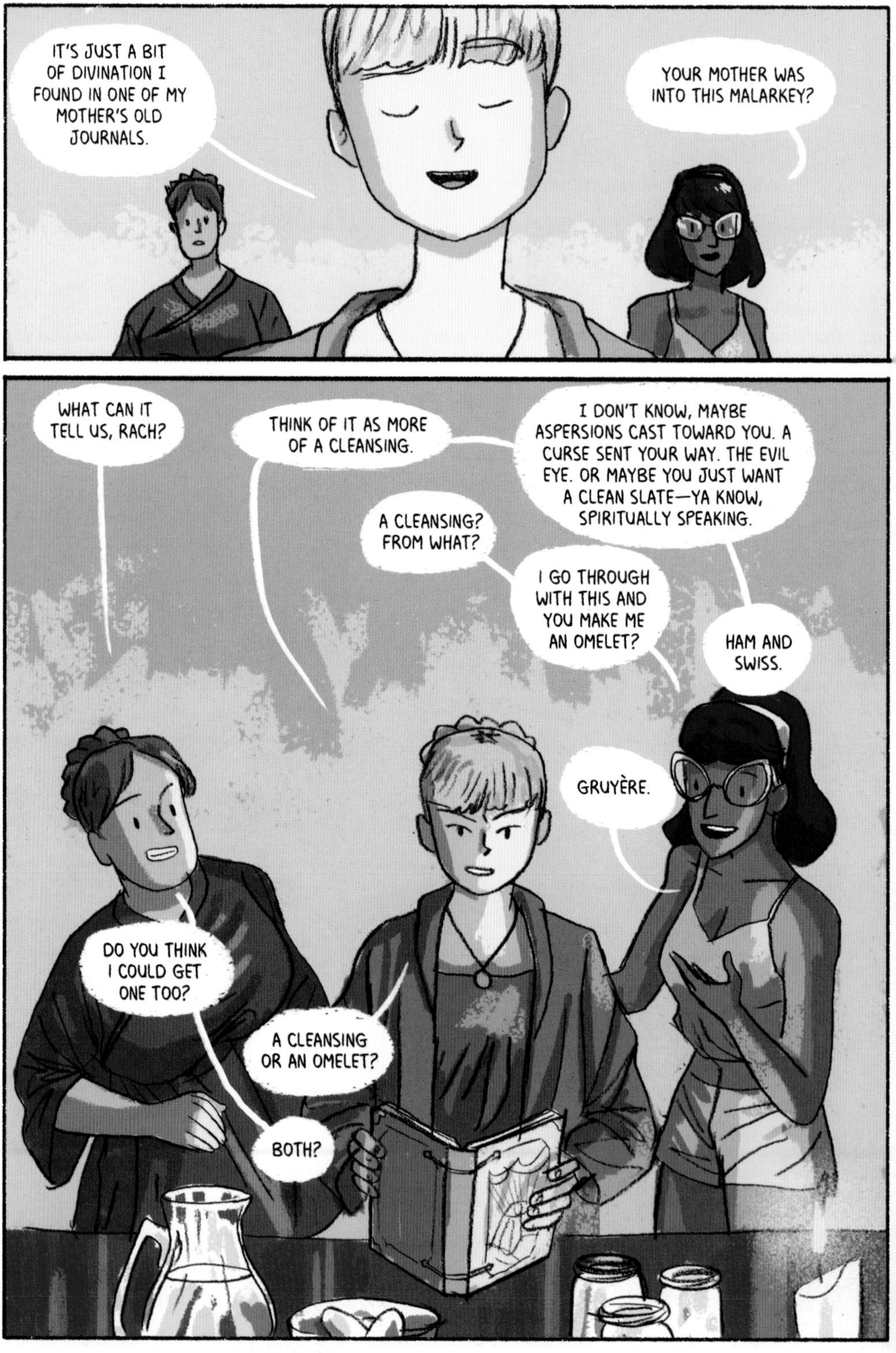
IT'S JUST A BIT OF DIVINATION I FOUND IN ONE OF MY MOTHER'S OLD JOURNALS.
YOUR MOTHER WAS INTO THIS MALARKEY?
WHAT CAN IT TELL US, RACH?
THINK OF IT AS MORE OF A CLEANSING.
I DON'T KNOW, MAYBE ASPERSIONS CAST TOWARD YOU. A CURSE SENT YOUR WAY. THE EVIL EYE. OR MAYBE YOU JUST WANT A CLEAN SLATE—YA KNOW, SPIRITUALLY SPEAKING.
A CLEANSING? FROM WHAT?
I GO THROUGH WITH THIS AND YOU MAKE ME AN OMELET?
HAM AND SWISS.
GRUYÈRE.
DO YOU THINK I COULD GET ONE TOO?
A CLEANSING OR AN OMELET?
BOTH?

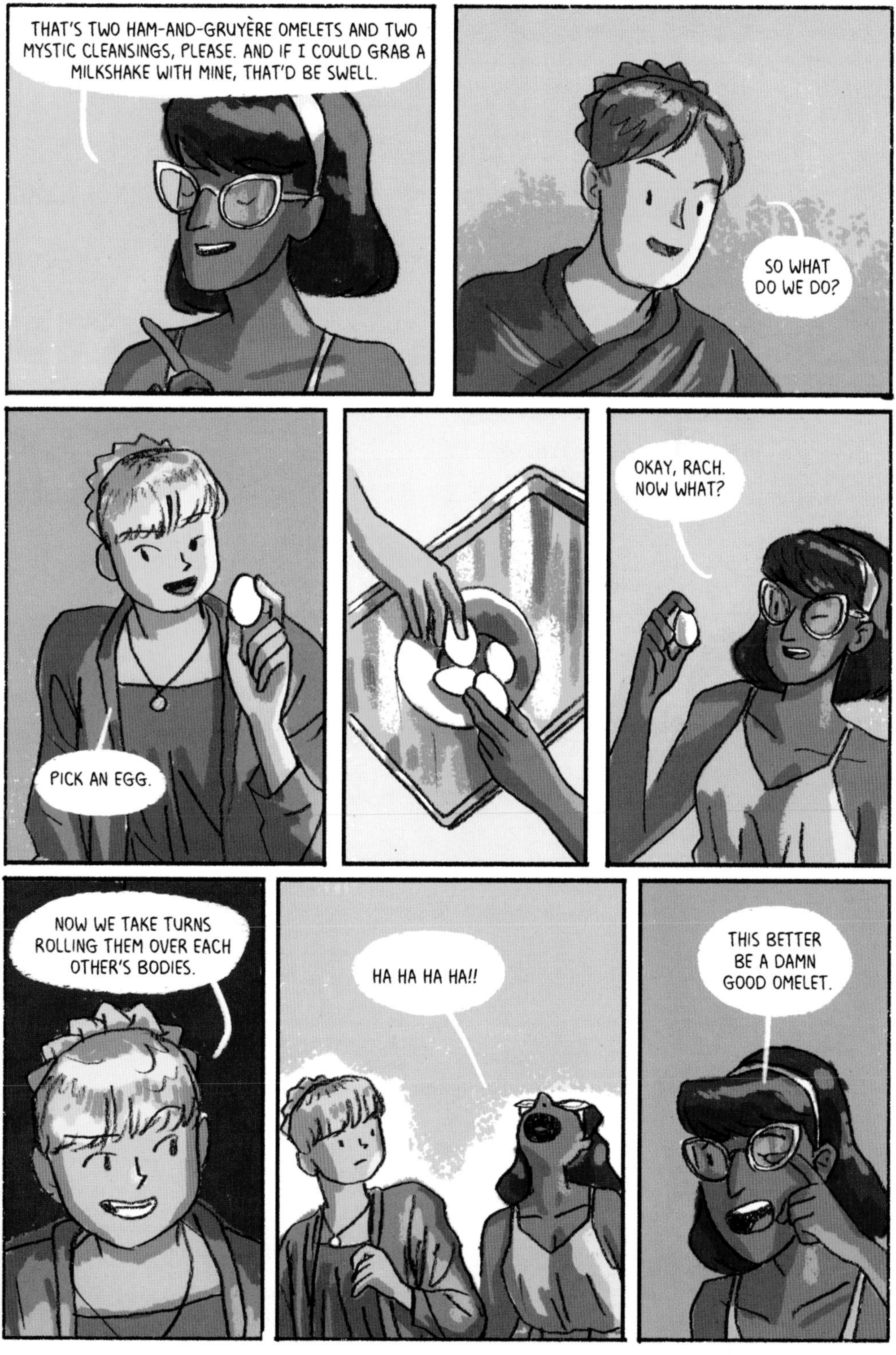
THAT'S TWO HAM-AND-GRUYÈRE OMELETS AND TWO MYSTIC CLEANSINGS, PLEASE. AND IF I COULD GRAB A MILKSHAKE WITH MINE, THAT'D BE SWELL.
SO WHAT DO WE DO?
PICK AN EGG.
OKAY, RACH. NOW WHAT?
NOW WE TAKE TURNS ROLLING THEM OVER EACH OTHER'S BODIES.
HA HA HA HA!!
THIS BETTER BE A DAMN GOOD OMELET.

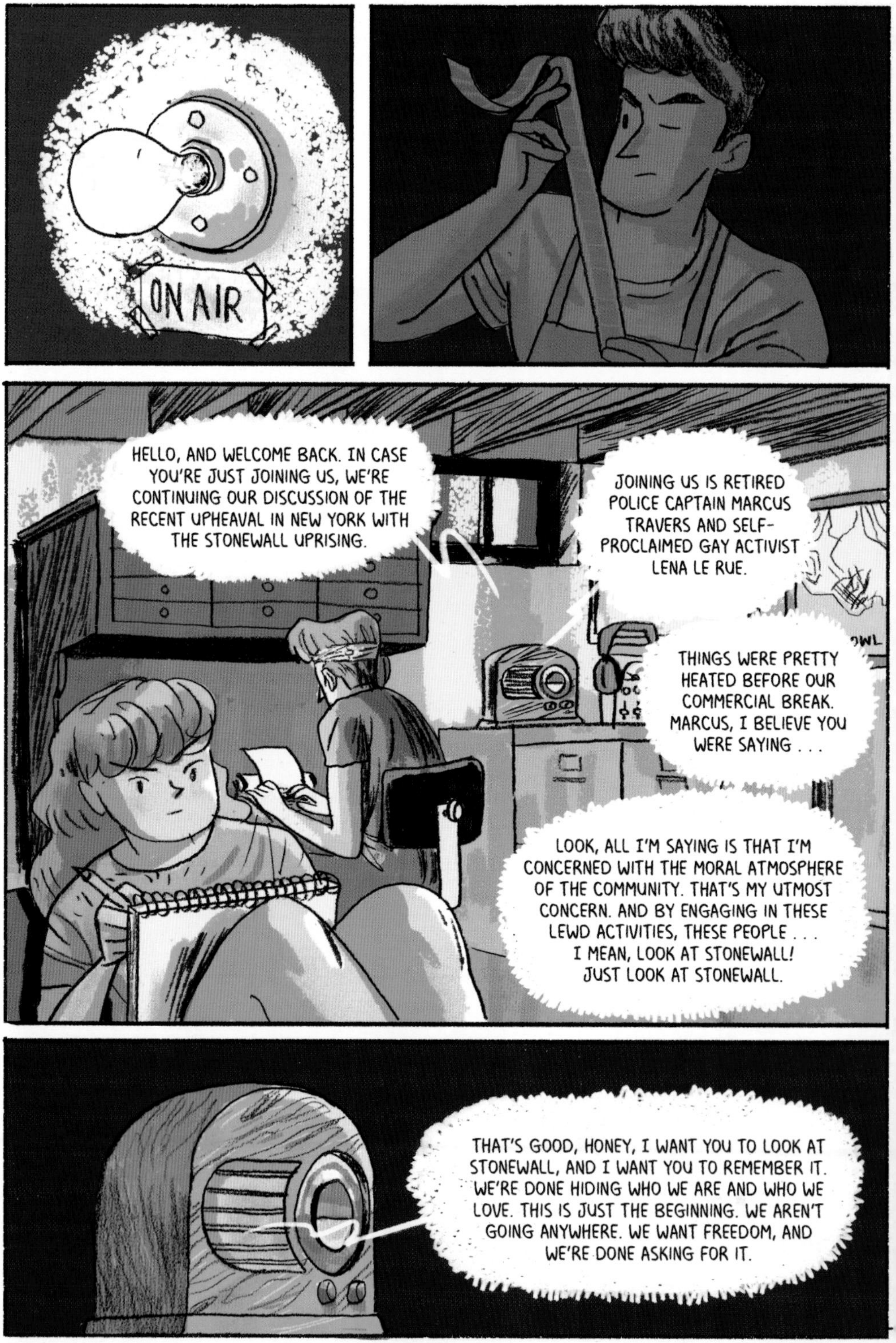
ON AIR
HELLO, AND WELCOME BACK. IN CASE YOU'RE JUST JOINING US, WE'RE CONTINUING OUR DISCUSSION OF THE RECENT UPHEAVAL IN NEW YORK WITH THE STONEWALL UPRISING.
JOINING US IS RETIRED POLICE CAPTAIN MARCUS TRAVERS AND SELF-PROCLAIMED GAY ACTIVIST LENA LE RUE.
THINGS WERE PRETTY HEATED BEFORE OUR COMMERCIAL BREAK. MARCUS, I BELIEVE YOU WERE SAYING . . .
LOOK, ALL I'M SAYING IS THAT I'M CONCERNED WITH THE MORAL ATMOSPHERE OF THE COMMUNITY. THAT'S MY UTMOST CONCERN. AND BY ENGAGING IN THESE LEWD ACTIVITIES, THESE PEOPLE . . . I MEAN, LOOK AT STONEWALL! JUST LOOK AT STONEWALL.
THAT'S GOOD, HONEY, I WANT YOU TO LOOK AT STONEWALL, AND I WANT YOU TO REMEMBER IT. WE'RE DONE HIDING WHO WE ARE AND WHO WE LOVE. THIS IS JUST THE BEGINNING. WE AREN'T GOING ANYWHERE. WE WANT FREEDOM, AND WE'RE DONE ASKING FOR IT.

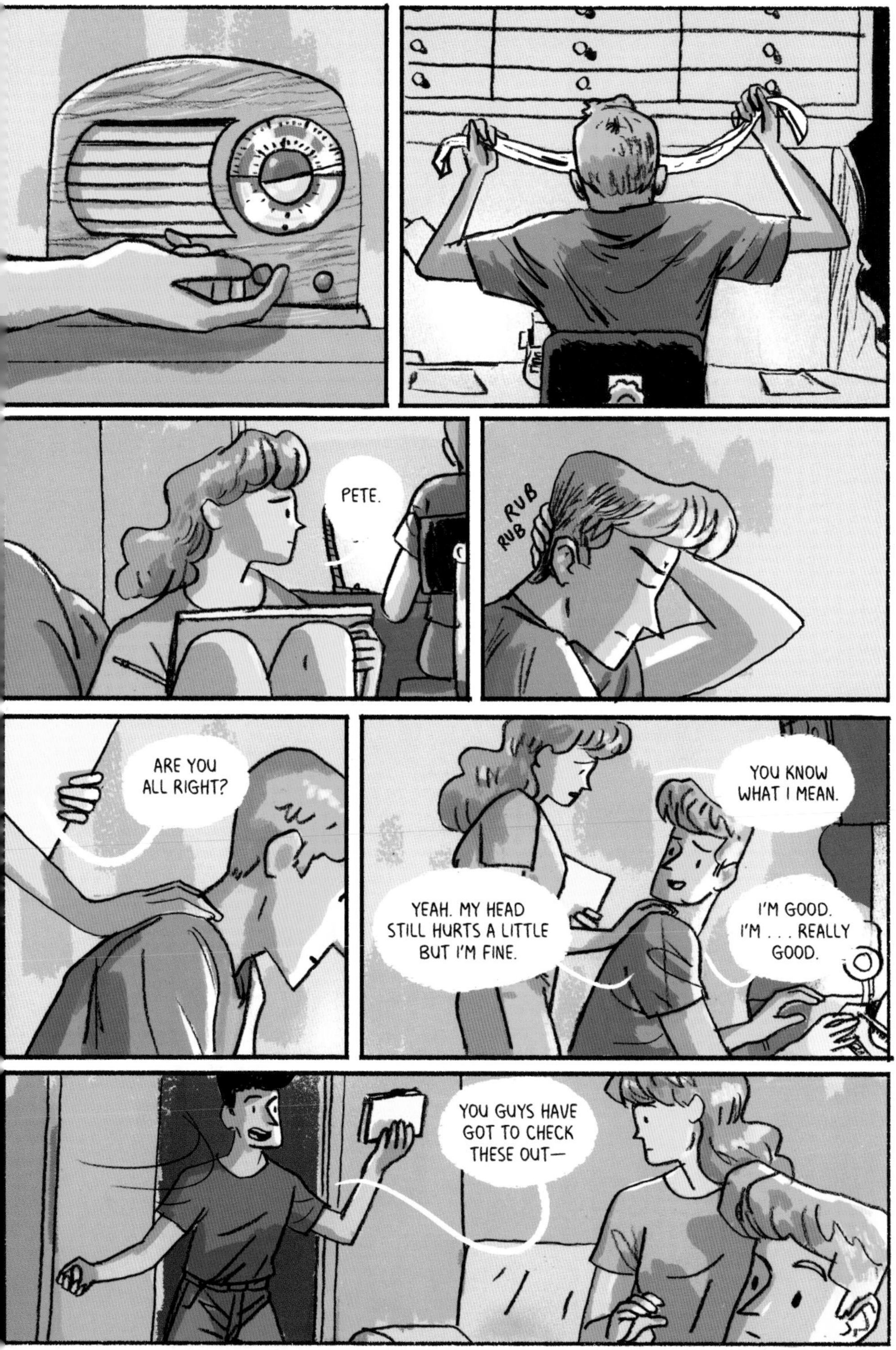
PETE.
RUB RUB
ARE YOU ALL RIGHT?
YEAH. MY HEAD STILL HURTS A LITTLE BUT I'M FINE.
YOU KNOW WHAT I MEAN.
I'M GOOD. I'M . . . REALLY GOOD.
YOU GUYS HAVE GOT TO CHECK THESE OUT—

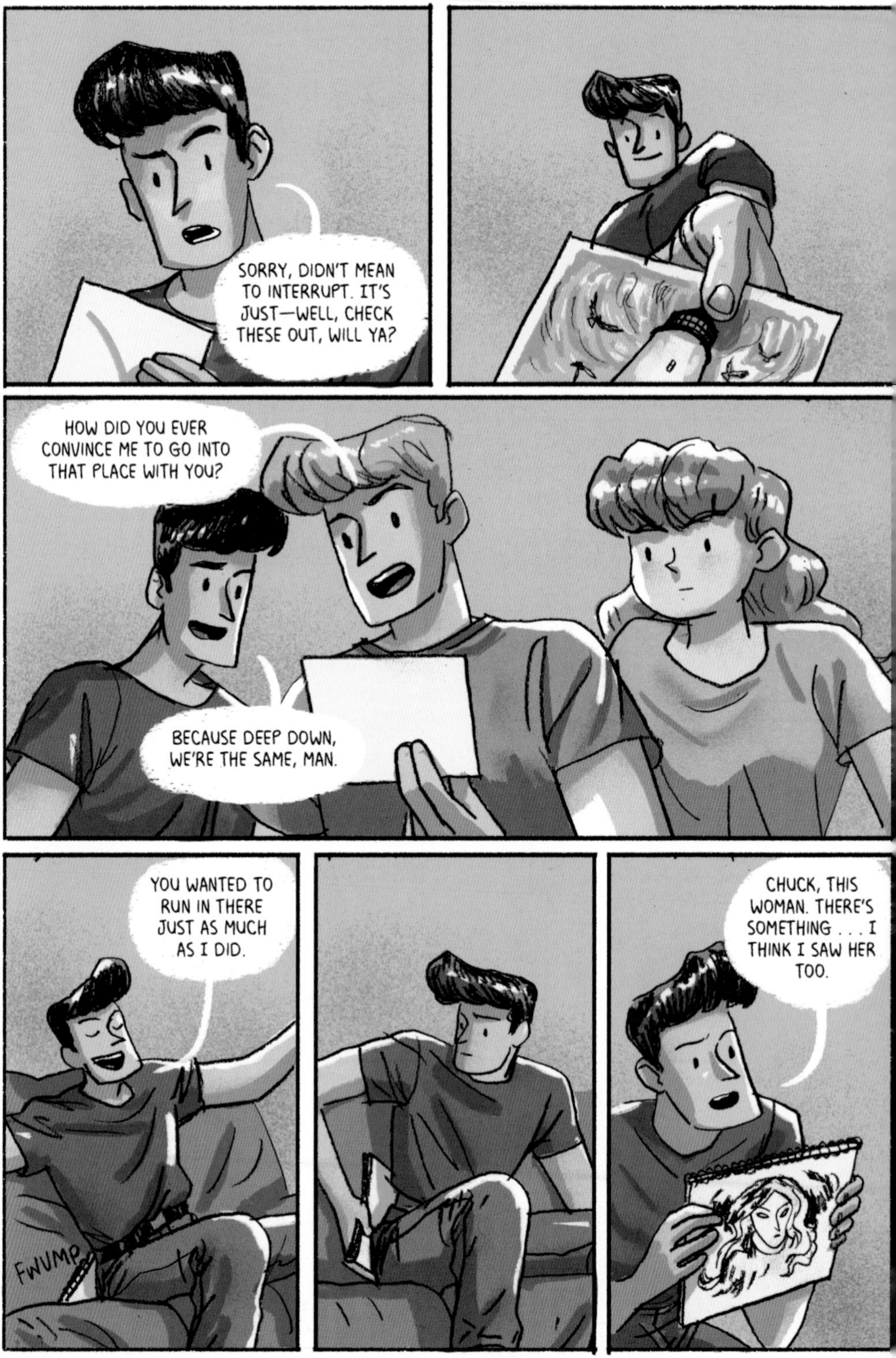
SORRY, DIDN'T MEAN TO INTERRUPT. IT'S JUST—WELL, CHECK THESE OUT, WILL YA?
HOW DID YOU EVER CONVINCE ME TO GO INTO THAT PLACE WITH YOU?
BECAUSE DEEP DOWN, WE'RE THE SAME, MAN.
YOU WANTED TO RUN IN THERE JUST AS MUCH AS I DID.
FWUMP
CHUCK, THIS WOMAN. THERE'S SOMETHING . . . I THINK I SAW HER TOO.

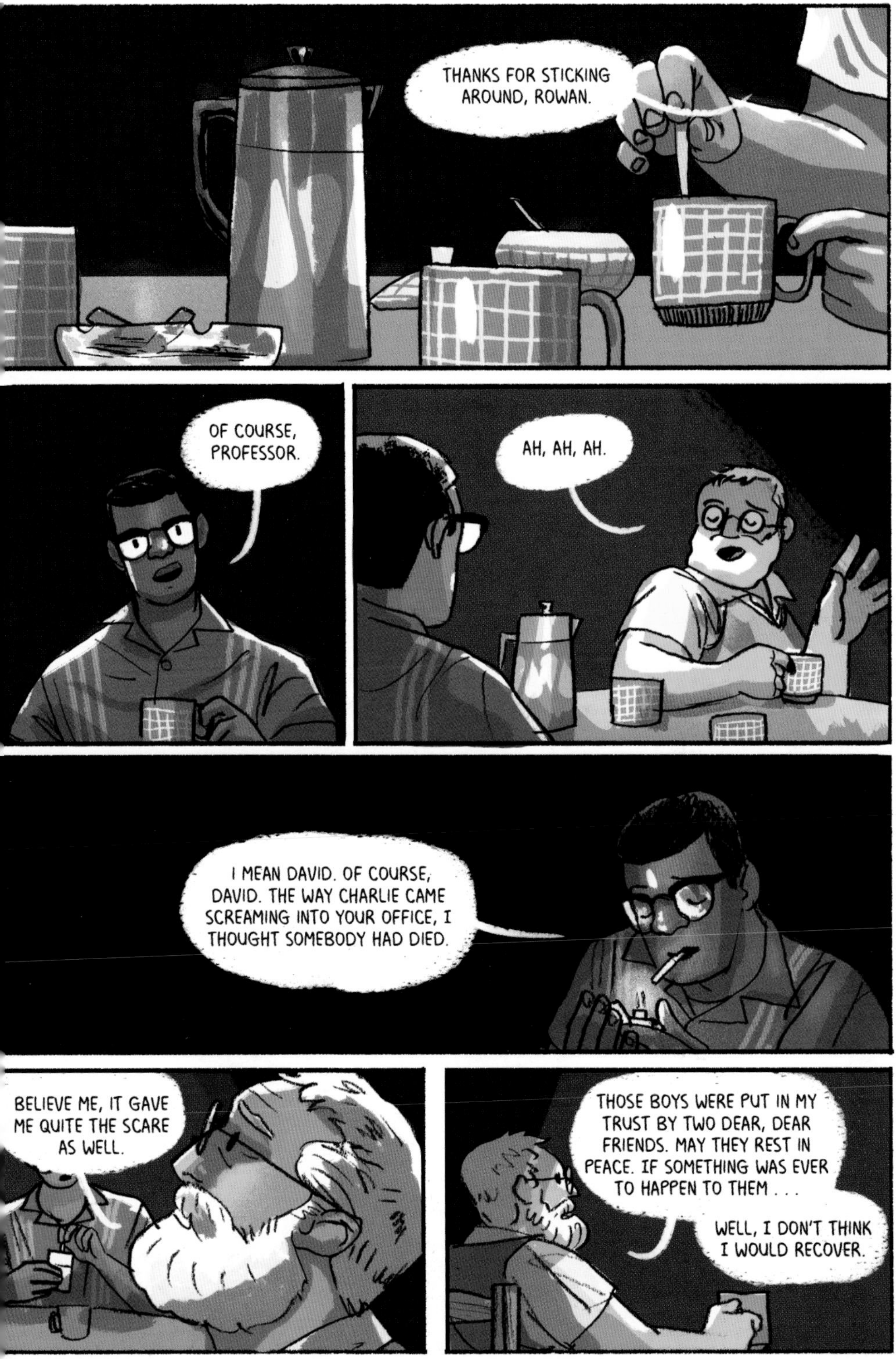
THANKS FOR STICKING AROUND, ROWAN.
OF COURSE, PROFESSOR.
AH, AH, AH.
I MEAN DAVID. OF COURSE, DAVID. THE WAY CHARLIE CAME SCREAMING INTO YOUR OFFICE, I THOUGHT SOMEBODY HAD DIED.
BELIEVE ME, IT GAVE ME QUITE THE SCARE AS WELL.
THOSE BOYS WERE PUT IN MY TRUST BY TWO DEAR, DEAR FRIENDS. MAY THEY REST IN PEACE. IF SOMETHING WAS EVER TO HAPPEN TO THEM . . .
WELL, I DON'T THINK I WOULD RECOVER.

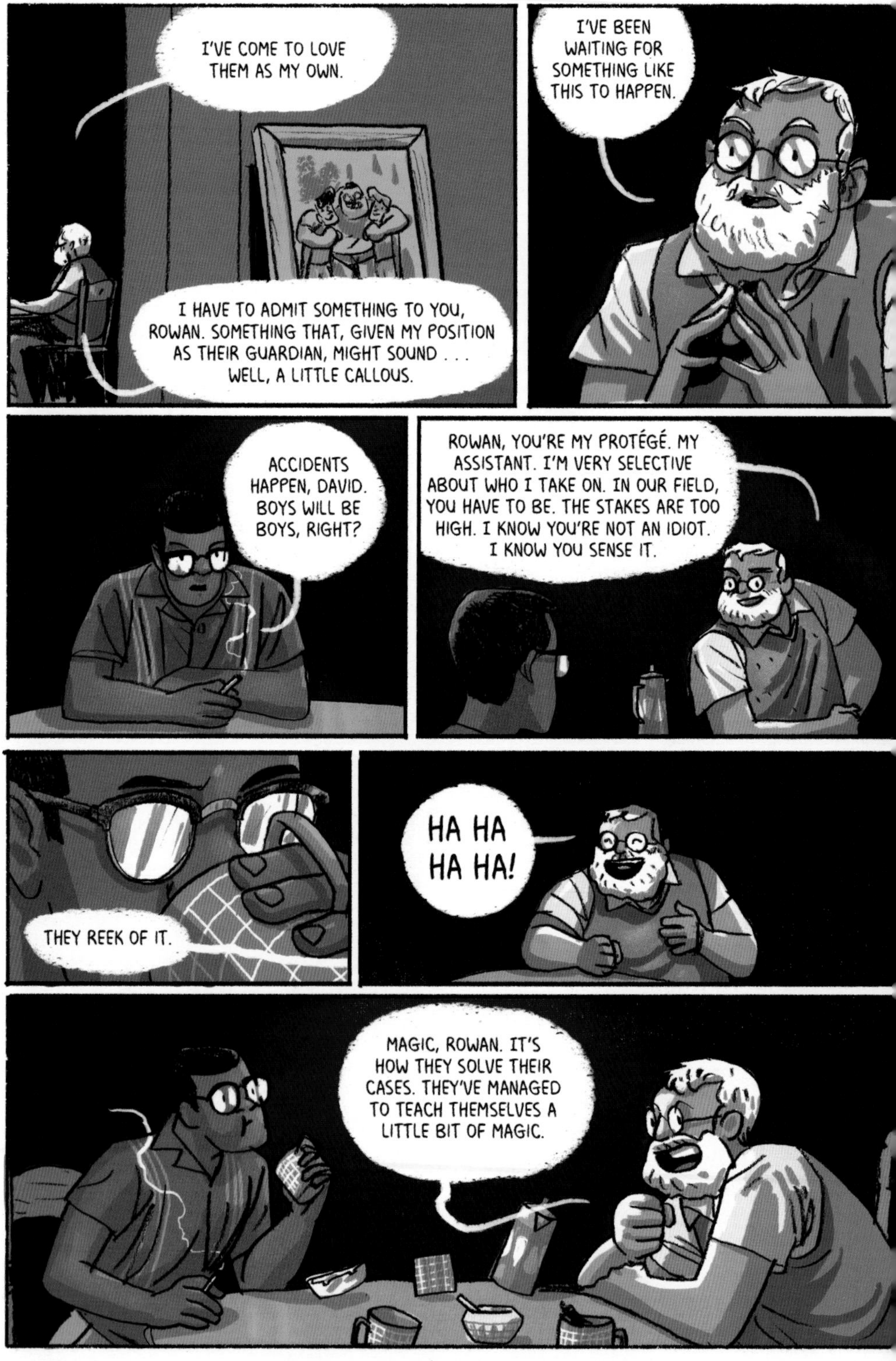
I'VE COME TO LOVE THEM AS MY OWN.
I HAVE TO ADMIT SOMETHING TO YOU, ROWAN. SOMETHING THAT, GIVEN MY POSITION AS THEIR GUARDIAN, MIGHT SOUND . . . WELL, A LITTLE CALLOUS.
I'VE BEEN WAITING FOR SOMETHING LIKE THIS TO HAPPEN.
ACCIDENTS HAPPEN, DAVID. BOYS WILL BE BOYS, RIGHT?
ROWAN, YOU'RE MY PROTÉGÉ. MY ASSISTANT. I'M VERY SELECTIVE ABOUT WHO I TAKE ON. IN OUR FIELD, YOU HAVE TO BE. THE STAKES ARE TOO HIGH. I KNOW YOU'RE NOT AN IDIOT. I KNOW YOU SENSE IT.
THEY REEK OF IT.
HA HA HA HA!
MAGIC, ROWAN. IT'S HOW THEY SOLVE THEIR CASES. THEY'VE MANAGED TO TEACH THEMSELVES A LITTLE BIT OF MAGIC.

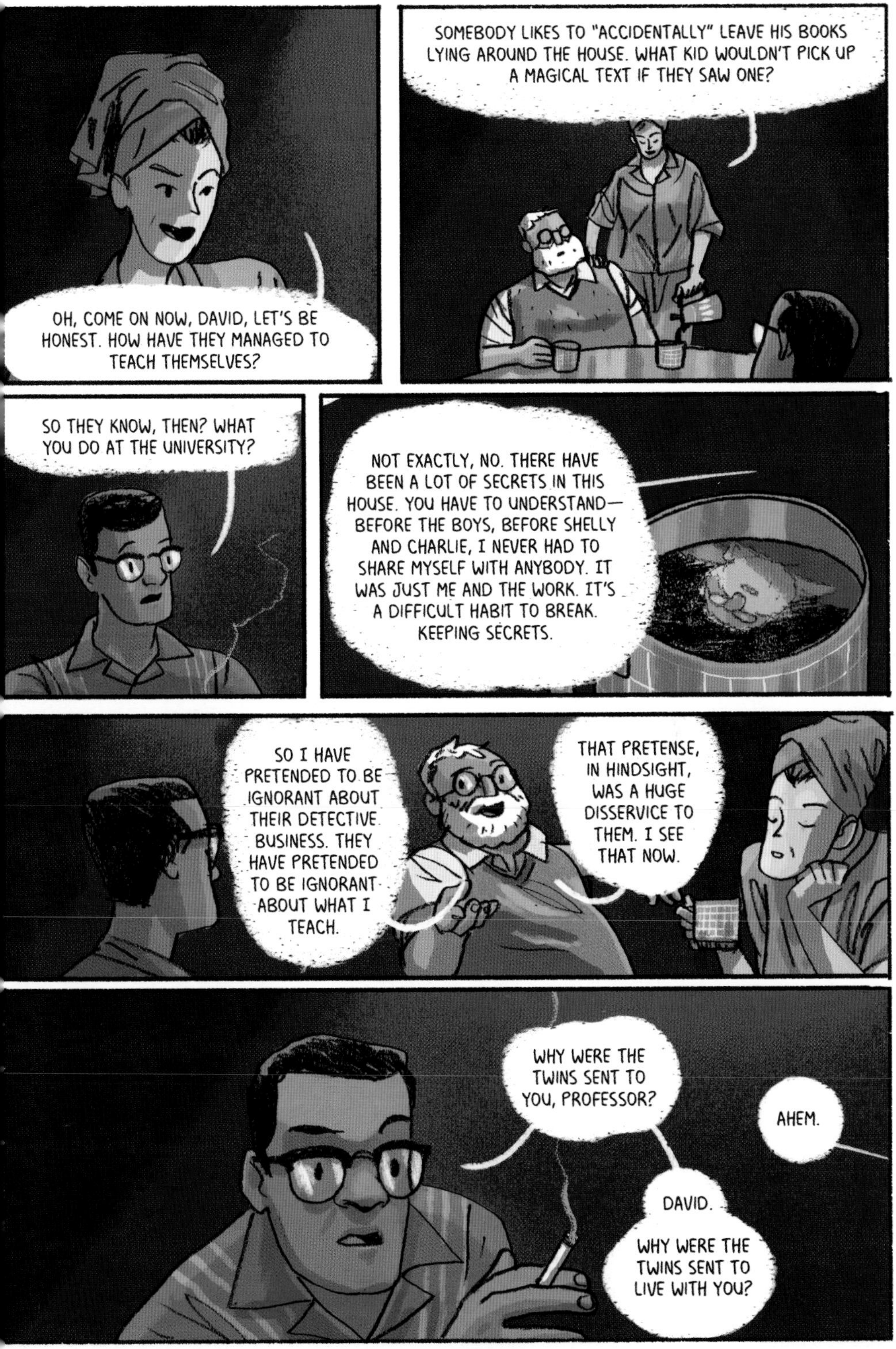
OH, COME ON NOW, DAVID, LET'S BE HONEST. HOW HAVE THEY MANAGED TO TEACH THEMSELVES?
SOMEBODY LIKES TO "ACCIDENTALLY" LEAVE HIS BOOKS LYING AROUND THE HOUSE. WHAT KID WOULDN'T PICK UP A MAGICAL TEXT IF THEY SAW ONE?
SO THEY KNOW, THEN? WHAT YOU DO AT THE UNIVERSITY?
NOT EXACTLY, NO. THERE HAVE BEEN A LOT OF SECRETS IN THIS HOUSE. YOU HAVE TO UNDERSTAND—BEFORE THE BOYS, BEFORE SHELLY AND CHARLIE, I NEVER HAD TO SHARE MYSELF WITH ANYBODY. IT WAS JUST ME AND THE WORK. IT'S A DIFFICULT HABIT TO BREAK. KEEPING SECRETS.
SO I HAVE PRETENDED TO BE IGNORANT ABOUT THEIR DETECTIVE BUSINESS. THEY HAVE PRETENDED TO BE IGNORANT ABOUT WHAT I TEACH.
THAT PRETENSE, IN HINDSIGHT, WAS A HUGE DISSERVICE TO THEM. I SEE THAT NOW.
WHY WERE THE TWINS SENT TO YOU, PROFESSOR?
AHEM.
DAVID.
WHY WERE THE TWINS SENT TO LIVE WITH YOU?

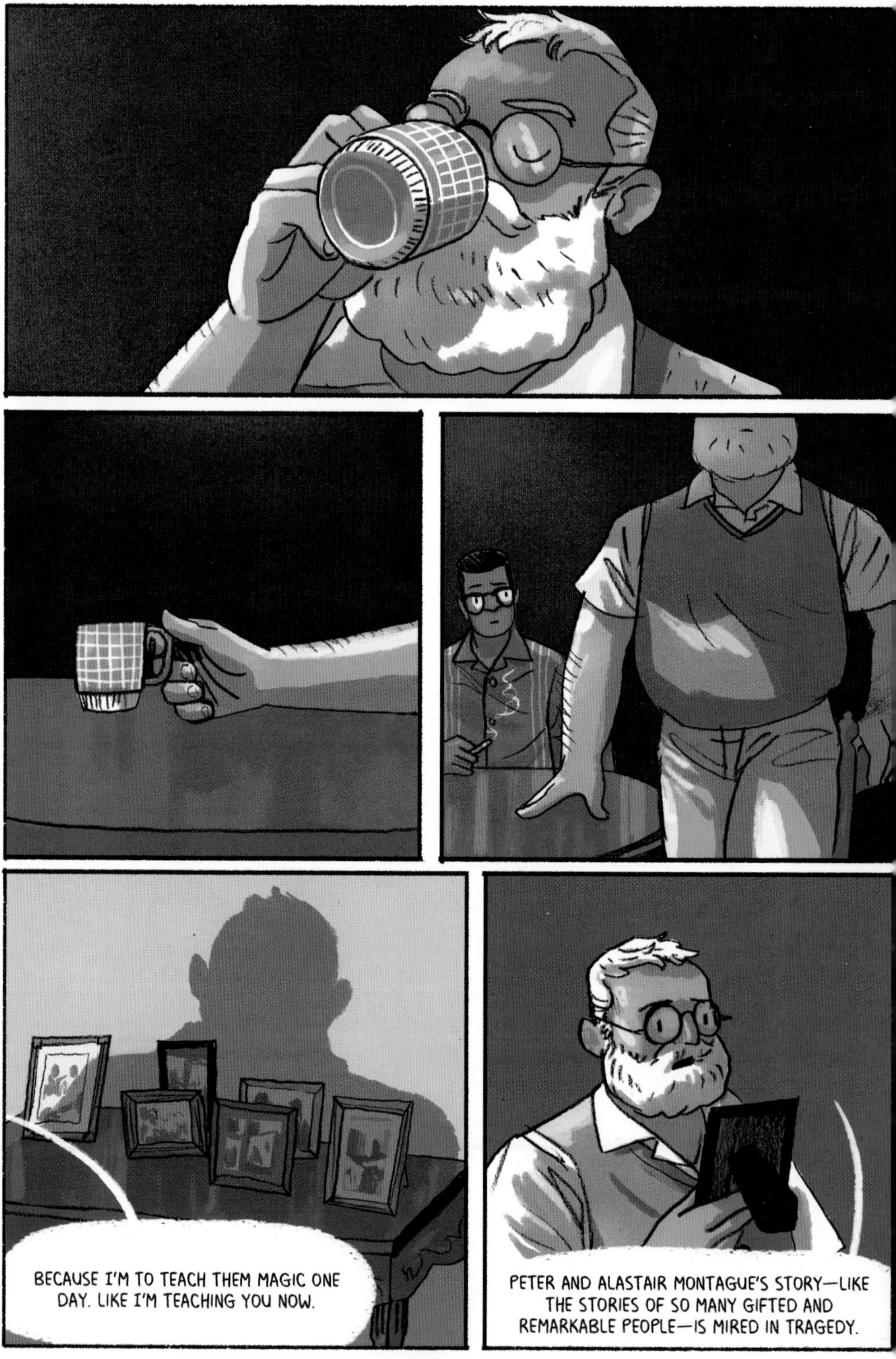
BECAUSE I'M TO TEACH THEM MAGIC ONE DAY. LIKE I'M TEACHING YOU NOW.
PETER AND ALASTAIR MONTAGUE'S STORY—LIKE THE STORIES OF SO MANY GIFTED AND REMARKABLE PEOPLE—IS MIRED IN TRAGEDY.

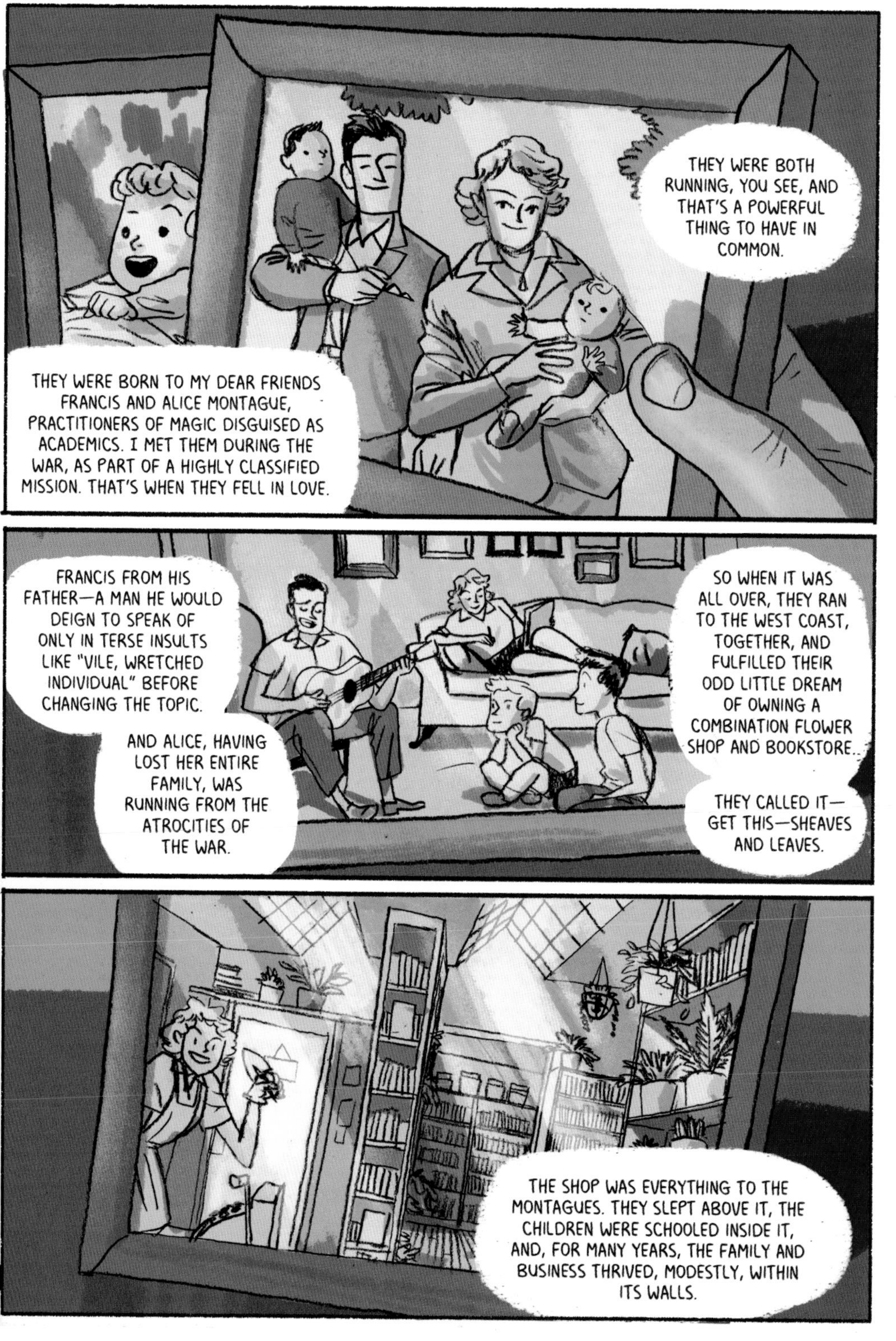
THEY WERE BORN TO MY DEAR FRIENDS FRANCIS AND ALICE MONTAGUE, PRACTITIONERS OF MAGIC DISGUISED AS ACADEMICS. I MET THEM DURING THE WAR, AS PART OF A HIGHLY CLASSIFIED MISSION. THAT'S WHEN THEY FELL IN LOVE.
THEY WERE BOTH RUNNING, YOU SEE, AND THAT'S A POWERFUL THING TO HAVE IN COMMON.
FRANCIS FROM HIS FATHER—A MAN HE WOULD DEIGN TO SPEAK OF ONLY IN TERSE INSULTS LIKE "VILE, WRETCHED INDIVIDUAL" BEFORE CHANGING THE TOPIC.
AND ALICE, HAVING LOST HER ENTIRE FAMILY, WAS RUNNING FROM THE ATROCITIES OF THE WAR.
SO WHEN IT WAS ALL OVER, THEY RAN TO THE WEST COAST, TOGETHER, AND FULFILLED THEIR ODD LITTLE DREAM OF OWNING A COMBINATION FLOWER SHOP AND BOOKSTORE.
THEY CALLED IT—GET THIS—SHEAVES AND LEAVES.
THE SHOP WAS EVERYTHING TO THE MONTAGUES. THEY SLEPT ABOVE IT, THE CHILDREN WERE SCHOOLED INSIDE IT, AND, FOR MANY YEARS, THE FAMILY AND BUSINESS THRIVED, MODESTLY, WITHIN ITS WALLS.

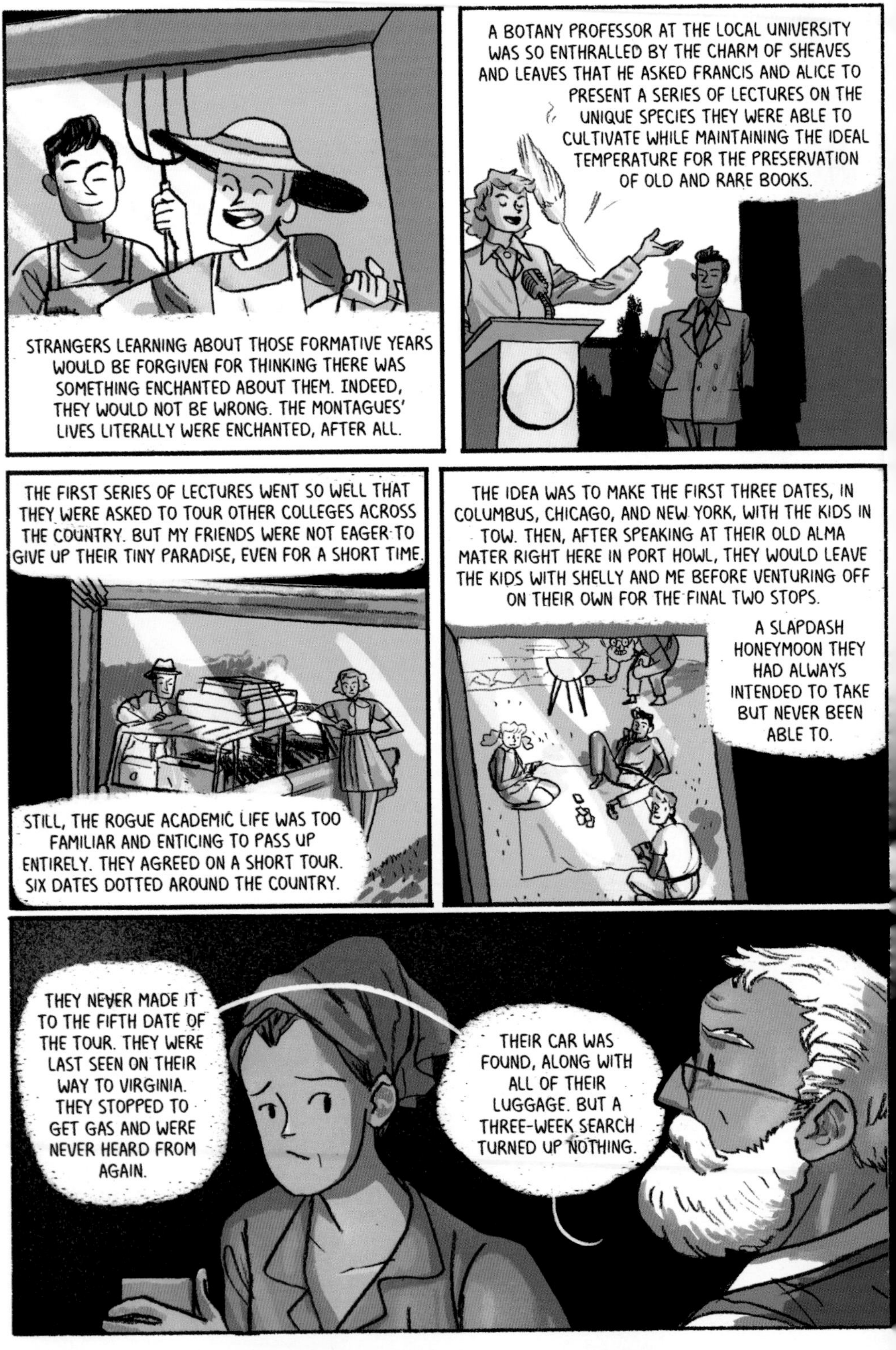
STRANGERS LEARNING ABOUT THOSE FORMATIVE YEARS WOULD BE FORGIVEN FOR THINKING THERE WAS SOMETHING ENCHANTED ABOUT THEM. INDEED, THEY WOULD NOT BE WRONG. THE MONTAGUES' LIVES LITERALLY WERE ENCHANTED, AFTER ALL.
A BOTANY PROFESSOR AT THE LOCAL UNIVERSITY WAS SO ENTHRALLED BY THE CHARM OF SHEAVES AND LEAVES THAT HE ASKED FRANCIS AND ALICE TO PRESENT A SERIES OF LECTURES ON THE UNIQUE SPECIES THEY WERE ABLE TO CULTIVATE WHILE MAINTAINING THE IDEAL TEMPERATURE FOR THE PRESERVATION OF OLD AND RARE BOOKS.
THE FIRST SERIES OF LECTURES WENT SO WELL THAT THEY WERE ASKED TO TOUR OTHER COLLEGES ACROSS THE COUNTRY. BUT MY FRIENDS WERE NOT EAGER TO GIVE UP THEIR TINY PARADISE, EVEN FOR A SHORT TIME.
STILL, THE ROGUE ACADEMIC LIFE WAS TOO FAMILIAR AND ENTICING TO PASS UP ENTIRELY. THEY AGREED ON A SHORT TOUR. SIX DATES DOTTED AROUND THE COUNTRY.
THE IDEA WAS TO MAKE THE FIRST THREE DATES, IN COLUMBUS, CHICAGO, AND NEW YORK, WITH THE KIDS IN TOW. THEN, AFTER SPEAKING AT THEIR OLD ALMA MATER RIGHT HERE IN PORT HOWL, THEY WOULD LEAVE THE KIDS WITH SHELLY AND ME BEFORE VENTURING OFF ON THEIR OWN FOR THE FINAL TWO STOPS.
A SLAPDASH HONEYMOON THEY HAD ALWAYS INTENDED TO TAKE BUT NEVER BEEN ABLE TO.
THEY NEVER MADE IT TO THE FIFTH DATE OF THE TOUR. THEY WERE LAST SEEN ON THEIR WAY TO VIRGINIA. THEY STOPPED TO GET GAS AND WERE NEVER HEARD FROM AGAIN.
THEIR CAR WAS FOUND, ALONG WITH ALL OF THEIR LUGGAGE. BUT A THREE-WEEK SEARCH TURNED UP NOTHING.

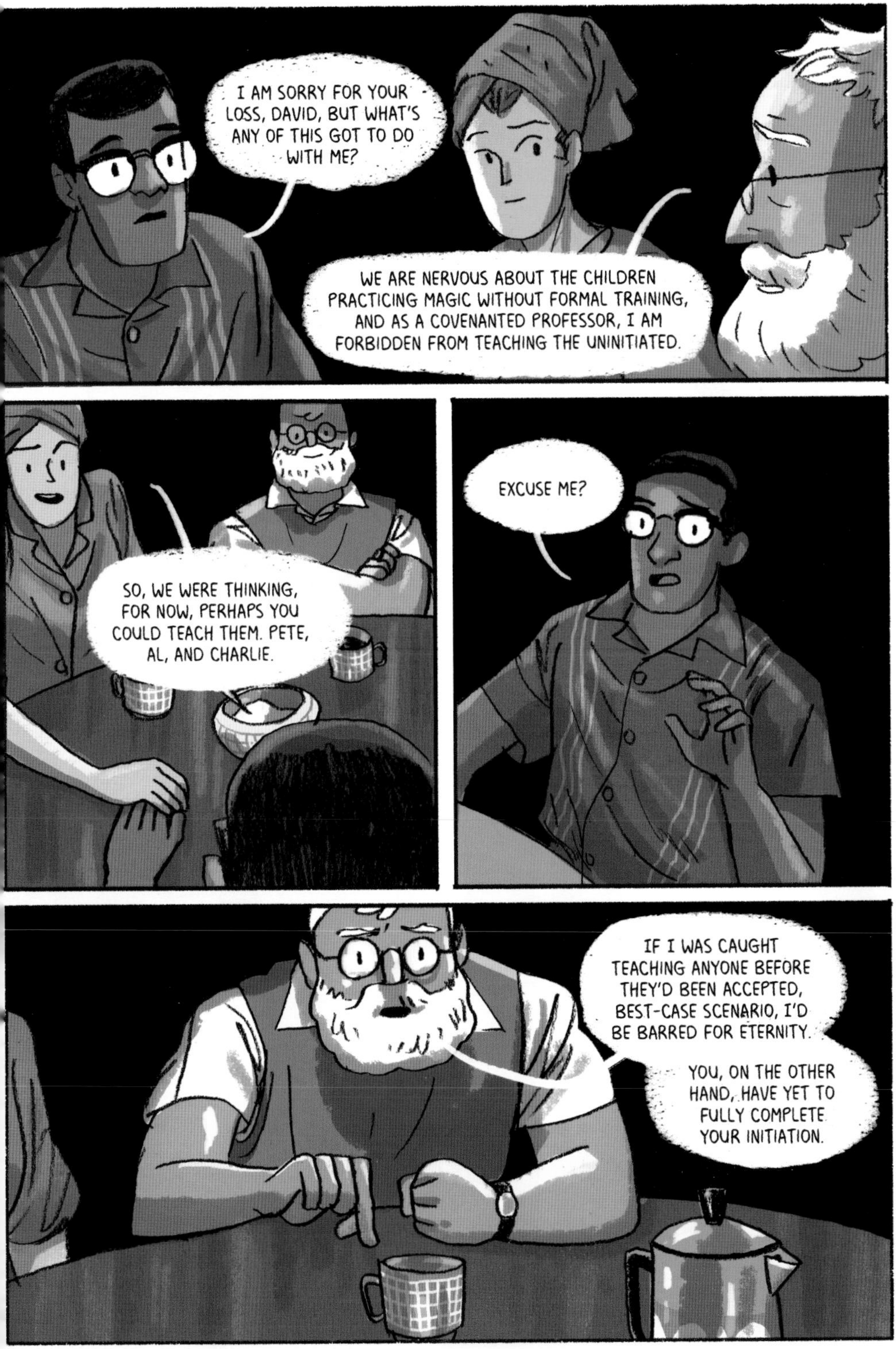
I AM SORRY FOR YOUR LOSS, DAVID, BUT WHAT'S ANY OF THIS GOT TO DO WITH ME?
WE ARE NERVOUS ABOUT THE CHILDREN PRACTICING MAGIC WITHOUT FORMAL TRAINING, AND AS A COVENANTED PROFESSOR, I AM FORBIDDEN FROM TEACHING THE UNINITIATED.
SO, WE WERE THINKING, FOR NOW, PERHAPS YOU COULD TEACH THEM. PETE, AL, AND CHARLIE.
EXCUSE ME?
IF I WAS CAUGHT TEACHING ANYONE BEFORE THEY'D BEEN ACCEPTED, BEST-CASE SCENARIO, I'D BE BARRED FOR ETERNITY.
YOU, ON THE OTHER HAND, HAVE YET TO FULLY COMPLETE YOUR INITIATION.

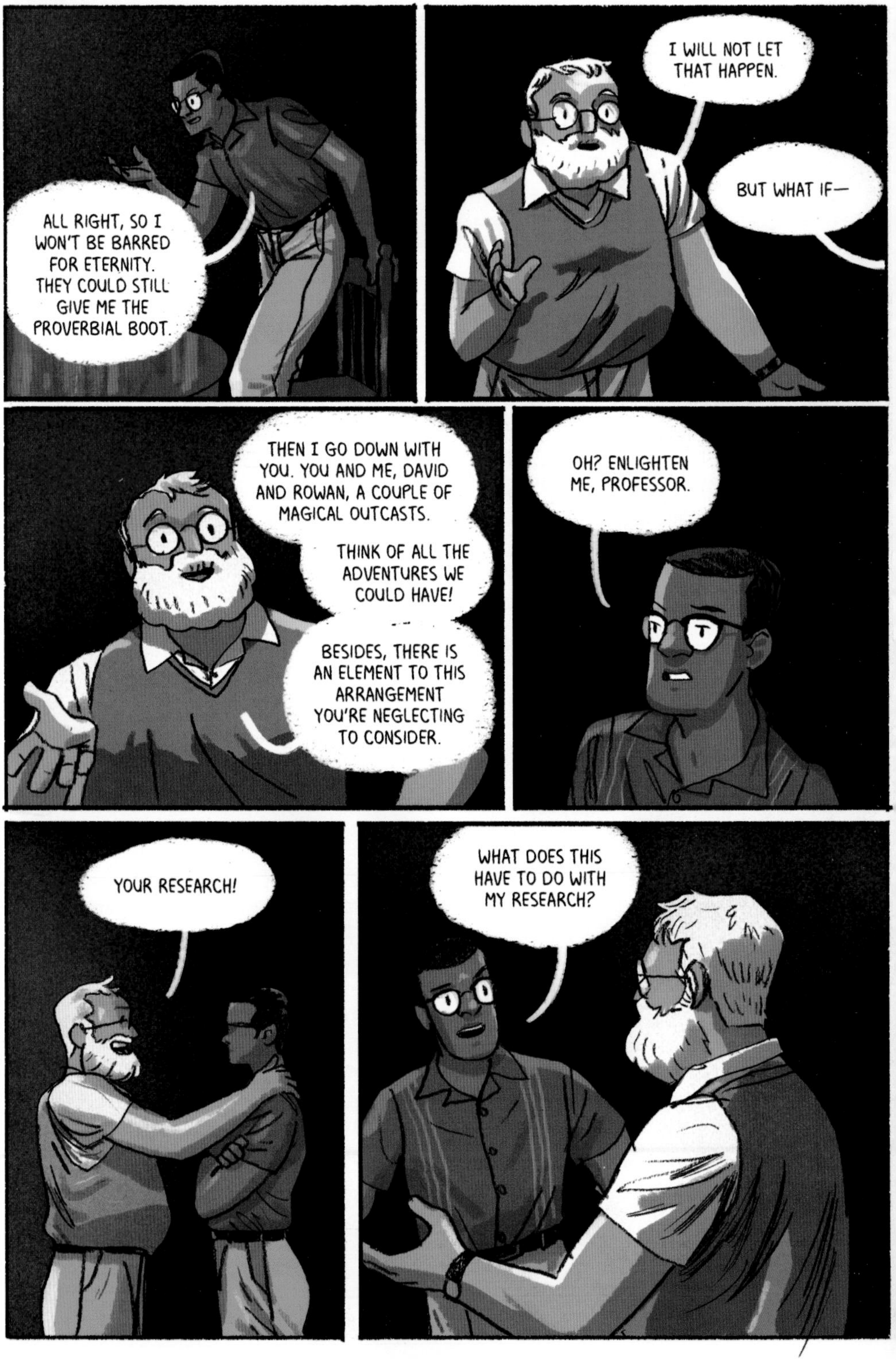
ALL RIGHT, SO I WON'T BE BARRED FOR ETERNITY. THEY COULD STILL GIVE ME THE PROVERBIAL BOOT.
I WILL NOT LET THAT HAPPEN.
BUT WHAT IF—
THEN I GO DOWN WITH YOU. YOU AND ME, DAVID AND ROWAN, A COUPLE OF MAGICAL OUTCASTS.
THINK OF ALL THE ADVENTURES WE COULD HAVE!
BESIDES, THERE IS AN ELEMENT TO THIS ARRANGEMENT YOU'RE NEGLECTING TO CONSIDER.
OH? ENLIGHTEN ME, PROFESSOR.
YOUR RESEARCH!
WHAT DOES THIS HAVE TO DO WITH MY RESEARCH?

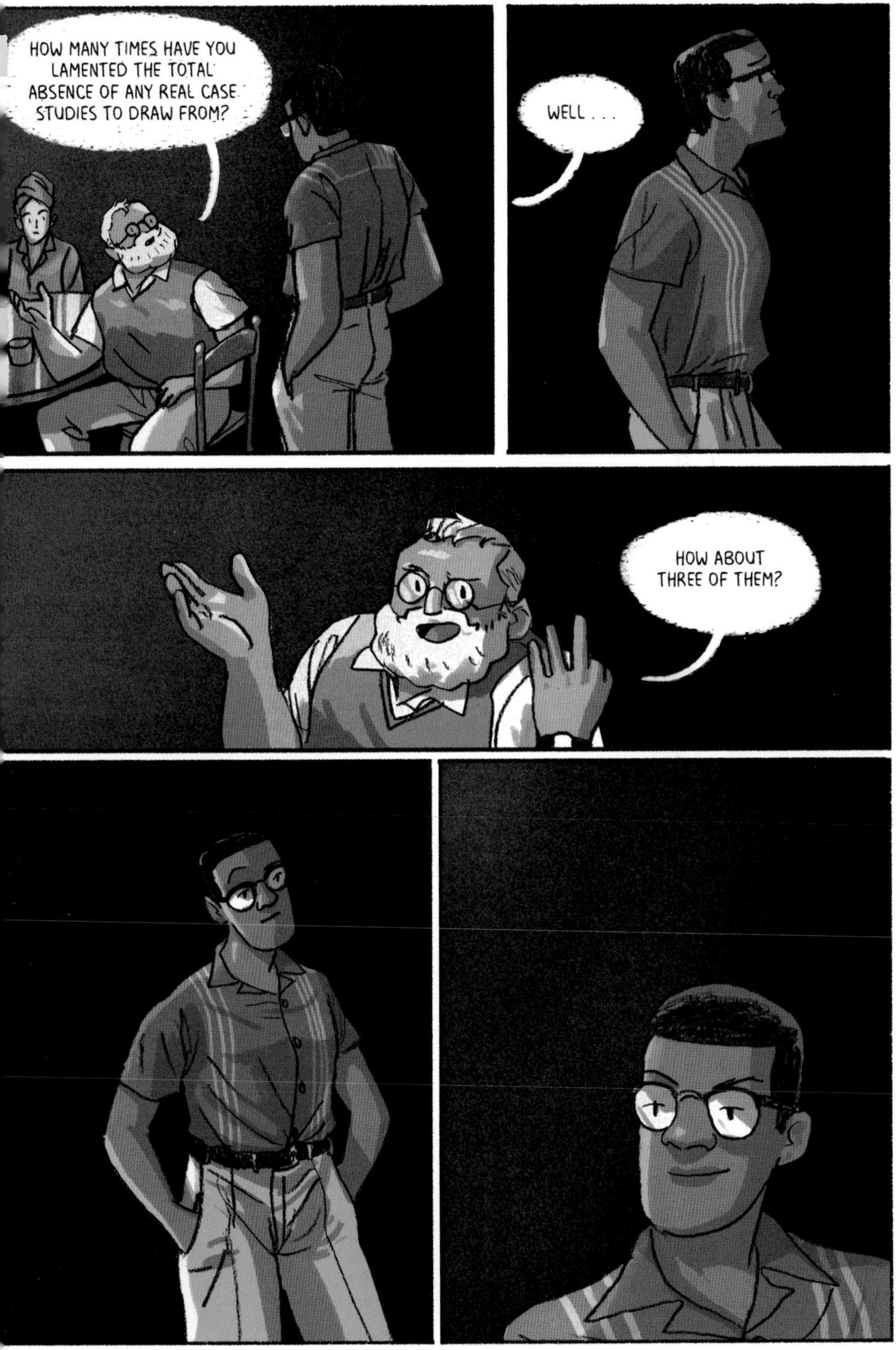
HOW MANY TIMES HAVE YOU LAMENTED THE TOTAL ABSENCE OF ANY REAL CASE STUDIES TO DRAW FROM?
WELL . . .
HOW ABOUT THREE OF THEM?

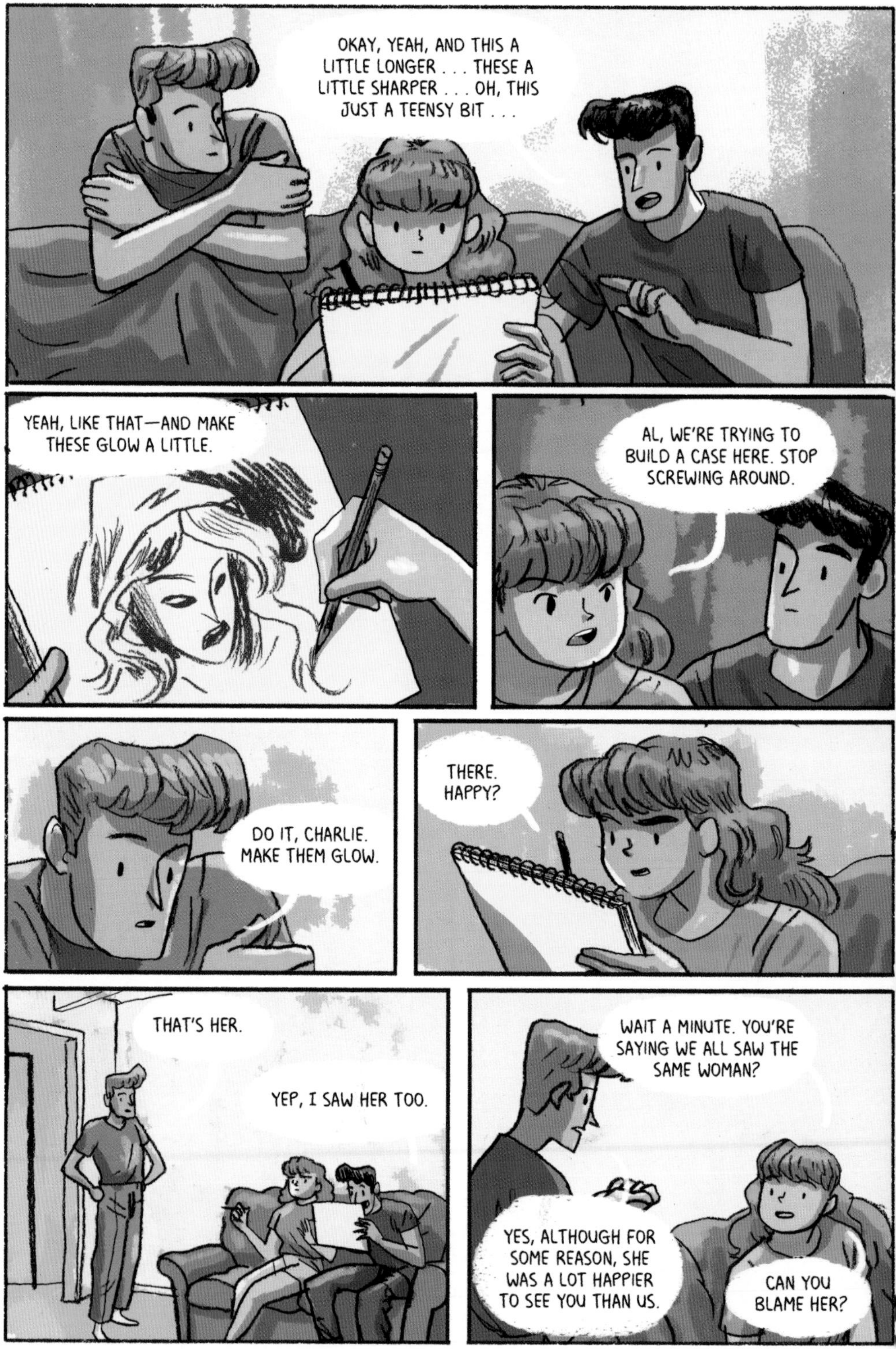
OKAY, YEAH, AND THIS A LITTLE LONGER . . . THESE A LITTLE SHARPER . . . OH, THIS JUST A TEENSY BIT . . .
YEAH, LIKE THAT—AND MAKE THESE GLOW A LITTLE.
AL, WE'RE TRYING TO BUILD A CASE HERE. STOP SCREWING AROUND.
DO IT, CHARLIE. MAKE THEM GLOW.
THERE. HAPPY?
THAT'S HER.
YEP, I SAW HER TOO.
WAIT A MINUTE. YOU'RE SAYING WE ALL SAW THE SAME WOMAN?
YES, ALTHOUGH FOR SOME REASON, SHE WAS A LOT HAPPIER TO SEE YOU THAN US.
CAN YOU BLAME HER?

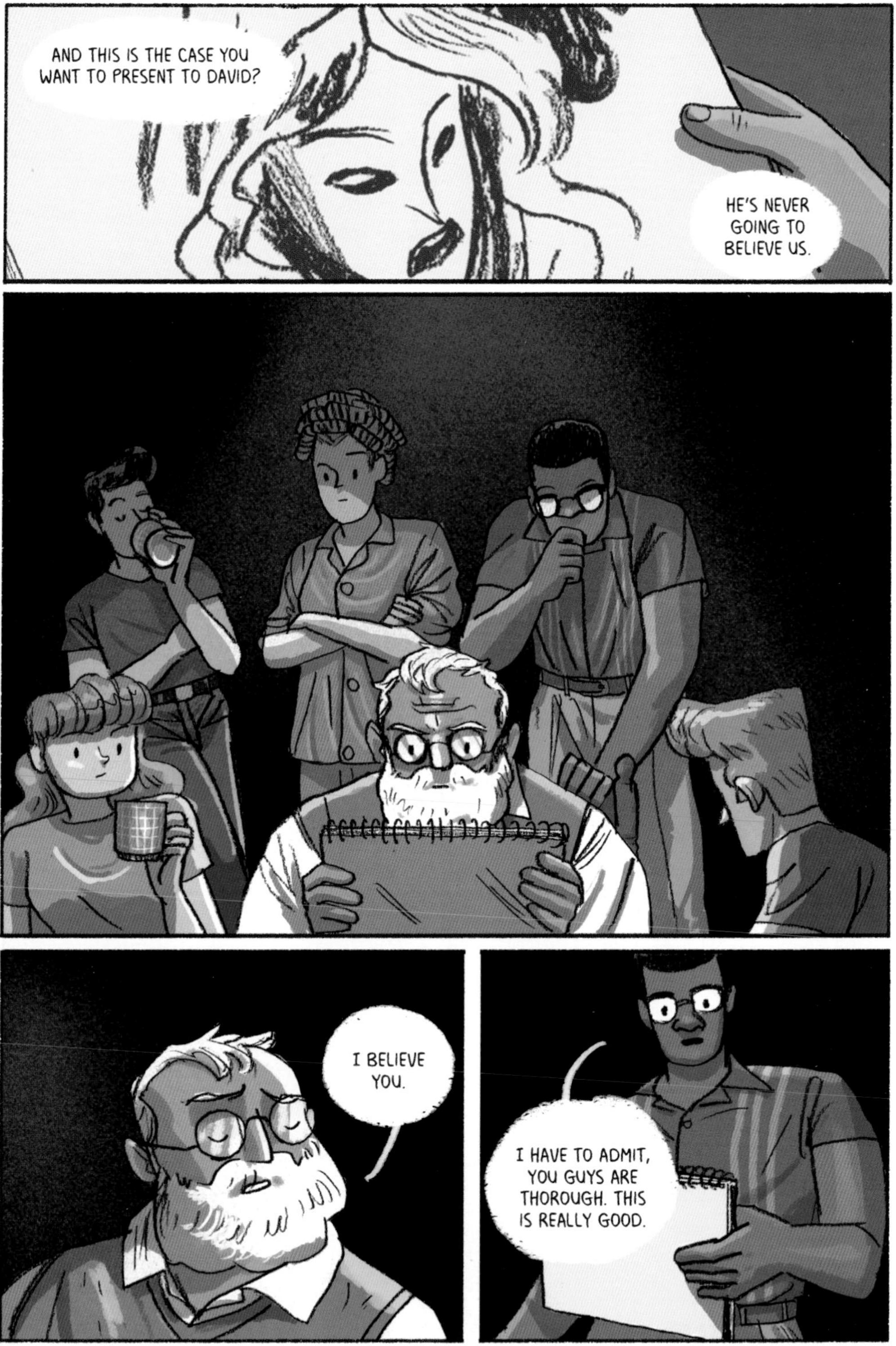
AND THIS IS THE CASE YOU WANT TO PRESENT TO DAVID?
HE'S NEVER GOING TO BELIEVE US.
I BELIEVE YOU.
I HAVE TO ADMIT, YOU GUYS ARE THOROUGH. THIS IS REALLY GOOD.

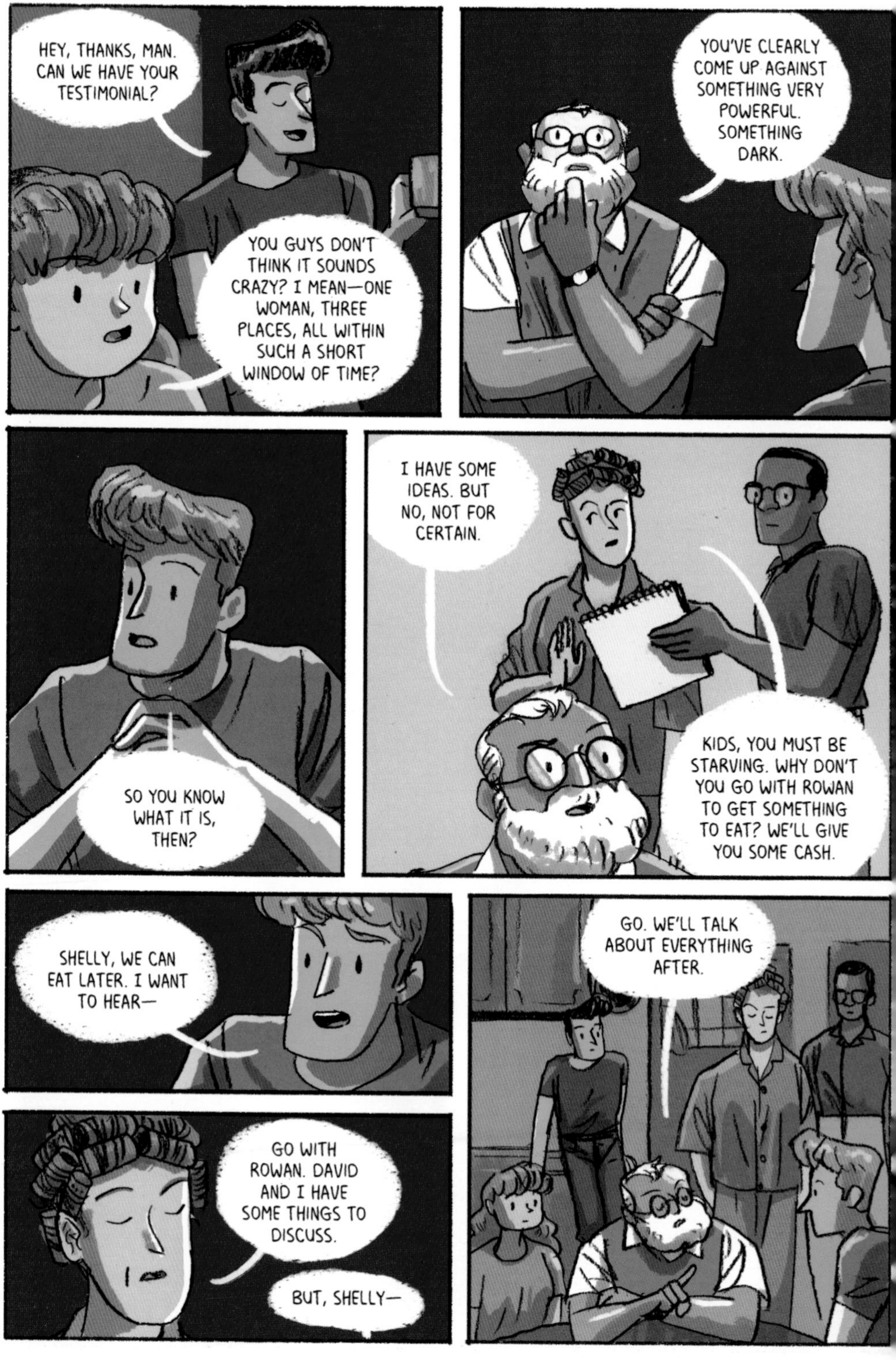
HEY, THANKS, MAN. CAN WE HAVE YOUR TESTIMONIAL?
YOU GUYS DON'T THINK IT SOUNDS CRAZY? I MEAN—ONE WOMAN, THREE PLACES, ALL WITHIN SUCH A SHORT WINDOW OF TIME?
YOU'VE CLEARLY COME UP AGAINST SOMETHING VERY POWERFUL. SOMETHING DARK.
SO YOU KNOW WHAT IT IS, THEN?
I HAVE SOME IDEAS. BUT NO, NOT FOR CERTAIN.
KIDS, YOU MUST BE STARVING. WHY DON'T YOU GO WITH ROWAN TO GET SOMETHING TO EAT? WE'LL GIVE YOU SOME CASH.
SHELLY, WE CAN EAT LATER. I WANT TO HEAR—
GO WITH ROWAN. DAVID AND I HAVE SOME THINGS TO DISCUSS.
BUT, SHELLY—
GO. WE'LL TALK ABOUT EVERYTHING AFTER.

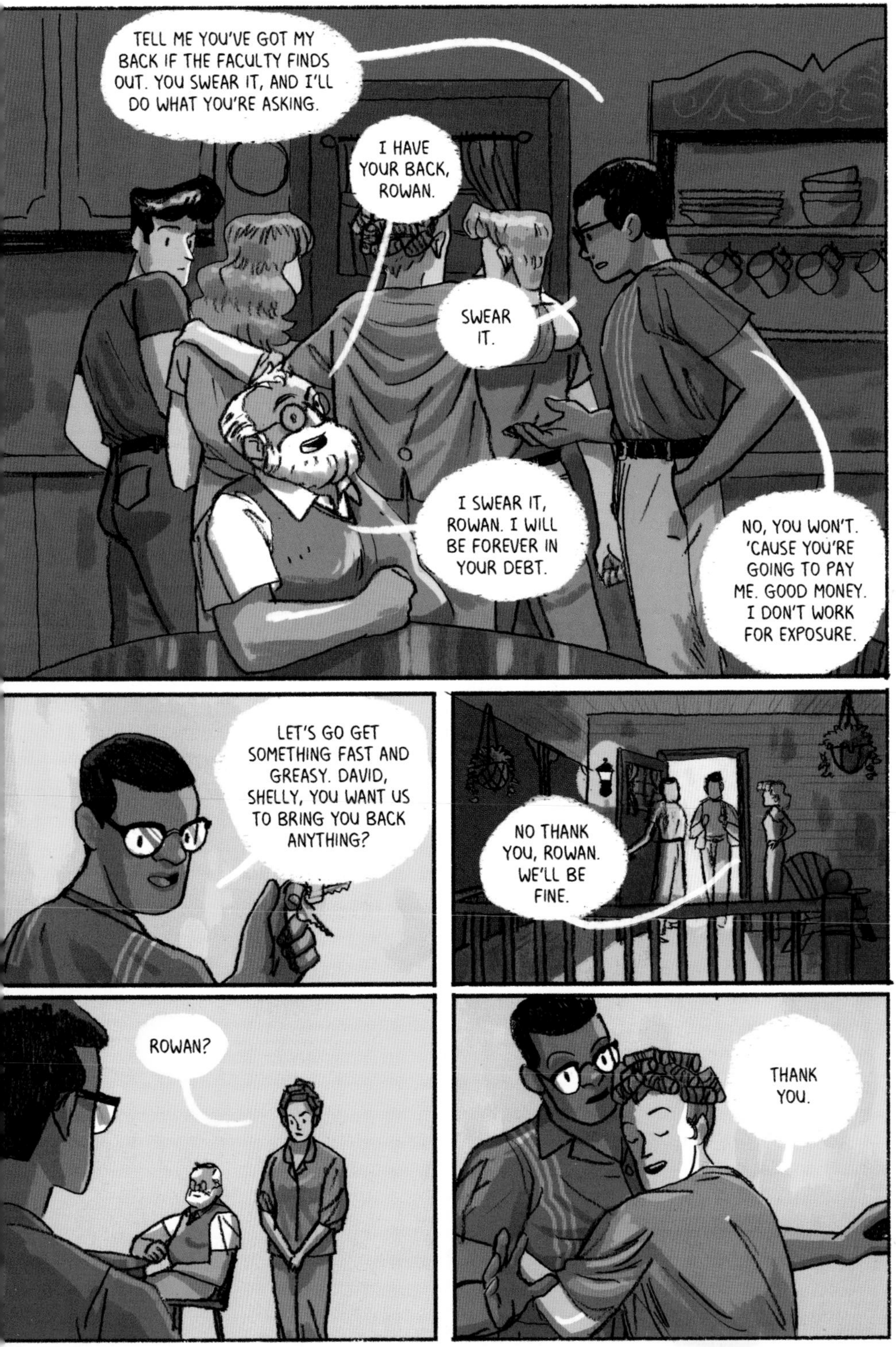
TELL ME YOU'VE GOT MY BACK IF THE FACULTY FINDS OUT. YOU SWEAR IT, AND I'LL DO WHAT YOU'RE ASKING.
I HAVE YOUR BACK, ROWAN.
SWEAR IT.
I SWEAR IT, ROWAN. I WILL BE FOREVER IN YOUR DEBT.
NO, YOU WON'T. 'CAUSE YOU'RE GOING TO PAY ME. GOOD MONEY. I DON'T WORK FOR EXPOSURE.
LET'S GO GET SOMETHING FAST AND GREASY. DAVID, SHELLY, YOU WANT US TO BRING YOU BACK ANYTHING?
NO THANK YOU, ROWAN. WE'LL BE FINE.
ROWAN?
THANK YOU.

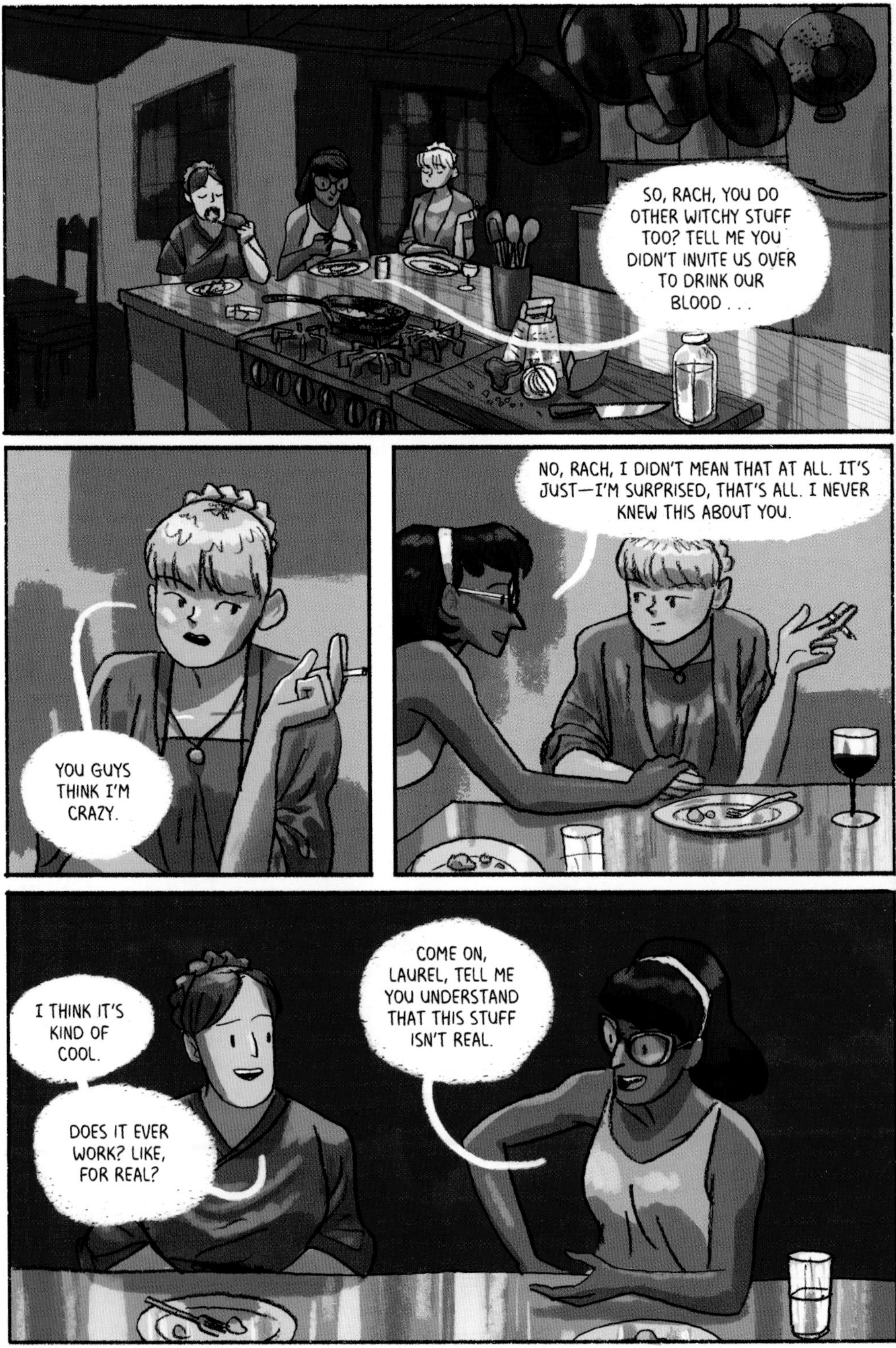
SO, RACH, YOU DO OTHER WITCHY STUFF TOO? TELL ME YOU DIDN'T INVITE US OVER TO DRINK OUR BLOOD . . .
YOU GUYS THINK I'M CRAZY.
NO, RACH, I DIDN'T MEAN THAT AT ALL. IT'S JUST—I'M SURPRISED, THAT'S ALL. I NEVER KNEW THIS ABOUT YOU.
I THINK IT'S KIND OF COOL.
DOES IT EVER WORK? LIKE, FOR REAL?
COME ON, LAUREL, TELL ME YOU UNDERSTAND THAT THIS STUFF ISN'T REAL.

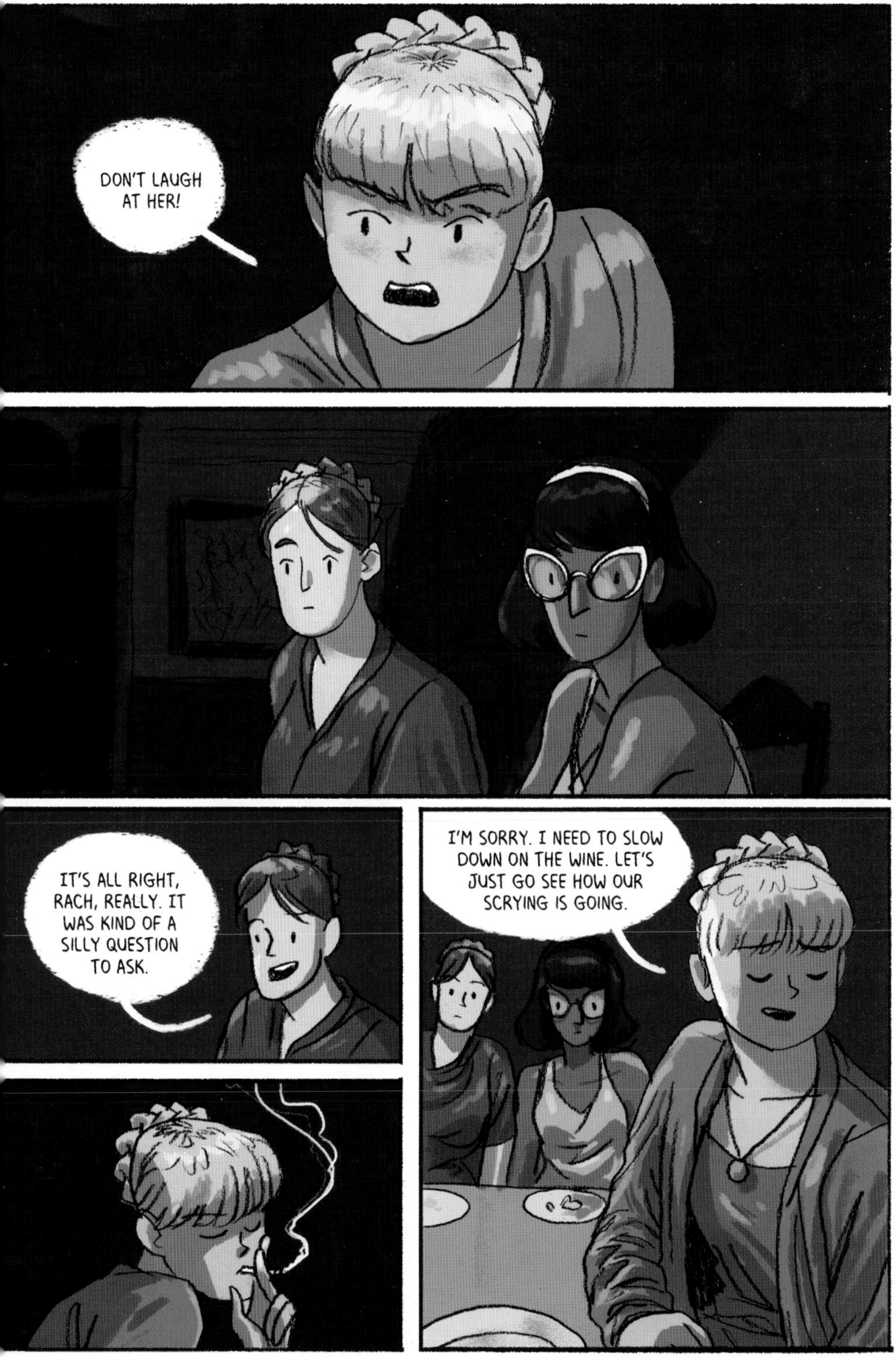
DON'T LAUGH AT HER!
IT'S ALL RIGHT, RACH, REALLY. IT WAS KIND OF A SILLY QUESTION TO ASK.
I'M SORRY. I NEED TO SLOW DOWN ON THE WINE. LET'S JUST GO SEE HOW OUR SCRYING IS GOING.

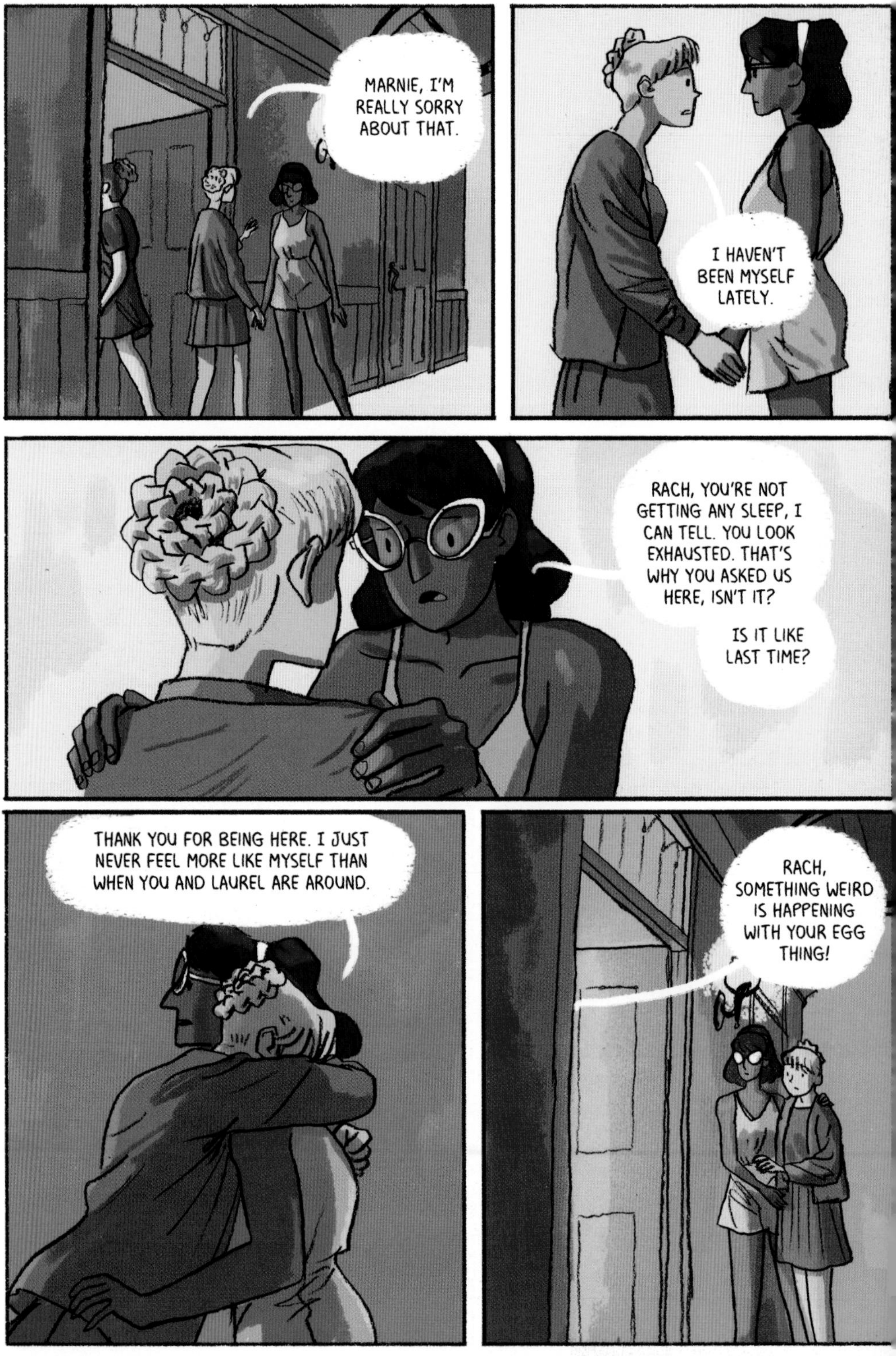
MARNIE, I'M REALLY SORRY ABOUT THAT.
I HAVEN'T BEEN MYSELF LATELY.
RACH, YOU'RE NOT GETTING ANY SLEEP, I CAN TELL. YOU LOOK EXHAUSTED. THAT'S WHY YOU ASKED US HERE, ISN'T IT?
IS IT LIKE LAST TIME?
THANK YOU FOR BEING HERE. I JUST NEVER FEEL MORE LIKE MYSELF THAN WHEN YOU AND LAUREL ARE AROUND.
RACH, SOMETHING WEIRD IS HAPPENING WITH YOUR EGG THING!

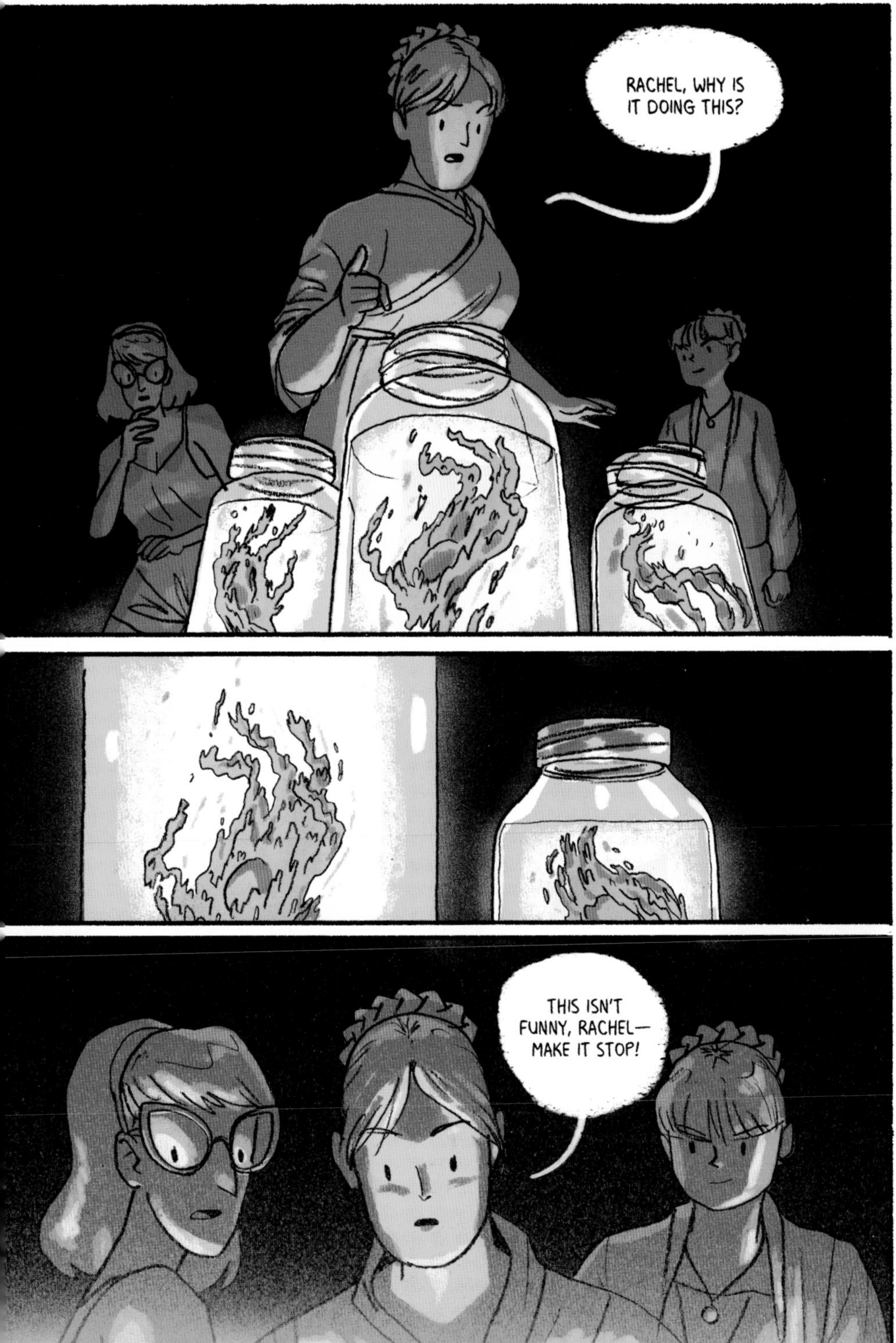
RACHEL, WHY IS IT DOING THIS?
THIS ISN'T FUNNY, RACHEL— MAKE IT STOP!

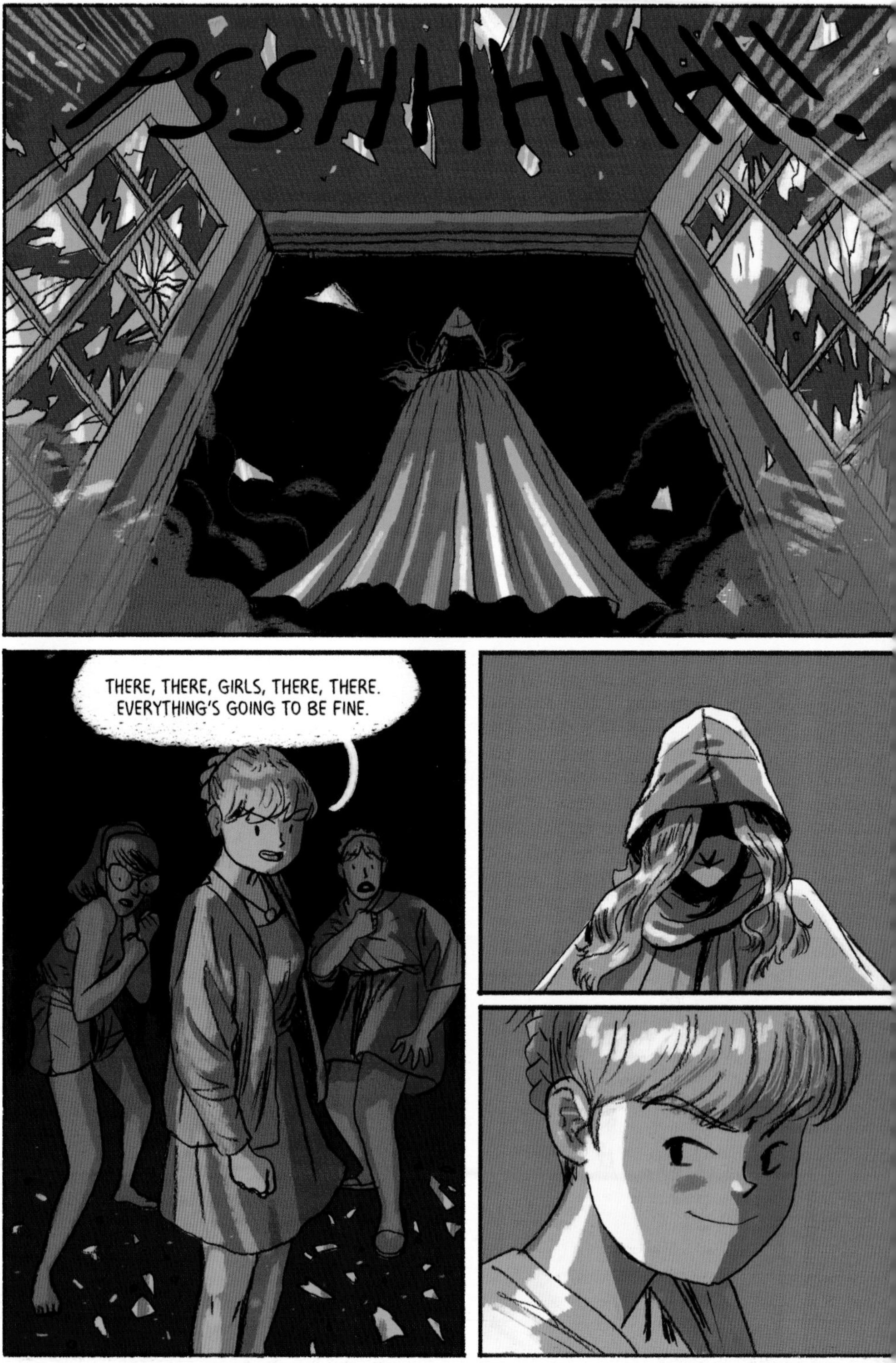
PSSHHHHH!!
THERE, THERE, GIRLS, THERE, THERE. EVERYTHING'S GOING TO BE FINE.

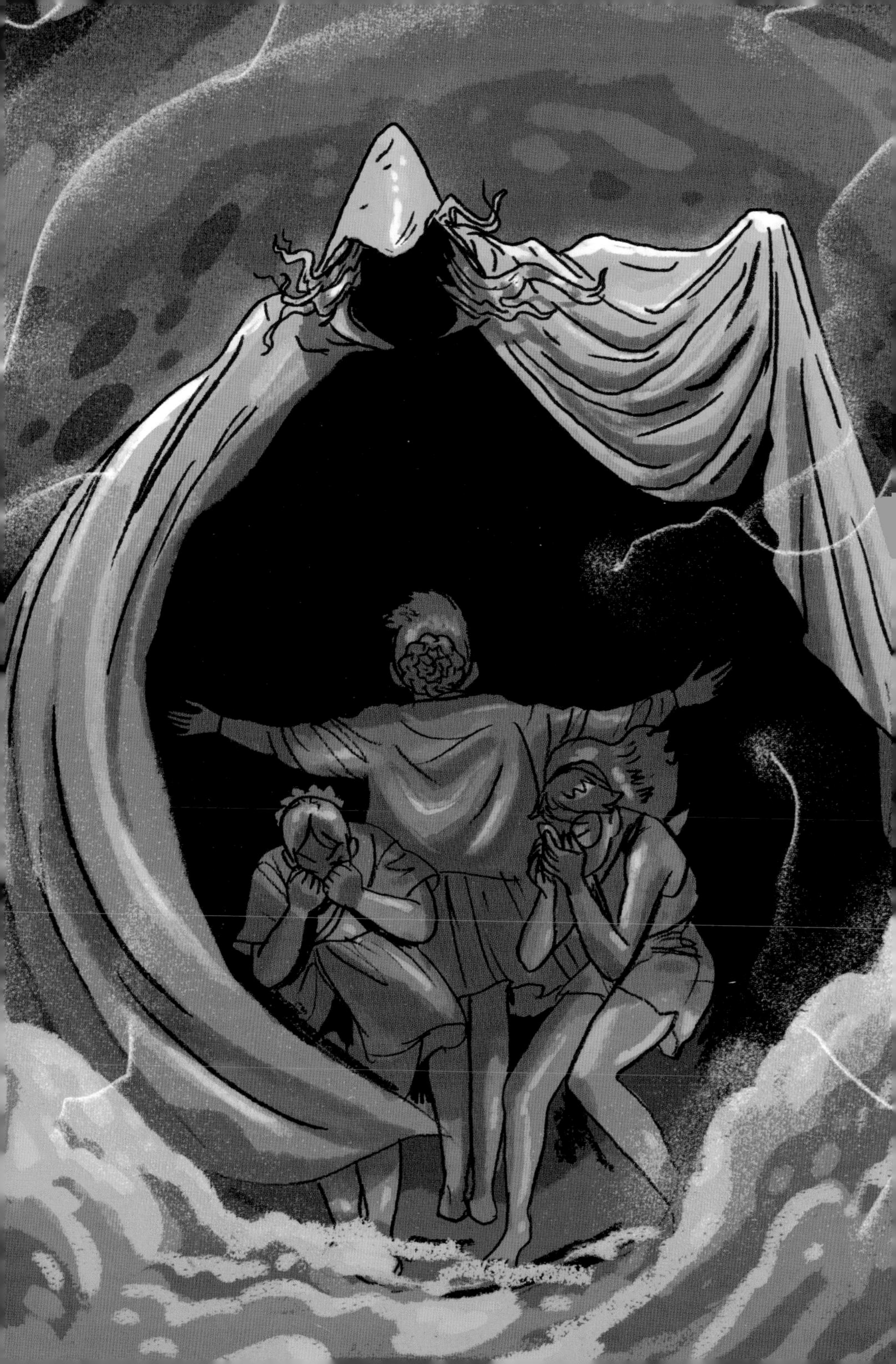

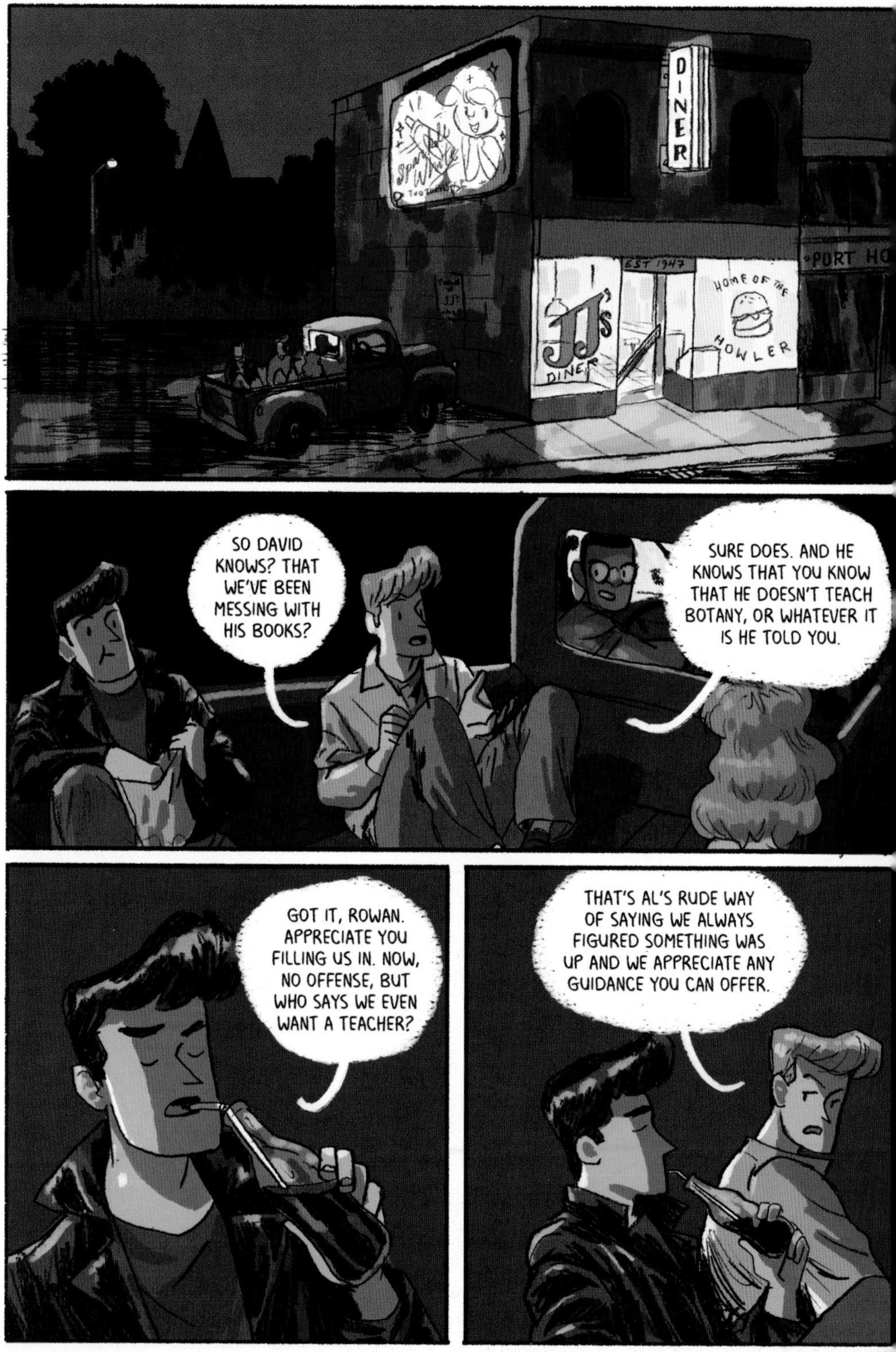
DINER
EST 1947
JJ's DINER
HOME OF THE HOWLER
SO DAVID KNOWS? THAT WE'VE BEEN MESSING WITH HIS BOOKS?
SURE DOES. AND HE KNOWS THAT YOU KNOW THAT HE DOESN'T TEACH BOTANY, OR WHATEVER IT IS HE TOLD YOU.
GOT IT, ROWAN. APPRECIATE YOU FILLING US IN. NOW, NO OFFENSE, BUT WHO SAYS WE EVEN WANT A TEACHER?
THAT'S AL'S RUDE WAY OF SAYING WE ALWAYS FIGURED SOMETHING WAS UP AND WE APPRECIATE ANY GUIDANCE YOU CAN OFFER.

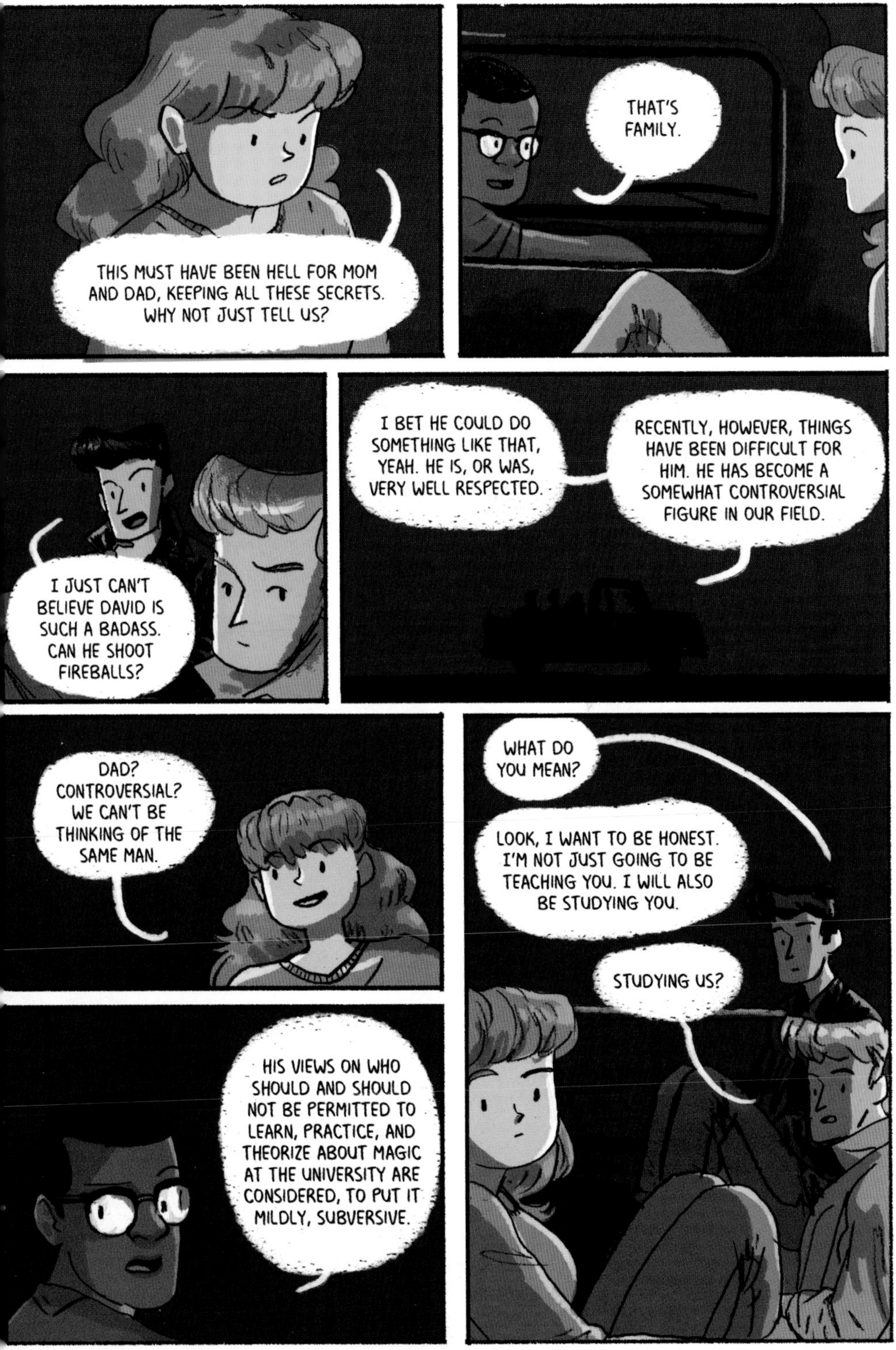
THIS MUST HAVE BEEN HELL FOR MOM AND DAD, KEEPING ALL THESE SECRETS. WHY NOT JUST TELL US?
THAT'S FAMILY.
I JUST CAN'T BELIEVE DAVID IS SUCH A BADASS. CAN HE SHOOT FIREBALLS?
I BET HE COULD DO SOMETHING LIKE THAT, YEAH. HE IS, OR WAS, VERY WELL RESPECTED.
RECENTLY, HOWEVER, THINGS HAVE BEEN DIFFICULT FOR HIM. HE HAS BECOME A SOMEWHAT CONTROVERSIAL FIGURE IN OUR FIELD.
DAD? CONTROVERSIAL? WE CAN'T BE THINKING OF THE SAME MAN.
HIS VIEWS ON WHO SHOULD AND SHOULD NOT BE PERMITTED TO LEARN, PRACTICE, AND THEORIZE ABOUT MAGIC AT THE UNIVERSITY ARE CONSIDERED, TO PUT IT MILDLY, SUBVERSIVE.
WHAT DO YOU MEAN?
LOOK, I WANT TO BE HONEST. I'M NOT JUST GOING TO BE TEACHING YOU. I WILL ALSO BE STUDYING YOU.
STUDYING US?

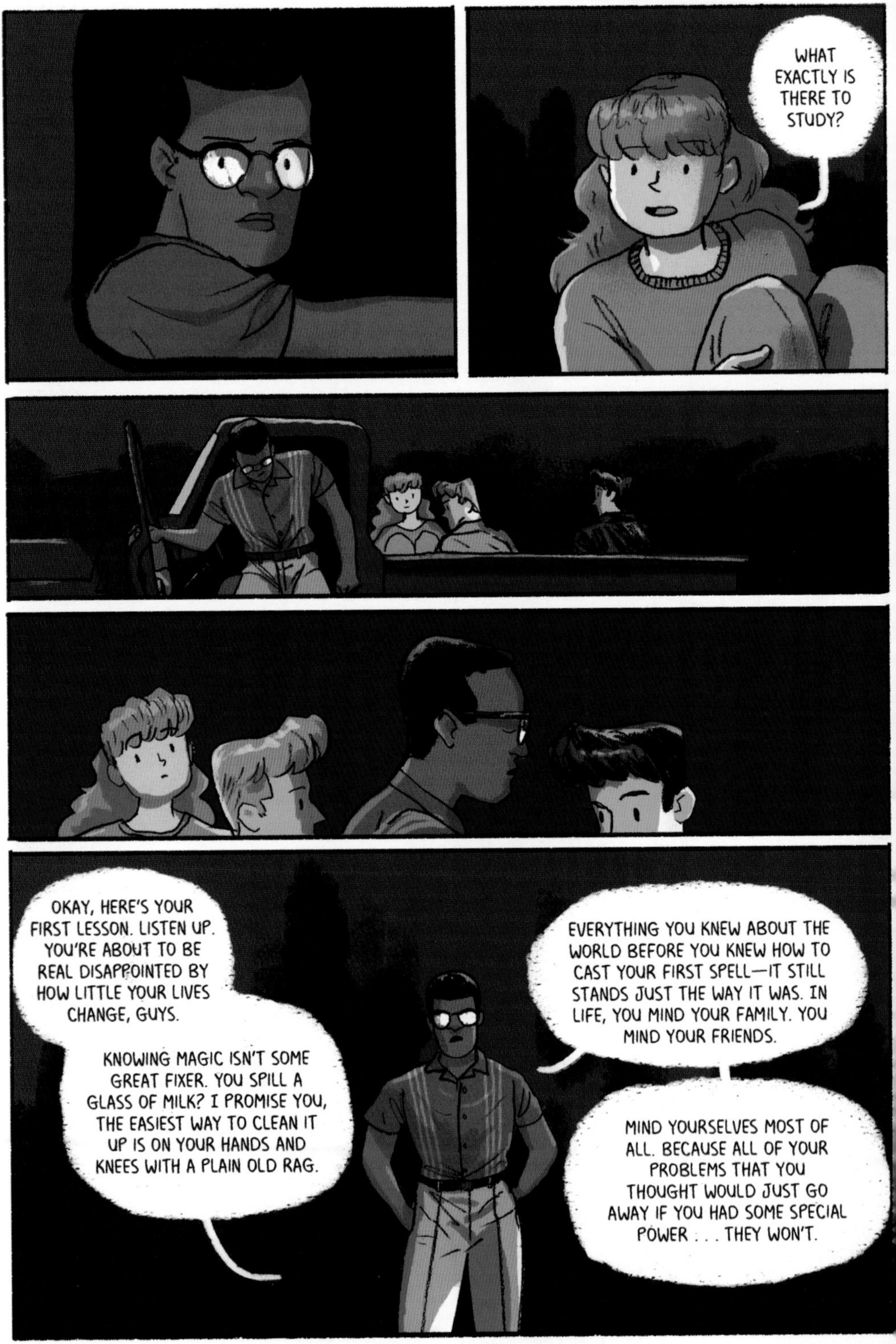
WHAT EXACTLY IS THERE TO STUDY?
OKAY, HERE'S YOUR FIRST LESSON. LISTEN UP. YOU'RE ABOUT TO BE REAL DISAPPOINTED BY HOW LITTLE YOUR LIVES CHANGE, GUYS.
KNOWING MAGIC ISN'T SOME GREAT FIXER. YOU SPILL A GLASS OF MILK? I PROMISE YOU, THE EASIEST WAY TO CLEAN IT UP IS ON YOUR HANDS AND KNEES WITH A PLAIN OLD RAG.
EVERYTHING YOU KNEW ABOUT THE WORLD BEFORE YOU KNEW HOW TO CAST YOUR FIRST SPELL—IT STILL STANDS JUST THE WAY IT WAS. IN LIFE, YOU MIND YOUR FAMILY. YOU MIND YOUR FRIENDS.
MIND YOURSELVES MOST OF ALL. BECAUSE ALL OF YOUR PROBLEMS THAT YOU THOUGHT WOULD JUST GO AWAY IF YOU HAD SOME SPECIAL POWER . . . THEY WON'T.

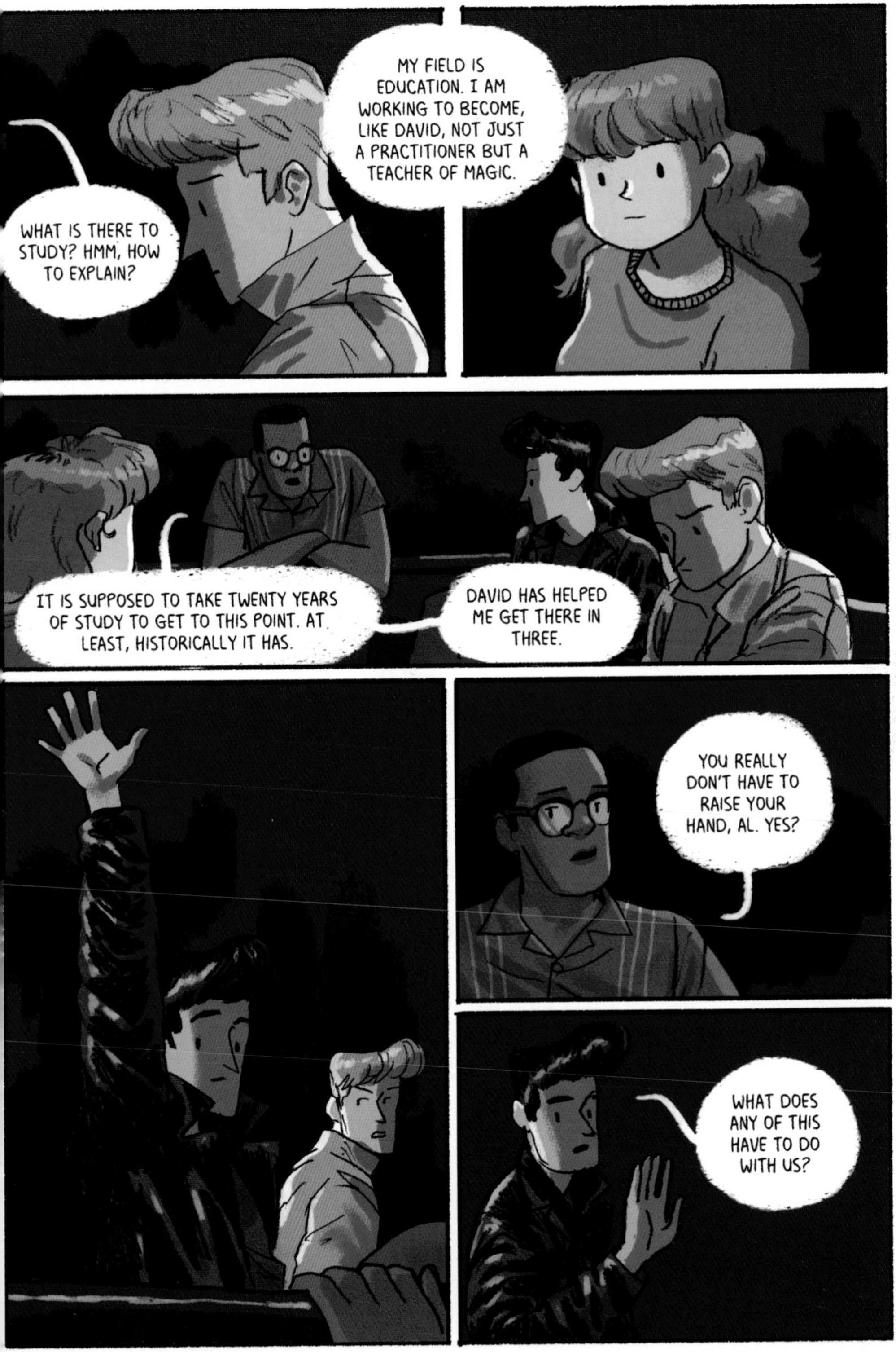
WHAT IS THERE TO STUDY? HMM, HOW TO EXPLAIN?
MY FIELD IS EDUCATION. I AM WORKING TO BECOME, LIKE DAVID, NOT JUST A PRACTITIONER BUT A TEACHER OF MAGIC.
IT IS SUPPOSED TO TAKE TWENTY YEARS OF STUDY TO GET TO THIS POINT. AT LEAST, HISTORICALLY IT HAS.
DAVID HAS HELPED ME GET THERE IN THREE.
YOU REALLY DON'T HAVE TO RAISE YOUR HAND, AL. YES?
WHAT DOES ANY OF THIS HAVE TO DO WITH US?

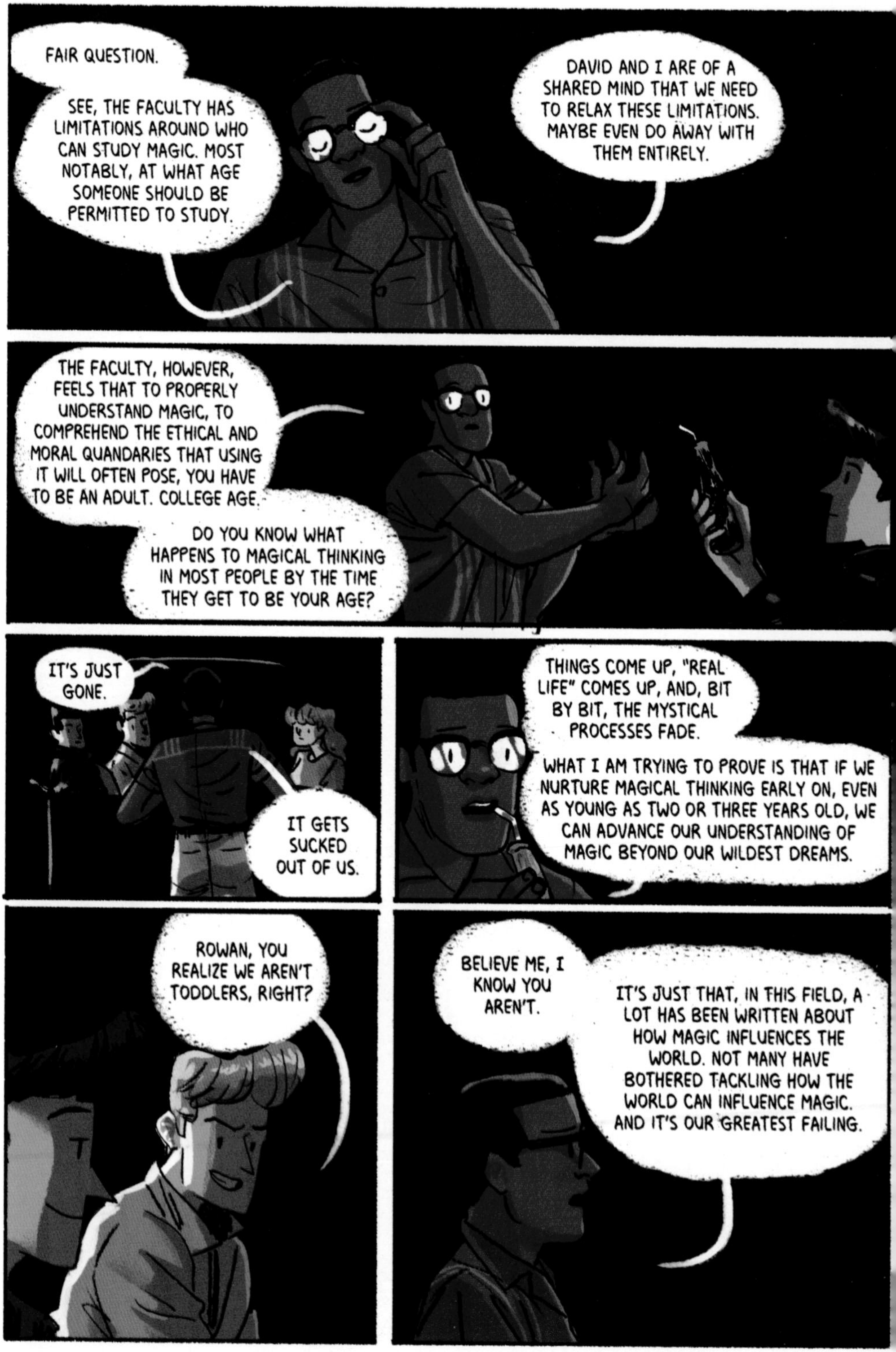
FAIR QUESTION.
SEE, THE FACULTY HAS LIMITATIONS AROUND WHO CAN STUDY MAGIC. MOST NOTABLY, AT WHAT AGE SOMEONE SHOULD BE PERMITTED TO STUDY.
DAVID AND I ARE OF A SHARED MIND THAT WE NEED TO RELAX THESE LIMITATIONS. MAYBE EVEN DO AWAY WITH THEM ENTIRELY.
THE FACULTY, HOWEVER, FEELS THAT TO PROPERLY UNDERSTAND MAGIC, TO COMPREHEND THE ETHICAL AND MORAL QUANDARIES THAT USING IT WILL OFTEN POSE, YOU HAVE TO BE AN ADULT. COLLEGE AGE.
DO YOU KNOW WHAT HAPPENS TO MAGICAL THINKING IN MOST PEOPLE BY THE TIME THEY GET TO BE YOUR AGE?
IT'S JUST GONE.
IT GETS SUCKED OUT OF US.
THINGS COME UP, "REAL LIFE" COMES UP, AND, BIT BY BIT, THE MYSTICAL PROCESSES FADE.
WHAT I AM TRYING TO PROVE IS THAT IF WE NURTURE MAGICAL THINKING EARLY ON, EVEN AS YOUNG AS TWO OR THREE YEARS OLD, WE CAN ADVANCE OUR UNDERSTANDING OF MAGIC BEYOND OUR WILDEST DREAMS.
ROWAN, YOU REALIZE WE AREN'T TODDLERS, RIGHT?
BELIEVE ME, I KNOW YOU AREN'T.
IT'S JUST THAT, IN THIS FIELD, A LOT HAS BEEN WRITTEN ABOUT HOW MAGIC INFLUENCES THE WORLD. NOT MANY HAVE BOTHERED TACKLING HOW THE WORLD CAN INFLUENCE MAGIC. AND IT'S OUR GREATEST FAILING.

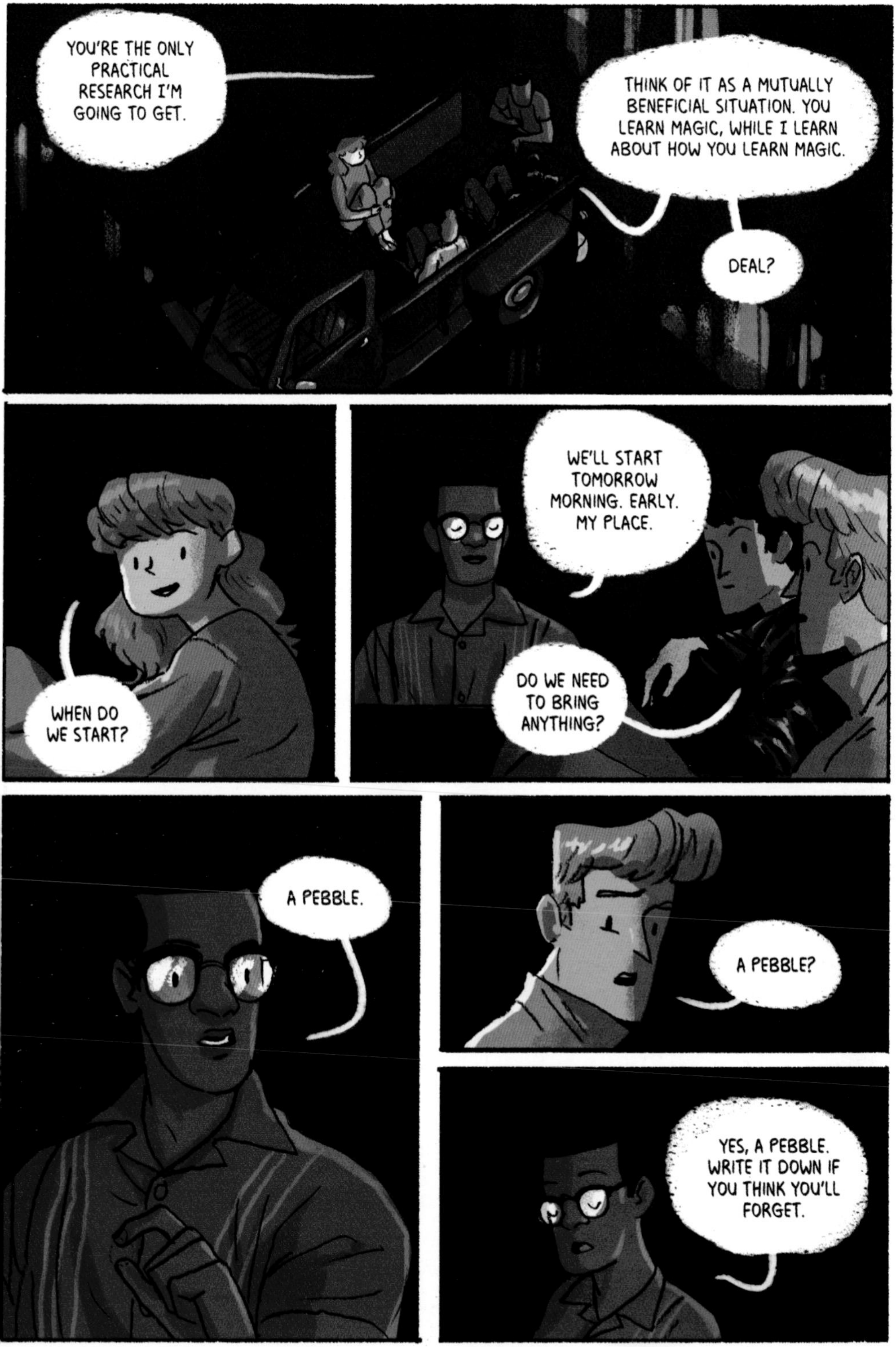
YOU'RE THE ONLY PRACTICAL RESEARCH I'M GOING TO GET.
THINK OF IT AS A MUTUALLY BENEFICIAL SITUATION. YOU LEARN MAGIC, WHILE I LEARN ABOUT HOW YOU LEARN MAGIC.
DEAL?
WHEN DO WE START?
WE'LL START TOMORROW MORNING. EARLY. MY PLACE.
DO WE NEED TO BRING ANYTHING?
A PEBBLE.
A PEBBLE?
YES, A PEBBLE. WRITE IT DOWN IF YOU THINK YOU'LL FORGET.

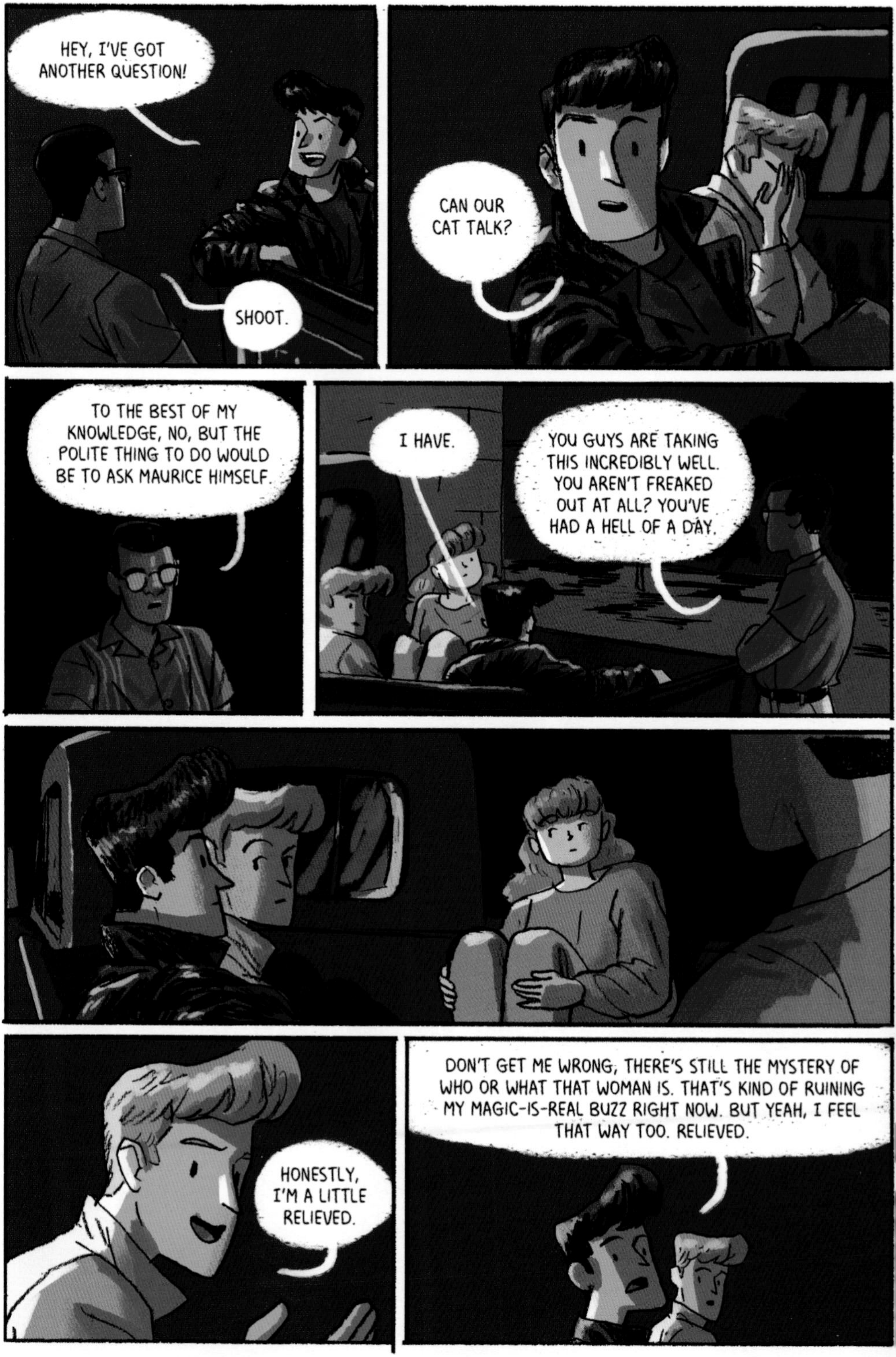
HEY, I'VE GOT ANOTHER QUESTION!
SHOOT.
CAN OUR CAT TALK?
TO THE BEST OF MY KNOWLEDGE, NO, BUT THE POLITE THING TO DO WOULD BE TO ASK MAURICE HIMSELF.
I HAVE.
YOU GUYS ARE TAKING THIS INCREDIBLY WELL. YOU AREN'T FREAKED OUT AT ALL? YOU'VE HAD A HELL OF A DAY.
HONESTLY, I'M A LITTLE RELIEVED.
DON'T GET ME WRONG, THERE'S STILL THE MYSTERY OF WHO OR WHAT THAT WOMAN IS. THAT'S KIND OF RUINING MY MAGIC-IS-REAL BUZZ RIGHT NOW. BUT YEAH, I FEEL THAT WAY TOO. RELIEVED.

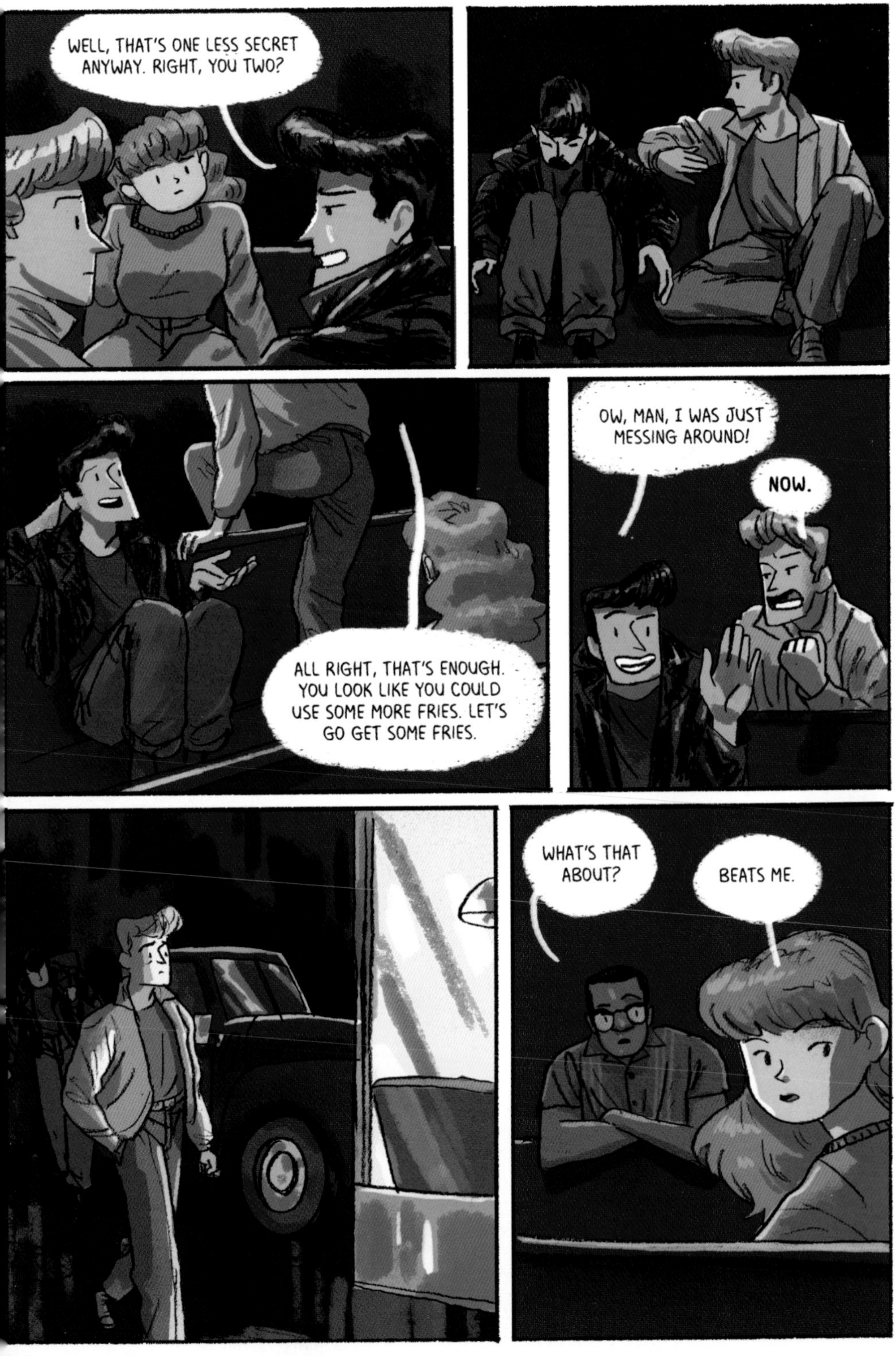
WELL, THAT'S ONE LESS SECRET ANYWAY. RIGHT, YOU TWO?
ALL RIGHT, THAT'S ENOUGH. YOU LOOK LIKE YOU COULD USE SOME MORE FRIES. LET'S GO GET SOME FRIES.
OW, MAN, I WAS JUST MESSING AROUND!
NOW.
WHAT'S THAT ABOUT?
BEATS ME.

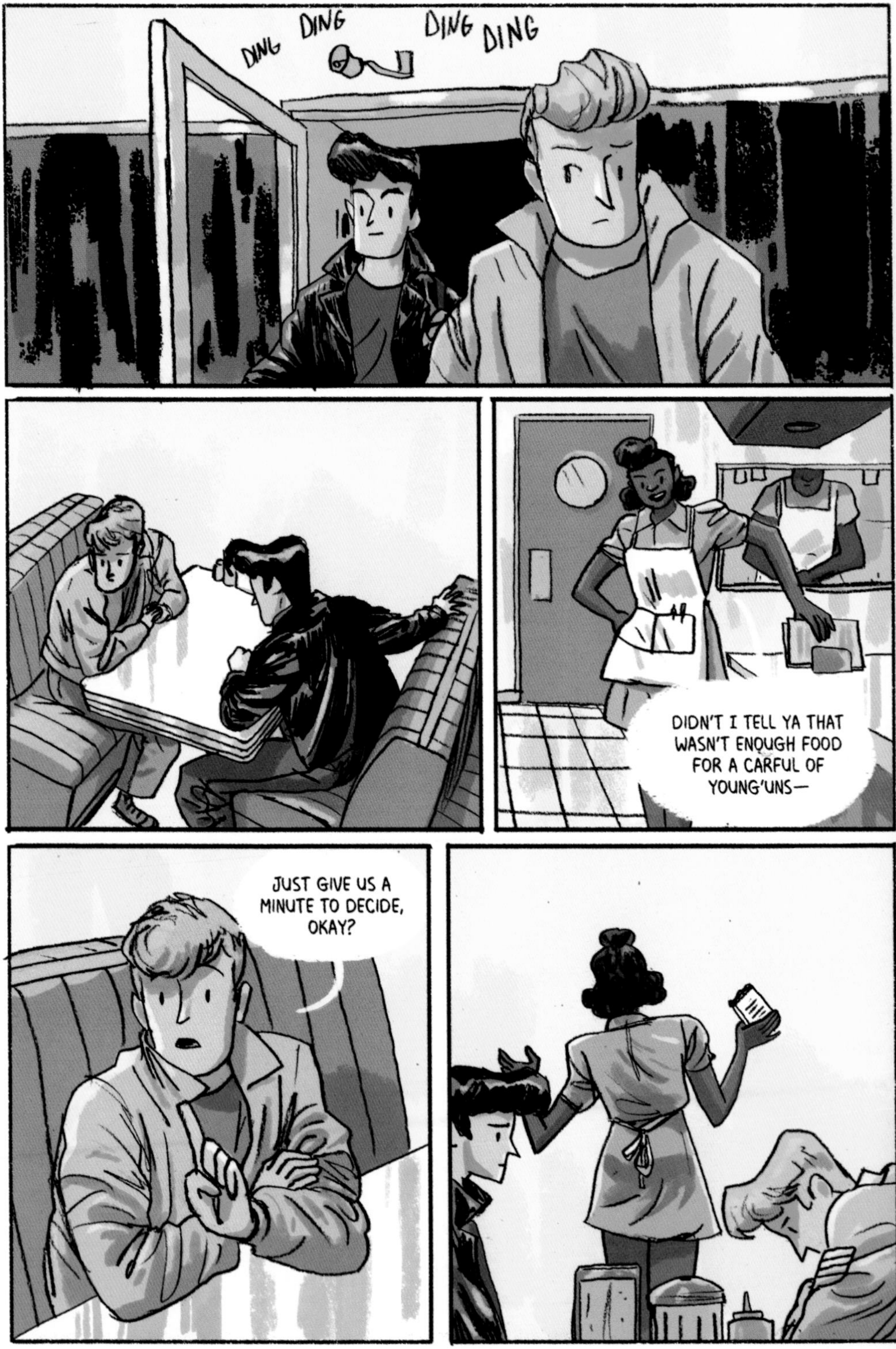
DING DING
DING DING
DIDN'T I TELL YA THAT WASN'T ENOUGH FOOD FOR A CARFUL OF YOUNG'UNS—
JUST GIVE US A MINUTE TO DECIDE, OKAY?

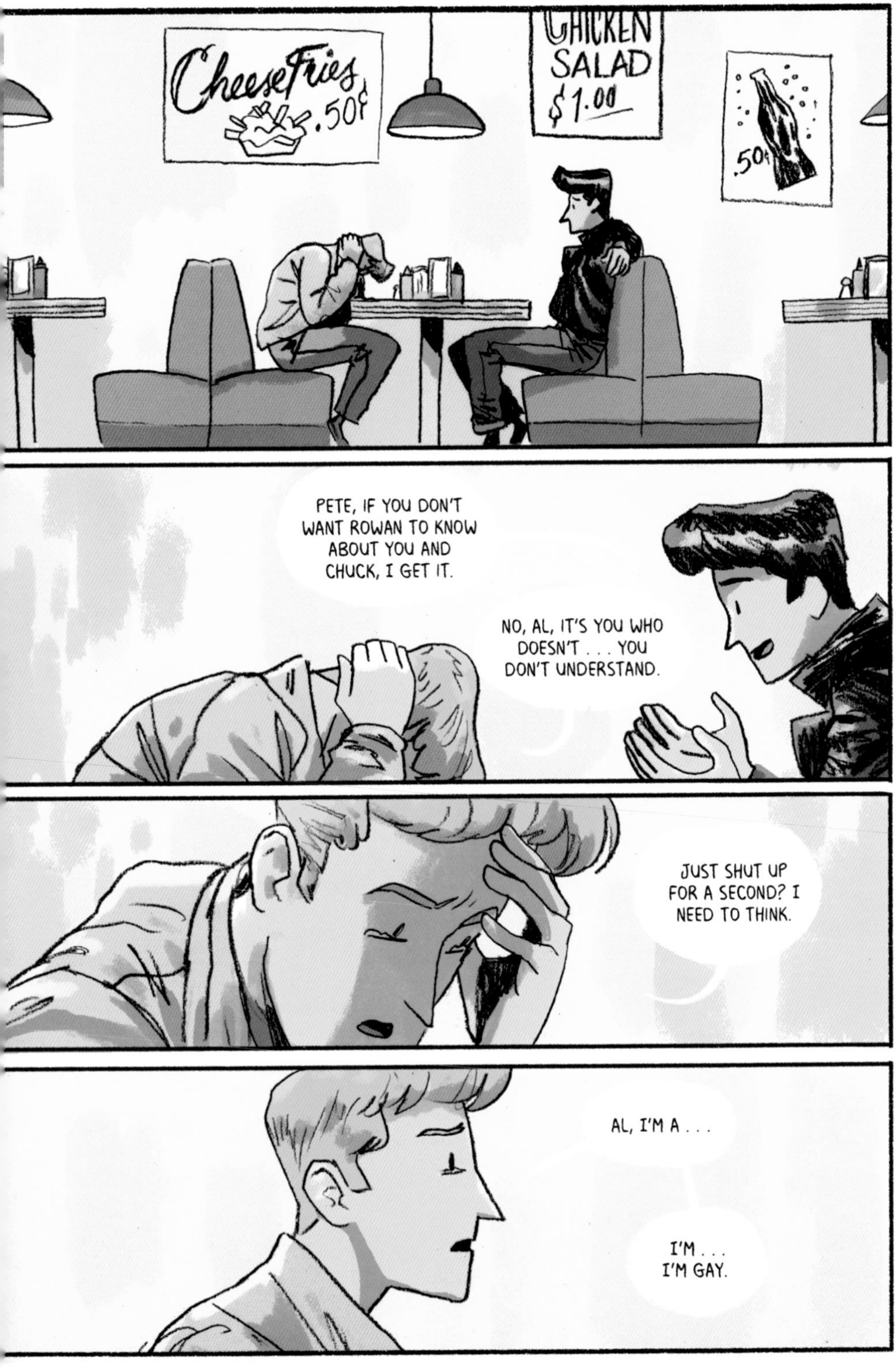

Cheese Fries .50¢
CHICKEN SALAD $1.00
.50¢
PETE, IF YOU DON'T WANT ROWAN TO KNOW ABOUT YOU AND CHUCK, I GET IT.
NO, AL, IT'S YOU WHO DOESN'T . . . YOU DON'T UNDERSTAND.
JUST SHUT UP FOR A SECOND? I NEED TO THINK.
AL, I'M A . . .
I'M . . . I'M GAY.

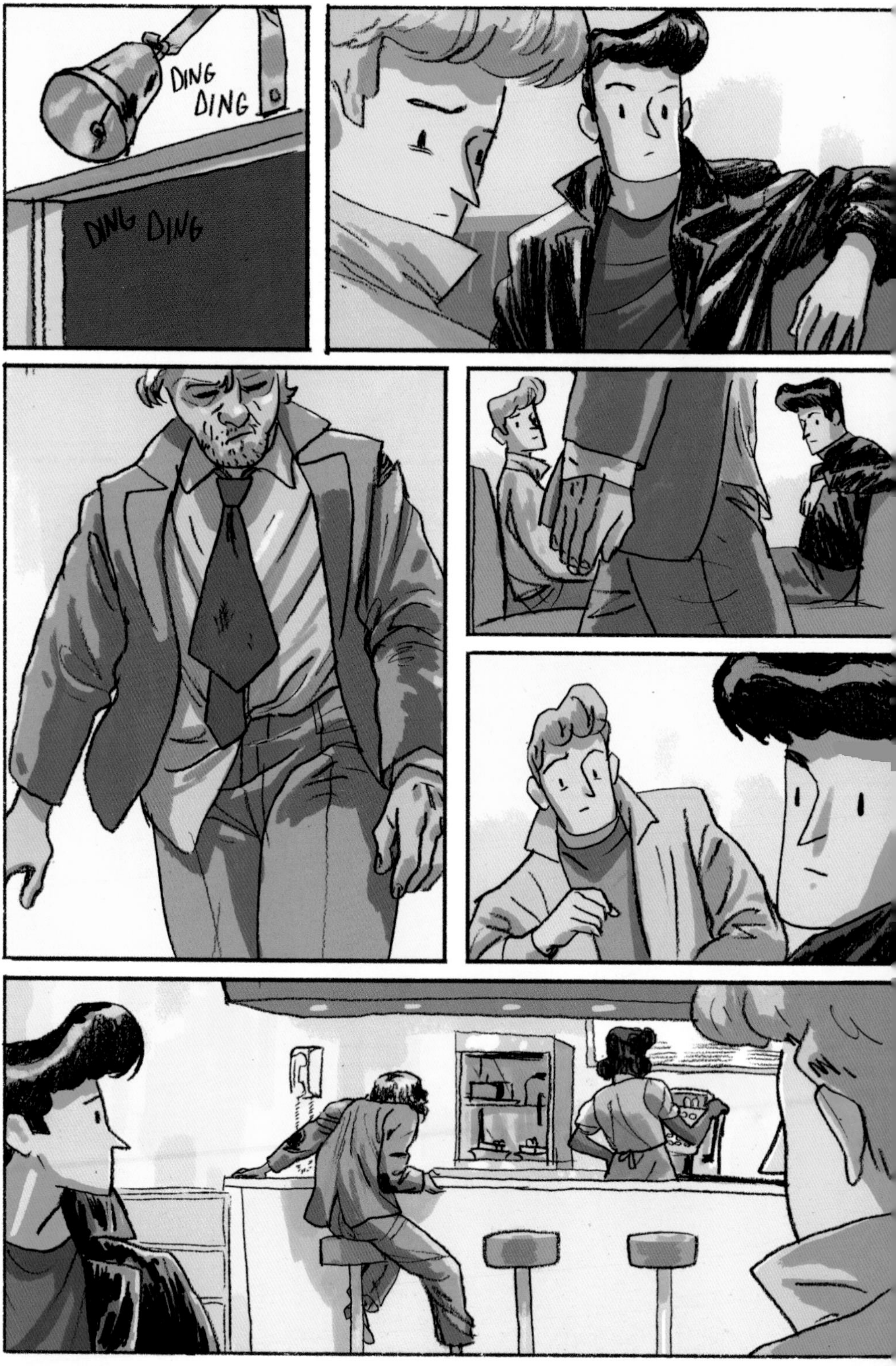
DING DING
DING DING

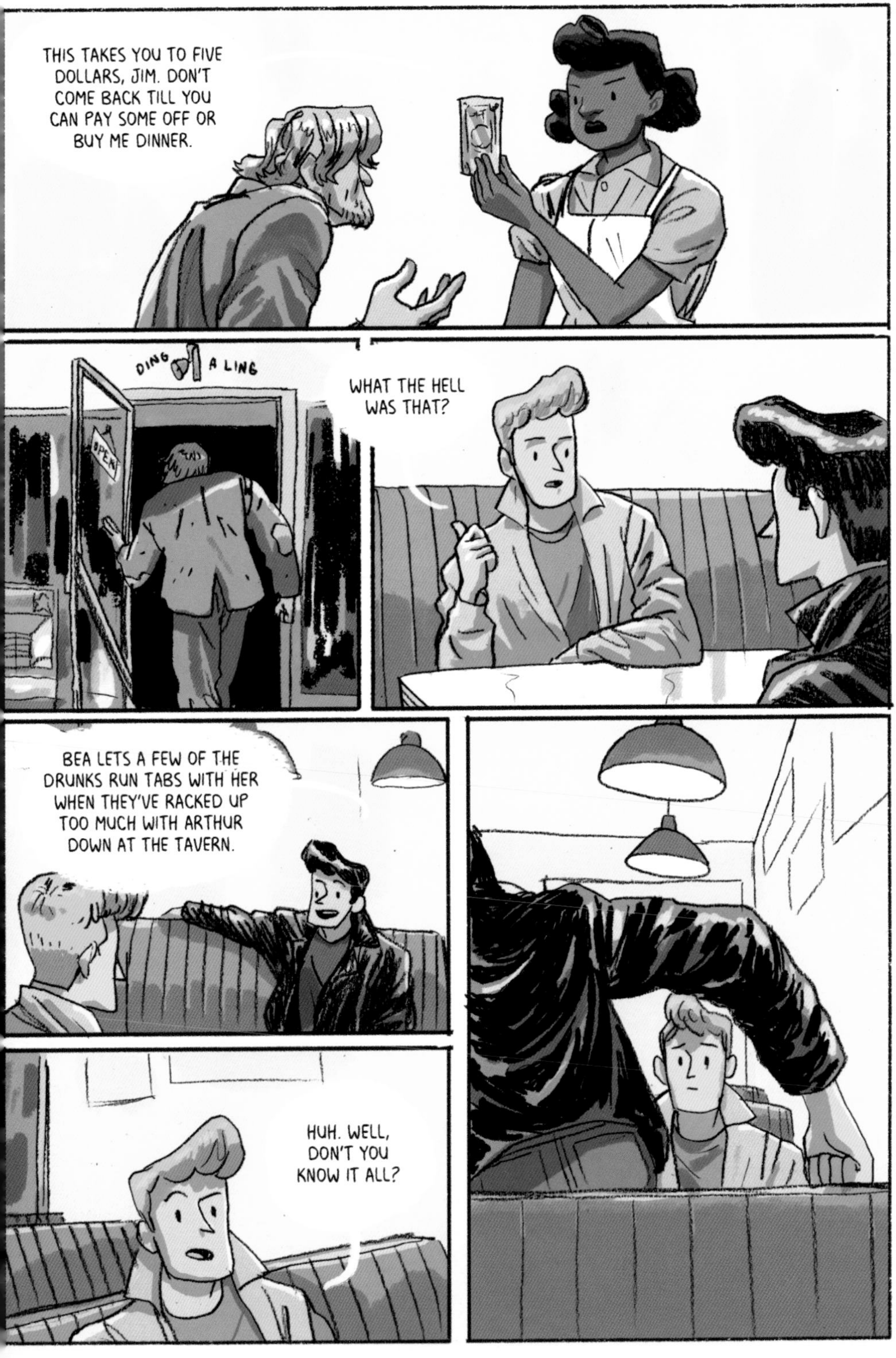
THIS TAKES YOU TO FIVE DOLLARS, JIM. DON'T COME BACK TILL YOU CAN PAY SOME OFF OR BUY ME DINNER.
DING A LING
OPEN
WHAT THE HELL WAS THAT?
BEA LETS A FEW OF THE DRUNKS RUN TABS WITH HER WHEN THEY'VE RACKED UP TOO MUCH WITH ARTHUR DOWN AT THE TAVERN.
HUH. WELL, DON'T YOU KNOW IT ALL?

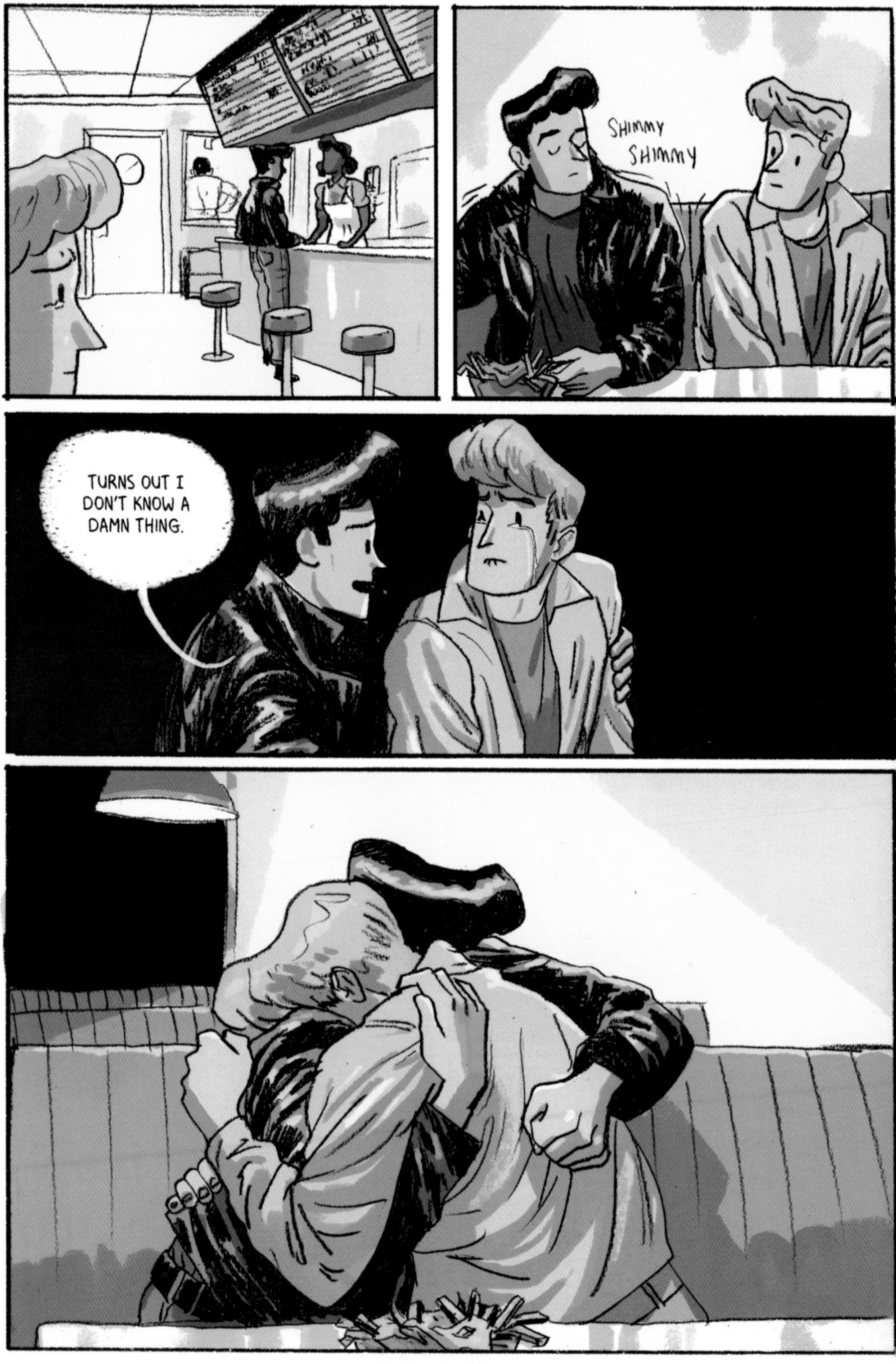
SHIMMY
SHIMMY
TURNS OUT I DON'T KNOW A DAMN THING.

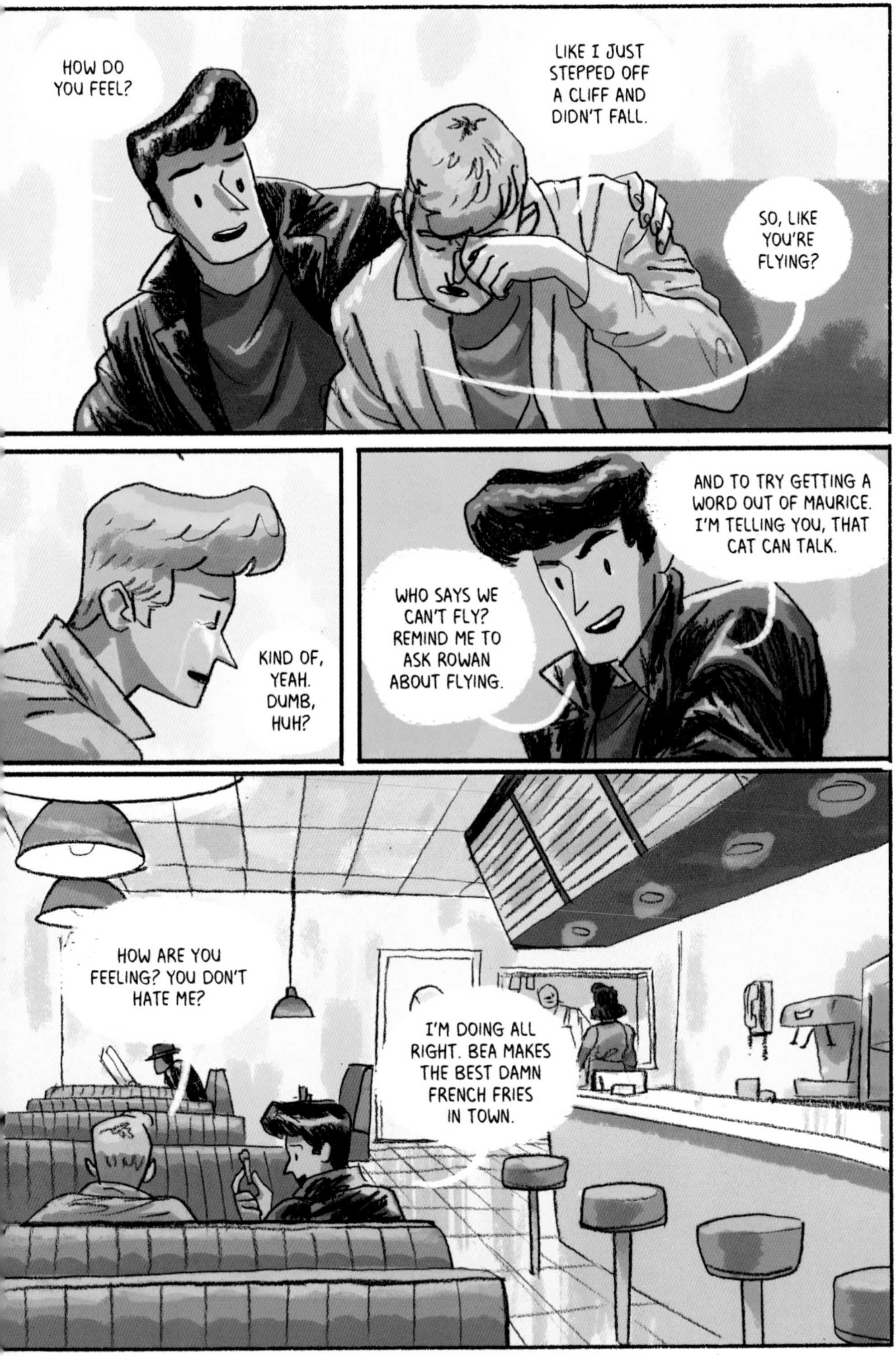
HOW DO YOU FEEL?
LIKE I JUST STEPPED OFF A CLIFF AND DIDN'T FALL.
SO, LIKE YOU'RE FLYING?
KIND OF, YEAH. DUMB, HUH?
WHO SAYS WE CAN'T FLY? REMIND ME TO ASK ROWAN ABOUT FLYING.
AND TO TRY GETTING A WORD OUT OF MAURICE. I'M TELLING YOU, THAT CAT CAN TALK.
HOW ARE YOU FEELING? YOU DON'T HATE ME?
I'M DOING ALL RIGHT. BEA MAKES THE BEST DAMN FRENCH FRIES IN TOWN.

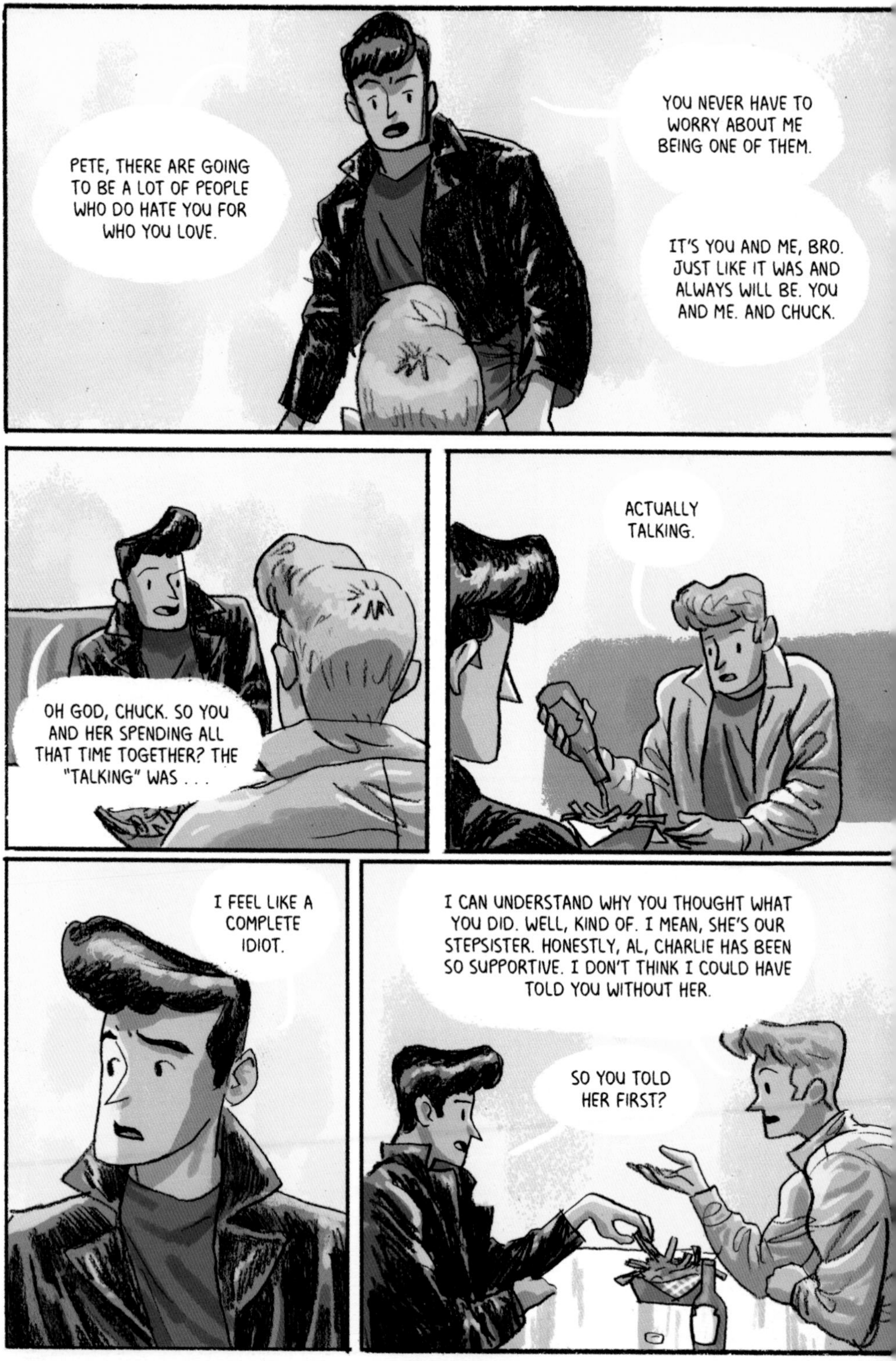
PETE, THERE ARE GOING TO BE A LOT OF PEOPLE WHO DO HATE YOU FOR WHO YOU LOVE.
YOU NEVER HAVE TO WORRY ABOUT ME BEING ONE OF THEM.
IT'S YOU AND ME, BRO. JUST LIKE IT WAS AND ALWAYS WILL BE. YOU AND ME. AND CHUCK.
OH GOD, CHUCK. SO YOU AND HER SPENDING ALL THAT TIME TOGETHER? THE "TALKING" WAS . . .
ACTUALLY TALKING.
I FEEL LIKE A COMPLETE IDIOT.
I CAN UNDERSTAND WHY YOU THOUGHT WHAT YOU DID. WELL, KIND OF. I MEAN, SHE'S OUR STEPSISTER. HONESTLY, AL, CHARLIE HAS BEEN SO SUPPORTIVE. I DON'T THINK I COULD HAVE TOLD YOU WITHOUT HER.
SO YOU TOLD HER FIRST?

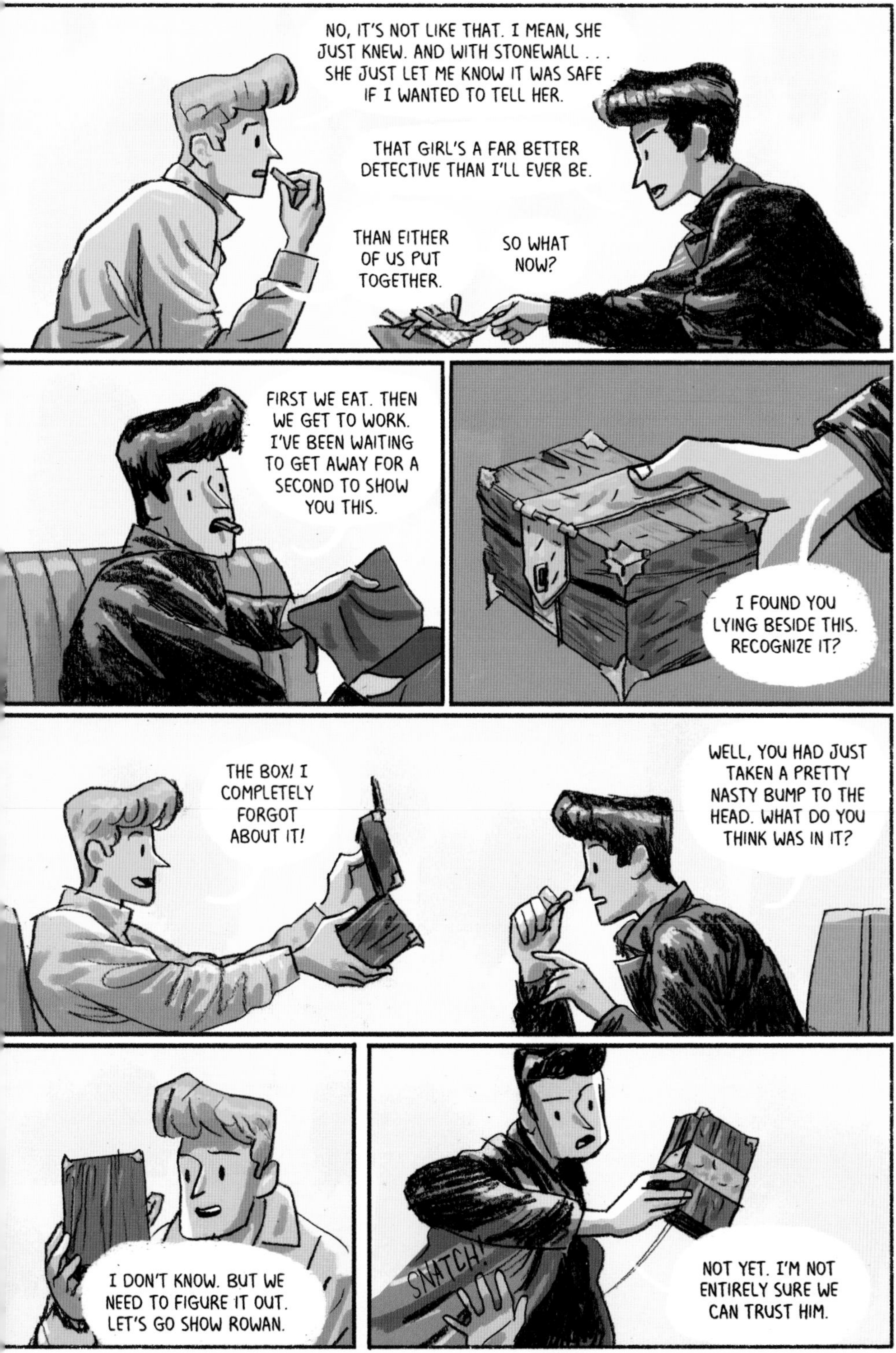
NO, IT'S NOT LIKE THAT. I MEAN, SHE JUST KNEW. AND WITH STONEWALL . . . SHE JUST LET ME KNOW IT WAS SAFE IF I WANTED TO TELL HER.
THAT GIRL'S A FAR BETTER DETECTIVE THAN I'LL EVER BE.
THAN EITHER OF US PUT TOGETHER.
SO WHAT NOW?
FIRST WE EAT. THEN WE GET TO WORK. I'VE BEEN WAITING TO GET AWAY FOR A SECOND TO SHOW YOU THIS.
I FOUND YOU LYING BESIDE THIS. RECOGNIZE IT?
THE BOX! I COMPLETELY FORGOT ABOUT IT!
WELL, YOU HAD JUST TAKEN A PRETTY NASTY BUMP TO THE HEAD. WHAT DO YOU THINK WAS IN IT?
I DON'T KNOW. BUT WE NEED TO FIGURE IT OUT. LET'S GO SHOW ROWAN.
SNATCH!
NOT YET. I'M NOT ENTIRELY SURE WE CAN TRUST HIM.

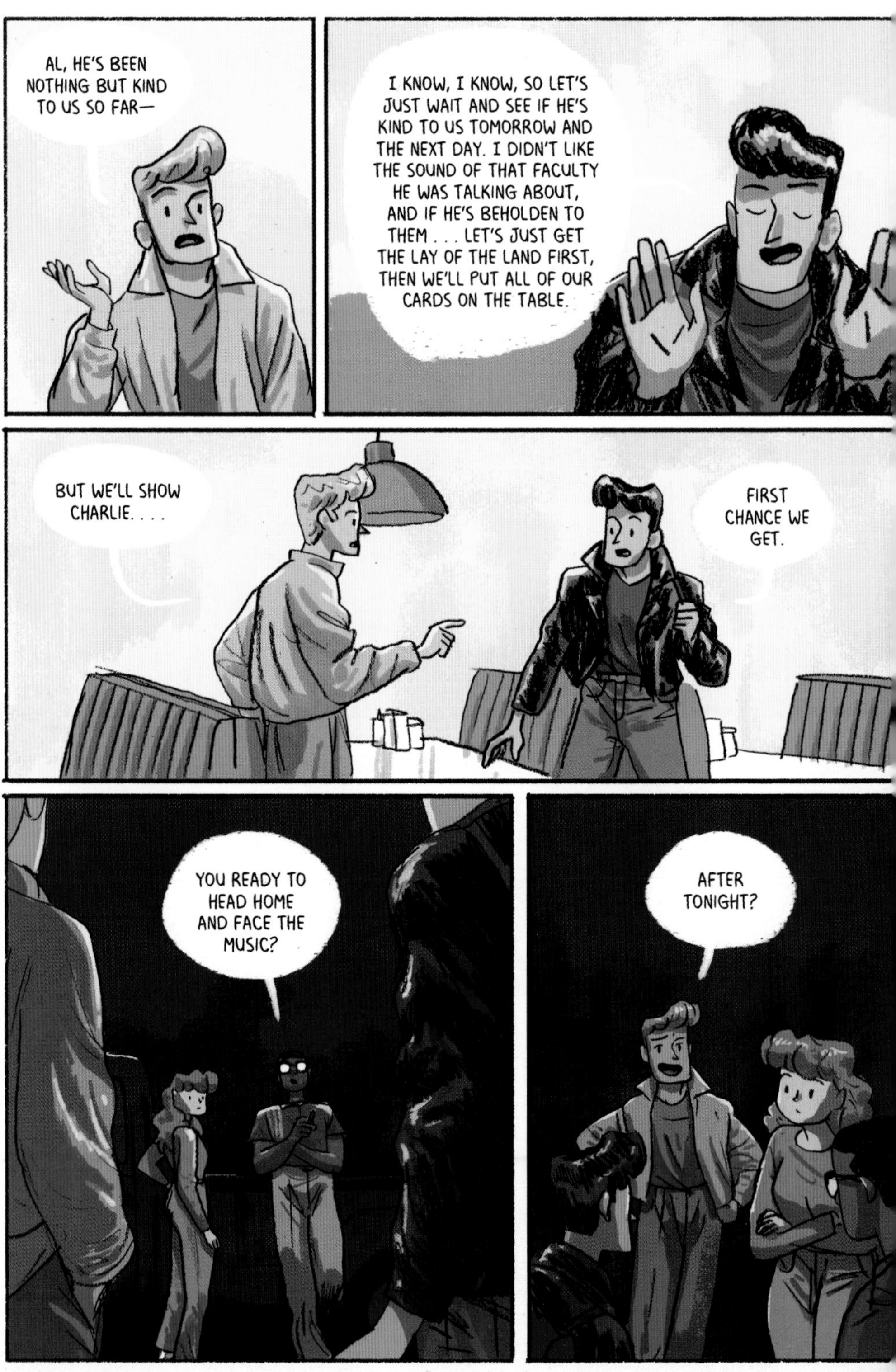
AL, HE'S BEEN NOTHING BUT KIND TO US SO FAR—
I KNOW, I KNOW, SO LET'S JUST WAIT AND SEE IF HE'S KIND TO US TOMORROW AND THE NEXT DAY. I DIDN'T LIKE THE SOUND OF THAT FACULTY HE WAS TALKING ABOUT, AND IF HE'S BEHOLDEN TO THEM . . . LET'S JUST GET THE LAY OF THE LAND FIRST, THEN WE'LL PUT ALL OF OUR CARDS ON THE TABLE.
BUT WE'LL SHOW CHARLIE. . . .
FIRST CHANCE WE GET.
YOU READY TO HEAD HOME AND FACE THE MUSIC?
AFTER TONIGHT?

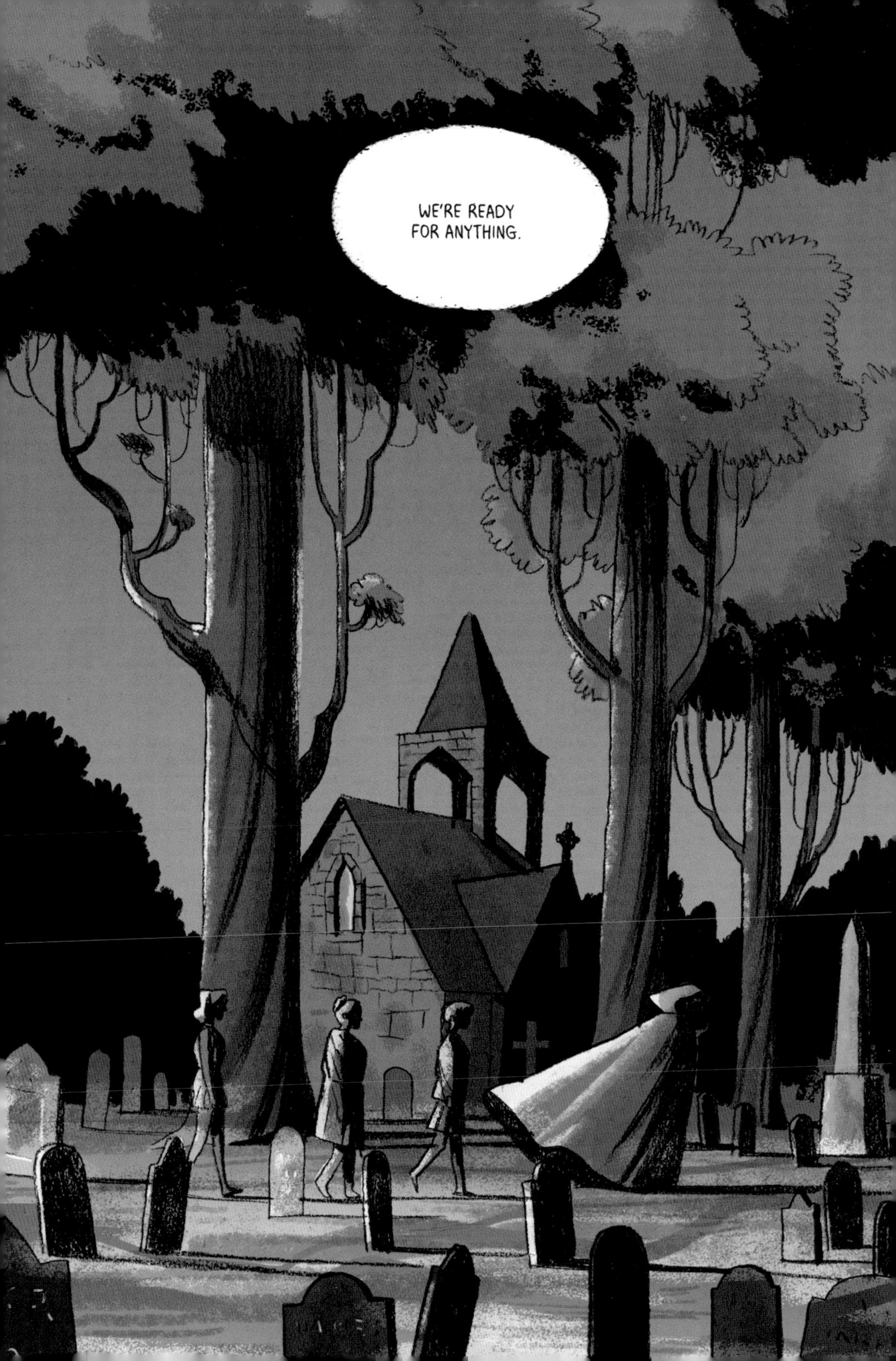
WE'RE READY FOR ANYTHING.

CHAPTER 3

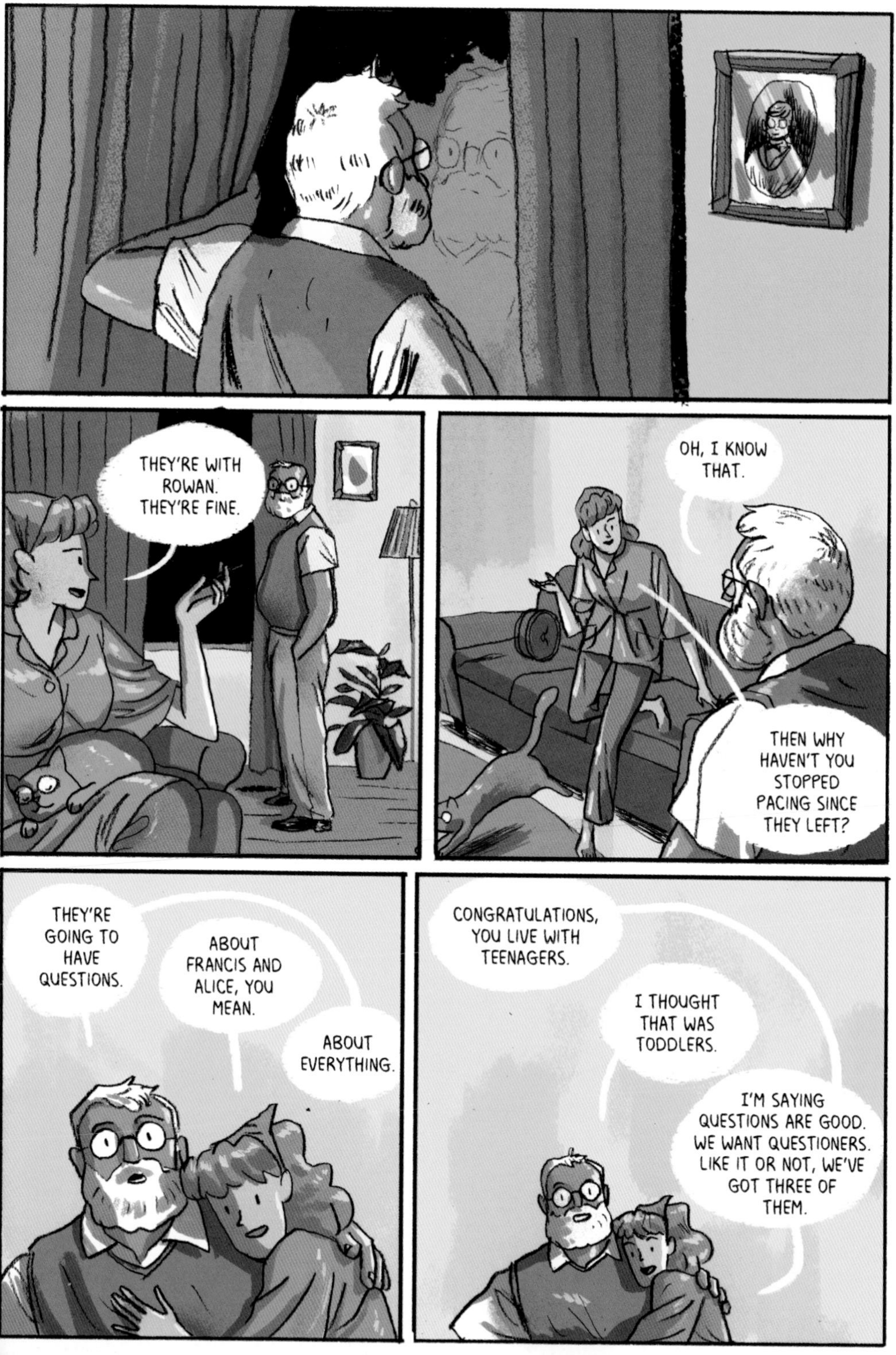
THEY'RE WITH ROWAN. THEY'RE FINE.
OH, I KNOW THAT.
THEN WHY HAVEN'T YOU STOPPED PACING SINCE THEY LEFT?
THEY'RE GOING TO HAVE QUESTIONS.
ABOUT FRANCIS AND ALICE, YOU MEAN.
ABOUT EVERYTHING.
CONGRATULATIONS, YOU LIVE WITH TEENAGERS.
I THOUGHT THAT WAS TODDLERS.
I'M SAYING QUESTIONS ARE GOOD. WE WANT QUESTIONERS. LIKE IT OR NOT, WE'VE GOT THREE OF THEM.

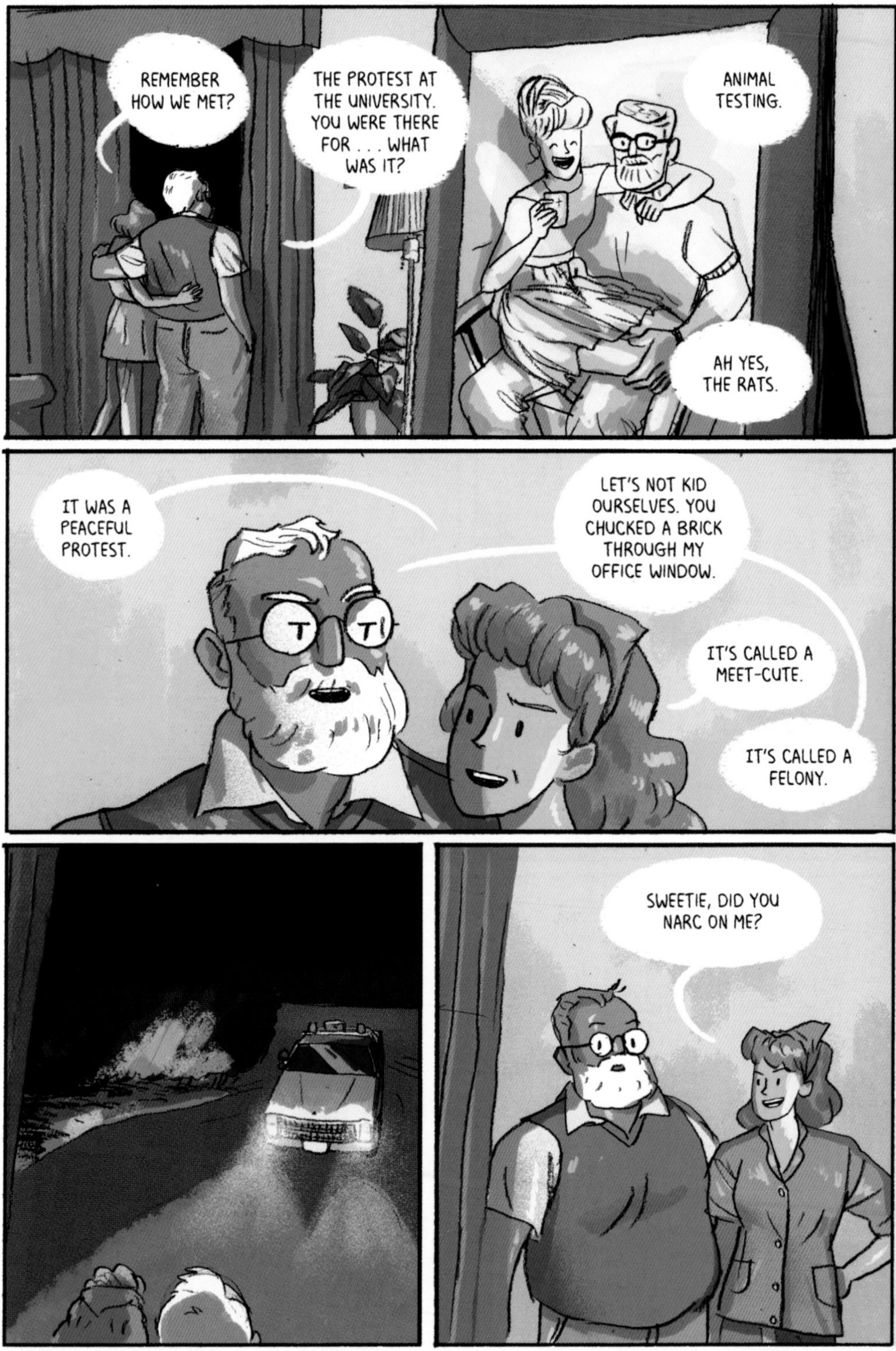
REMEMBER HOW WE MET?
THE PROTEST AT THE UNIVERSITY. YOU WERE THERE FOR . . . WHAT WAS IT?
ANIMAL TESTING.
AH YES, THE RATS.
IT WAS A PEACEFUL PROTEST.
LET'S NOT KID OURSELVES. YOU CHUCKED A BRICK THROUGH MY OFFICE WINDOW.
IT'S CALLED A MEET-CUTE.
IT'S CALLED A FELONY.
SWEETIE, DID YOU NARC ON ME?

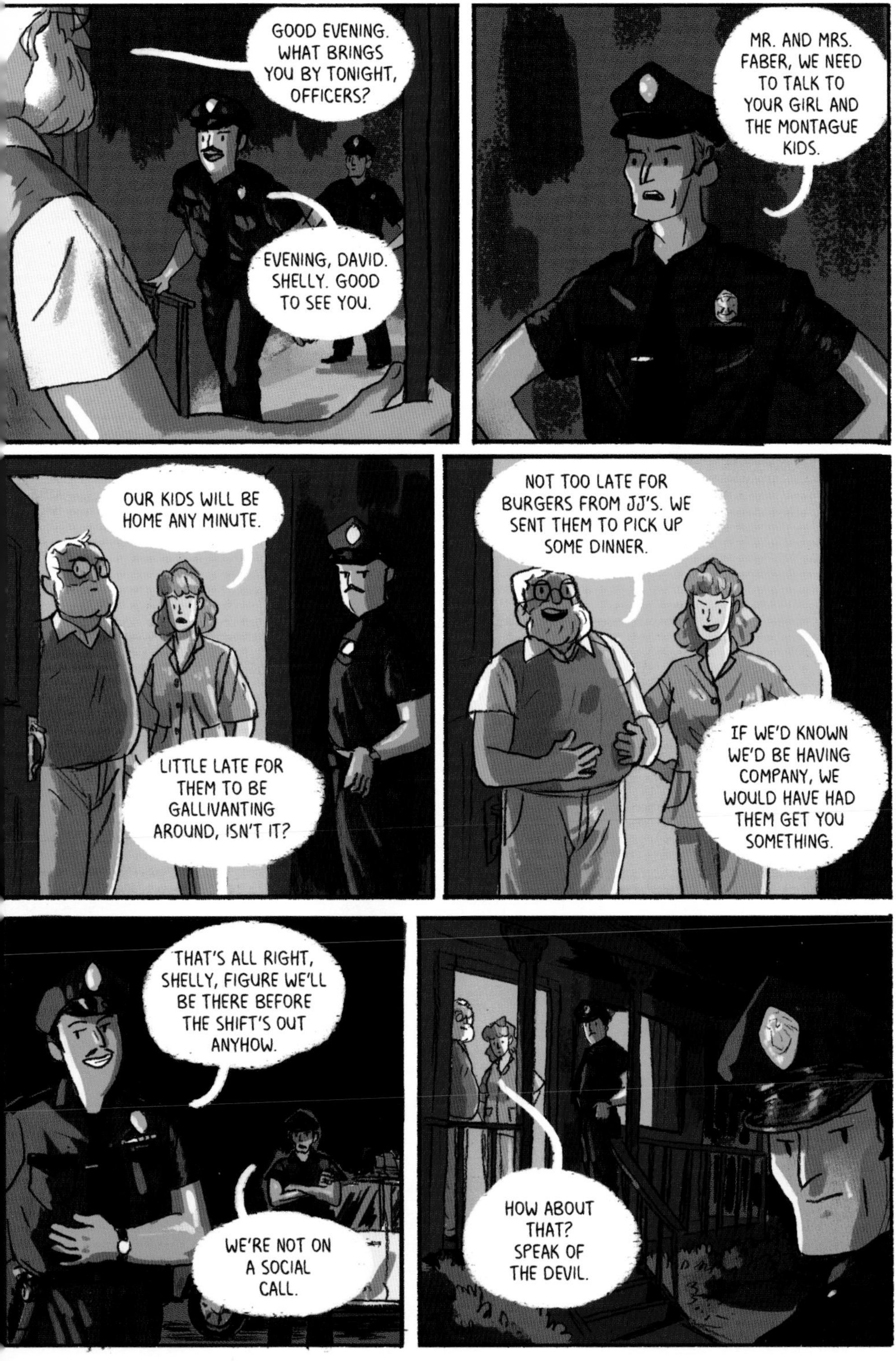
GOOD EVENING. WHAT BRINGS YOU BY TONIGHT, OFFICERS?
EVENING, DAVID. SHELLY. GOOD TO SEE YOU.
MR. AND MRS. FABER, WE NEED TO TALK TO YOUR GIRL AND THE MONTAGUE KIDS.
OUR KIDS WILL BE HOME ANY MINUTE.
LITTLE LATE FOR THEM TO BE GALLIVANTING AROUND, ISN'T IT?
NOT TOO LATE FOR BURGERS FROM JJ'S. WE SENT THEM TO PICK UP SOME DINNER.
IF WE'D KNOWN WE'D BE HAVING COMPANY, WE WOULD HAVE HAD THEM GET YOU SOMETHING.
THAT'S ALL RIGHT, SHELLY, FIGURE WE'LL BE THERE BEFORE THE SHIFT'S OUT ANYHOW.
WE'RE NOT ON A SOCIAL CALL.
HOW ABOUT THAT? SPEAK OF THE DEVIL.

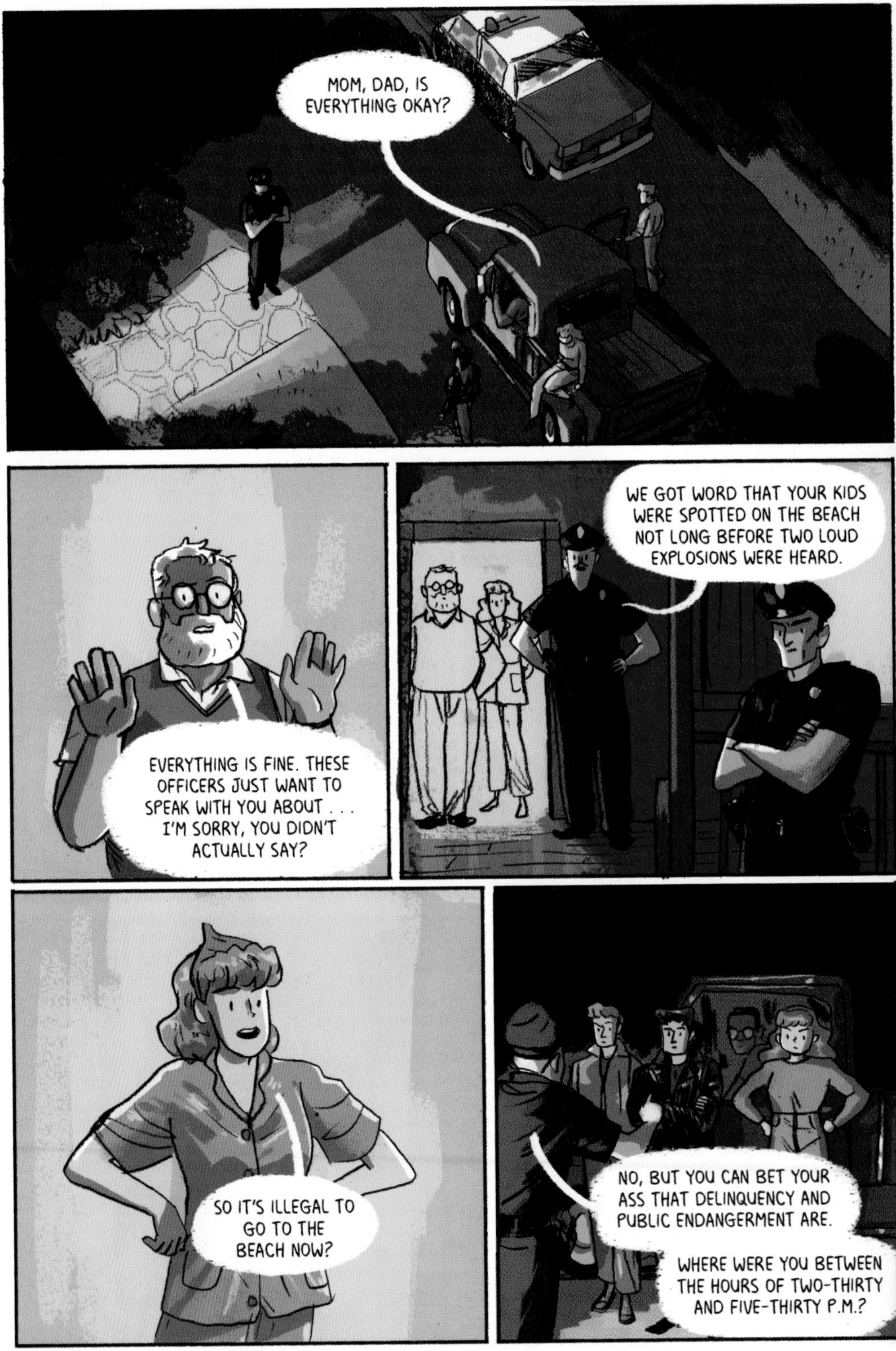
MOM, DAD, IS EVERYTHING OKAY?
EVERYTHING IS FINE. THESE OFFICERS JUST WANT TO SPEAK WITH YOU ABOUT . . . I'M SORRY, YOU DIDN'T ACTUALLY SAY?
WE GOT WORD THAT YOUR KIDS WERE SPOTTED ON THE BEACH NOT LONG BEFORE TWO LOUD EXPLOSIONS WERE HEARD.
SO IT'S ILLEGAL TO GO TO THE BEACH NOW?
NO, BUT YOU CAN BET YOUR ASS THAT DELINQUENCY AND PUBLIC ENDANGERMENT ARE.
WHERE WERE YOU BETWEEN THE HOURS OF TWO-THIRTY AND FIVE-THIRTY P.M.?

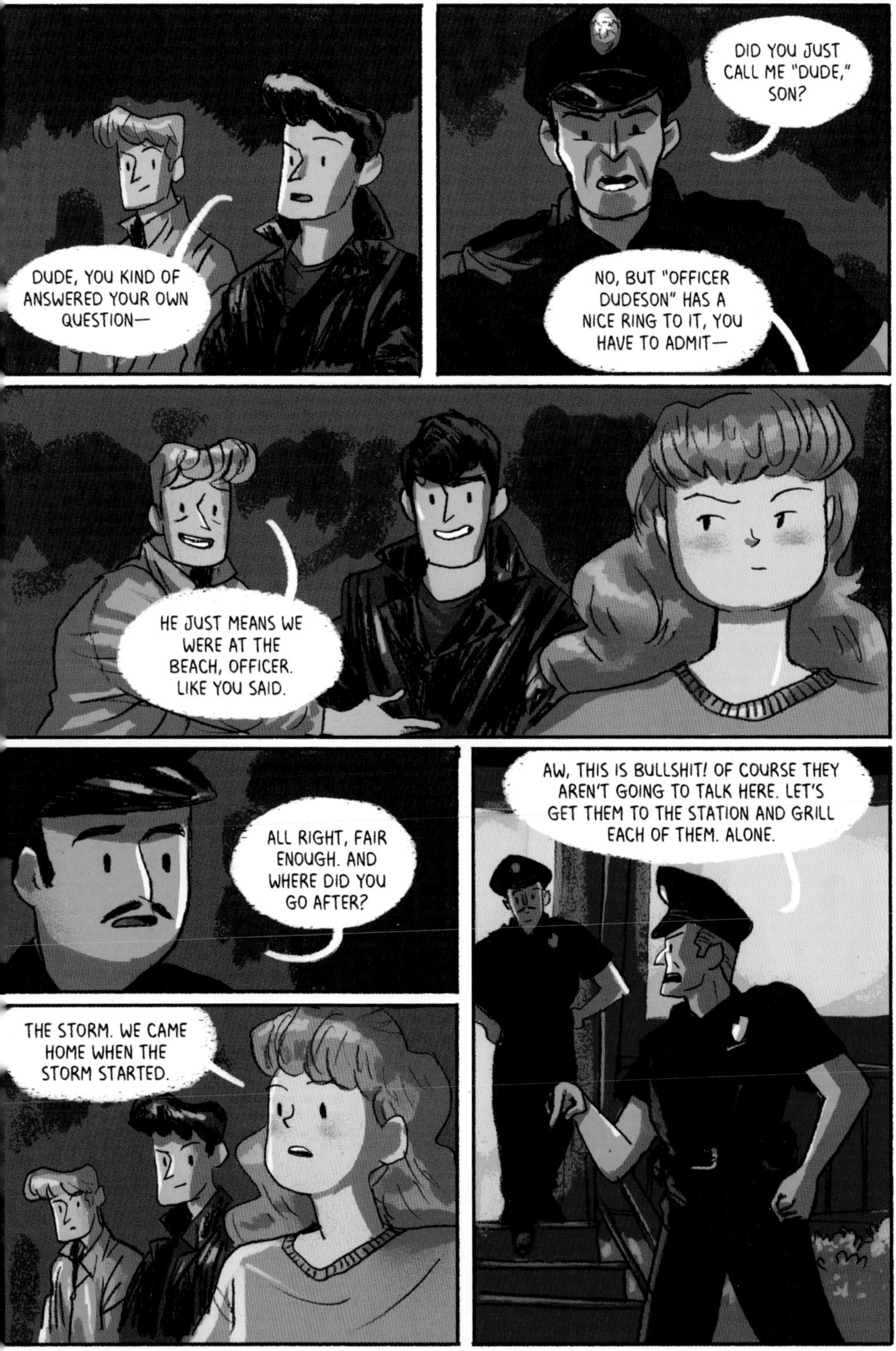
DUDE, YOU KIND OF ANSWERED YOUR OWN QUESTION—
DID YOU JUST CALL ME "DUDE," SON?
NO, BUT "OFFICER DUDESON" HAS A NICE RING TO IT, YOU HAVE TO ADMIT—
HE JUST MEANS WE WERE AT THE BEACH, OFFICER. LIKE YOU SAID.
ALL RIGHT, FAIR ENOUGH. AND WHERE DID YOU GO AFTER?
THE STORM. WE CAME HOME WHEN THE STORM STARTED.
AW, THIS IS BULLSHIT! OF COURSE THEY AREN'T GOING TO TALK HERE. LET'S GET THEM TO THE STATION AND GRILL EACH OF THEM. ALONE.

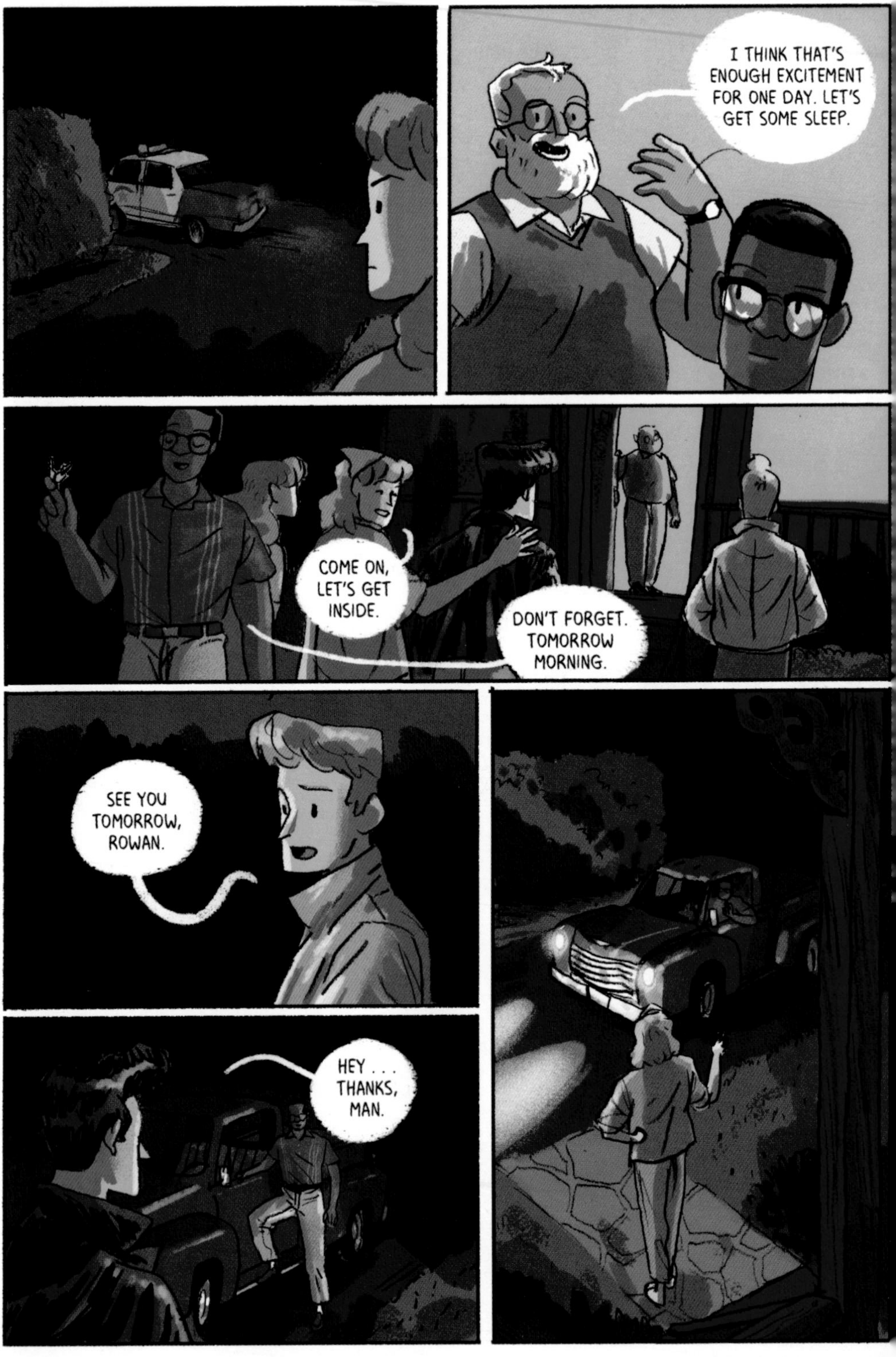
I THINK THAT'S ENOUGH EXCITEMENT FOR ONE DAY. LET'S GET SOME SLEEP.
COME ON, LET'S GET INSIDE.
DON'T FORGET. TOMORROW MORNING.
SEE YOU TOMORROW, ROWAN.
HEY . . . THANKS, MAN.

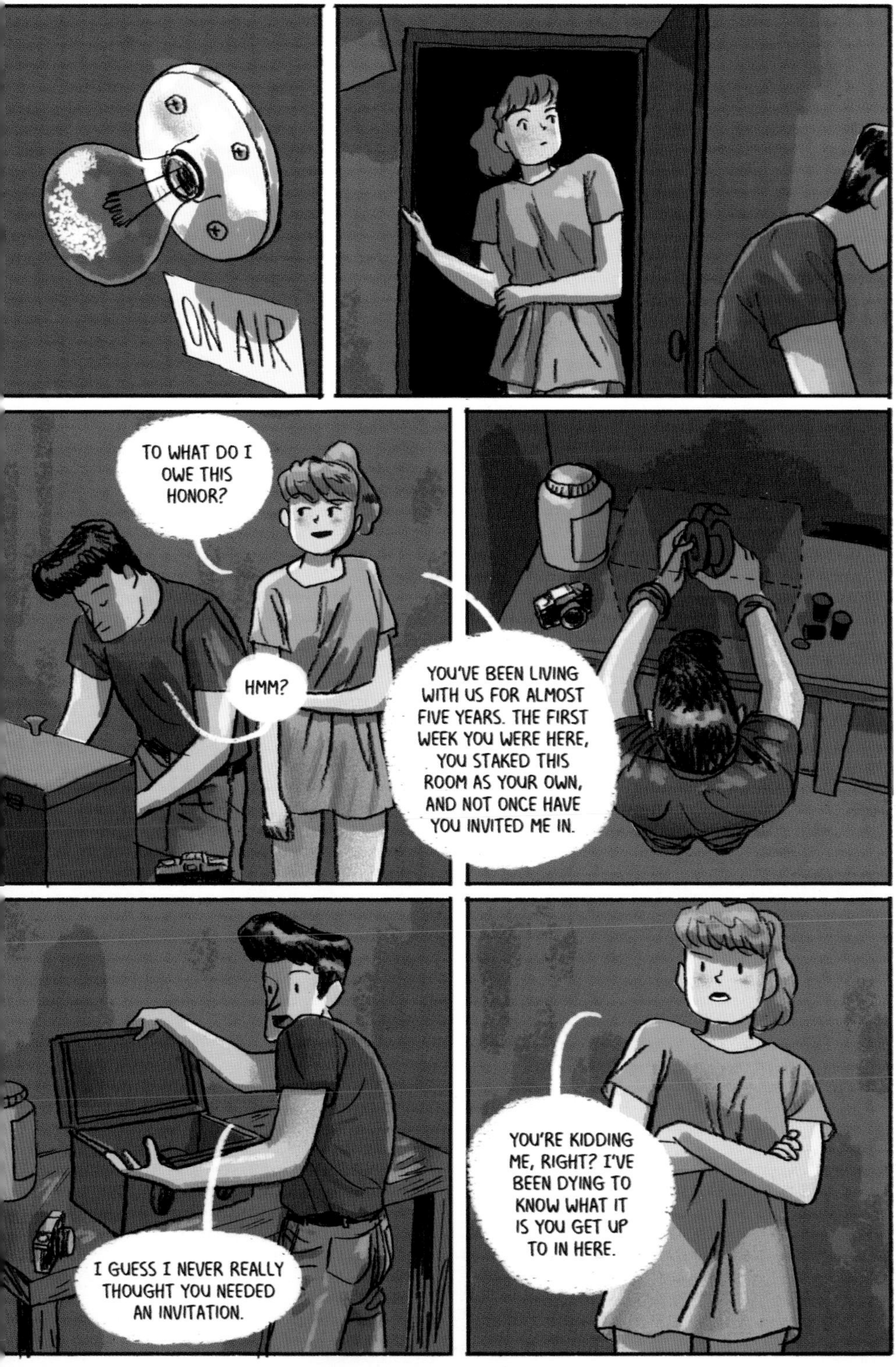
ON AIR
TO WHAT DO I OWE THIS HONOR?
HMM?
YOU'VE BEEN LIVING WITH US FOR ALMOST FIVE YEARS. THE FIRST WEEK YOU WERE HERE, YOU STAKED THIS ROOM AS YOUR OWN, AND NOT ONCE HAVE YOU INVITED ME IN.
I GUESS I NEVER REALLY THOUGHT YOU NEEDED AN INVITATION.
YOU'RE KIDDING ME, RIGHT? I'VE BEEN DYING TO KNOW WHAT IT IS YOU GET UP TO IN HERE.

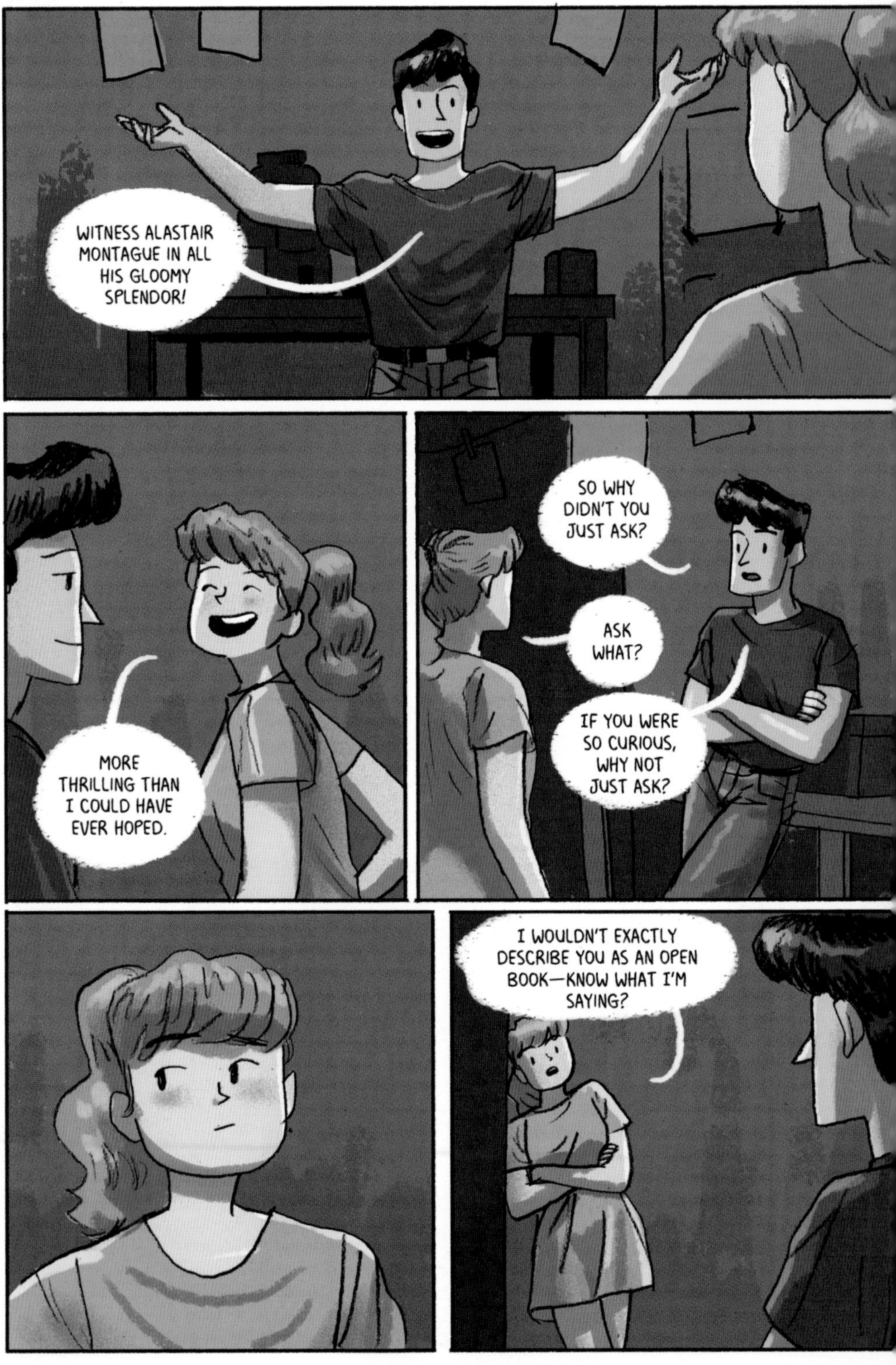
WITNESS ALASTAIR MONTAGUE IN ALL HIS GLOOMY SPLENDOR!
MORE THRILLING THAN I COULD HAVE EVER HOPED.
SO WHY DIDN'T YOU JUST ASK?
ASK WHAT?
IF YOU WERE SO CURIOUS, WHY NOT JUST ASK?
I WOULDN'T EXACTLY DESCRIBE YOU AS AN OPEN BOOK—KNOW WHAT I'M SAYING?

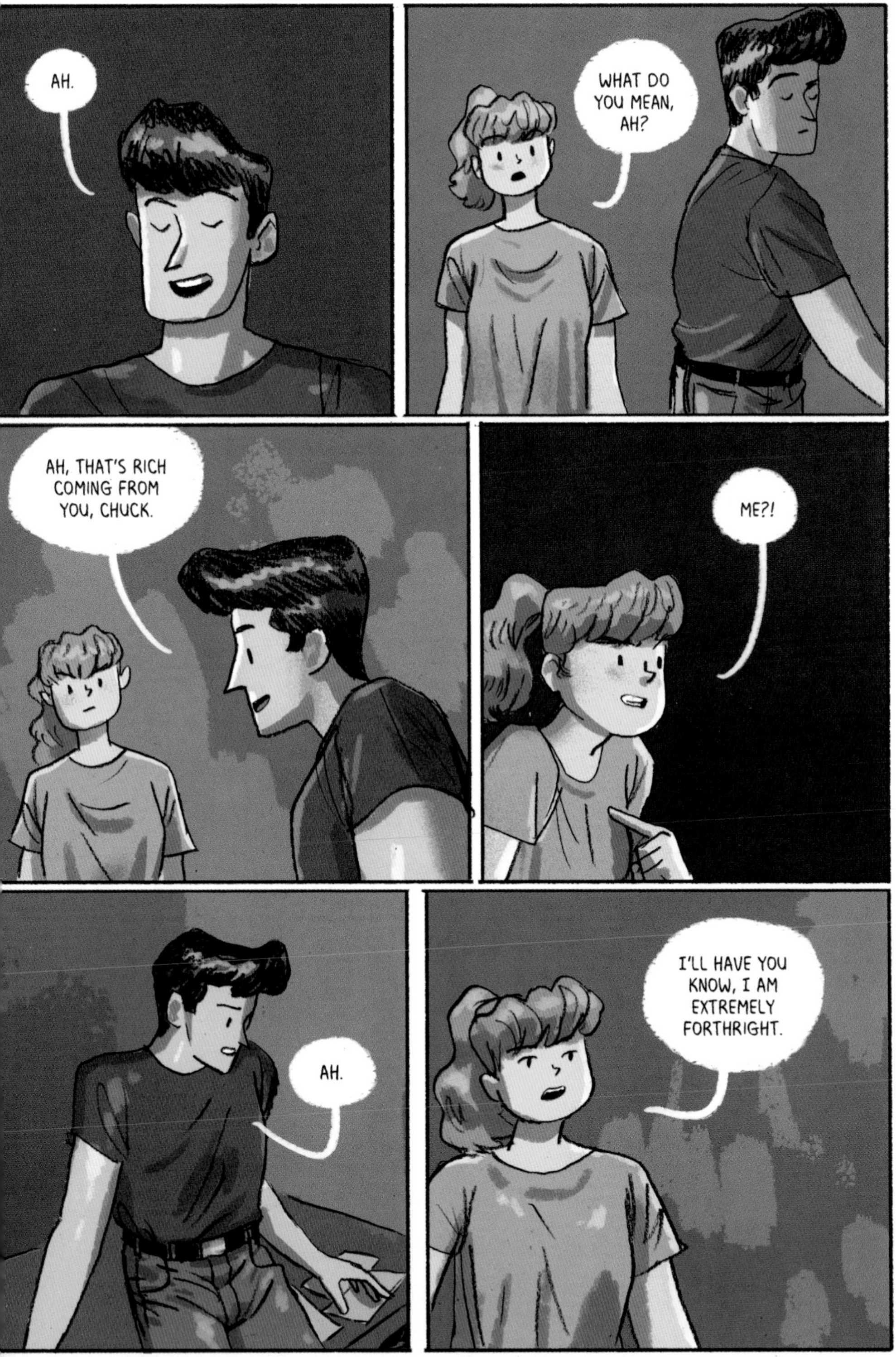
AH.
WHAT DO YOU MEAN, AH?
AH, THAT'S RICH COMING FROM YOU, CHUCK.
ME?!
AH.
I'LL HAVE YOU KNOW, I AM EXTREMELY FORTHRIGHT.

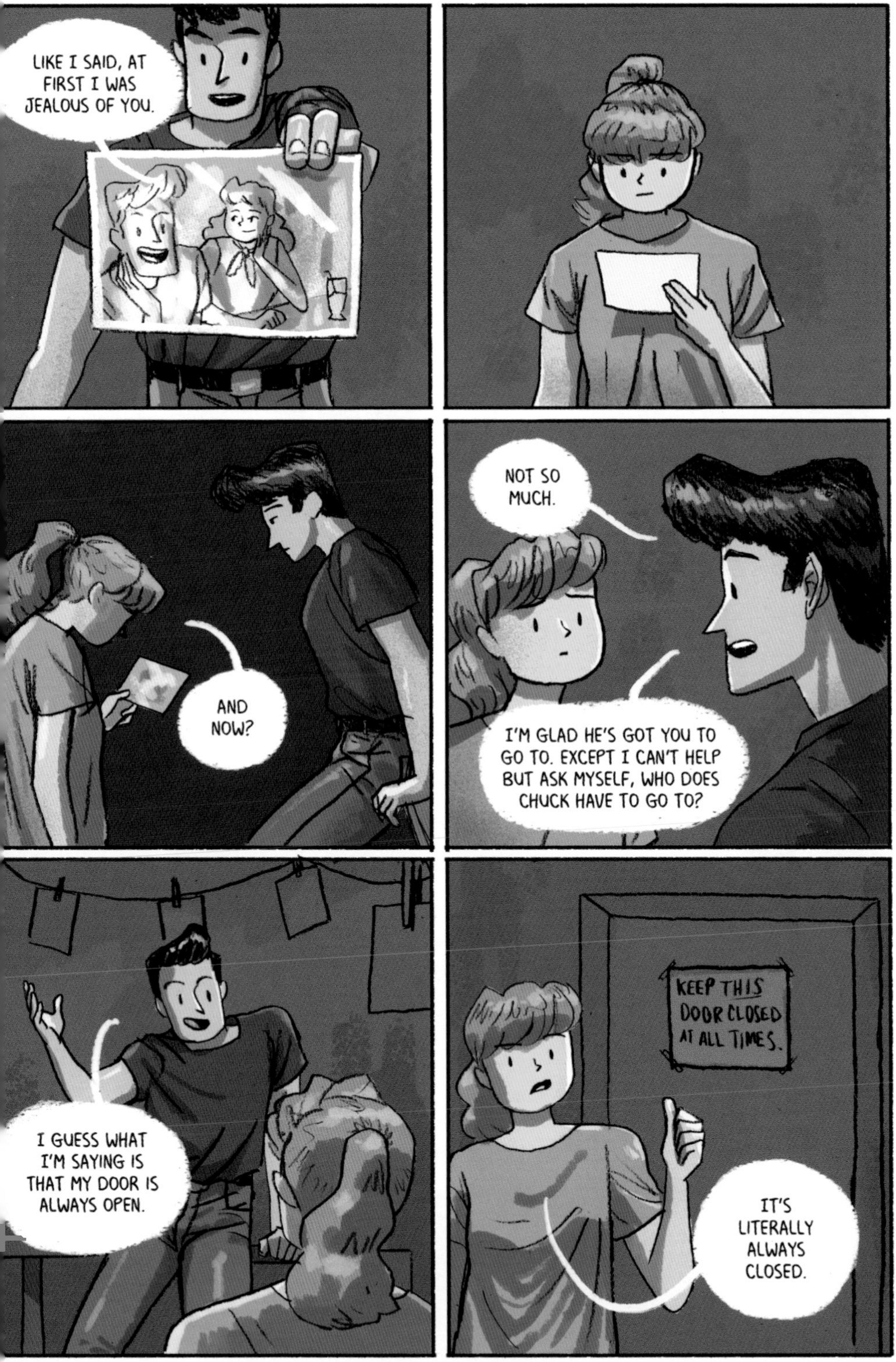
LIKE I SAID, AT FIRST I WAS JEALOUS OF YOU.
AND NOW?
NOT SO MUCH.
I'M GLAD HE'S GOT YOU TO GO TO. EXCEPT I CAN'T HELP BUT ASK MYSELF, WHO DOES CHUCK HAVE TO GO TO?
I GUESS WHAT I'M SAYING IS THAT MY DOOR IS ALWAYS OPEN.
KEEP THIS DOOR CLOSED AT ALL TIMES.
IT'S LITERALLY ALWAYS CLOSED.

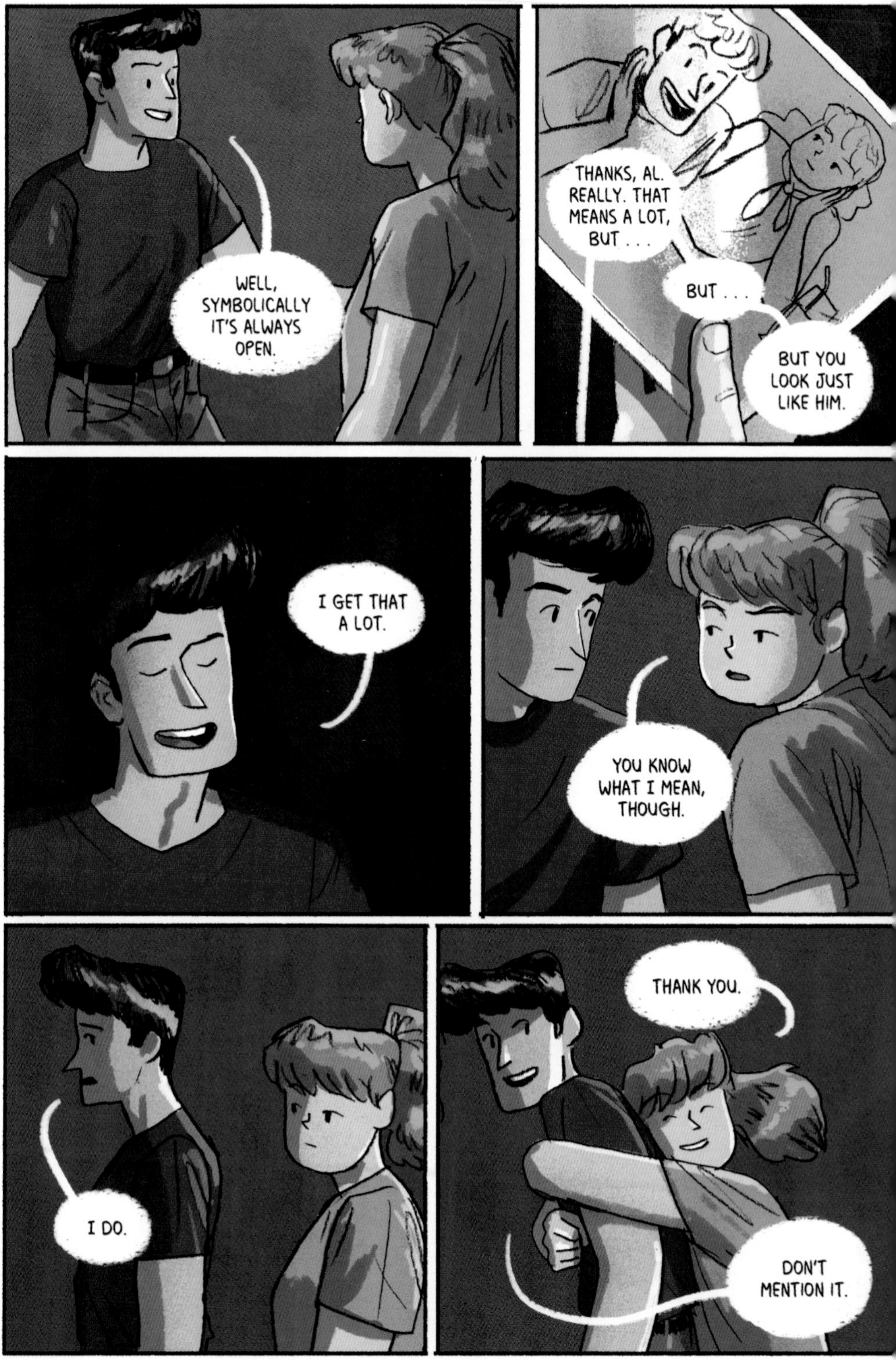
WELL, SYMBOLICALLY IT'S ALWAYS OPEN.
THANKS, AL. REALLY. THAT MEANS A LOT, BUT . . .
BUT . . .
BUT YOU LOOK JUST LIKE HIM.
I GET THAT A LOT.
YOU KNOW WHAT I MEAN, THOUGH.
I DO.
THANK YOU.
DON'T MENTION IT.

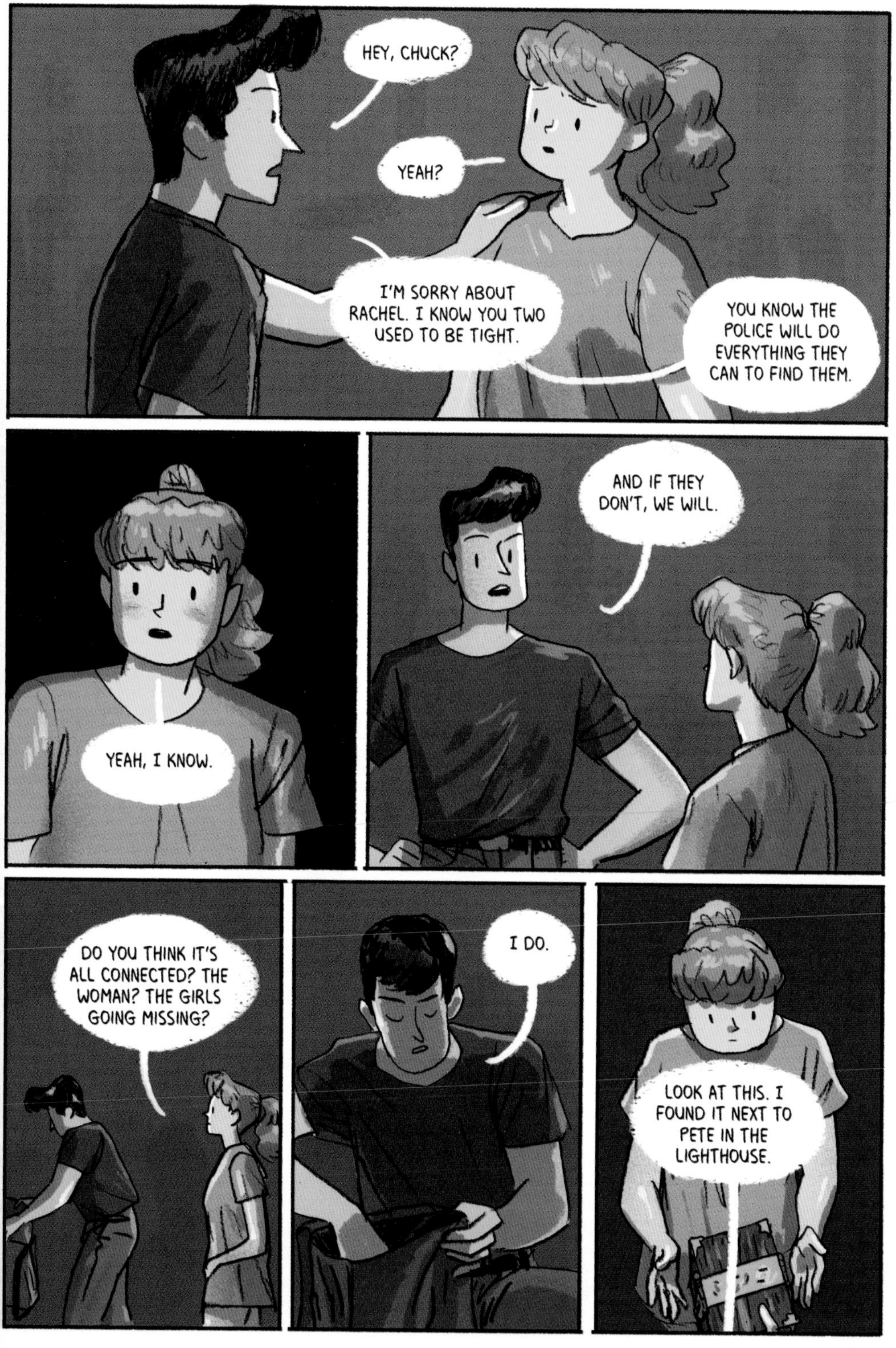
HEY, CHUCK?
YEAH?
I'M SORRY ABOUT RACHEL. I KNOW YOU TWO USED TO BE TIGHT.
YOU KNOW THE POLICE WILL DO EVERYTHING THEY CAN TO FIND THEM.
YEAH, I KNOW.
AND IF THEY DON'T, WE WILL.
DO YOU THINK IT'S ALL CONNECTED? THE WOMAN? THE GIRLS GOING MISSING?
I DO.
LOOK AT THIS. I FOUND IT NEXT TO PETE IN THE LIGHTHOUSE.

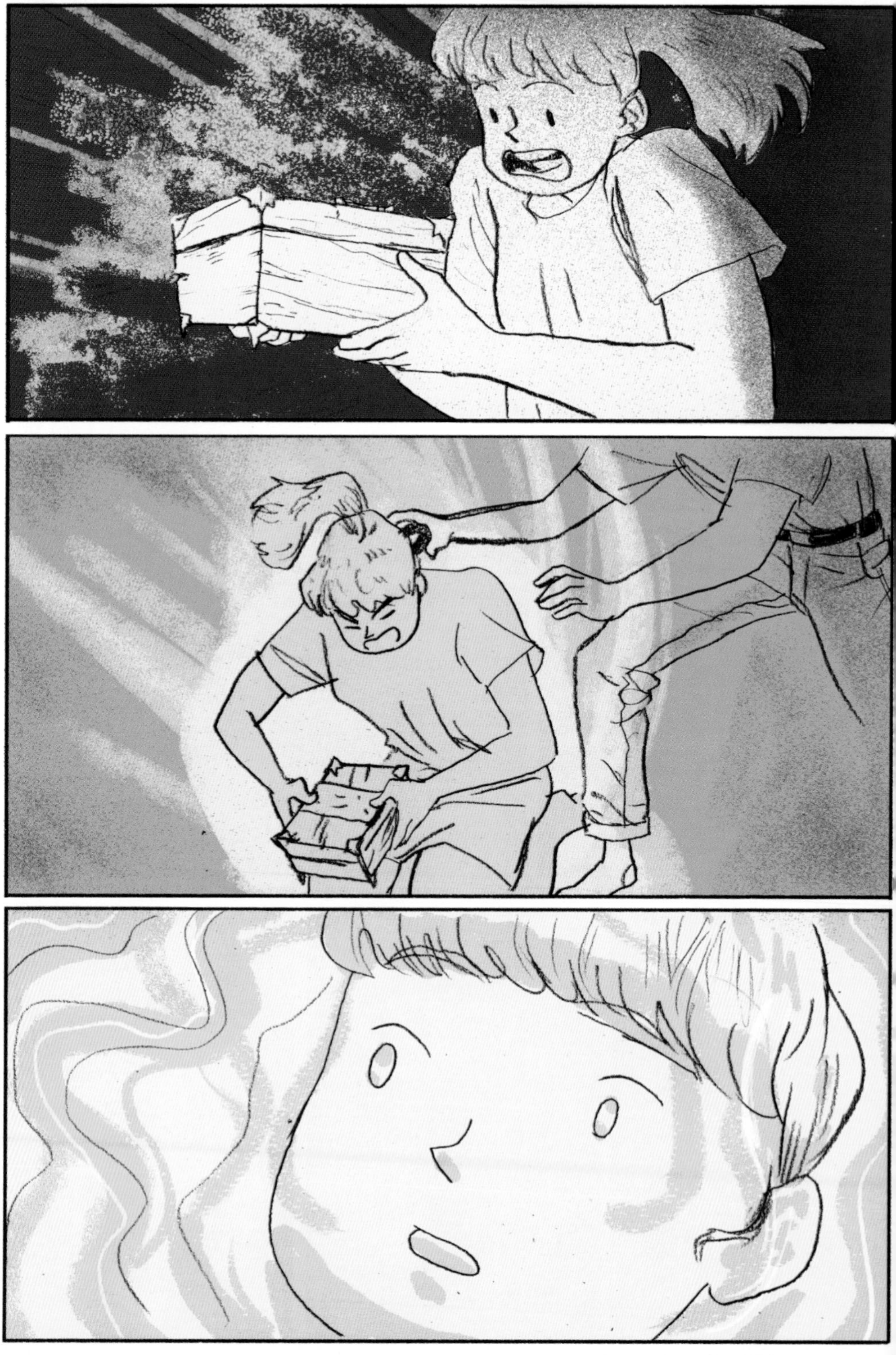

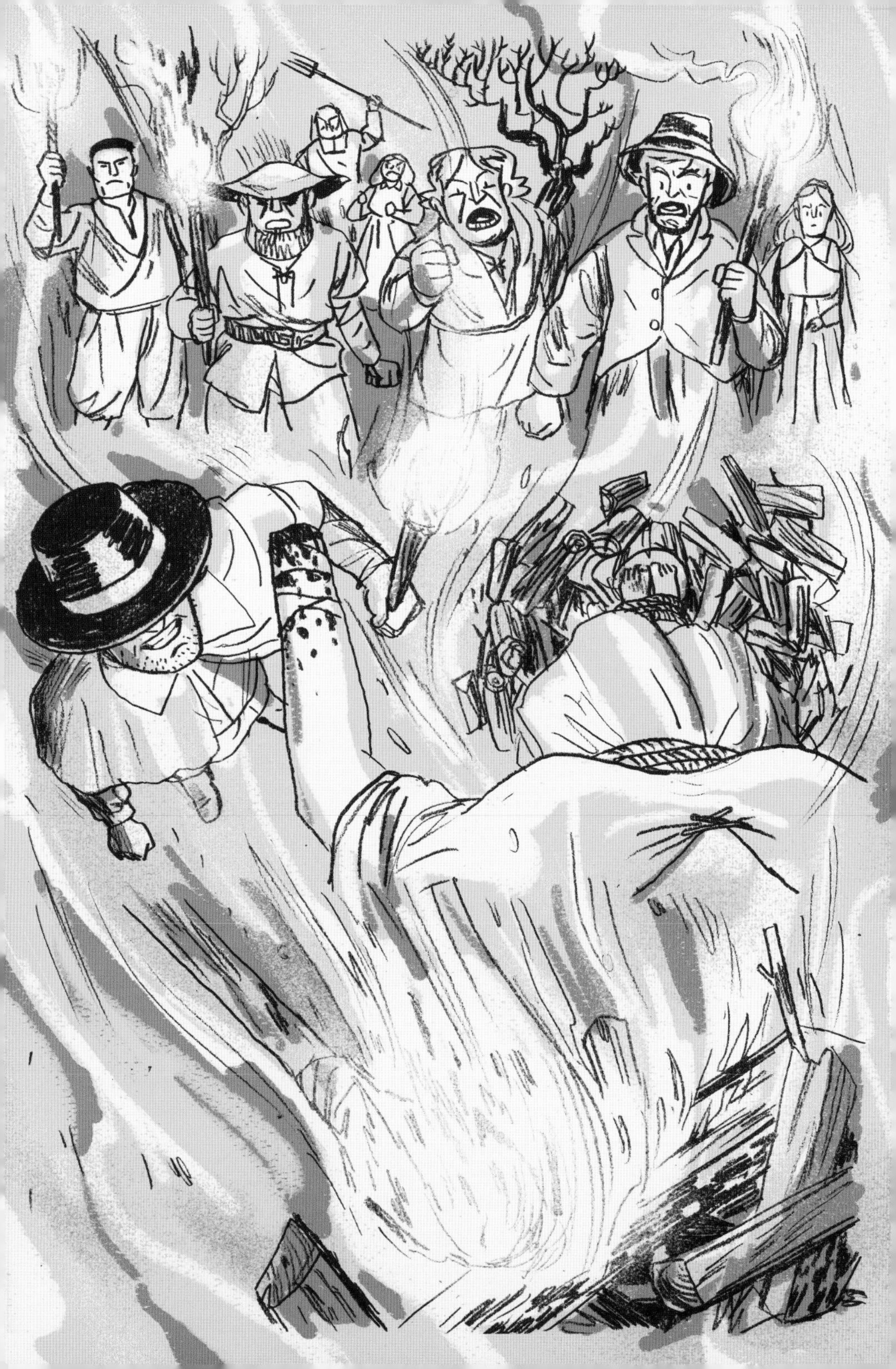

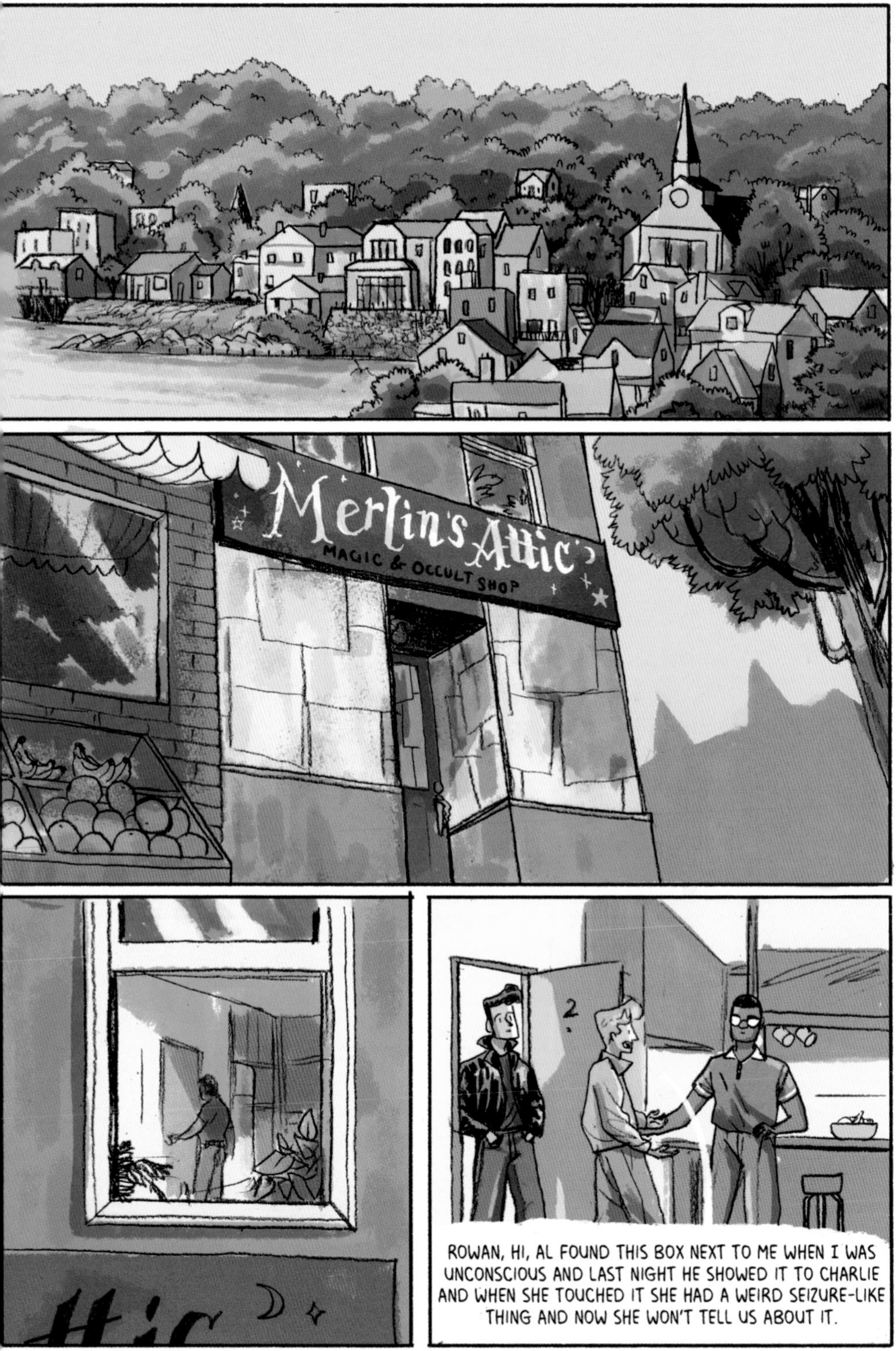
Merlin's Attic
MAGIC & OCCULT SHOP
2
ROWAN, HI, AL FOUND THIS BOX NEXT TO ME WHEN I WAS UNCONSCIOUS AND LAST NIGHT HE SHOWED IT TO CHARLIE AND WHEN SHE TOUCHED IT SHE HAD A WEIRD SEIZURE-LIKE THING AND NOW SHE WON'T TELL US ABOUT IT.

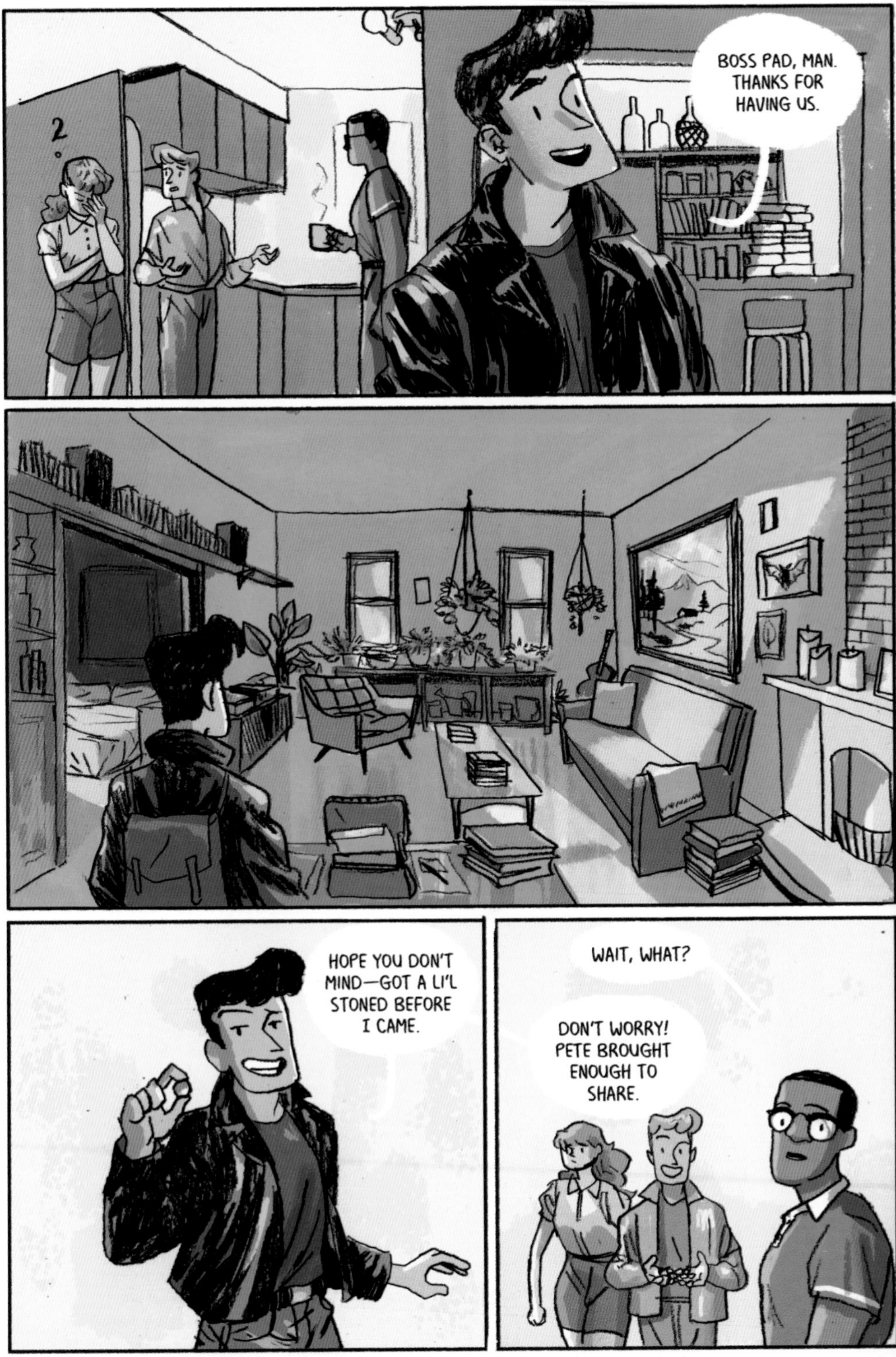
2
BOSS PAD, MAN. THANKS FOR HAVING US.
HOPE YOU DON'T MIND—GOT A LI'L STONED BEFORE I CAME.
WAIT, WHAT?
DON'T WORRY! PETE BROUGHT ENOUGH TO SHARE.

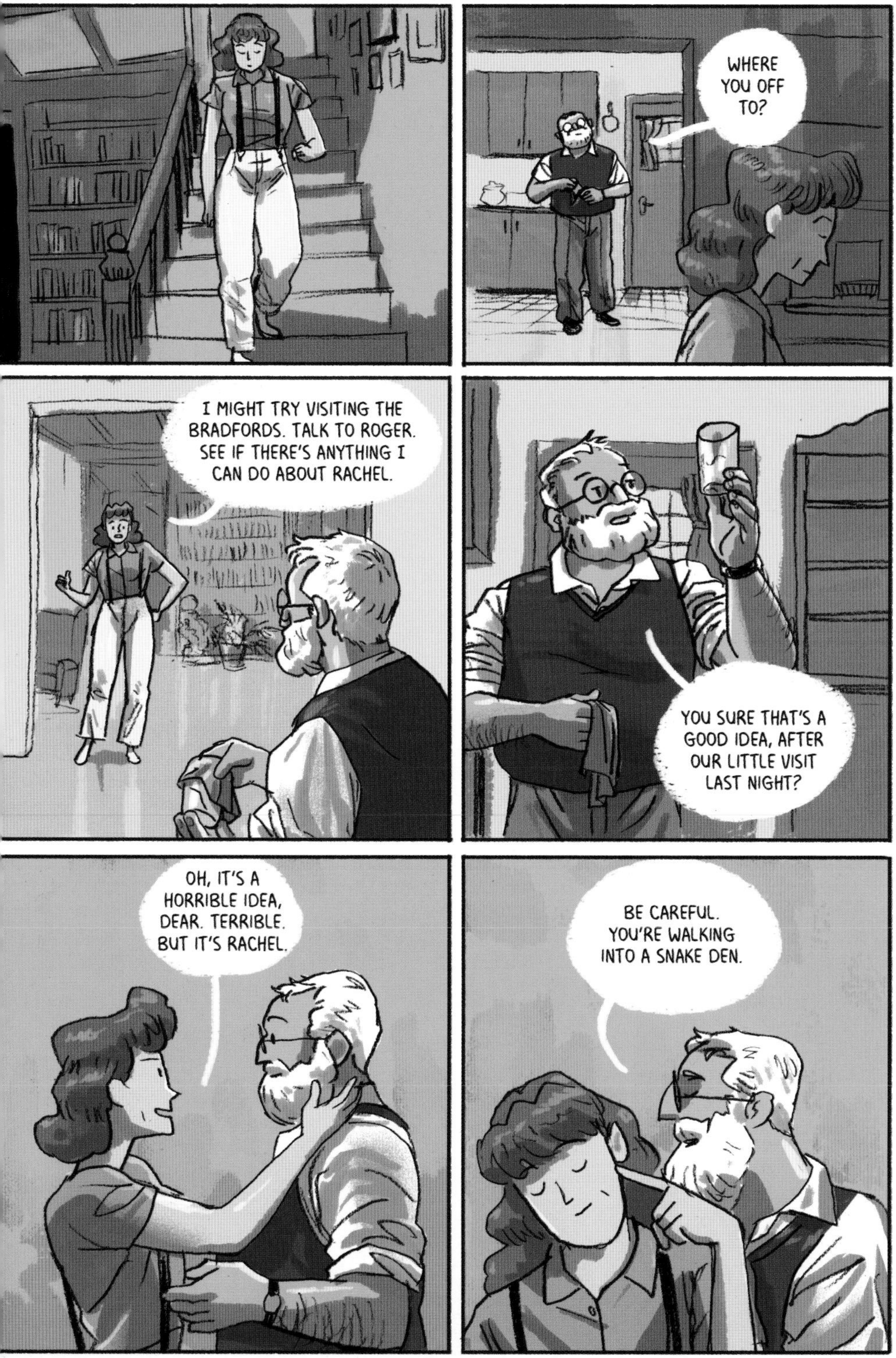
WHERE YOU OFF TO?
I MIGHT TRY VISITING THE BRADFORDS. TALK TO ROGER. SEE IF THERE'S ANYTHING I CAN DO ABOUT RACHEL.
YOU SURE THAT'S A GOOD IDEA, AFTER OUR LITTLE VISIT LAST NIGHT?
OH, IT'S A HORRIBLE IDEA, DEAR. TERRIBLE. BUT IT'S RACHEL.
BE CAREFUL. YOU'RE WALKING INTO A SNAKE DEN.

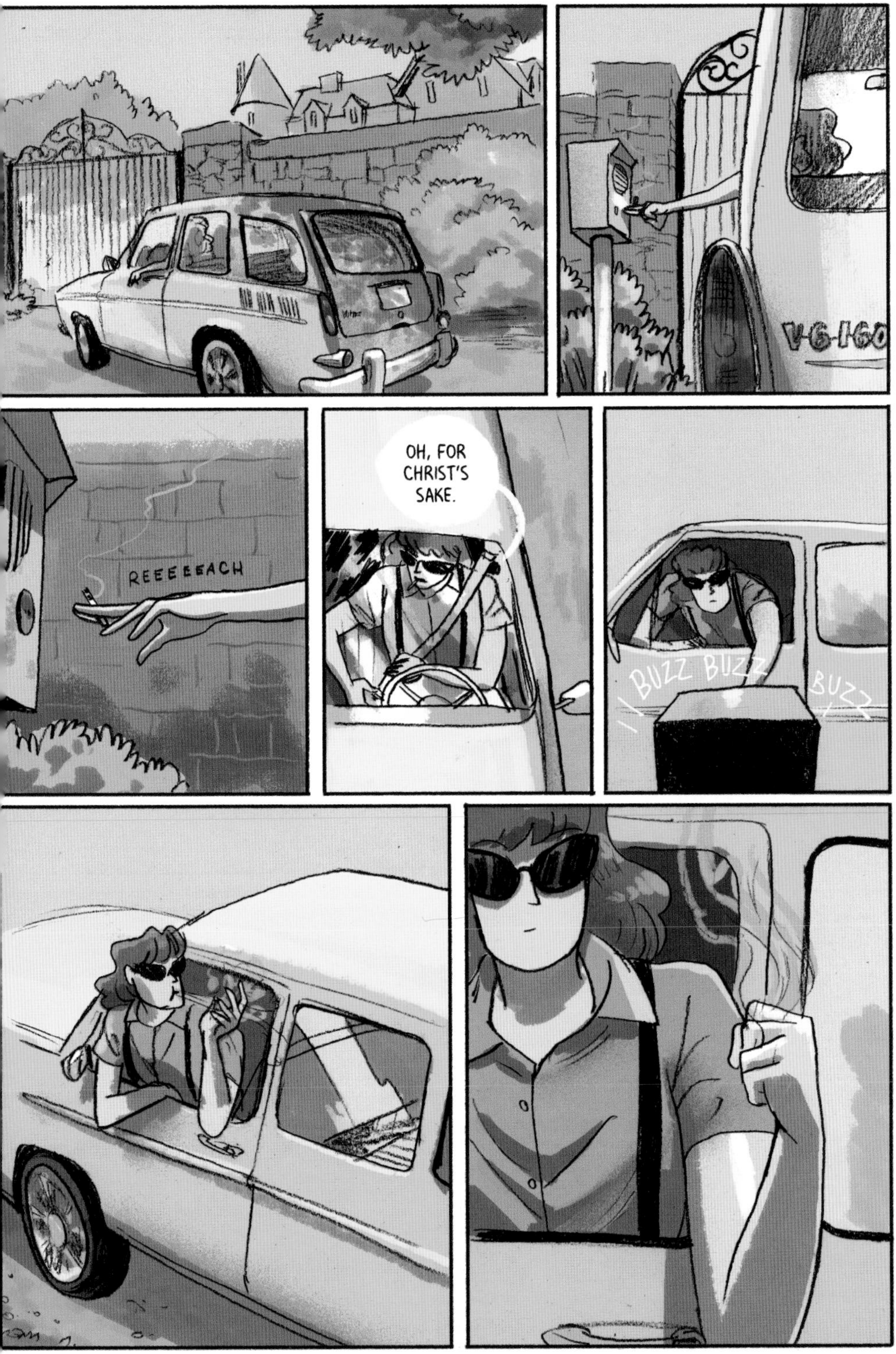
REEEEEEACH
OH, FOR CHRIST'S SAKE.
BUZZ BUZZ
BUZZ

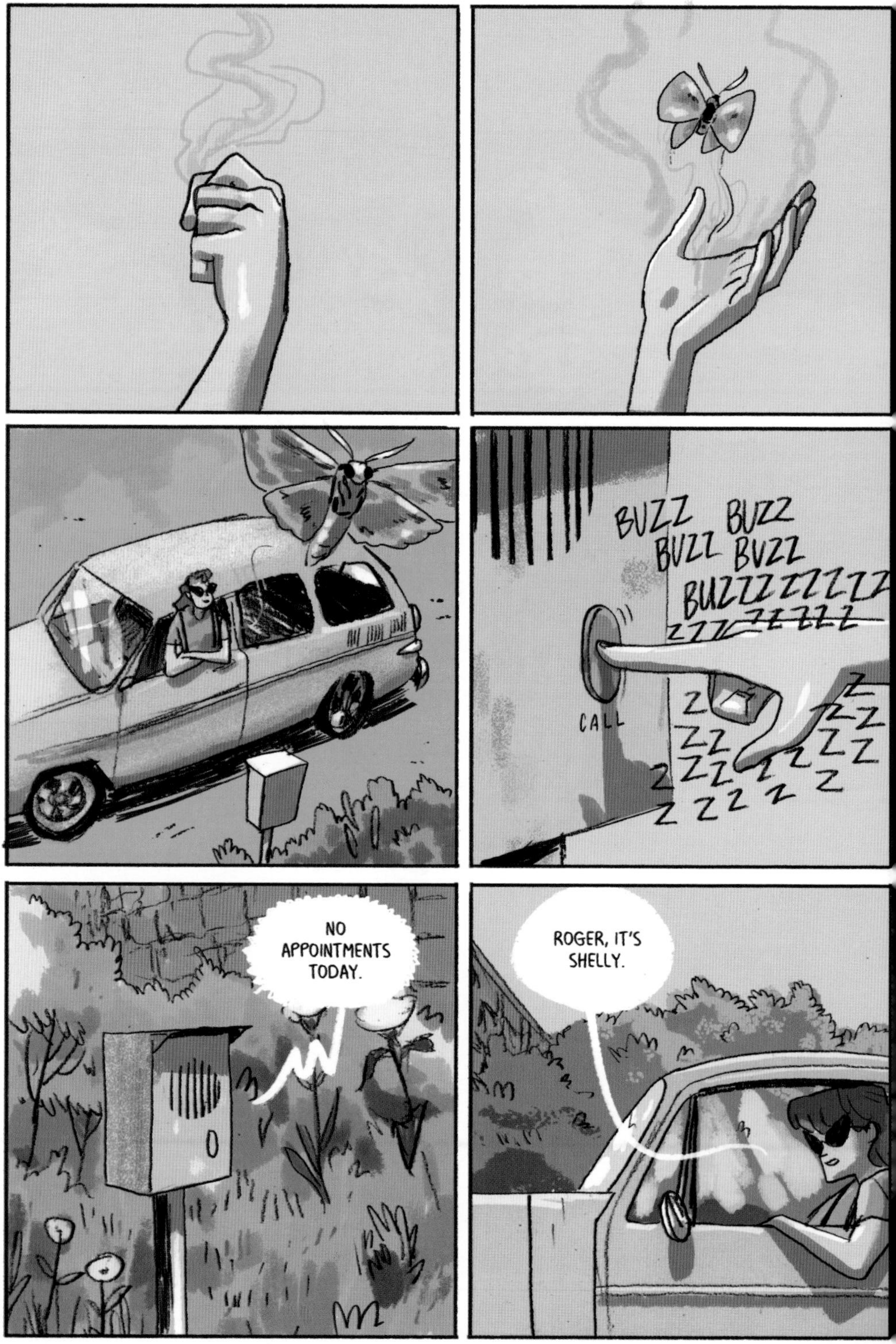
BUZZ BUZZ
BUZZ BUZZ
BUZZZZZZZZ
CALL
NO APPOINTMENTS TODAY.
ROGER, IT'S SHELLY.

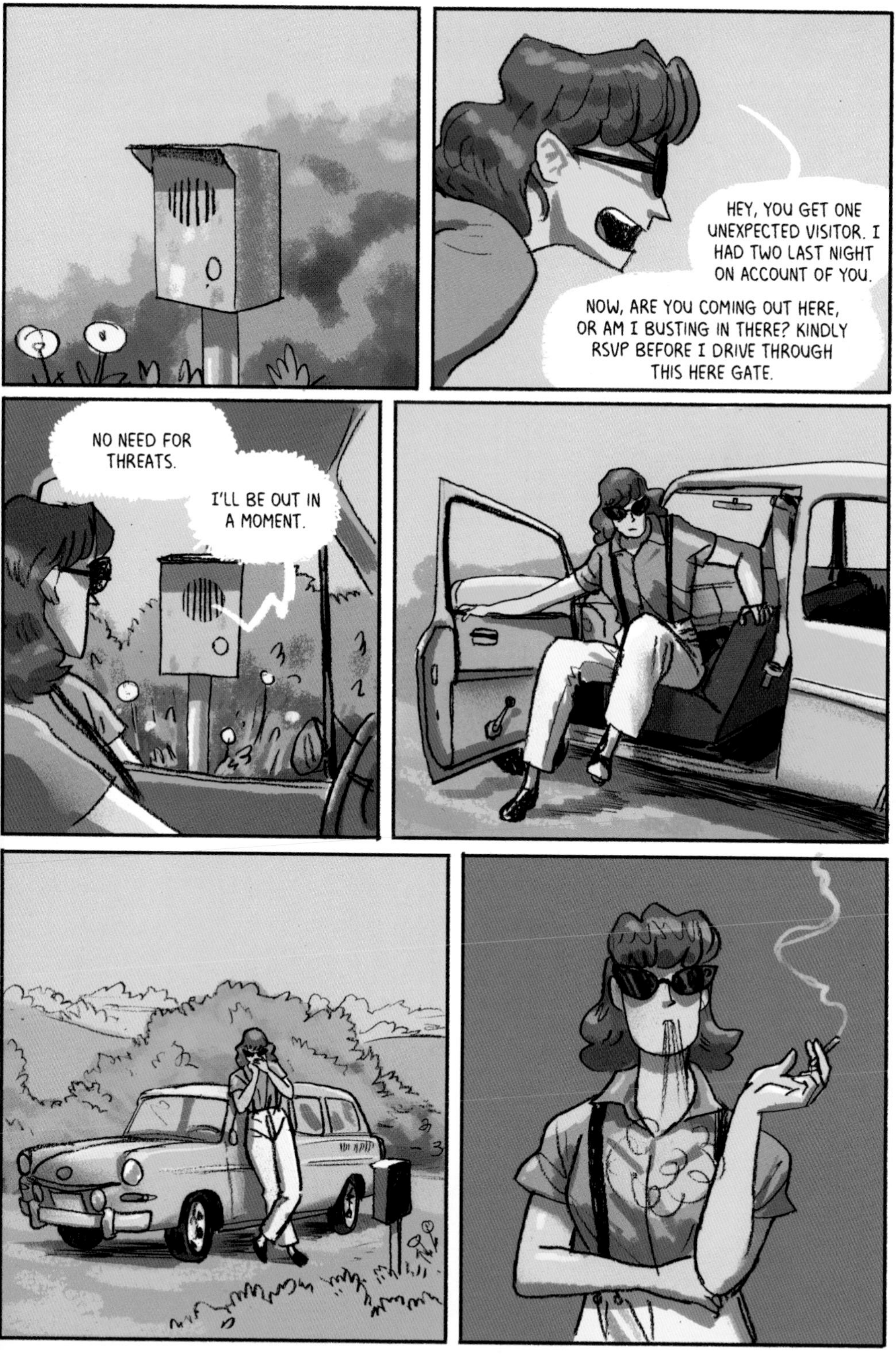
HEY, YOU GET ONE UNEXPECTED VISITOR. I HAD TWO LAST NIGHT ON ACCOUNT OF YOU.
NOW, ARE YOU COMING OUT HERE, OR AM I BUSTING IN THERE? KINDLY RSVP BEFORE I DRIVE THROUGH THIS HERE GATE.
NO NEED FOR THREATS.
I'LL BE OUT IN A MOMENT.

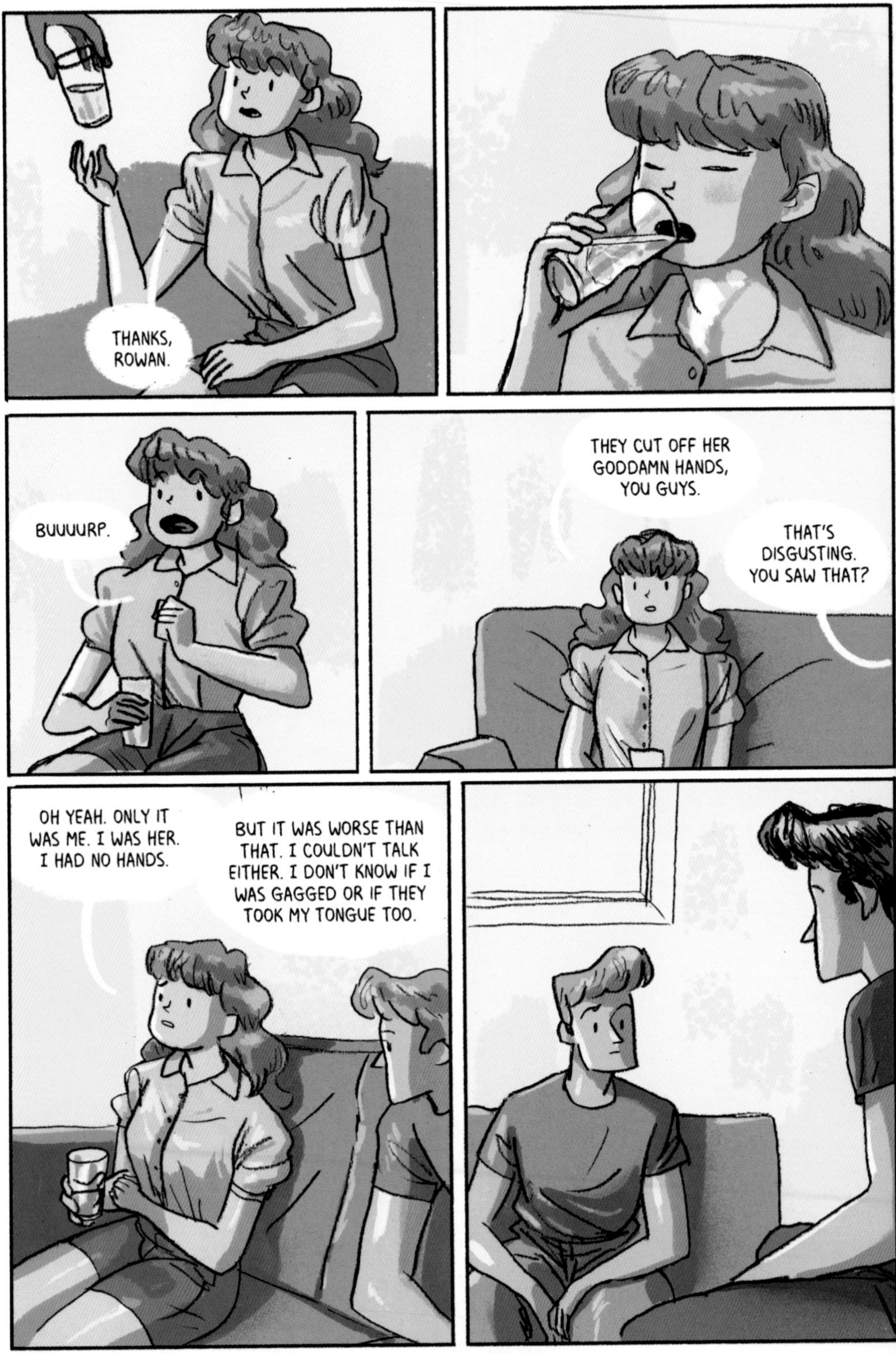

THANKS, ROWAN.
BUUUURP.
THEY CUT OFF HER GODDAMN HANDS, YOU GUYS.
THAT'S DISGUSTING. YOU SAW THAT?
OH YEAH. ONLY IT WAS ME. I WAS HER. I HAD NO HANDS.
BUT IT WAS WORSE THAN THAT. I COULDN'T TALK EITHER. I DON'T KNOW IF I WAS GAGGED OR IF THEY TOOK MY TONGUE TOO.

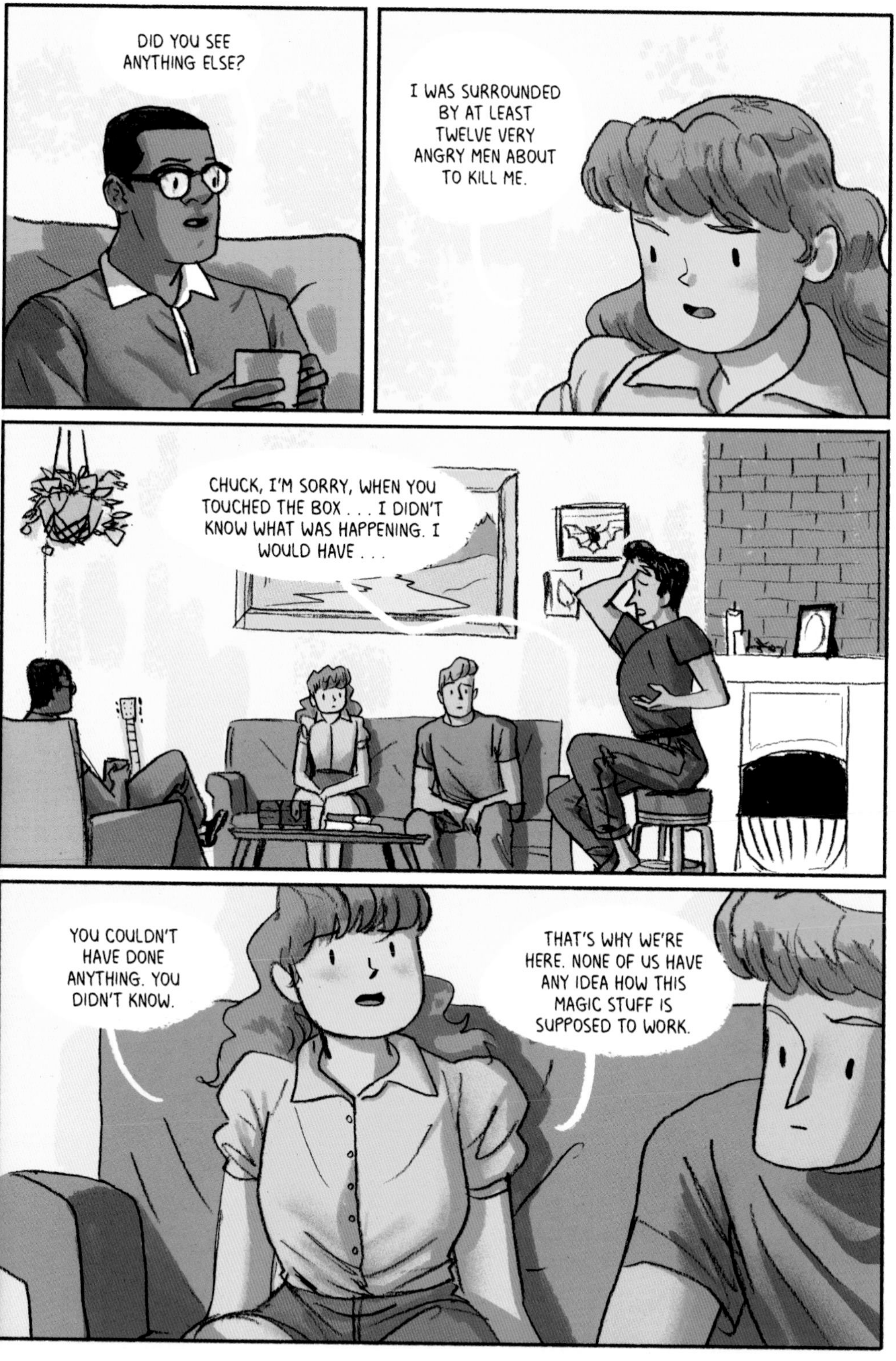
DID YOU SEE ANYTHING ELSE?
I WAS SURROUNDED BY AT LEAST TWELVE VERY ANGRY MEN ABOUT TO KILL ME.
CHUCK, I'M SORRY, WHEN YOU TOUCHED THE BOX . . . I DIDN'T KNOW WHAT WAS HAPPENING. I WOULD HAVE . . .
YOU COULDN'T HAVE DONE ANYTHING. YOU DIDN'T KNOW.
THAT'S WHY WE'RE HERE. NONE OF US HAVE ANY IDEA HOW THIS MAGIC STUFF IS SUPPOSED TO WORK.

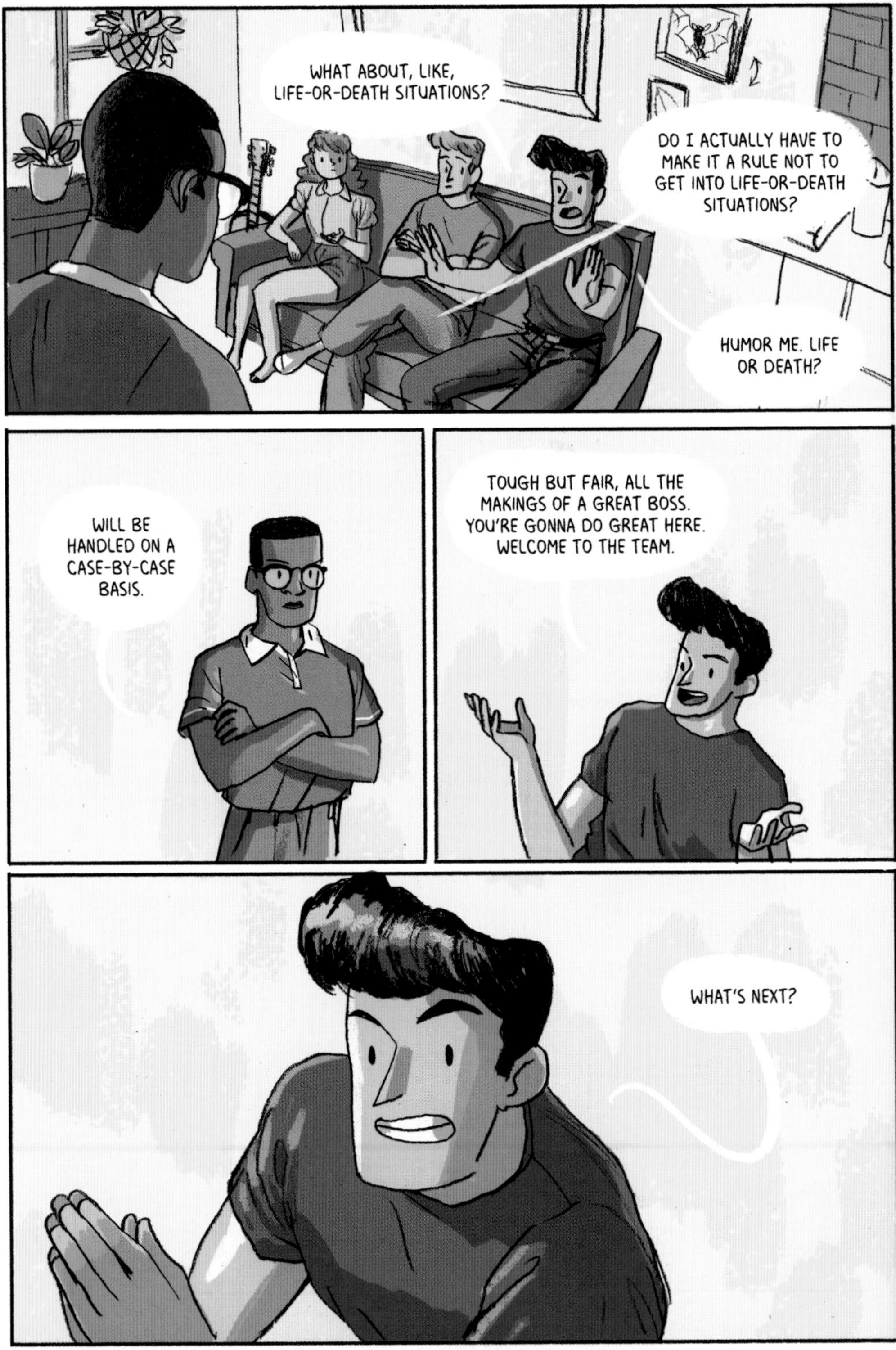
WHAT ABOUT, LIKE, LIFE-OR-DEATH SITUATIONS?
DO I ACTUALLY HAVE TO MAKE IT A RULE NOT TO GET INTO LIFE-OR-DEATH SITUATIONS?
HUMOR ME. LIFE OR DEATH?
WILL BE HANDLED ON A CASE-BY-CASE BASIS.
TOUGH BUT FAIR, ALL THE MAKINGS OF A GREAT BOSS. YOU'RE GONNA DO GREAT HERE. WELCOME TO THE TEAM.
WHAT'S NEXT?

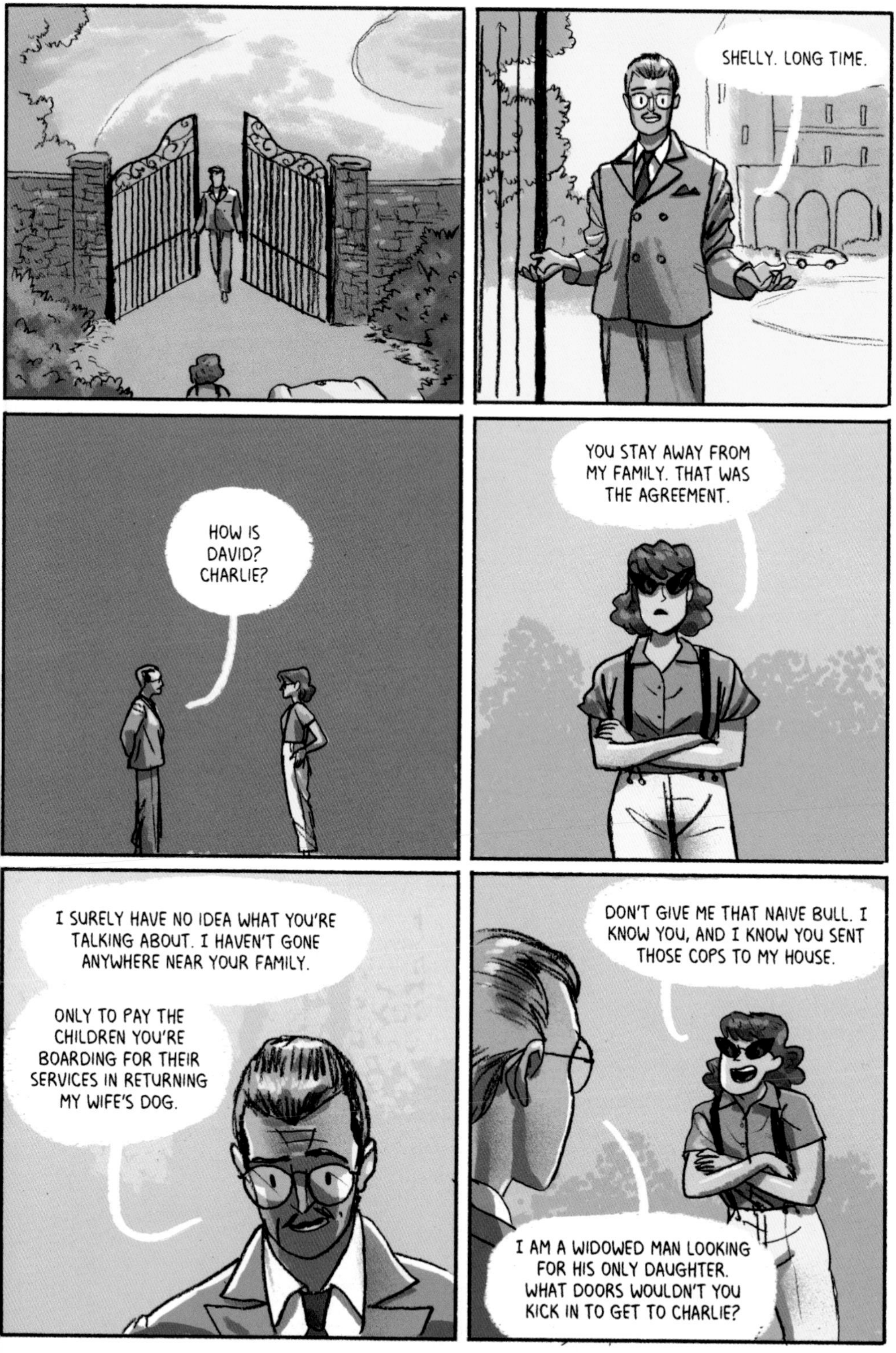
SHELLY. LONG TIME.
HOW IS DAVID? CHARLIE?
YOU STAY AWAY FROM MY FAMILY. THAT WAS THE AGREEMENT.
I SURELY HAVE NO IDEA WHAT YOU'RE TALKING ABOUT. I HAVEN'T GONE ANYWHERE NEAR YOUR FAMILY.
ONLY TO PAY THE CHILDREN YOU'RE BOARDING FOR THEIR SERVICES IN RETURNING MY WIFE'S DOG.
DON'T GIVE ME THAT NAIVE BULL. I KNOW YOU, AND I KNOW YOU SENT THOSE COPS TO MY HOUSE.
I AM A WIDOWED MAN LOOKING FOR HIS ONLY DAUGHTER. WHAT DOORS WOULDN'T YOU KICK IN TO GET TO CHARLIE?

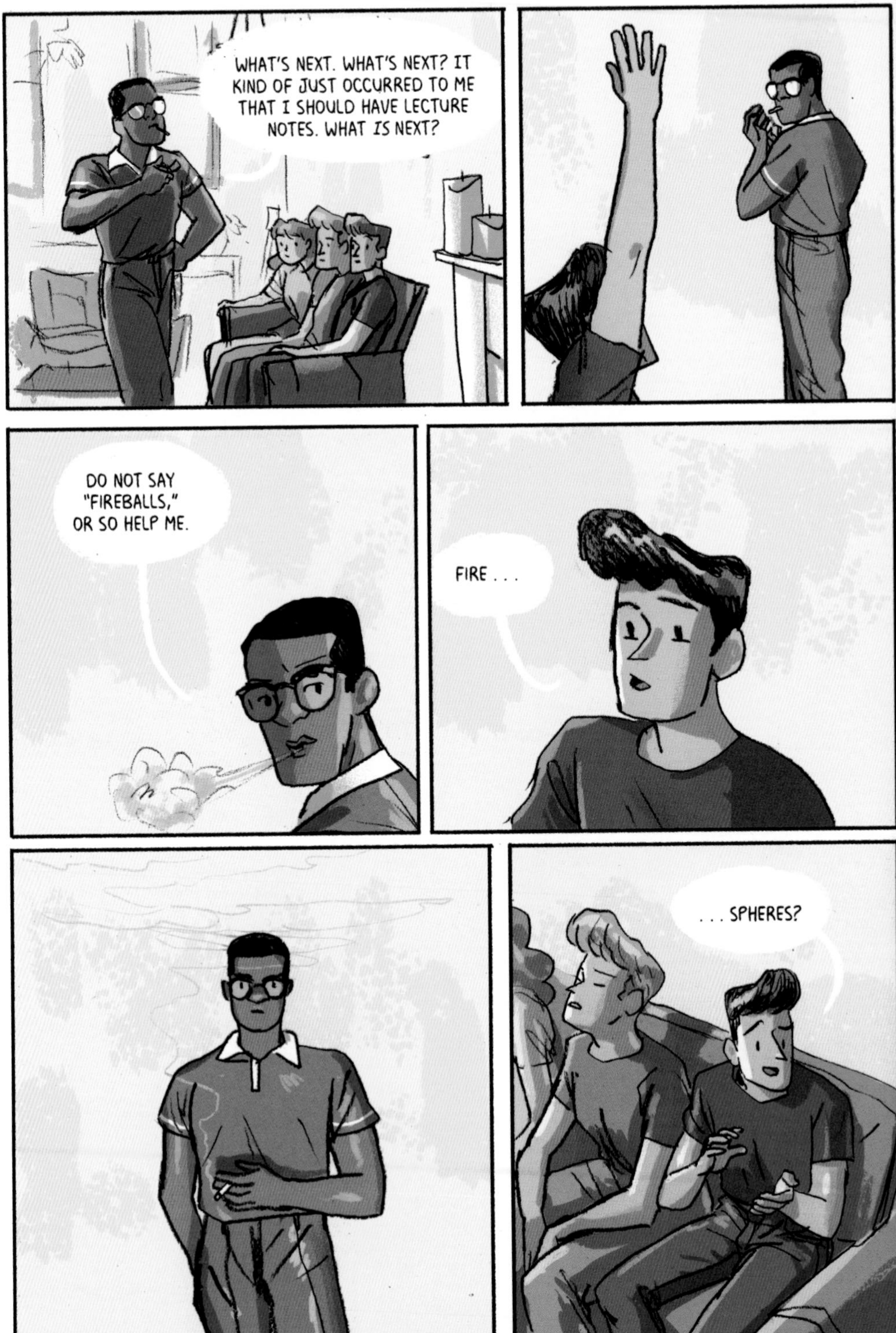
WHAT'S NEXT. WHAT'S NEXT? IT KIND OF JUST OCCURRED TO ME THAT I SHOULD HAVE LECTURE NOTES. WHAT *IS* NEXT?
DO NOT SAY "FIREBALLS," OR SO HELP ME.
FIRE . . .
. . . SPHERES?

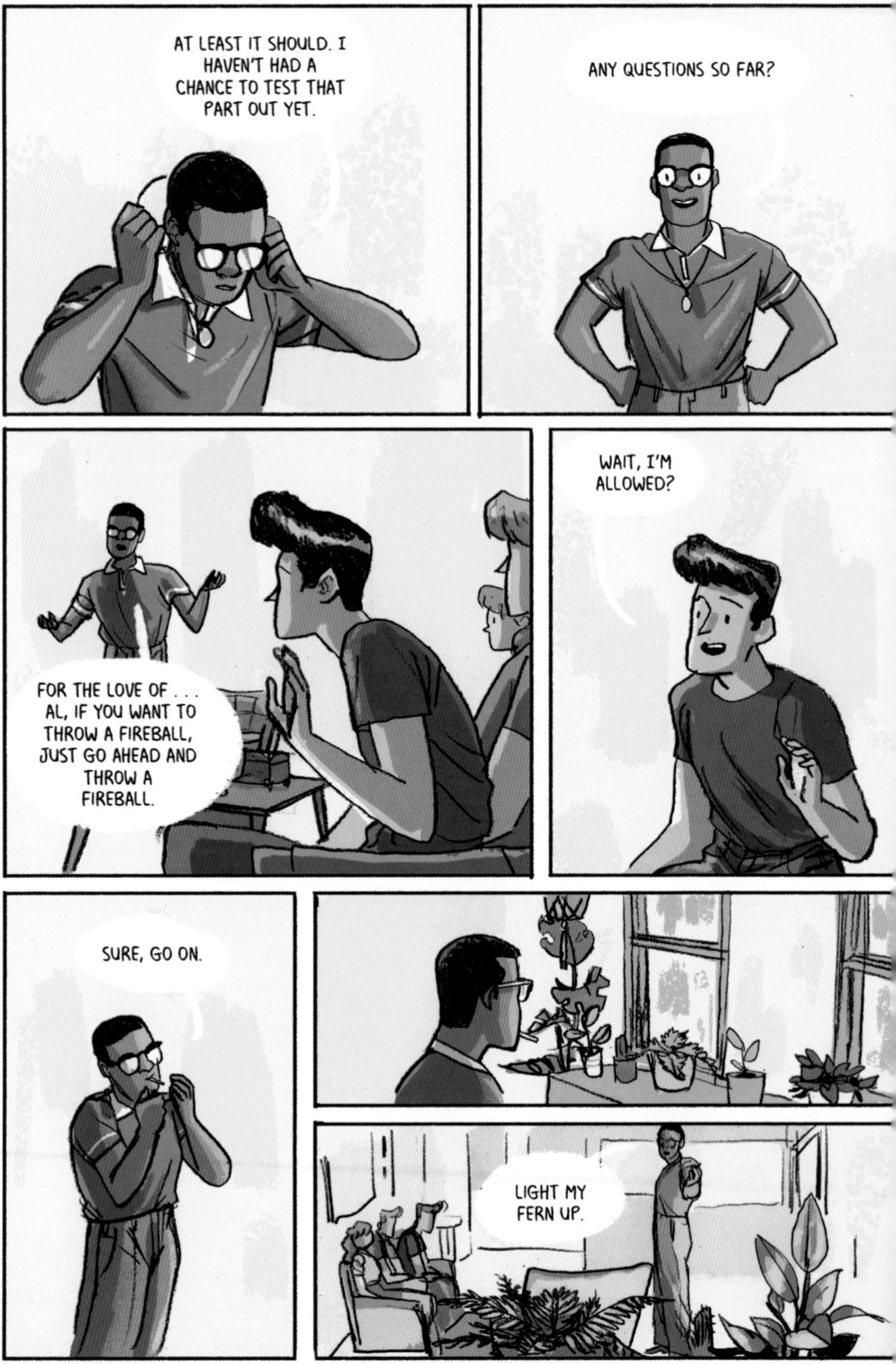
AT LEAST IT SHOULD. I HAVEN'T HAD A CHANCE TO TEST THAT PART OUT YET.
ANY QUESTIONS SO FAR?
FOR THE LOVE OF . . . AL, IF YOU WANT TO THROW A FIREBALL, JUST GO AHEAD AND THROW A FIREBALL.
WAIT, I'M ALLOWED?
SURE, GO ON.
LIGHT MY FERN UP.

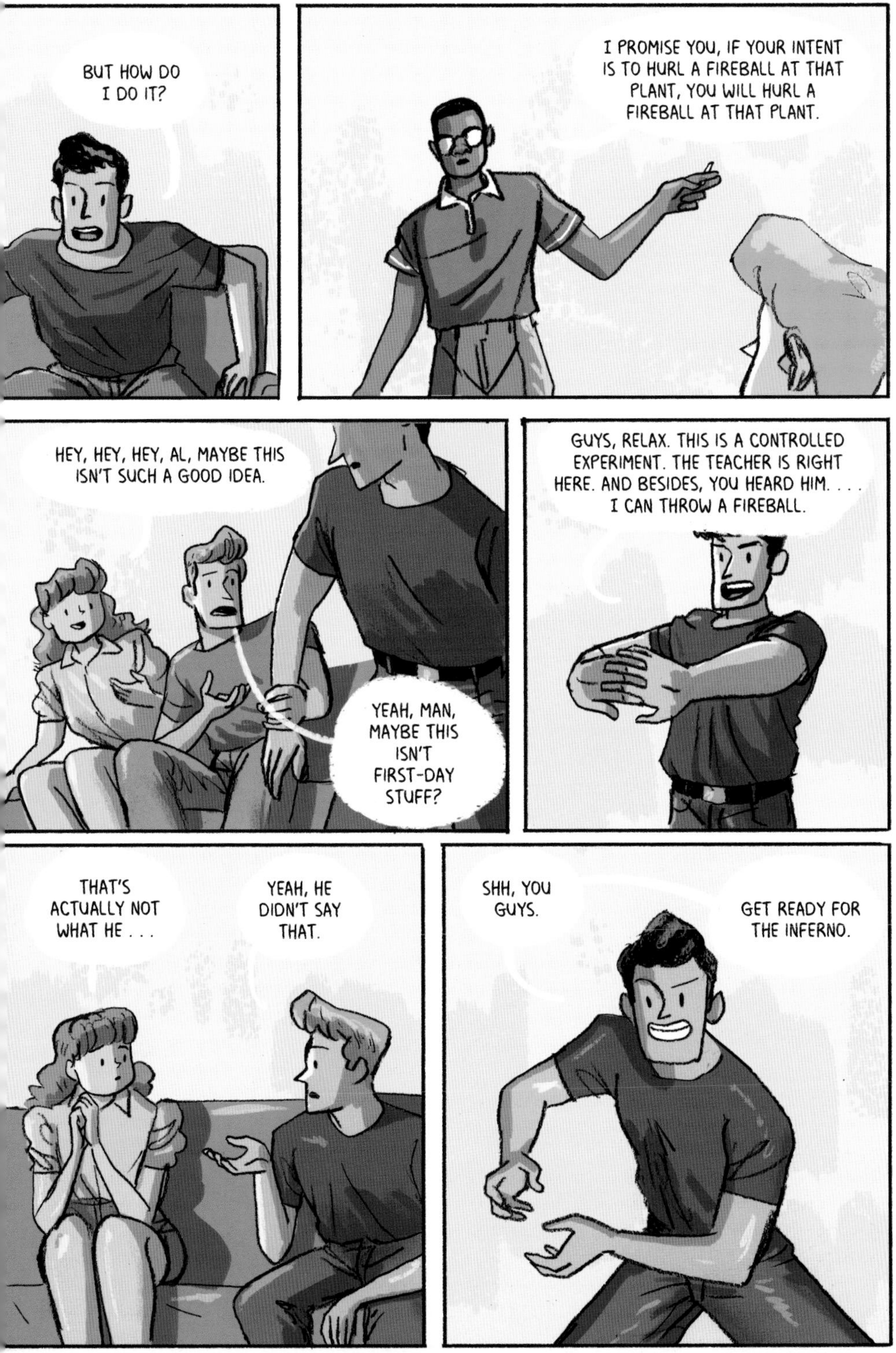
BUT HOW DO I DO IT?
I PROMISE YOU, IF YOUR INTENT IS TO HURL A FIREBALL AT THAT PLANT, YOU WILL HURL A FIREBALL AT THAT PLANT.
HEY, HEY, HEY, AL, MAYBE THIS ISN'T SUCH A GOOD IDEA.
YEAH, MAN, MAYBE THIS ISN'T FIRST-DAY STUFF?
GUYS, RELAX. THIS IS A CONTROLLED EXPERIMENT. THE TEACHER IS RIGHT HERE. AND BESIDES, YOU HEARD HIM. . . . I CAN THROW A FIREBALL.
THAT'S ACTUALLY NOT WHAT HE . . .
YEAH, HE DIDN'T SAY THAT.
SHH, YOU GUYS.
GET READY FOR THE INFERNO.

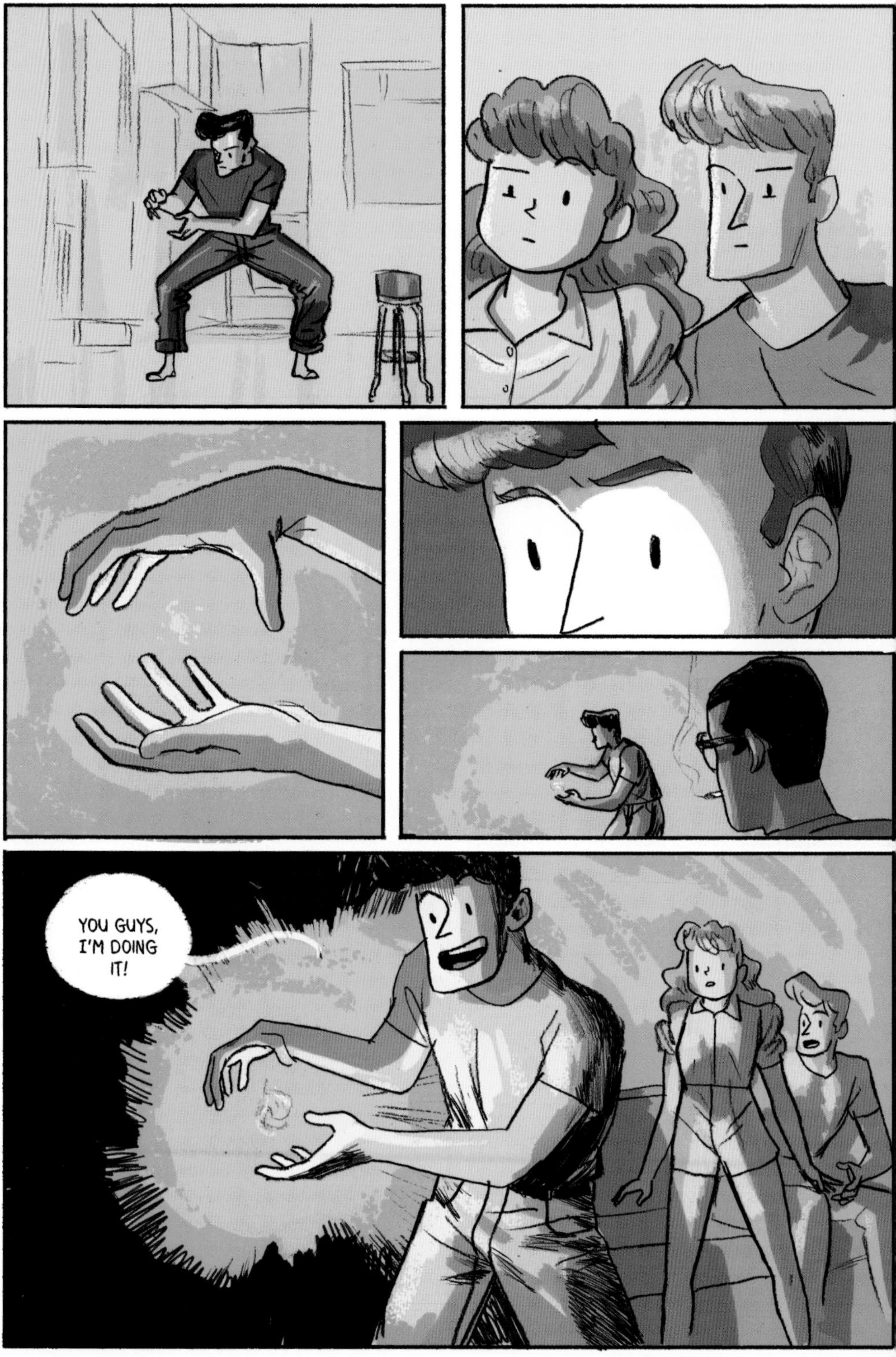
YOU GUYS, I'M DOING IT!

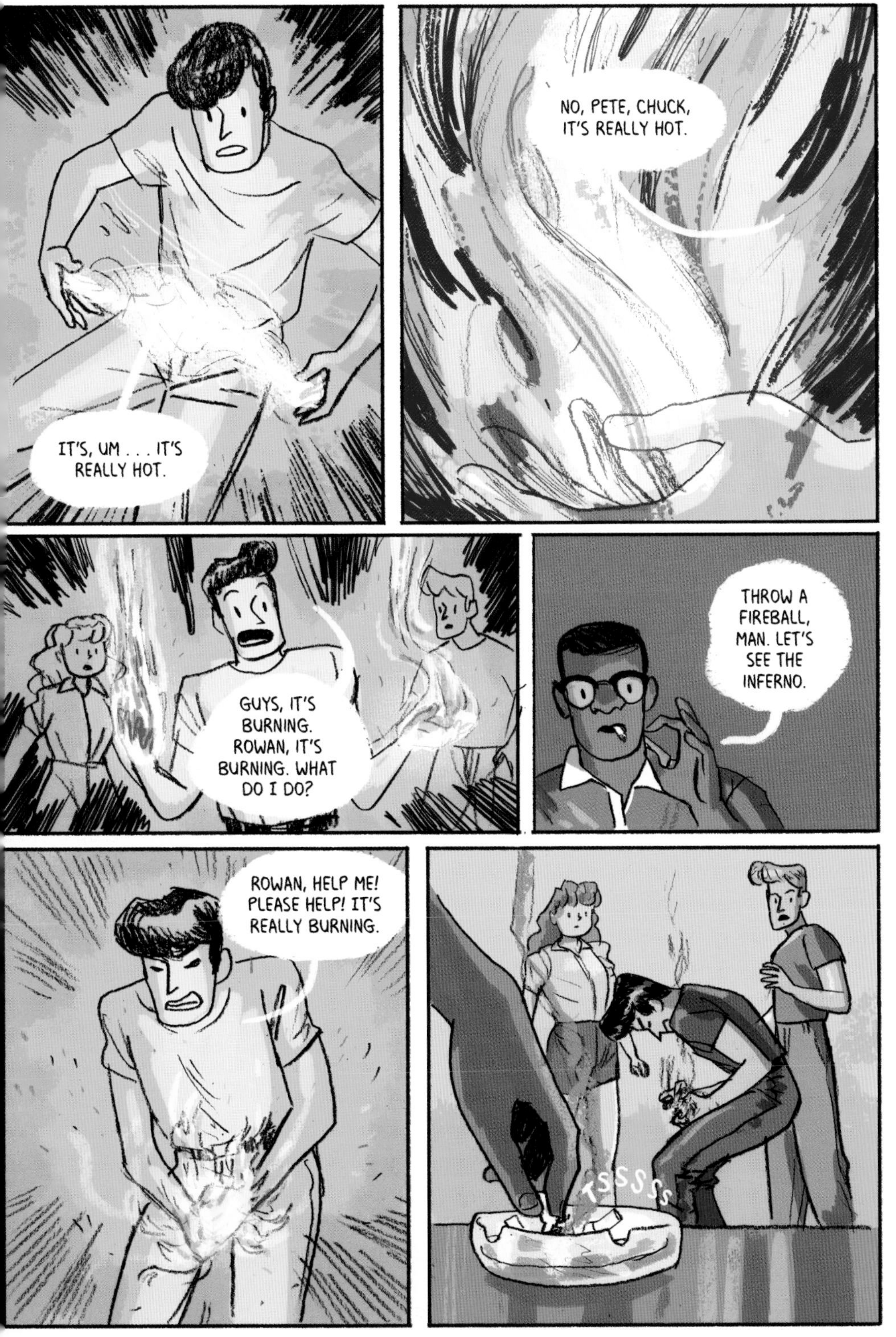
IT'S, UM . . . IT'S REALLY HOT.
NO, PETE, CHUCK, IT'S REALLY HOT.
GUYS, IT'S BURNING. ROWAN, IT'S BURNING. WHAT DO I DO?
THROW A FIREBALL, MAN. LET'S SEE THE INFERNO.
ROWAN, HELP ME! PLEASE HELP! IT'S REALLY BURNING.
TSSSSS

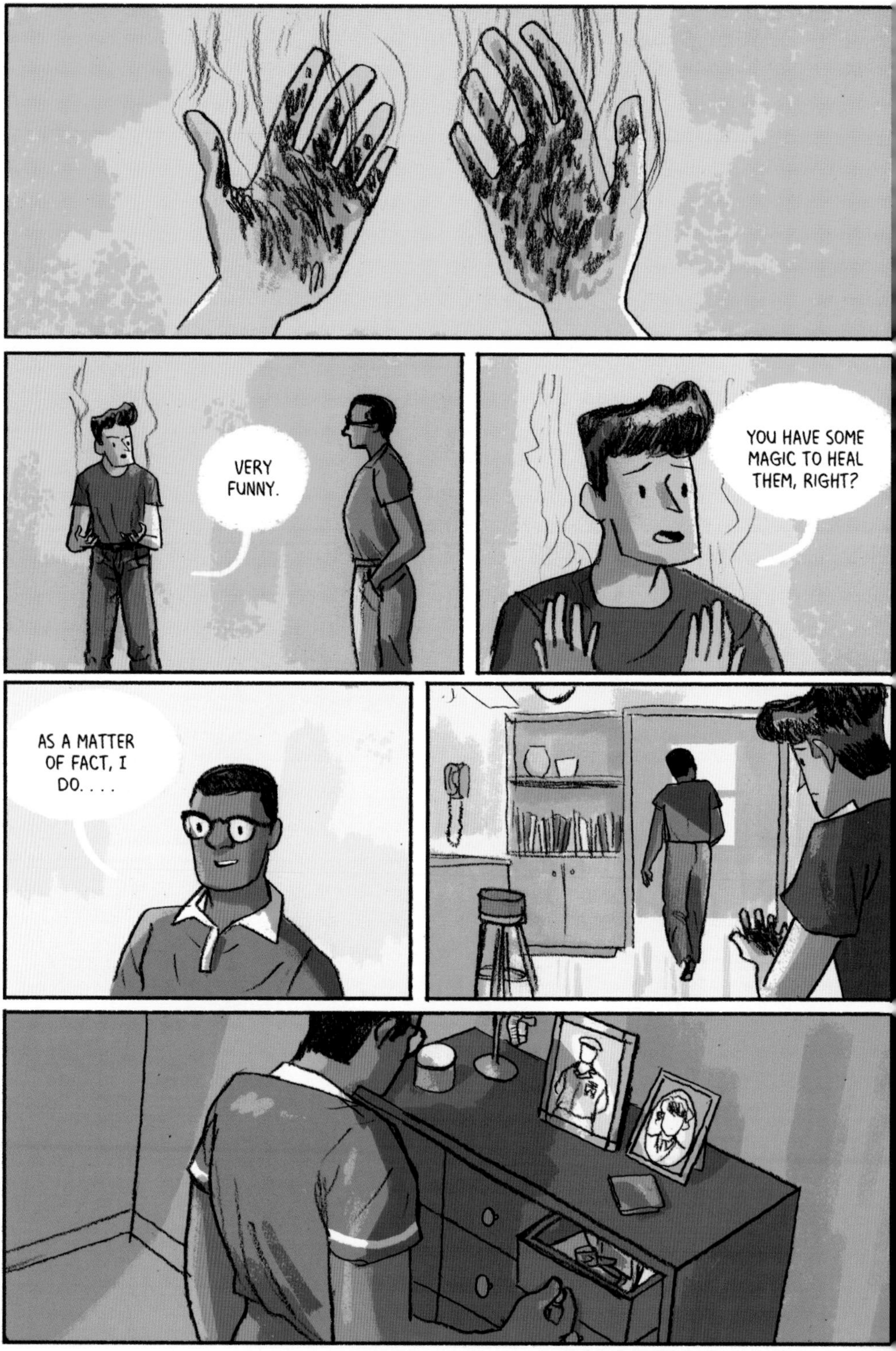

VERY FUNNY.
YOU HAVE SOME MAGIC TO HEAL THEM, RIGHT?
AS A MATTER OF FACT, I DO. . . .

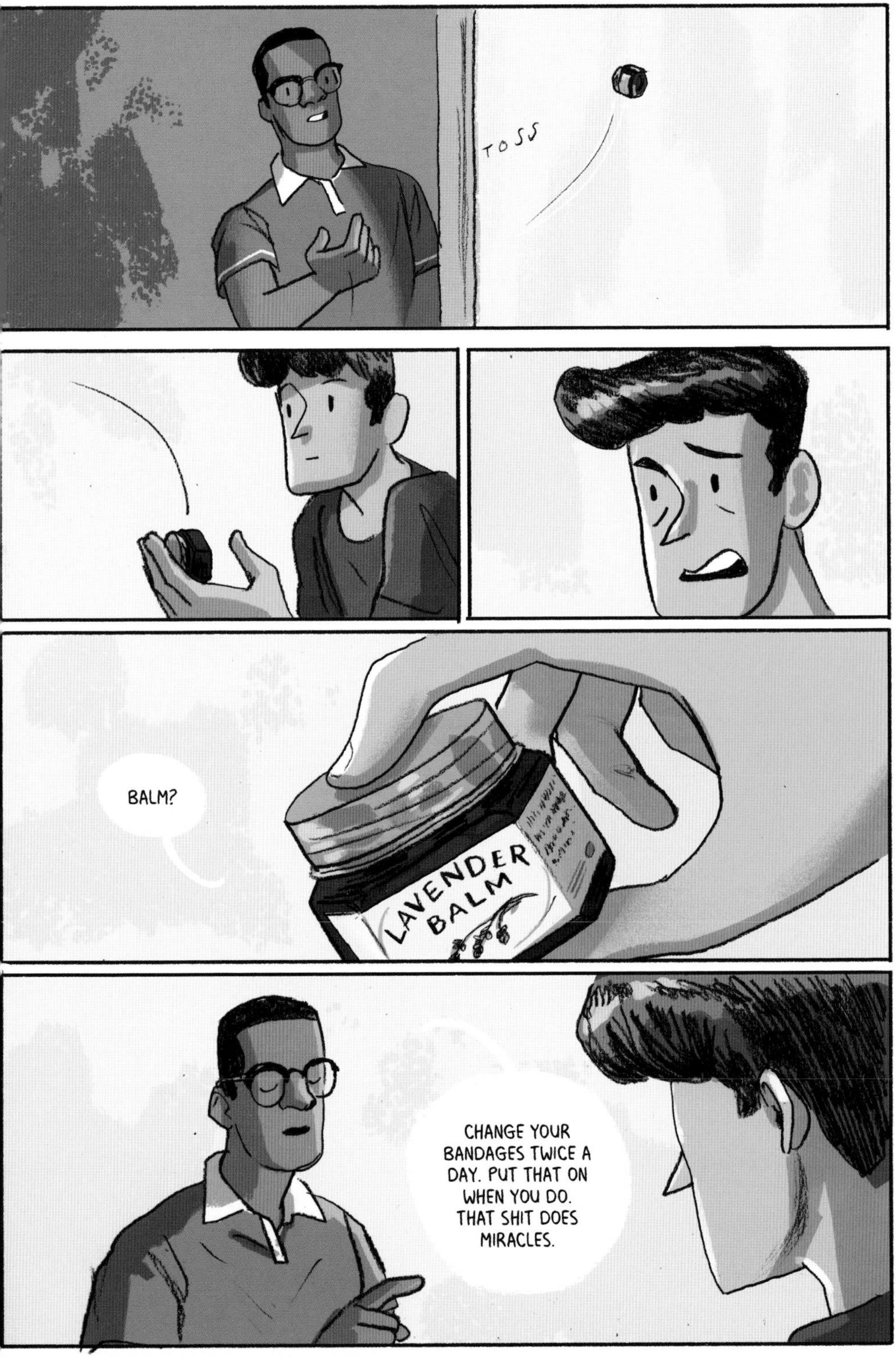
TOSS
BALM?
LAVENDER BALM
CHANGE YOUR BANDAGES TWICE A DAY. PUT THAT ON WHEN YOU DO. THAT SHIT DOES MIRACLES.

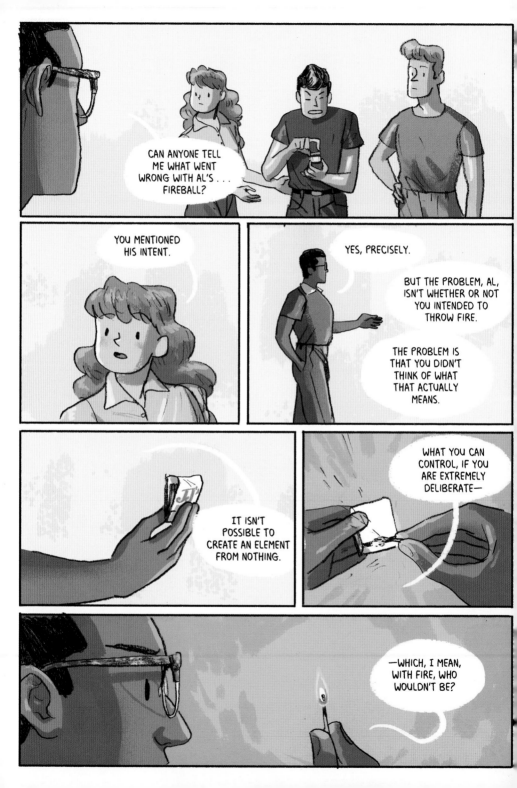

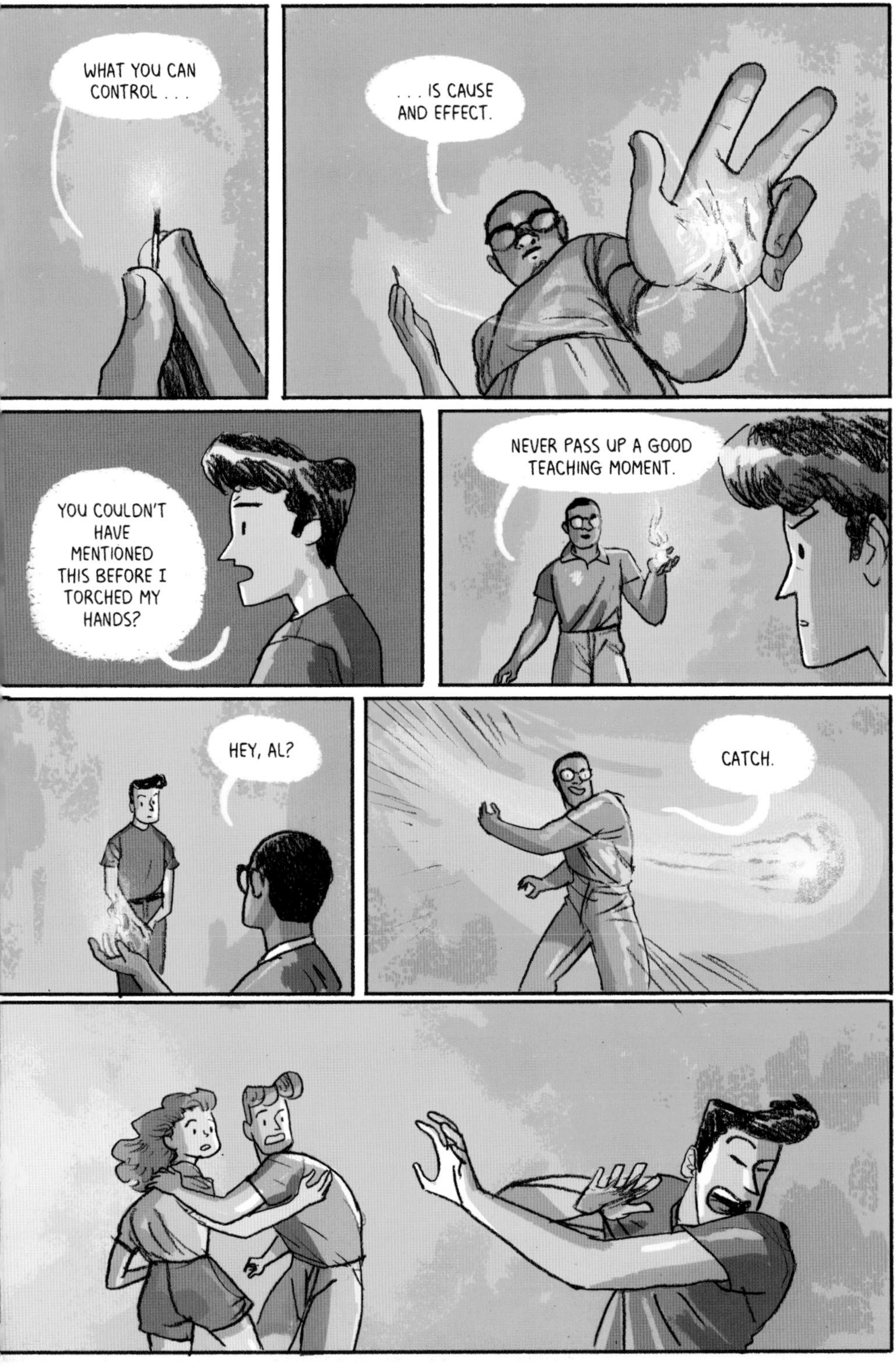
WHAT YOU CAN CONTROL . . .
. . . IS CAUSE AND EFFECT.
YOU COULDN'T HAVE MENTIONED THIS BEFORE I TORCHED MY HANDS?
NEVER PASS UP A GOOD TEACHING MOMENT.
HEY, AL?
CATCH.

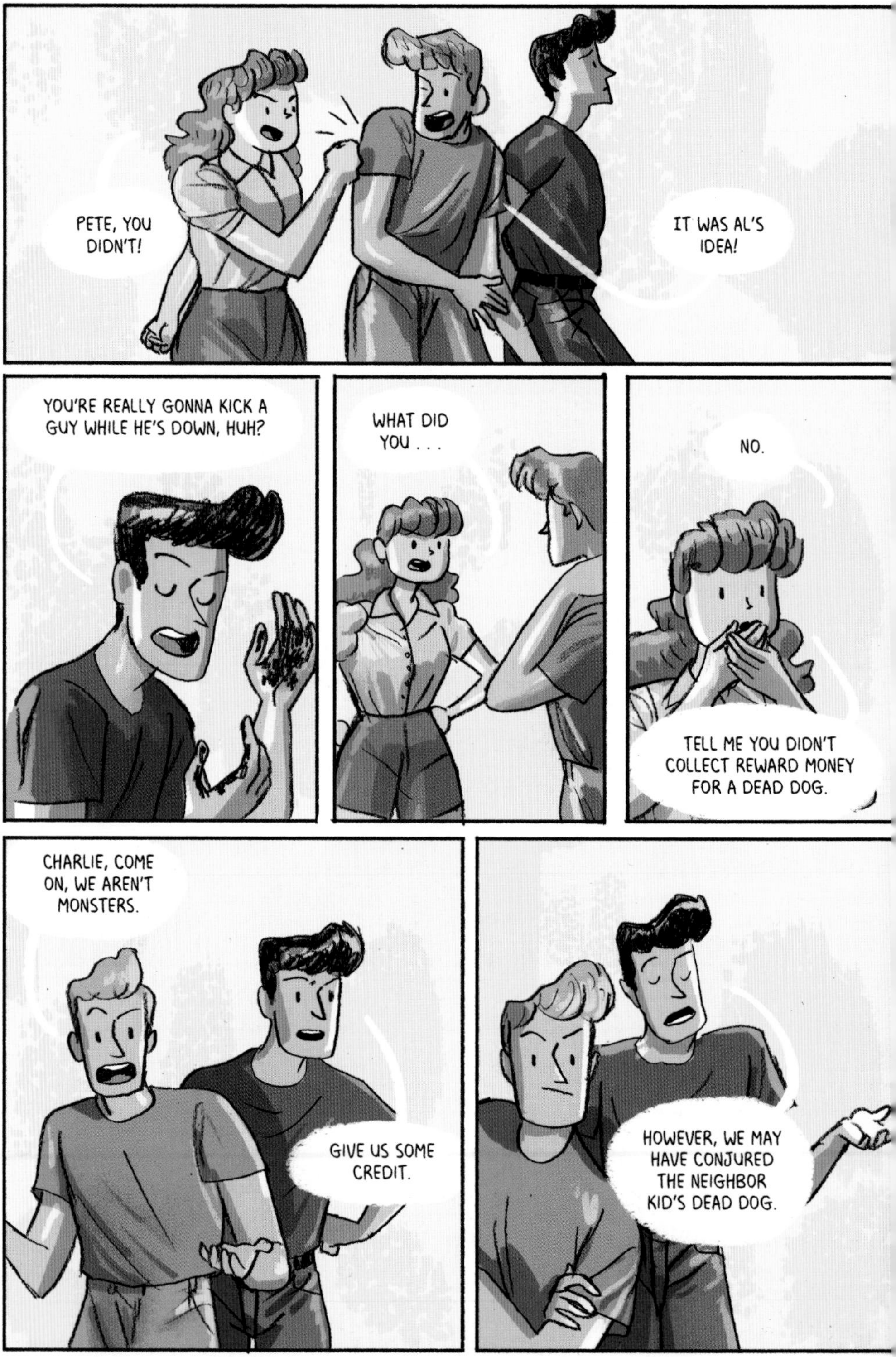
PETE, YOU DIDN'T!
IT WAS AL'S IDEA!
YOU'RE REALLY GONNA KICK A GUY WHILE HE'S DOWN, HUH?
WHAT DID YOU . . .
NO.
TELL ME YOU DIDN'T COLLECT REWARD MONEY FOR A DEAD DOG.
CHARLIE, COME ON, WE AREN'T MONSTERS.
GIVE US SOME CREDIT.
HOWEVER, WE MAY HAVE CONJURED THE NEIGHBOR KID'S DEAD DOG.

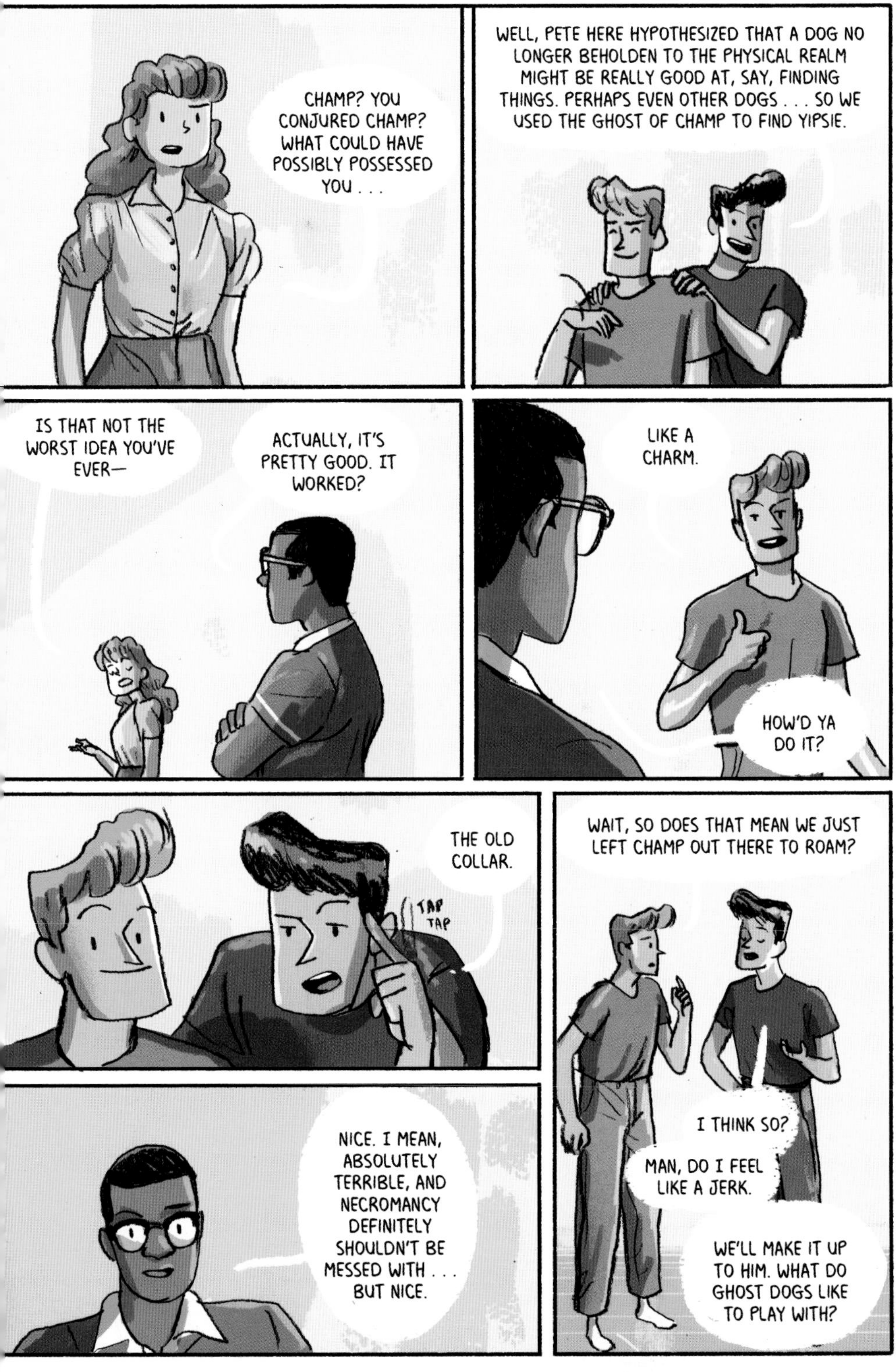
CHAMP? YOU CONJURED CHAMP? WHAT COULD HAVE POSSIBLY POSSESSED YOU . . .
WELL, PETE HERE HYPOTHESIZED THAT A DOG NO LONGER BEHOLDEN TO THE PHYSICAL REALM MIGHT BE REALLY GOOD AT, SAY, FINDING THINGS. PERHAPS EVEN OTHER DOGS . . . SO WE USED THE GHOST OF CHAMP TO FIND YIPSIE.
IS THAT NOT THE WORST IDEA YOU'VE EVER—
ACTUALLY, IT'S PRETTY GOOD. IT WORKED?
LIKE A CHARM.
HOW'D YA DO IT?
THE OLD COLLAR.
TAP TAP
NICE. I MEAN, ABSOLUTELY TERRIBLE, AND NECROMANCY DEFINITELY SHOULDN'T BE MESSED WITH . . . BUT NICE.
WAIT, SO DOES THAT MEAN WE JUST LEFT CHAMP OUT THERE TO ROAM?
I THINK SO?
MAN, DO I FEEL LIKE A JERK.
WE'LL MAKE IT UP TO HIM. WHAT DO GHOST DOGS LIKE TO PLAY WITH?

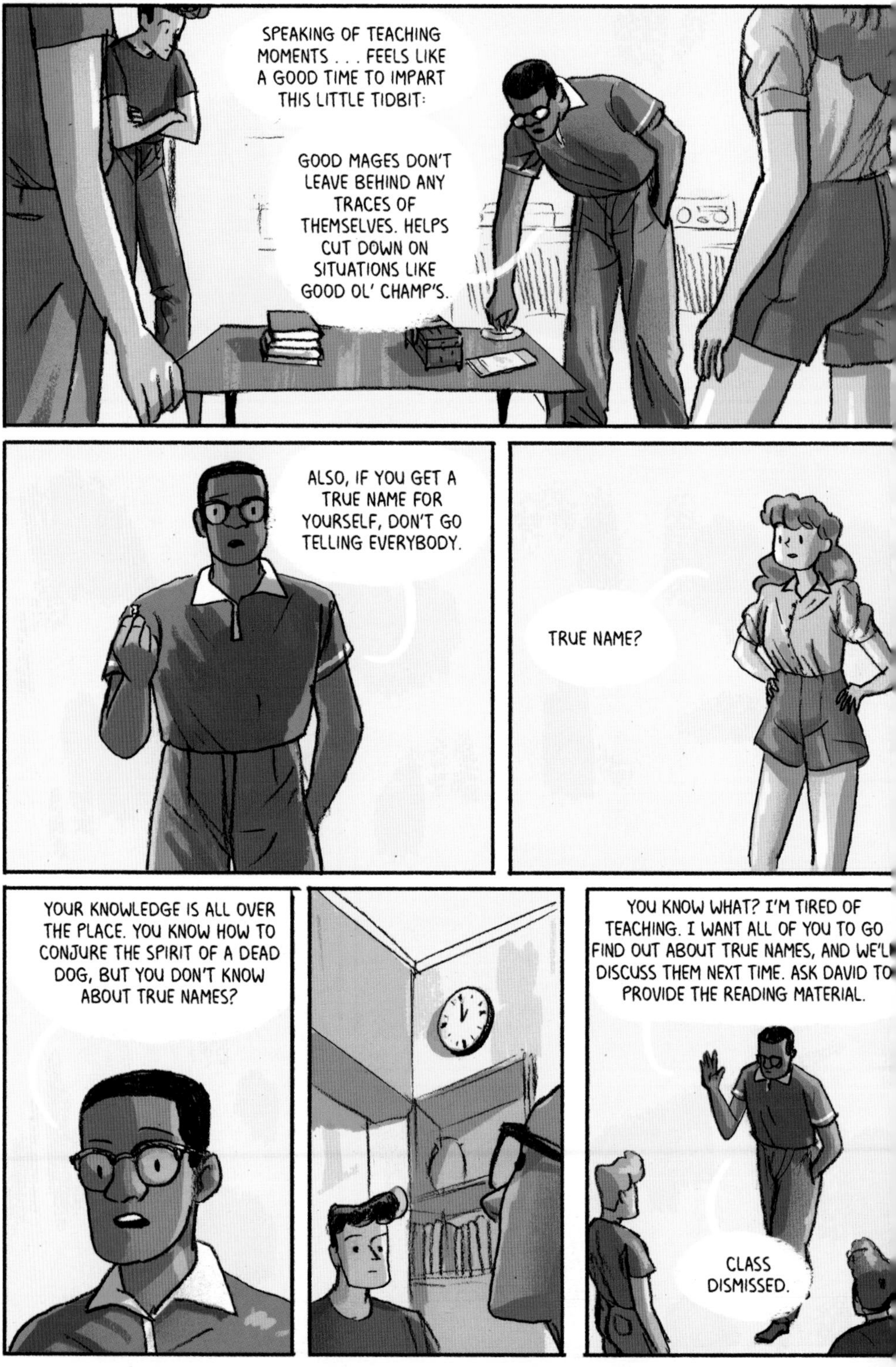
SPEAKING OF TEACHING MOMENTS . . . FEELS LIKE A GOOD TIME TO IMPART THIS LITTLE TIDBIT:
GOOD MAGES DON'T LEAVE BEHIND ANY TRACES OF THEMSELVES. HELPS CUT DOWN ON SITUATIONS LIKE GOOD OL' CHAMP'S.
ALSO, IF YOU GET A TRUE NAME FOR YOURSELF, DON'T GO TELLING EVERYBODY.
TRUE NAME?
YOUR KNOWLEDGE IS ALL OVER THE PLACE. YOU KNOW HOW TO CONJURE THE SPIRIT OF A DEAD DOG, BUT YOU DON'T KNOW ABOUT TRUE NAMES?
YOU KNOW WHAT? I'M TIRED OF TEACHING. I WANT ALL OF YOU TO GO FIND OUT ABOUT TRUE NAMES, AND WE'LL DISCUSS THEM NEXT TIME. ASK DAVID TO PROVIDE THE READING MATERIAL.
CLASS DISMISSED.

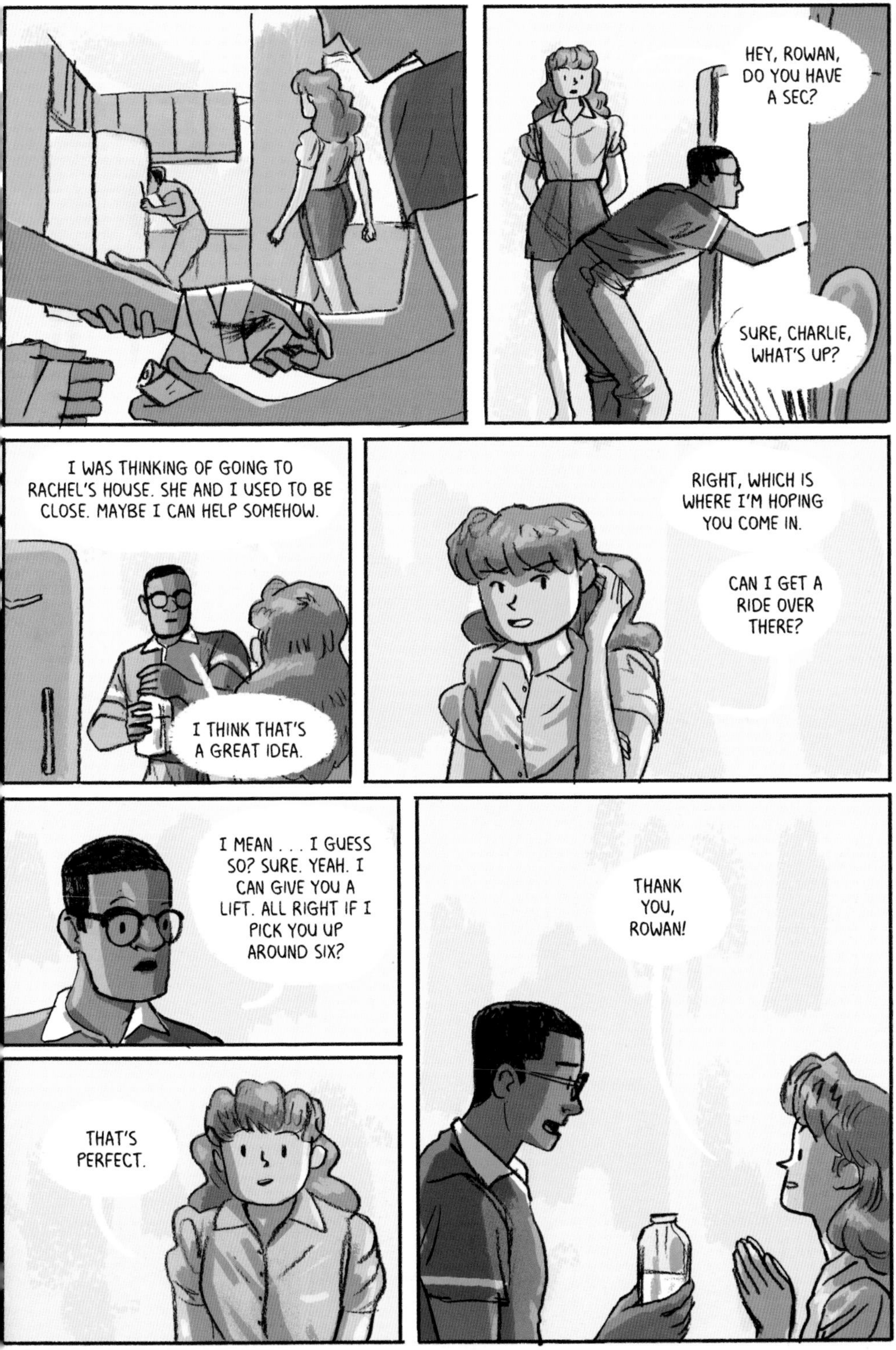
HEY, ROWAN, DO YOU HAVE A SEC?
SURE, CHARLIE, WHAT'S UP?
I WAS THINKING OF GOING TO RACHEL'S HOUSE. SHE AND I USED TO BE CLOSE. MAYBE I CAN HELP SOMEHOW.
I THINK THAT'S A GREAT IDEA.
RIGHT, WHICH IS WHERE I'M HOPING YOU COME IN.
CAN I GET A RIDE OVER THERE?
I MEAN . . . I GUESS SO? SURE. YEAH. I CAN GIVE YOU A LIFT. ALL RIGHT IF I PICK YOU UP AROUND SIX?
THAT'S PERFECT.
THANK YOU, ROWAN!

CHAPTER 4

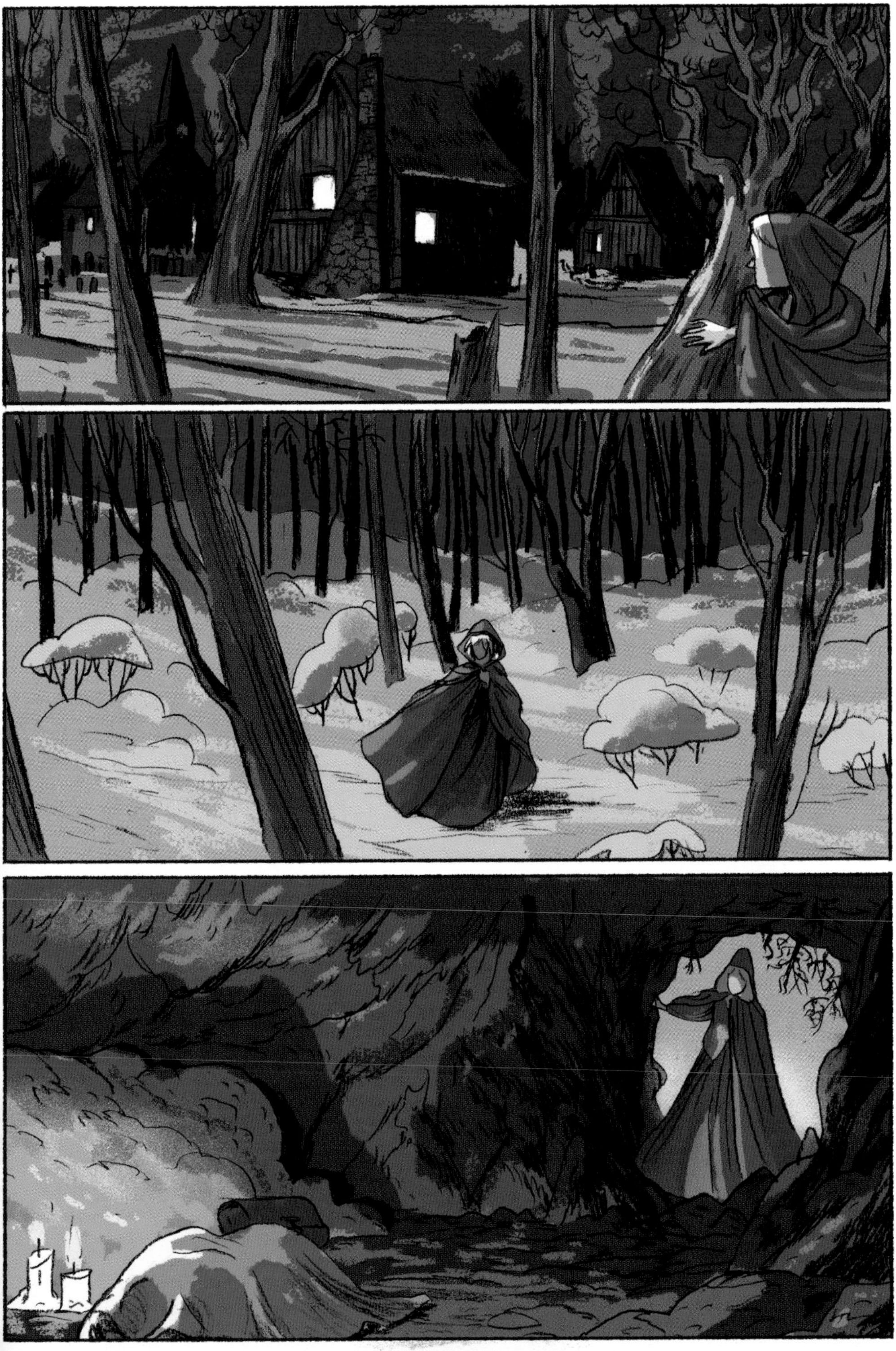

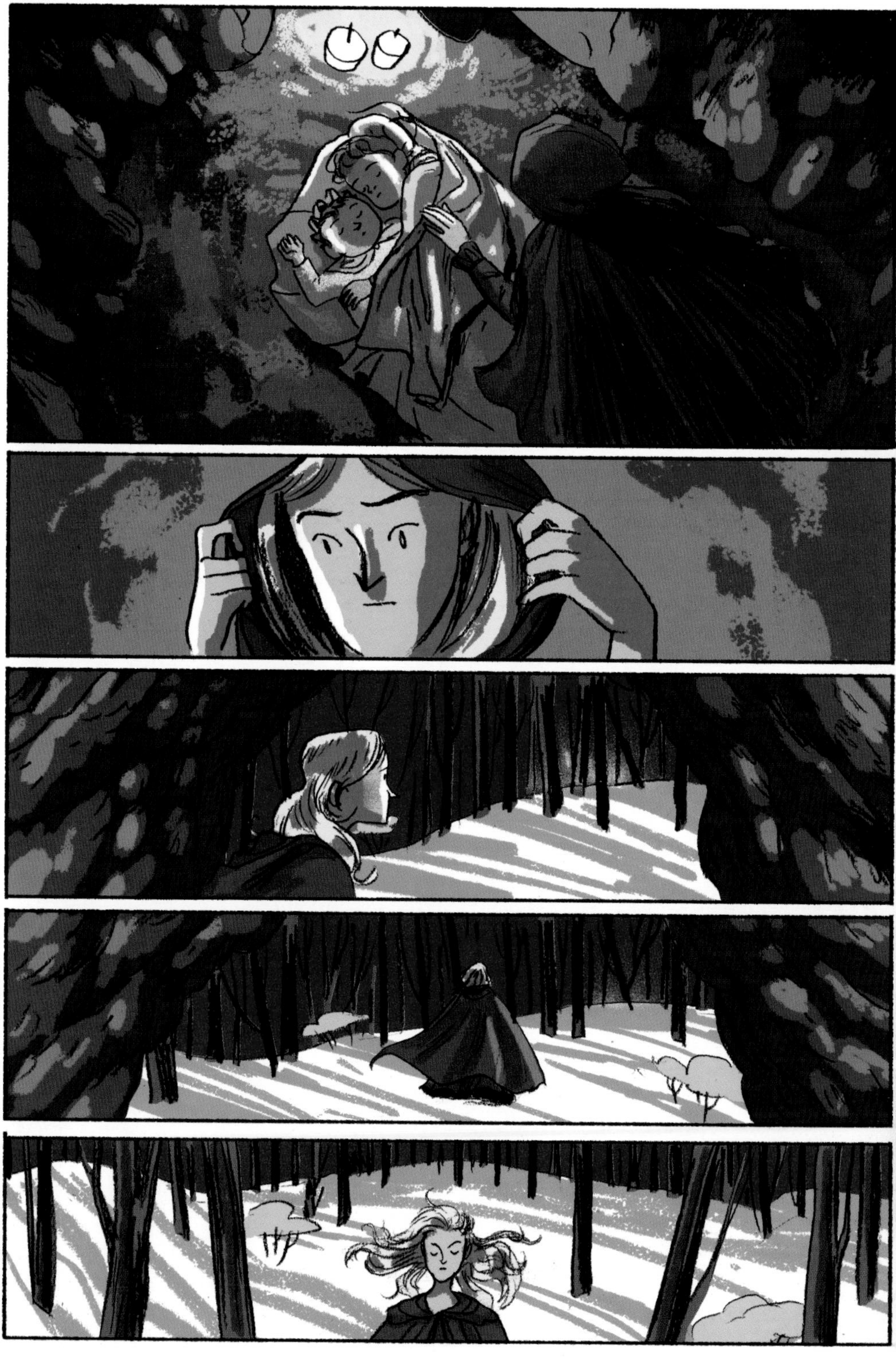

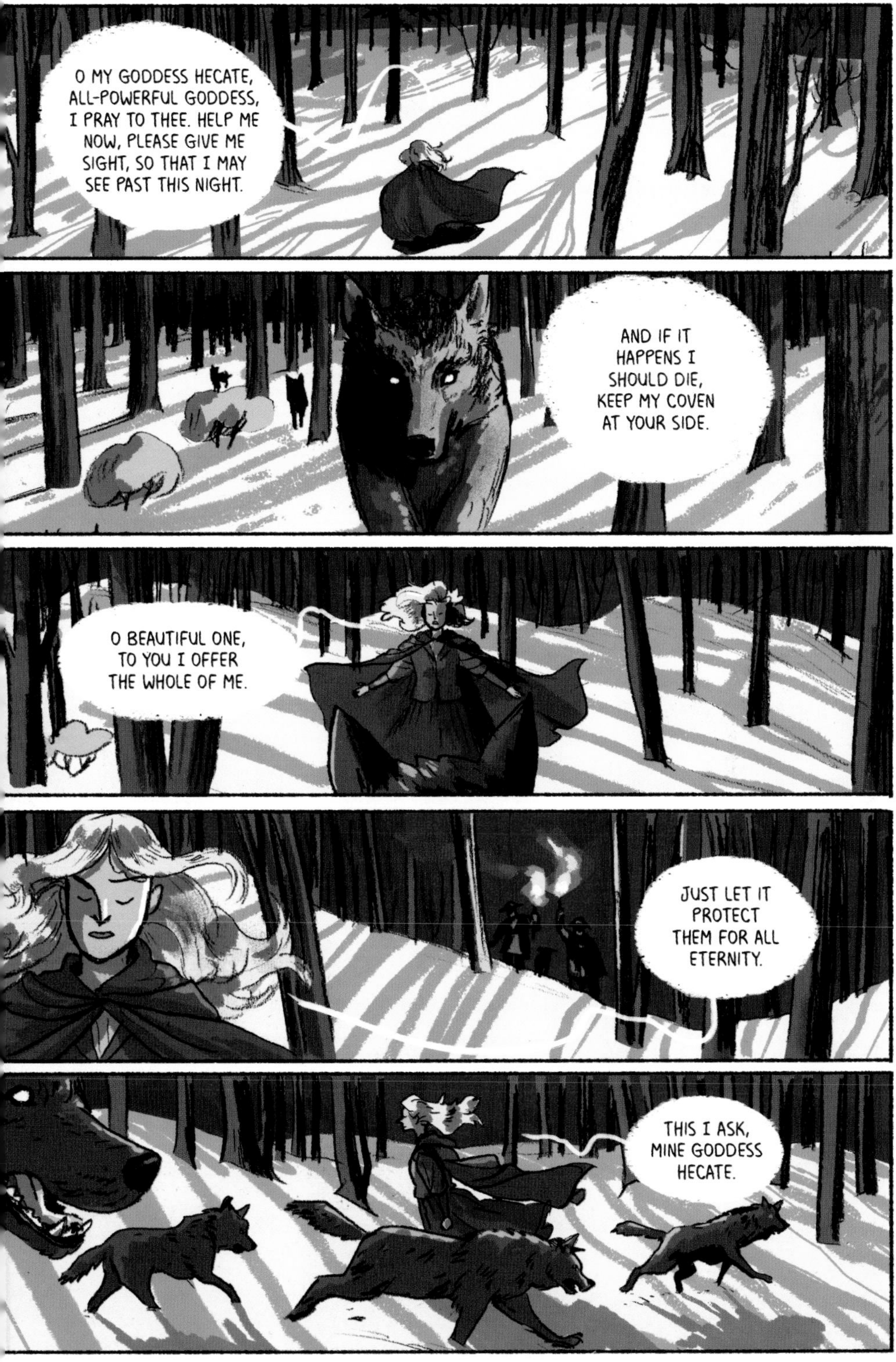
O MY GODDESS HECATE, ALL-POWERFUL GODDESS, I PRAY TO THEE. HELP ME NOW, PLEASE GIVE ME SIGHT, SO THAT I MAY SEE PAST THIS NIGHT.
AND IF IT HAPPENS I SHOULD DIE, KEEP MY COVEN AT YOUR SIDE.
O BEAUTIFUL ONE, TO YOU I OFFER THE WHOLE OF ME.
JUST LET IT PROTECT THEM FOR ALL ETERNITY.
THIS I ASK, MINE GODDESS HECATE.

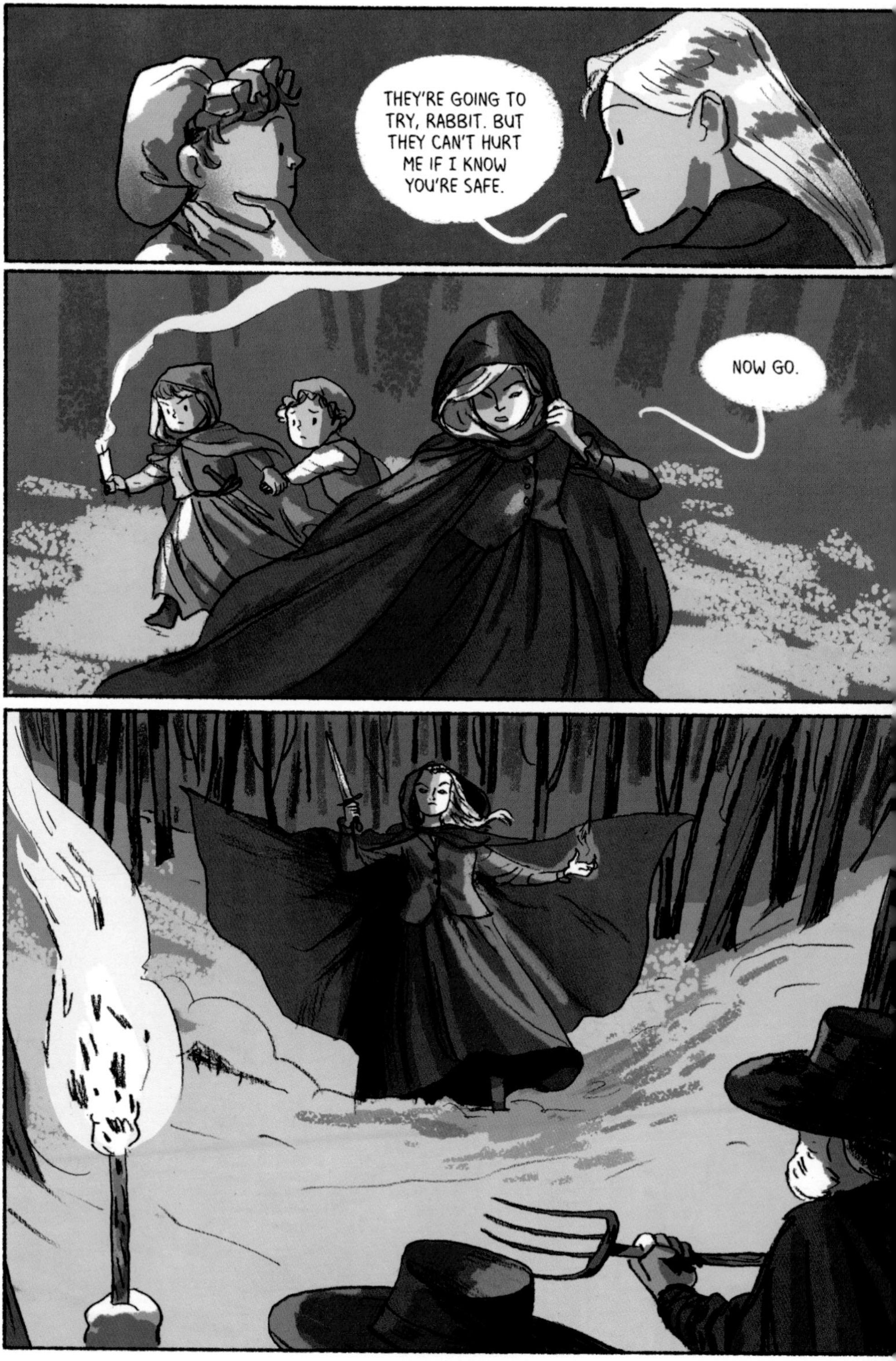
THEY'RE GOING TO TRY, RABBIT. BUT THEY CAN'T HURT ME IF I KNOW YOU'RE SAFE.
NOW GO.

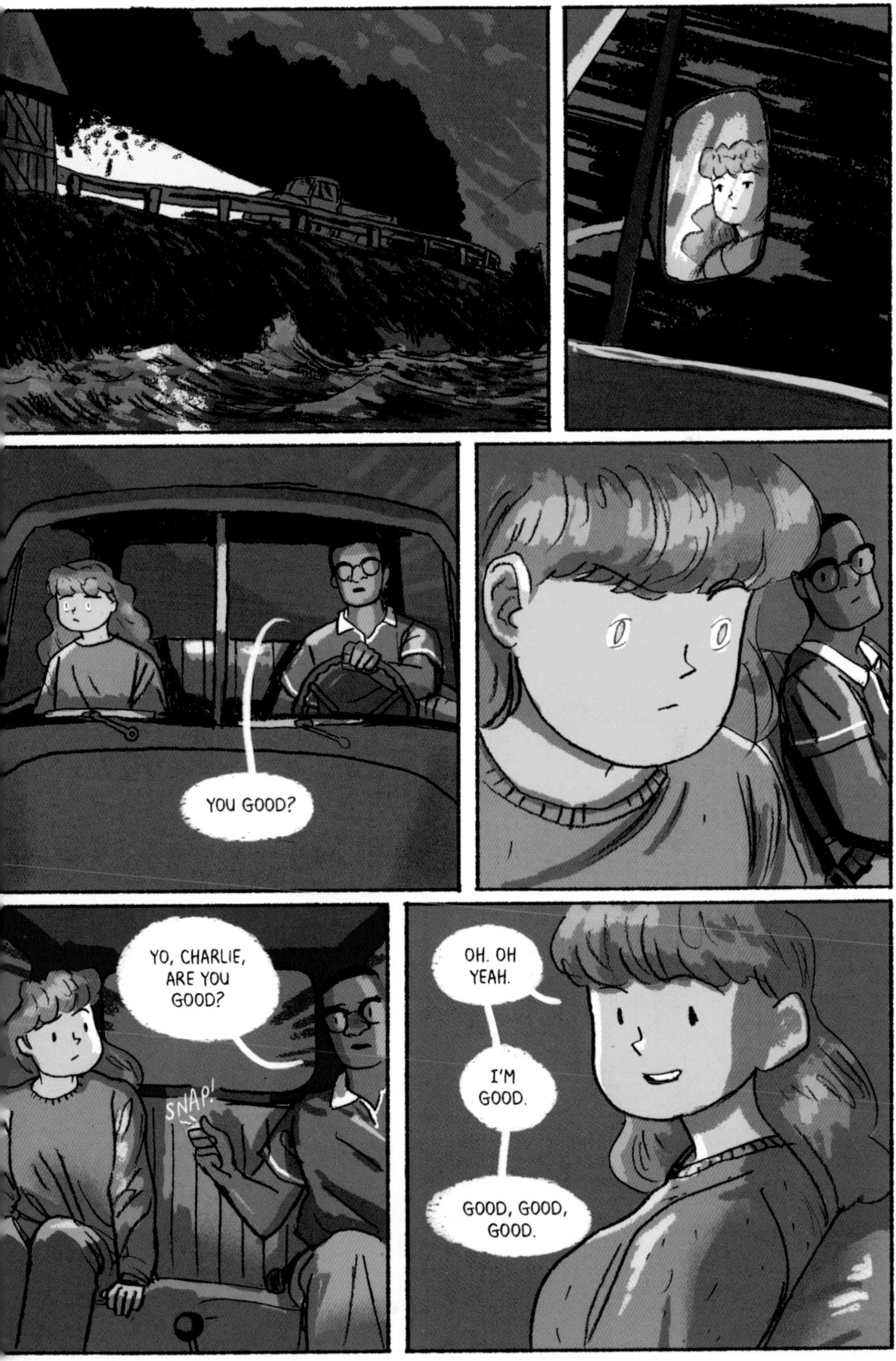
YOU GOOD?
YO, CHARLIE, ARE YOU GOOD?
SNAP!
OH. OH YEAH.
I'M GOOD.
GOOD, GOOD, GOOD.

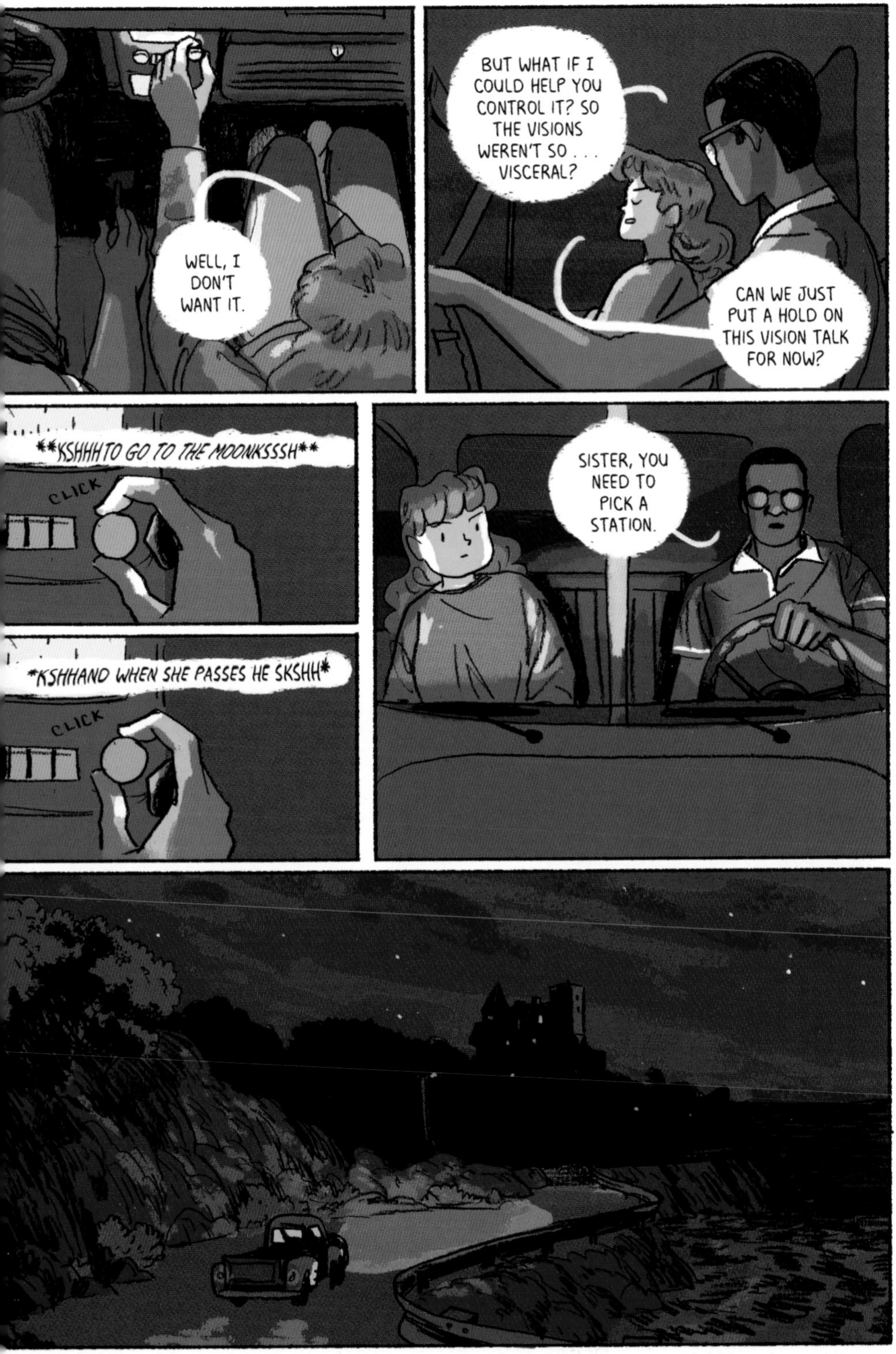
WELL, I DON'T WANT IT.
BUT WHAT IF I COULD HELP YOU CONTROL IT? SO THE VISIONS WEREN'T SO . . . VISCERAL?
CAN WE JUST PUT A HOLD ON THIS VISION TALK FOR NOW?
KSHHH TO GO TO THE MOONKSSSH
CLICK
KSHHAND WHEN SHE PASSES HE SKSHH
CLICK
SISTER, YOU NEED TO PICK A STATION.

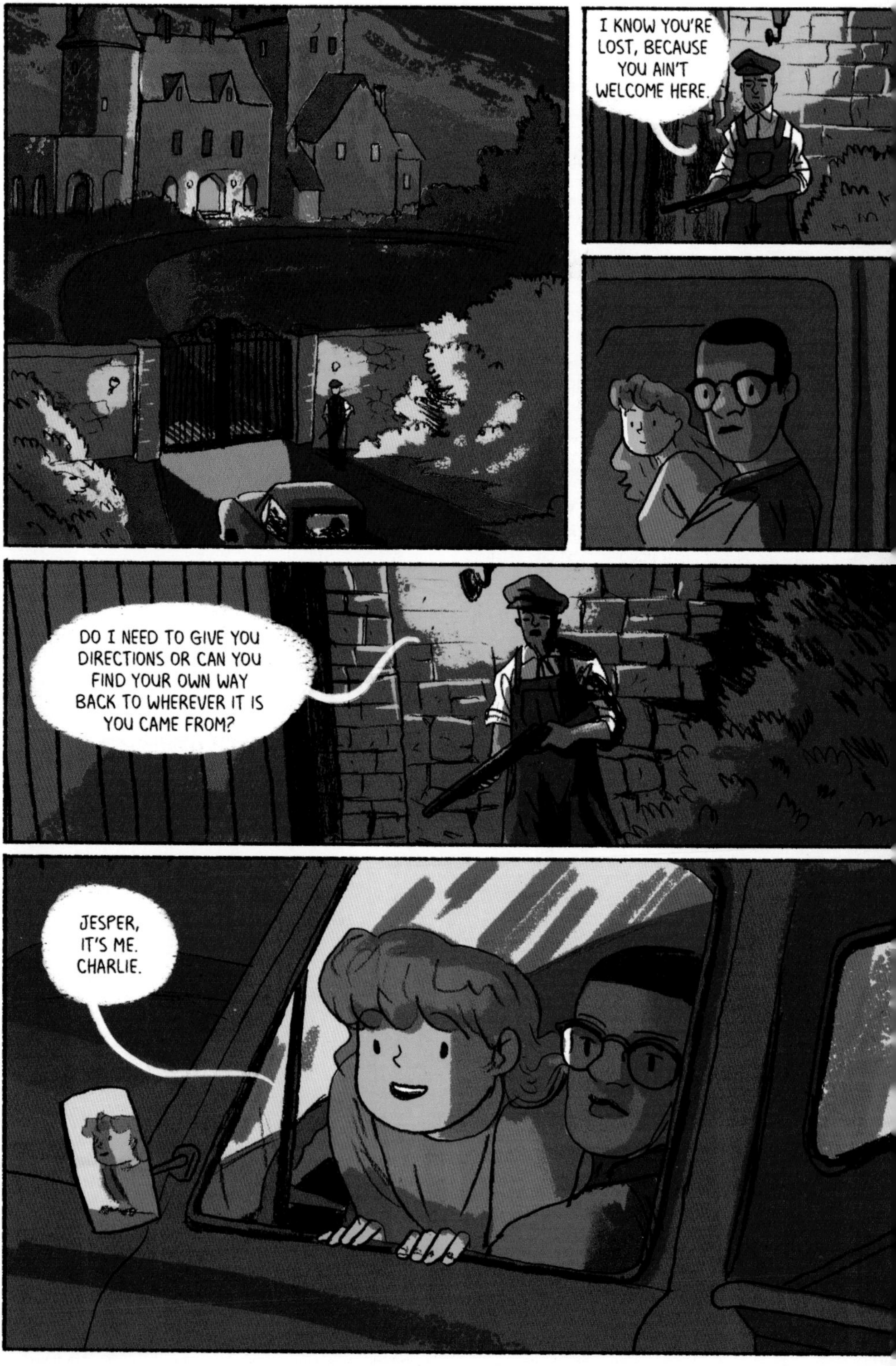
I KNOW YOU'RE LOST, BECAUSE YOU AIN'T WELCOME HERE.
DO I NEED TO GIVE YOU DIRECTIONS OR CAN YOU FIND YOUR OWN WAY BACK TO WHEREVER IT IS YOU CAME FROM?
JESPER, IT'S ME. CHARLIE.

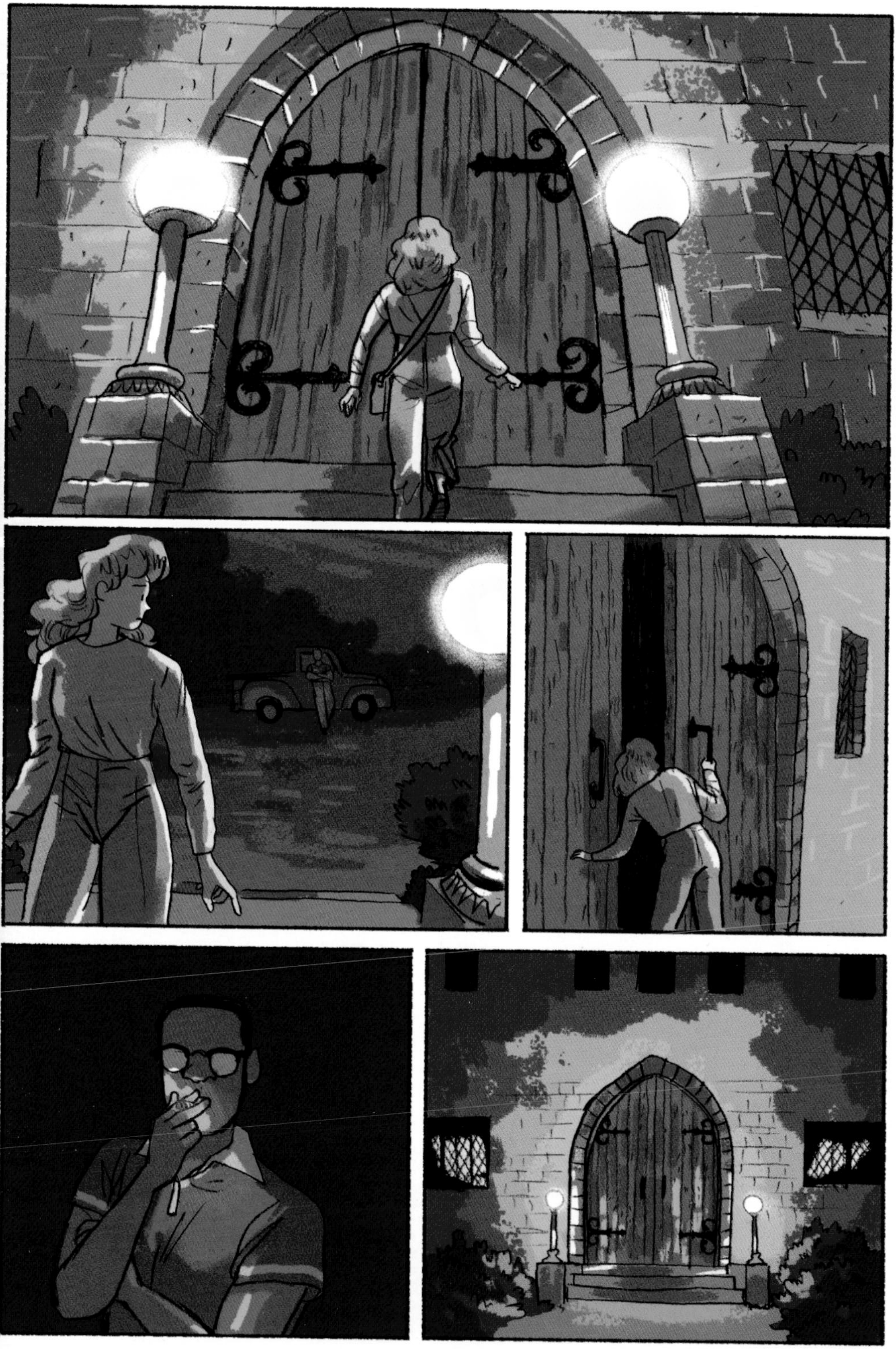

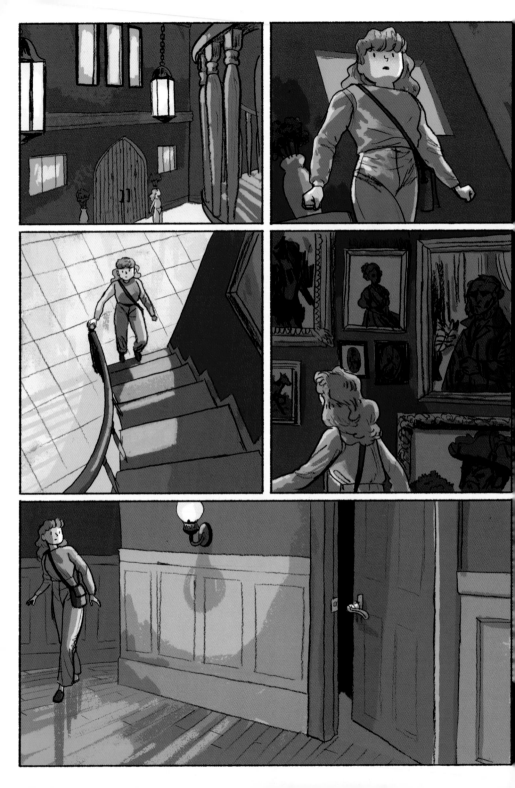

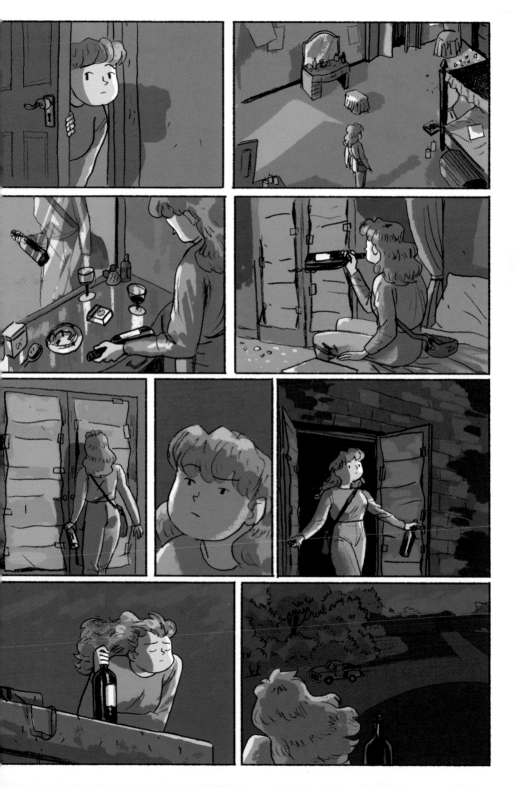

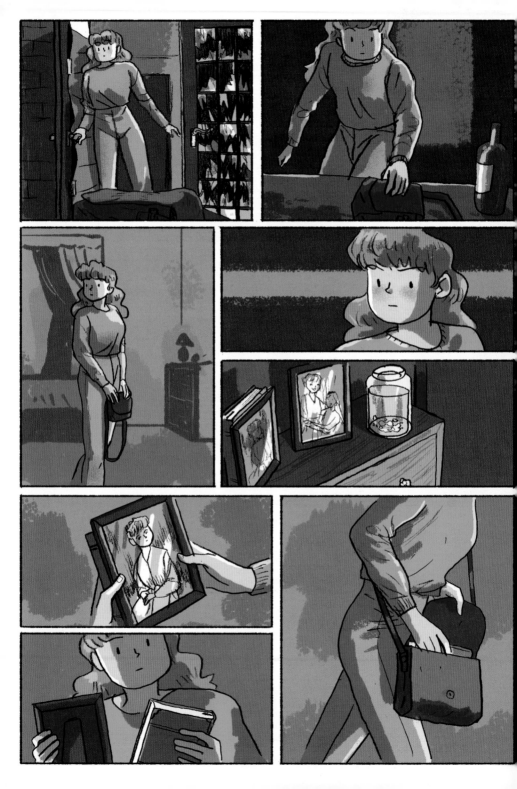

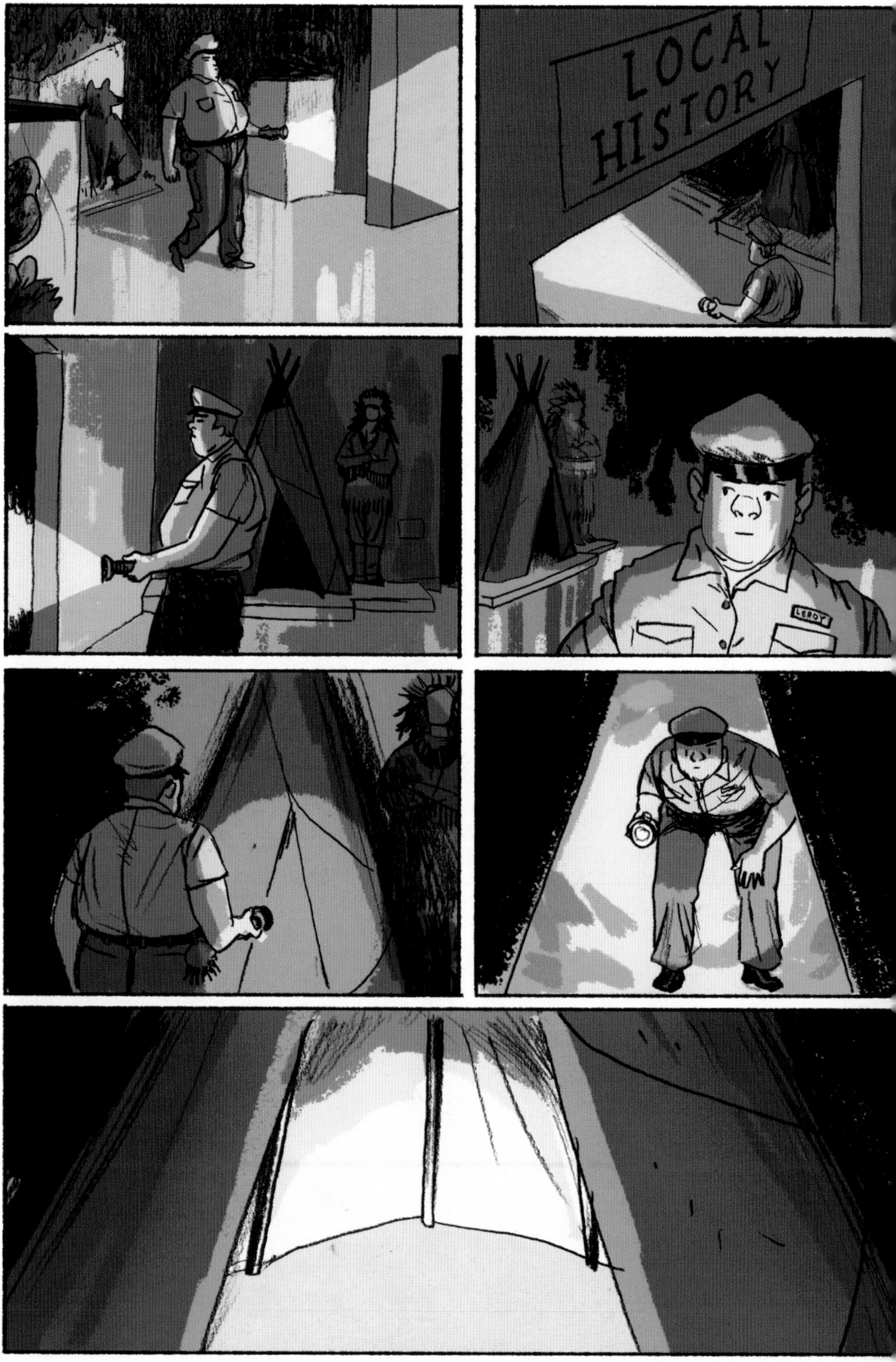
LOCAL HISTORY
LEROY

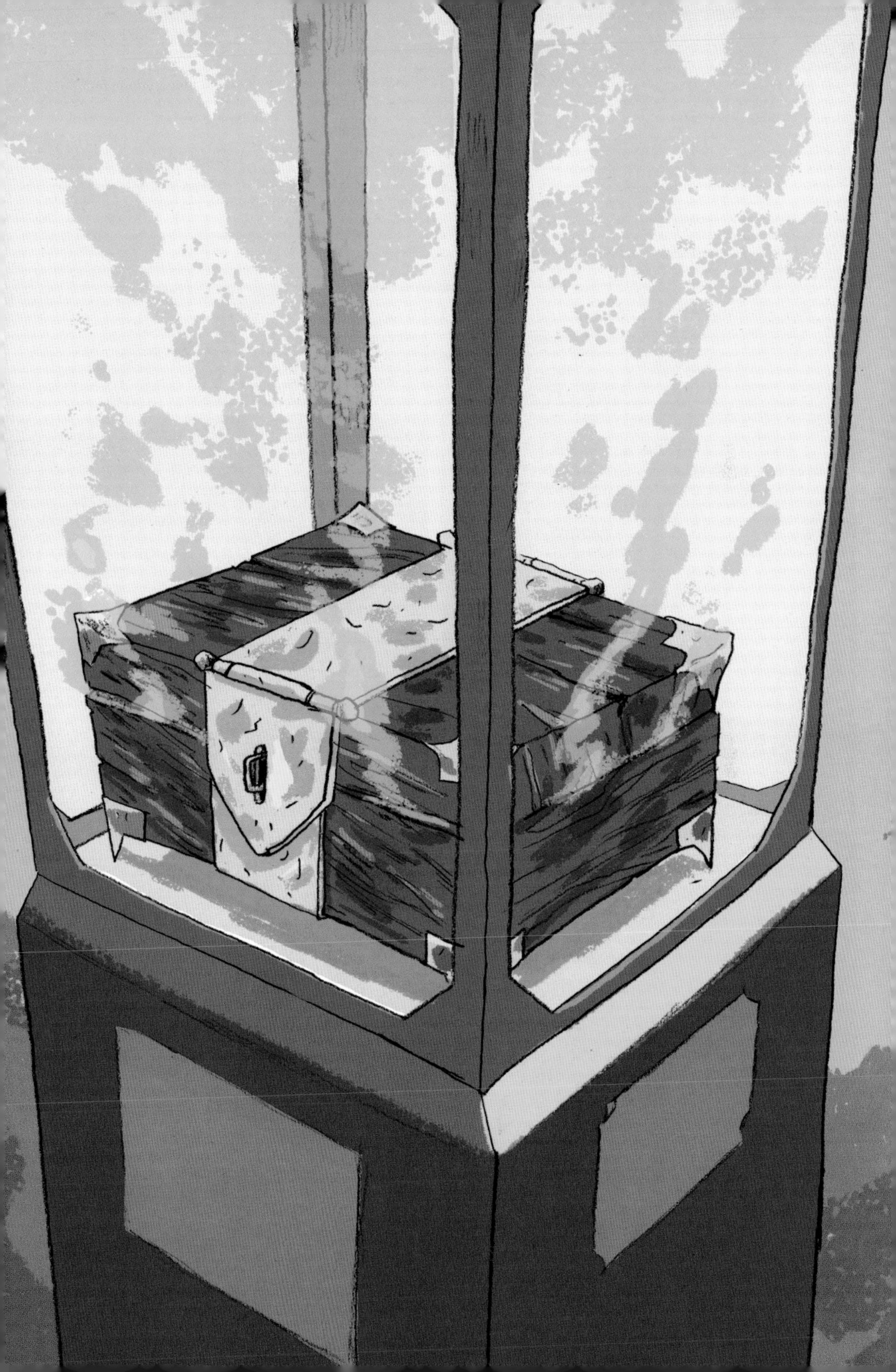

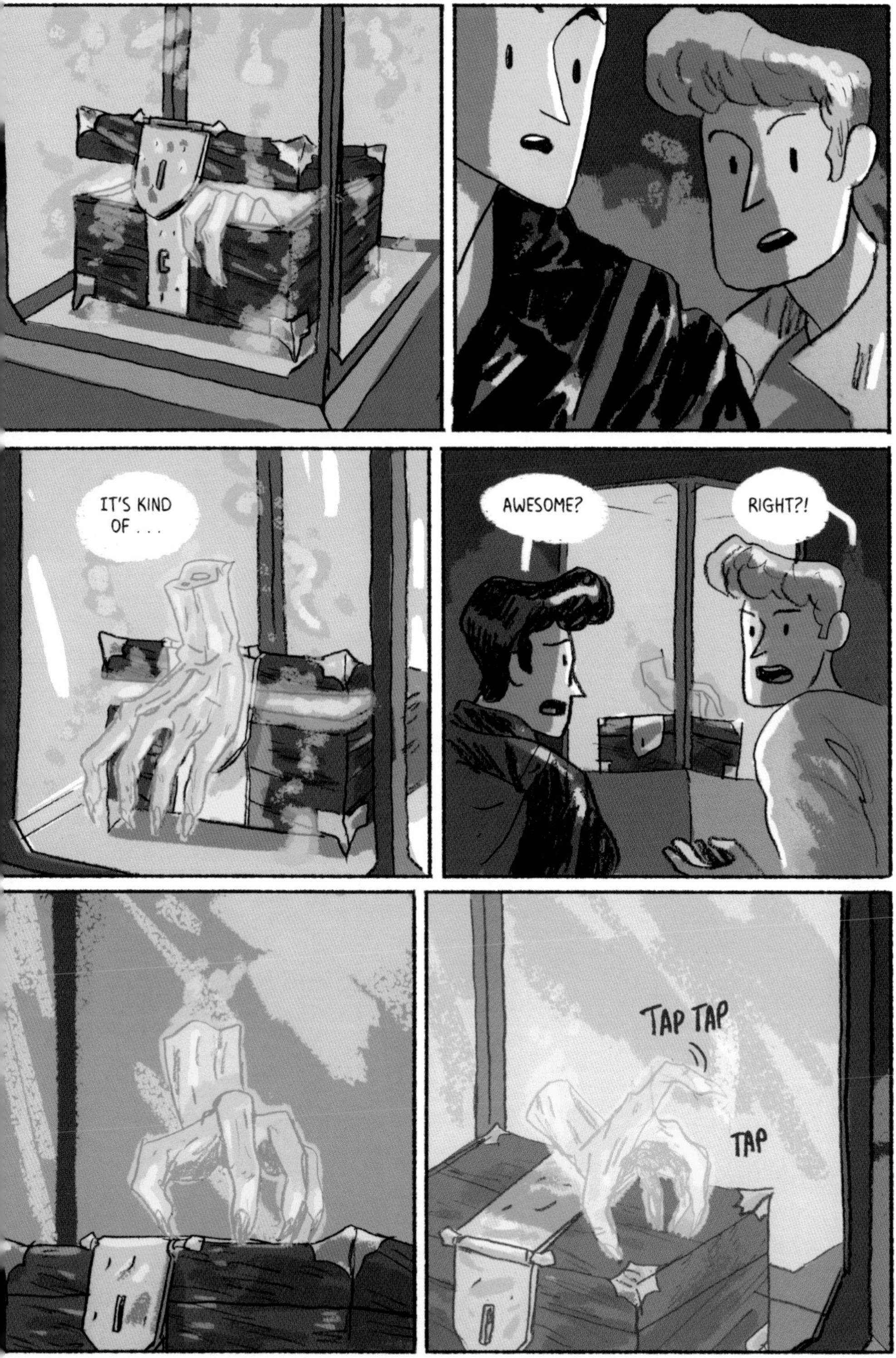
IT'S KIND OF . . .
AWESOME?
RIGHT?!
TAP TAP
TAP

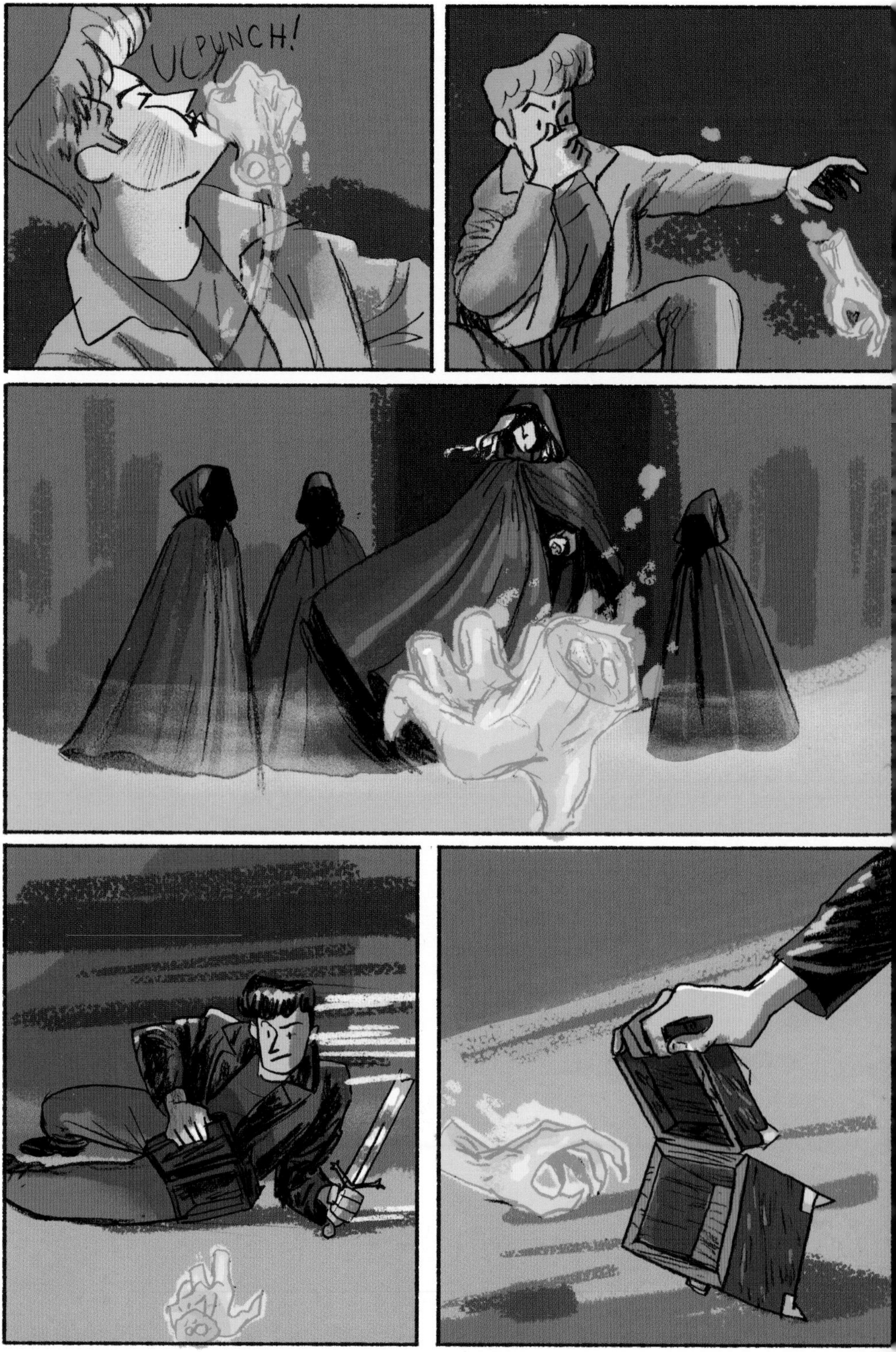
ULPUNCH!

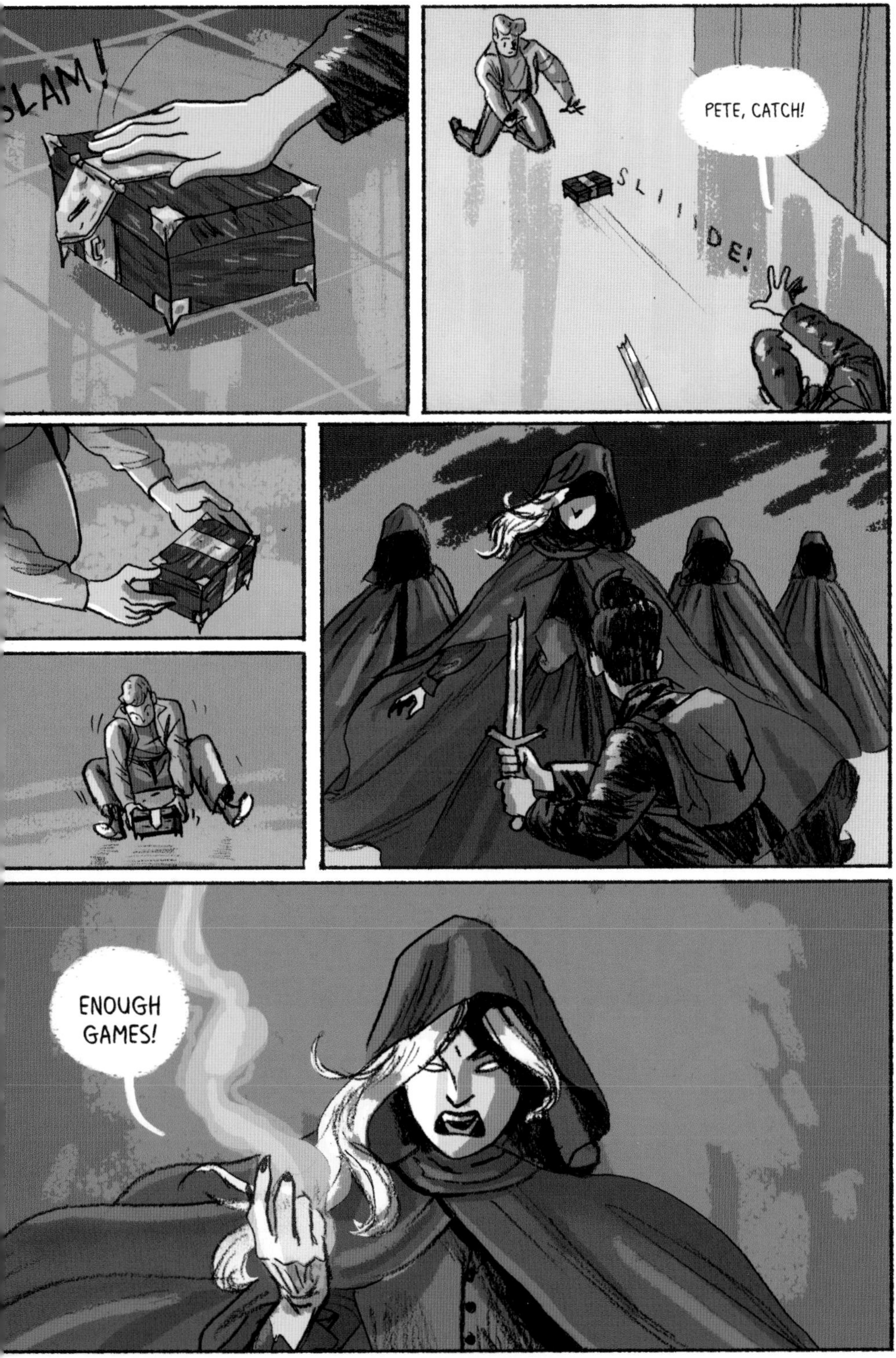
SLAM!
PETE, CATCH!
SLIIIIDE!
ENOUGH GAMES!

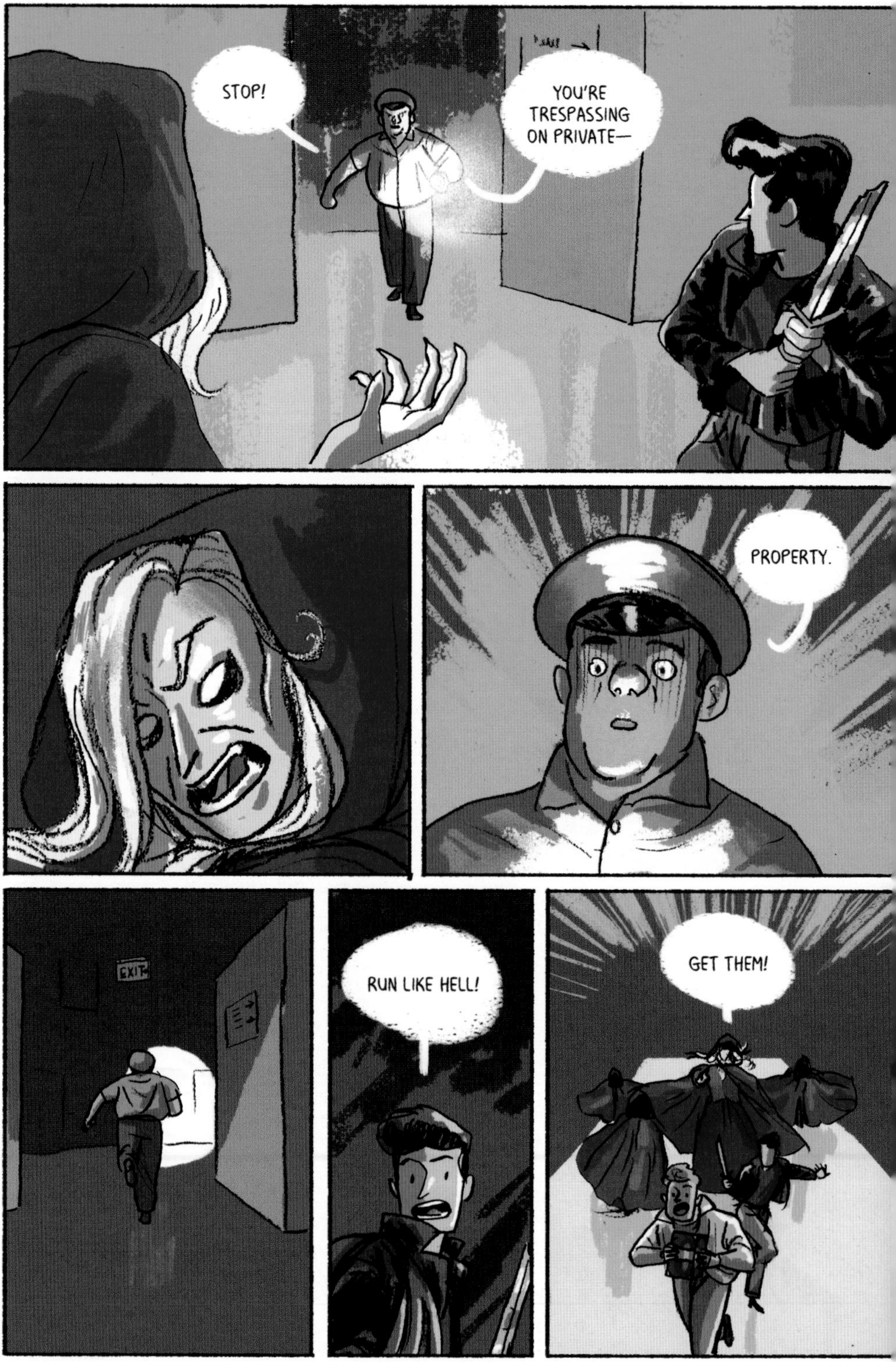

STOP!
YOU'RE TRESPASSING ON PRIVATE—
PROPERTY.
RUN LIKE HELL!
GET THEM!

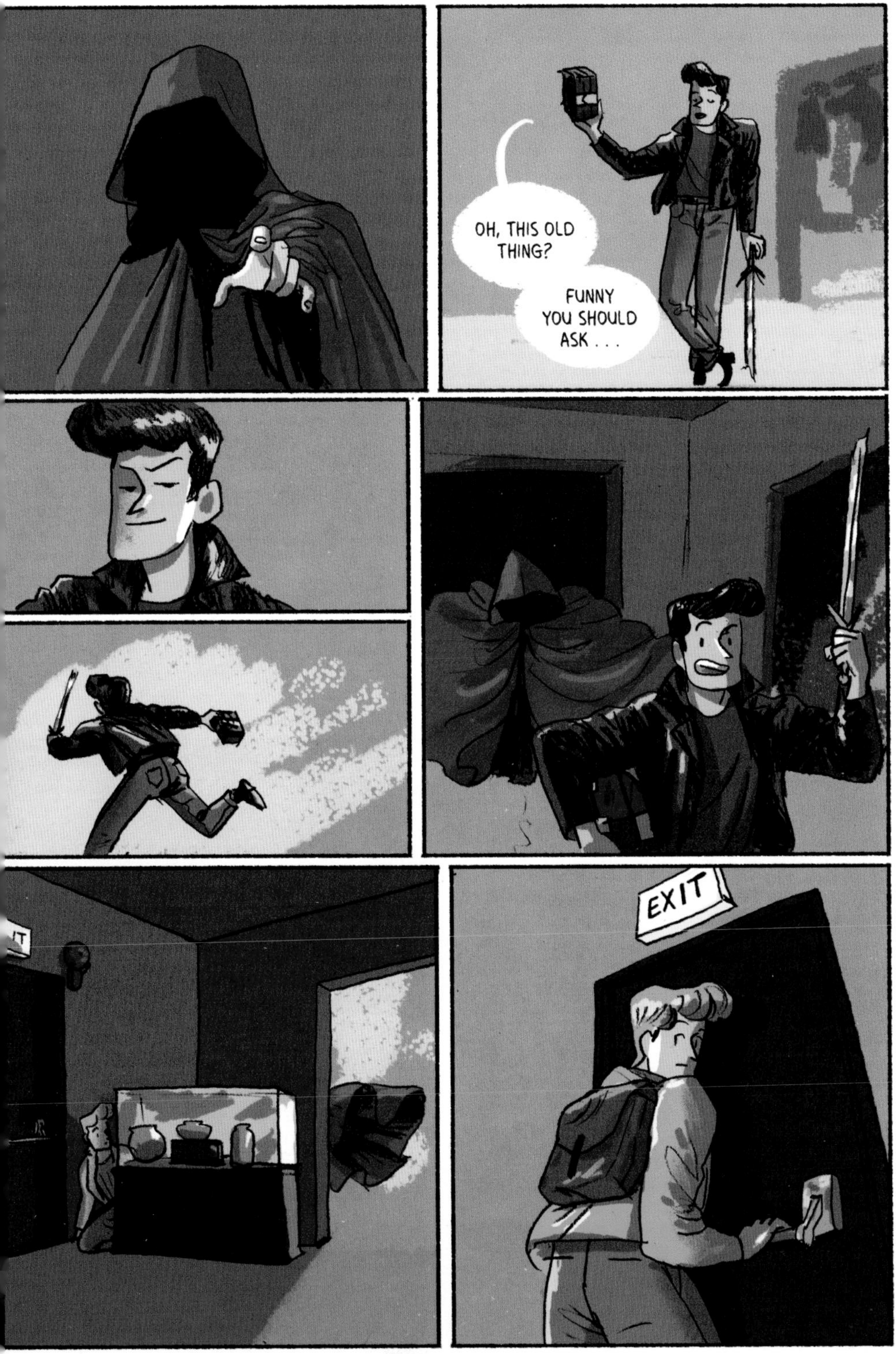
OH, THIS OLD THING?
FUNNY YOU SHOULD ASK . . .
EXIT

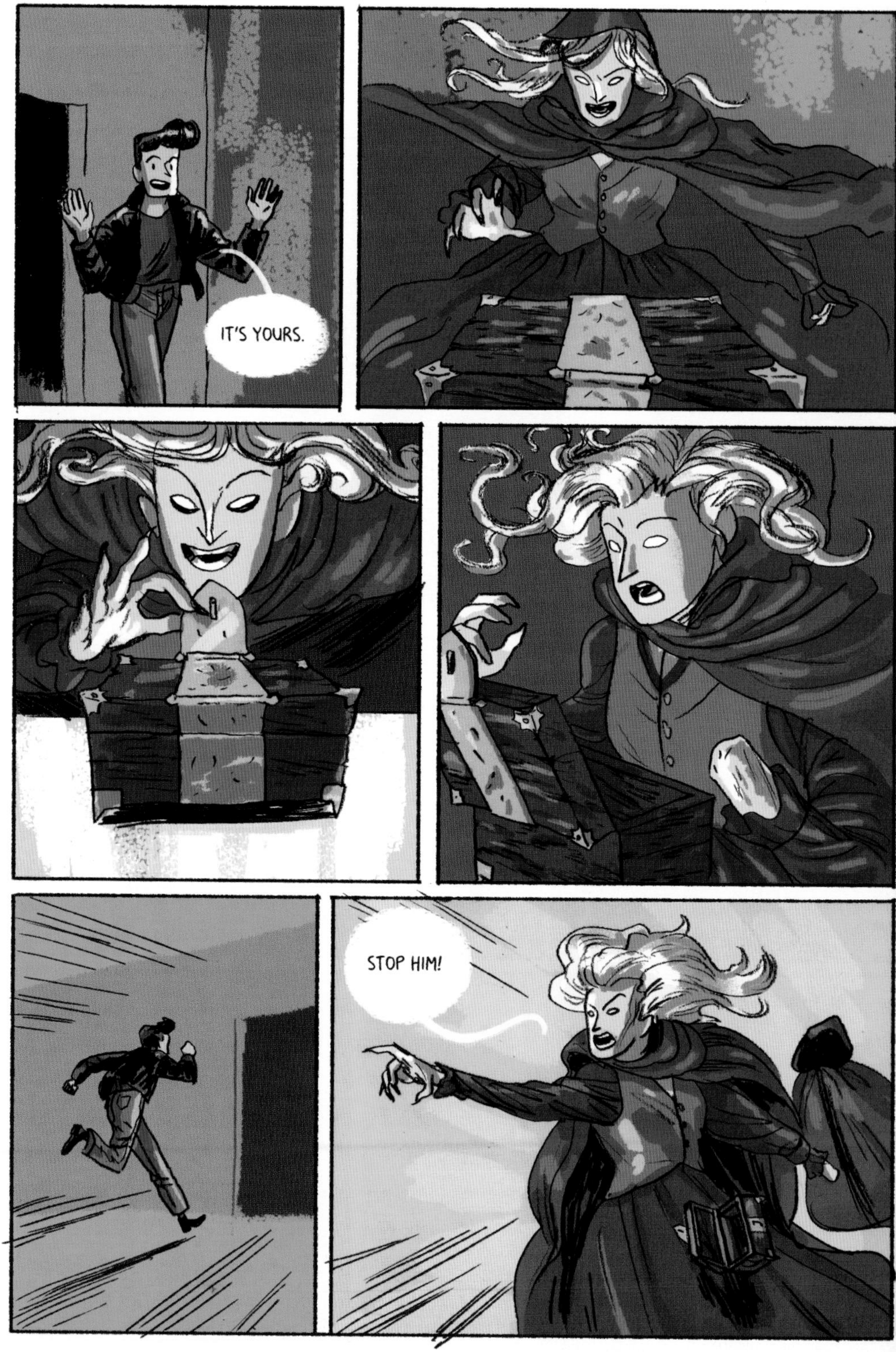
IT'S YOURS.
STOP HIM!

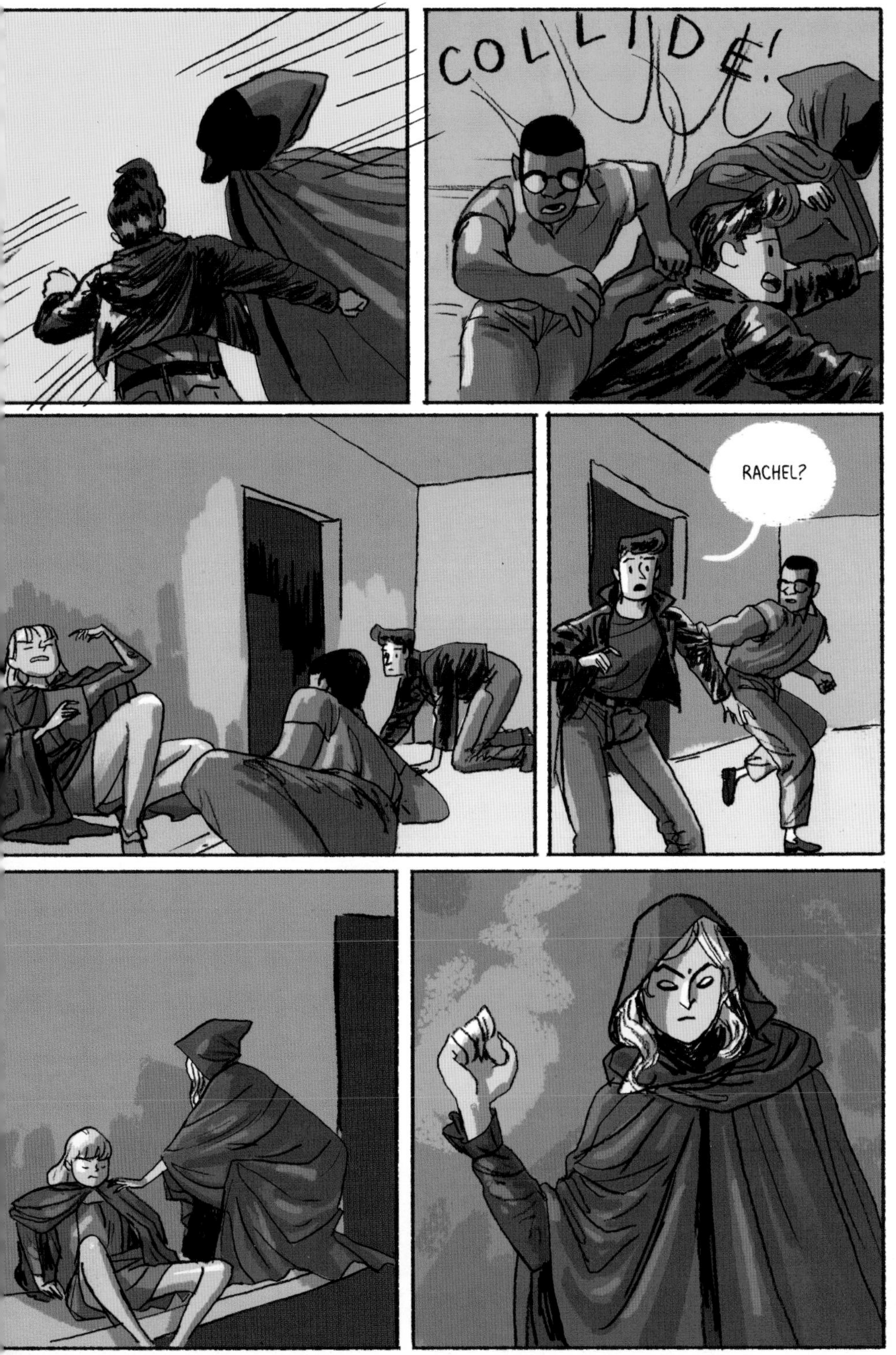
COLLIDE!
RACHEL?

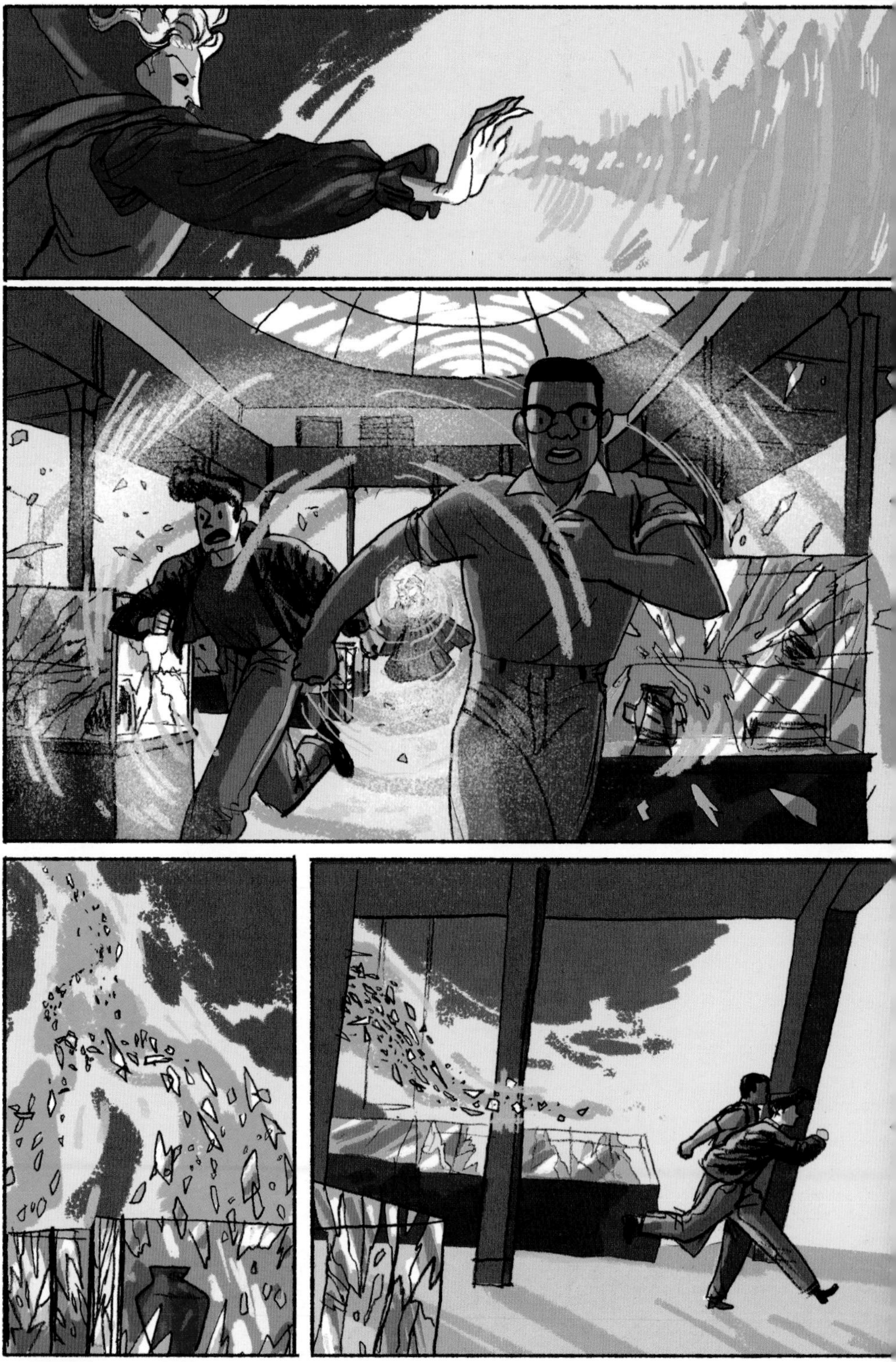

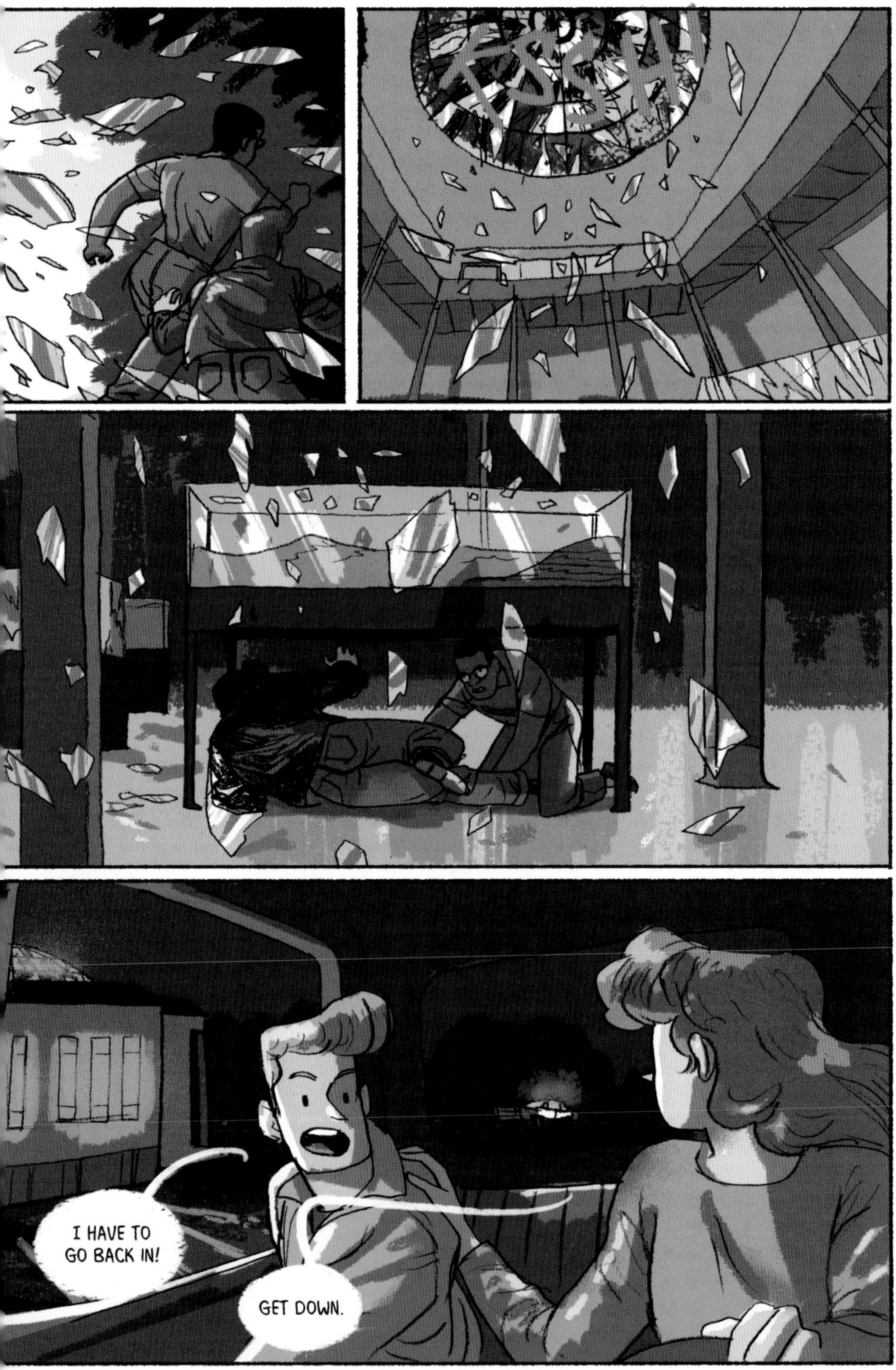
KRSSH
I HAVE TO GO BACK IN!
GET DOWN.

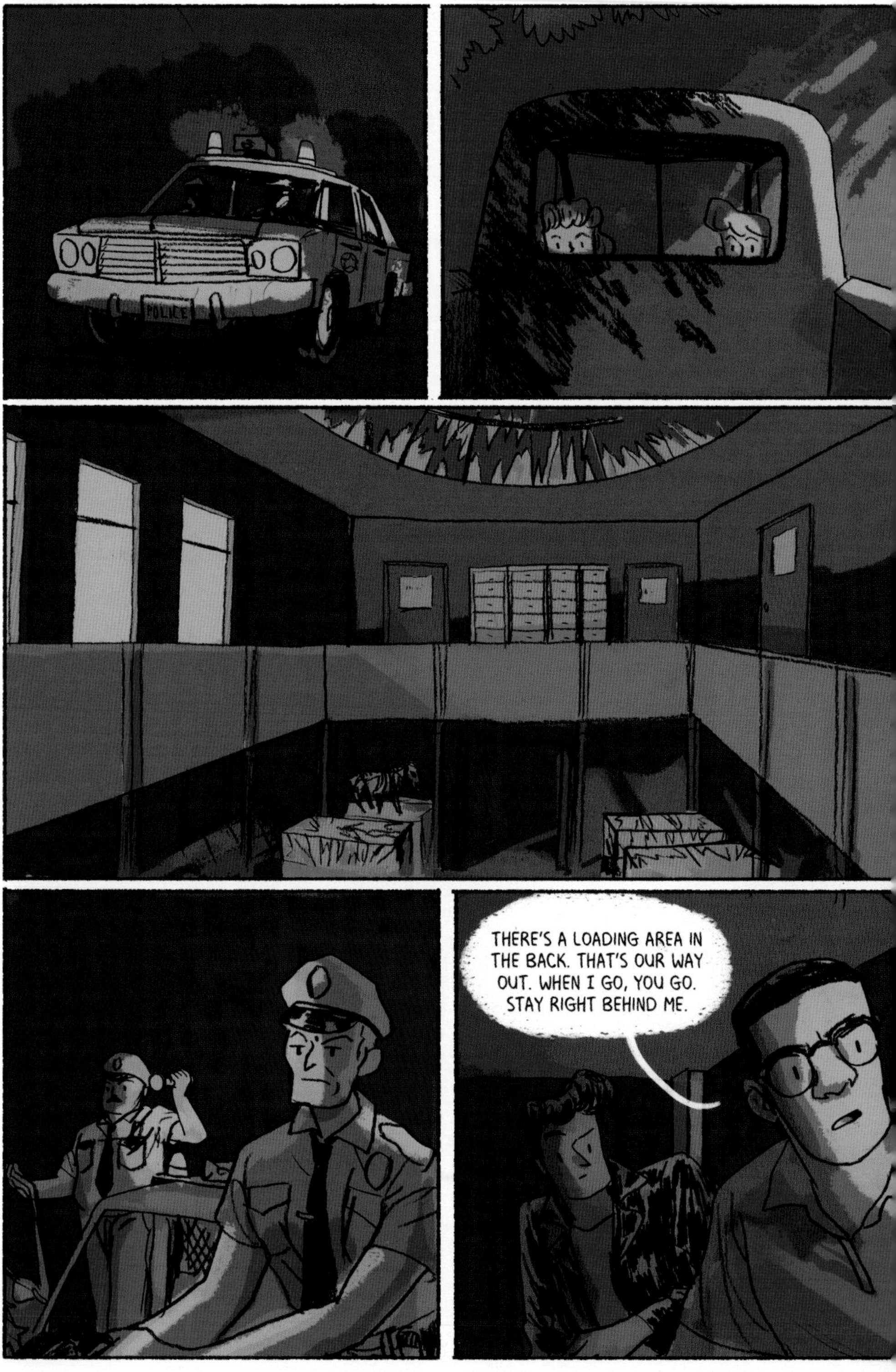
POLICE
THERE'S A LOADING AREA IN THE BACK. THAT'S OUR WAY OUT. WHEN I GO, YOU GO. STAY RIGHT BEHIND ME.

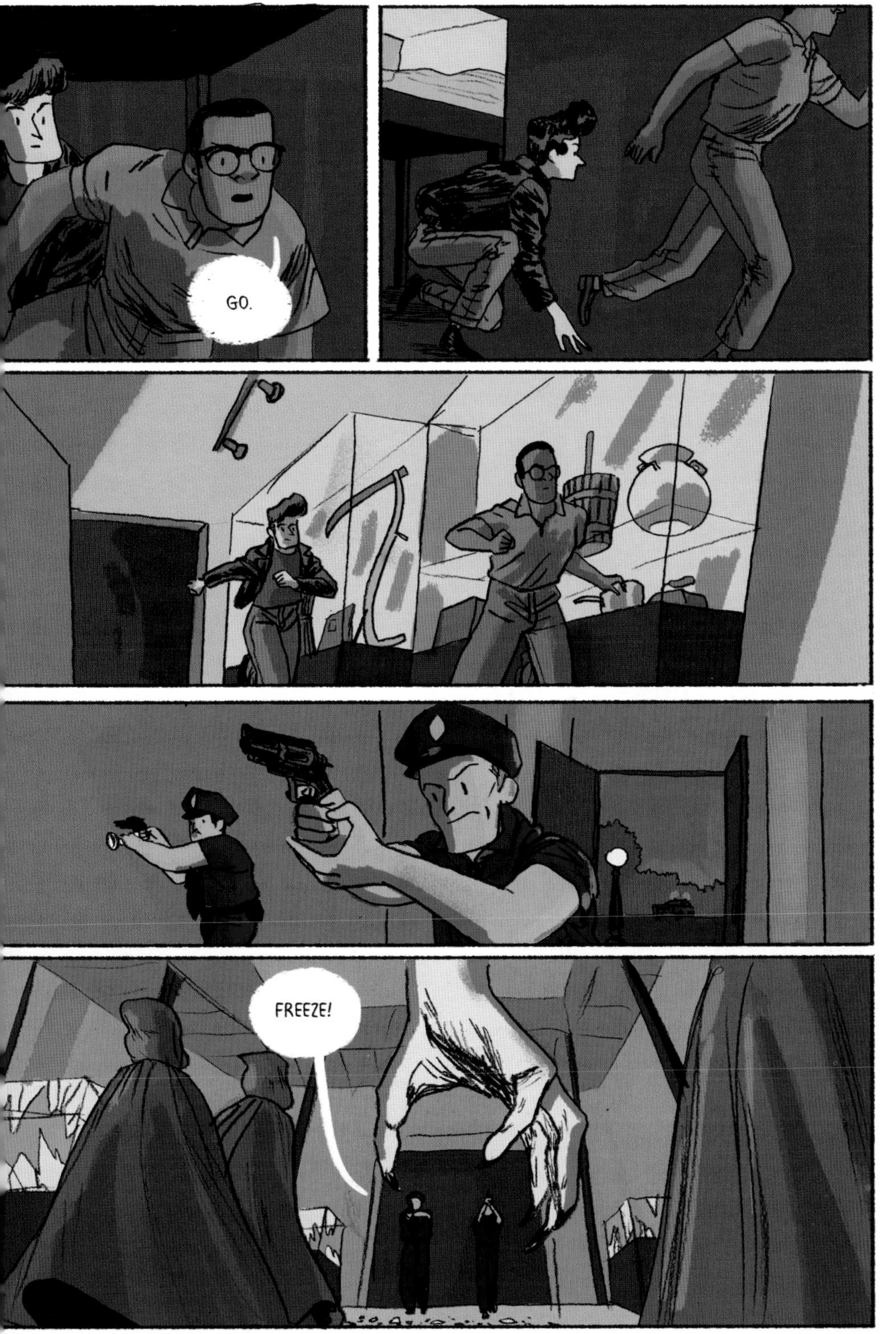
GO.
FREEZE!

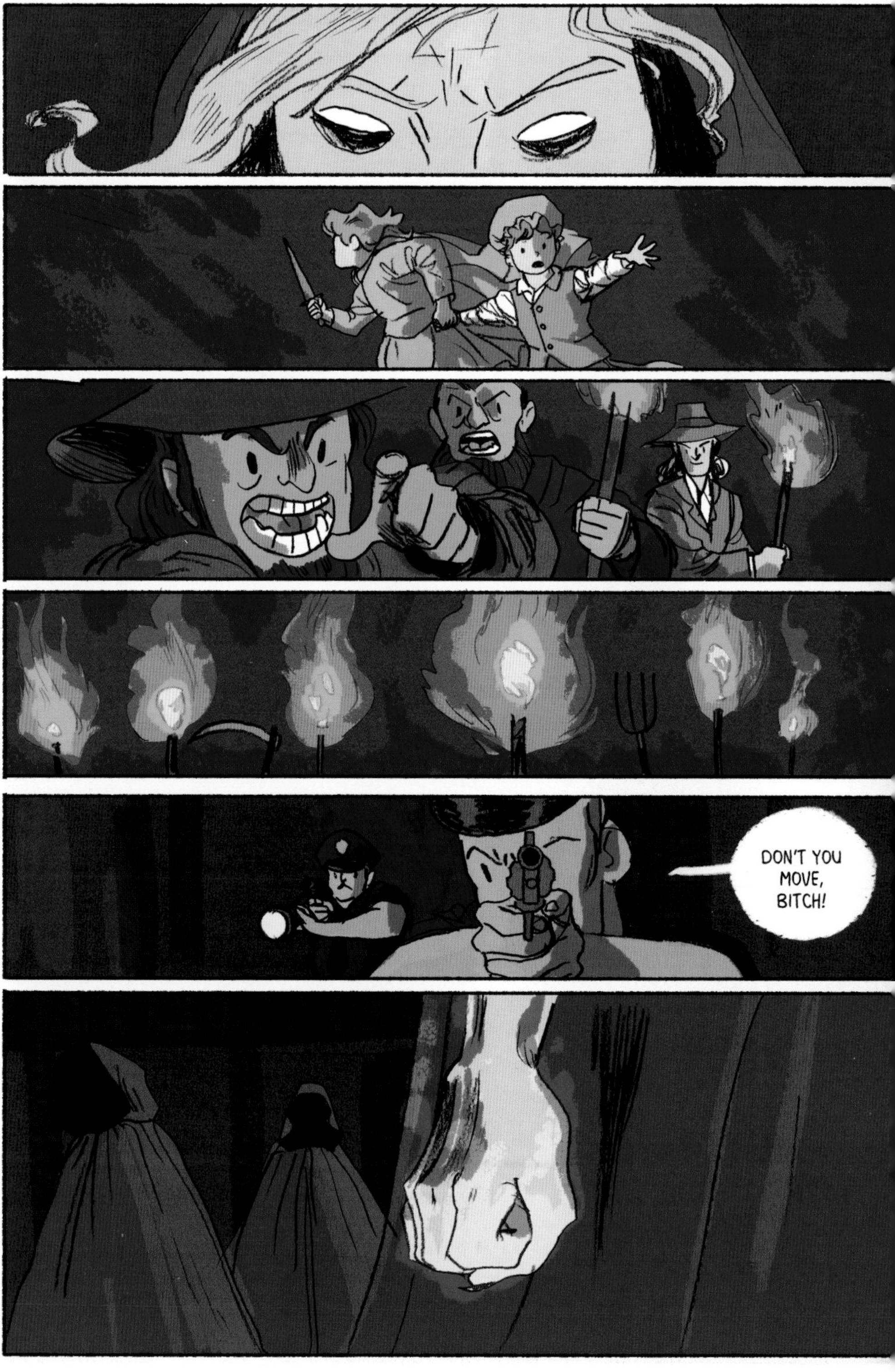
DON'T YOU MOVE, BITCH!

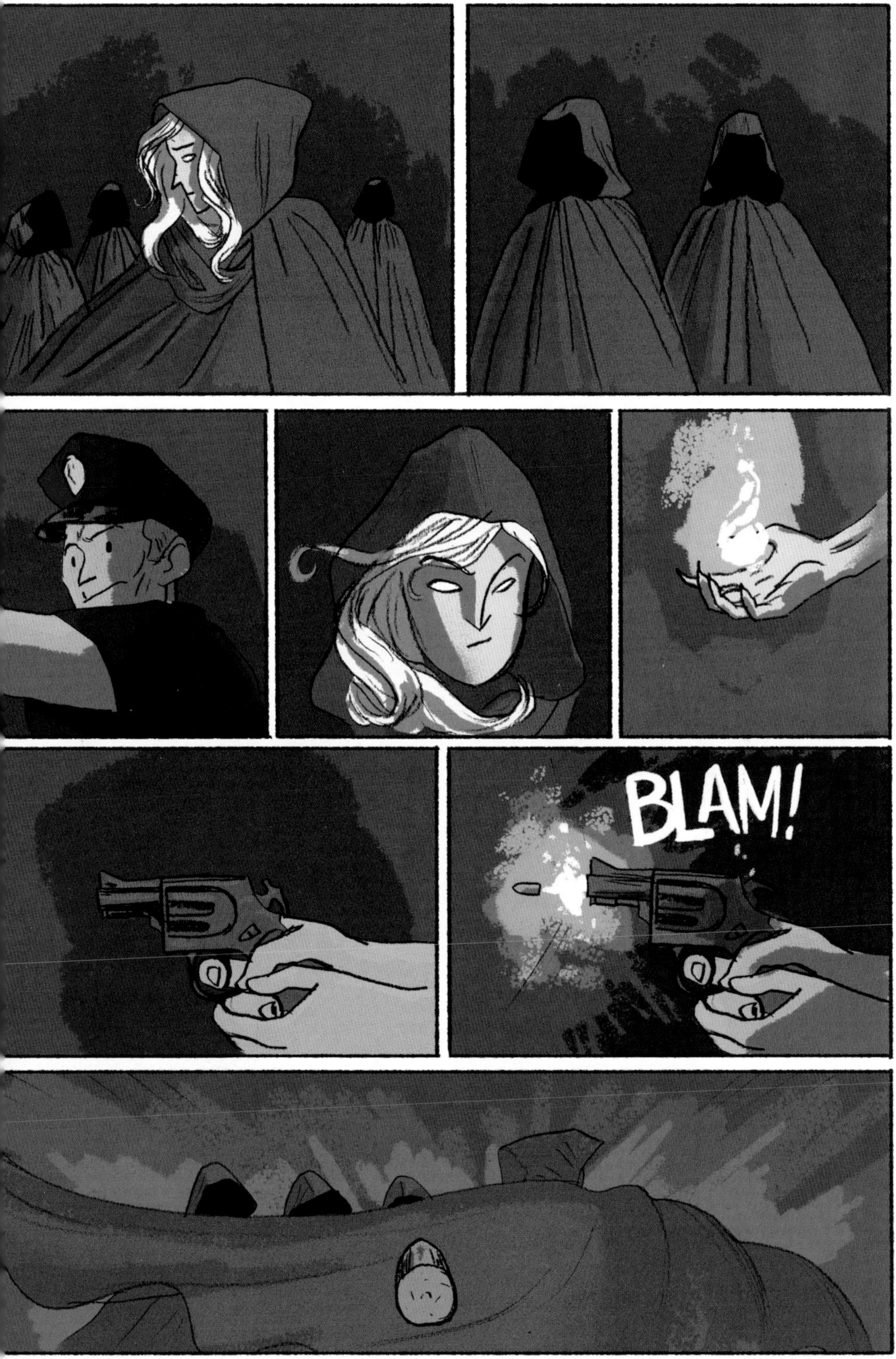
BLAM!

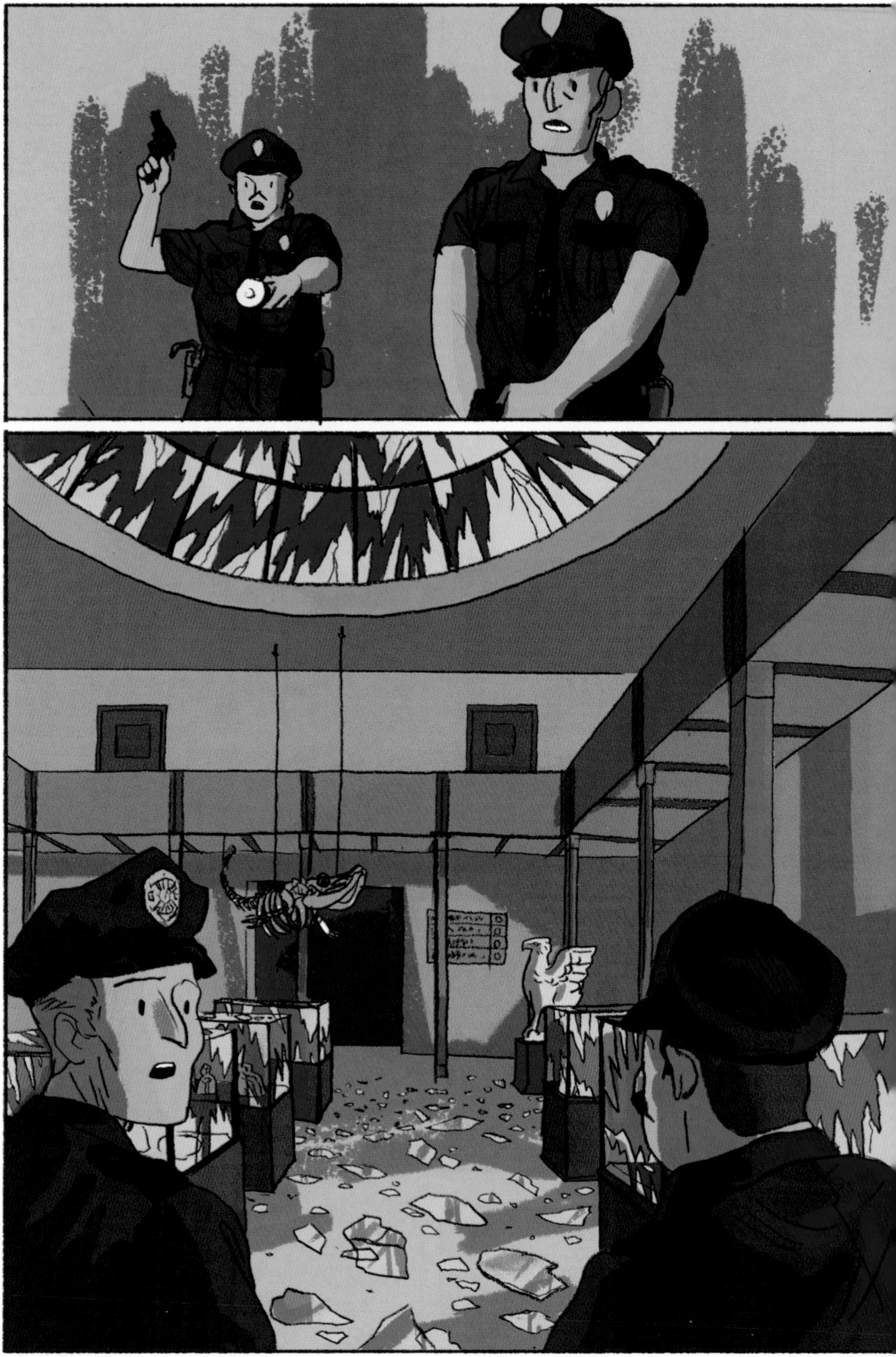

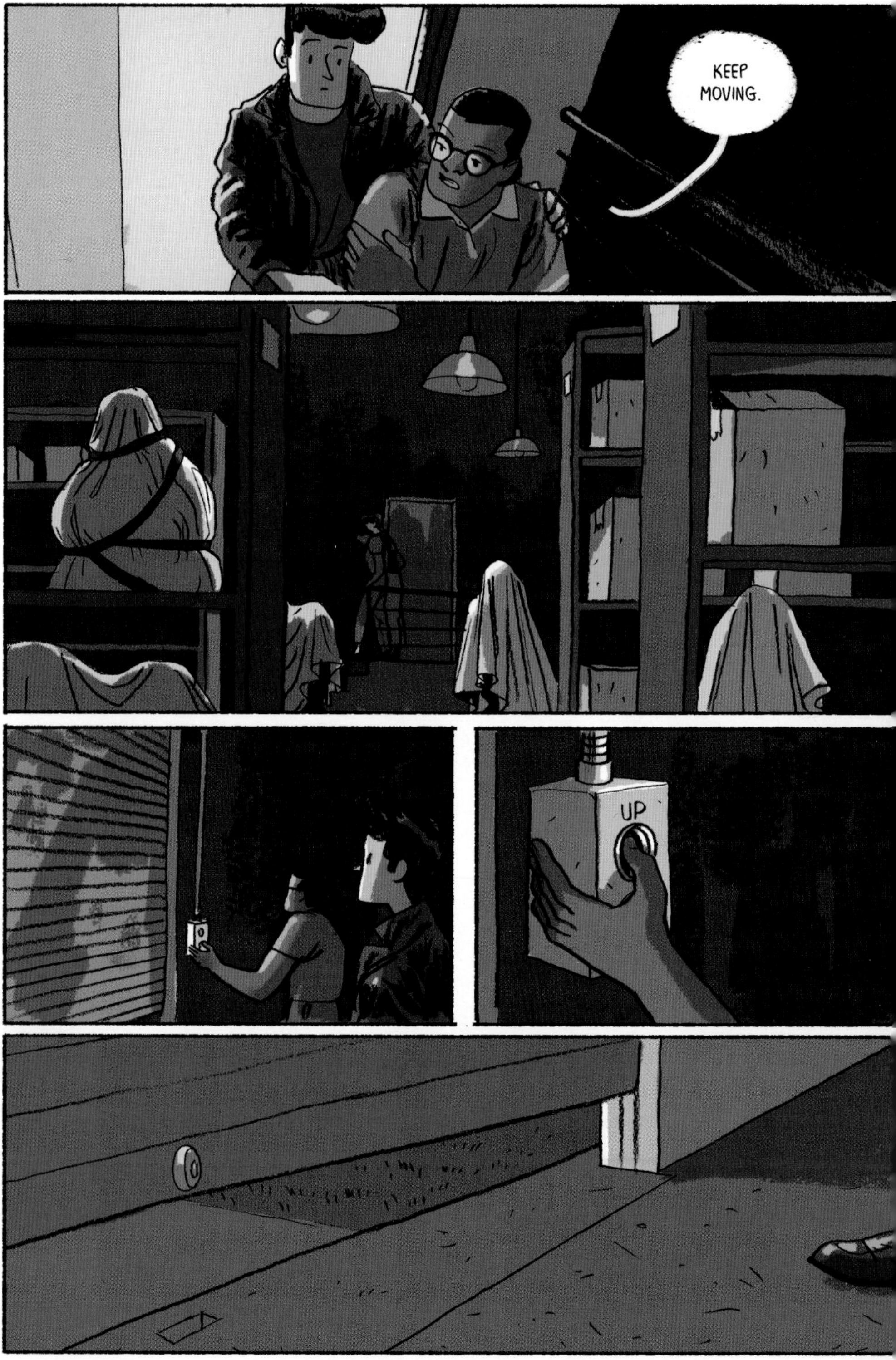
KEEP MOVING.
UP

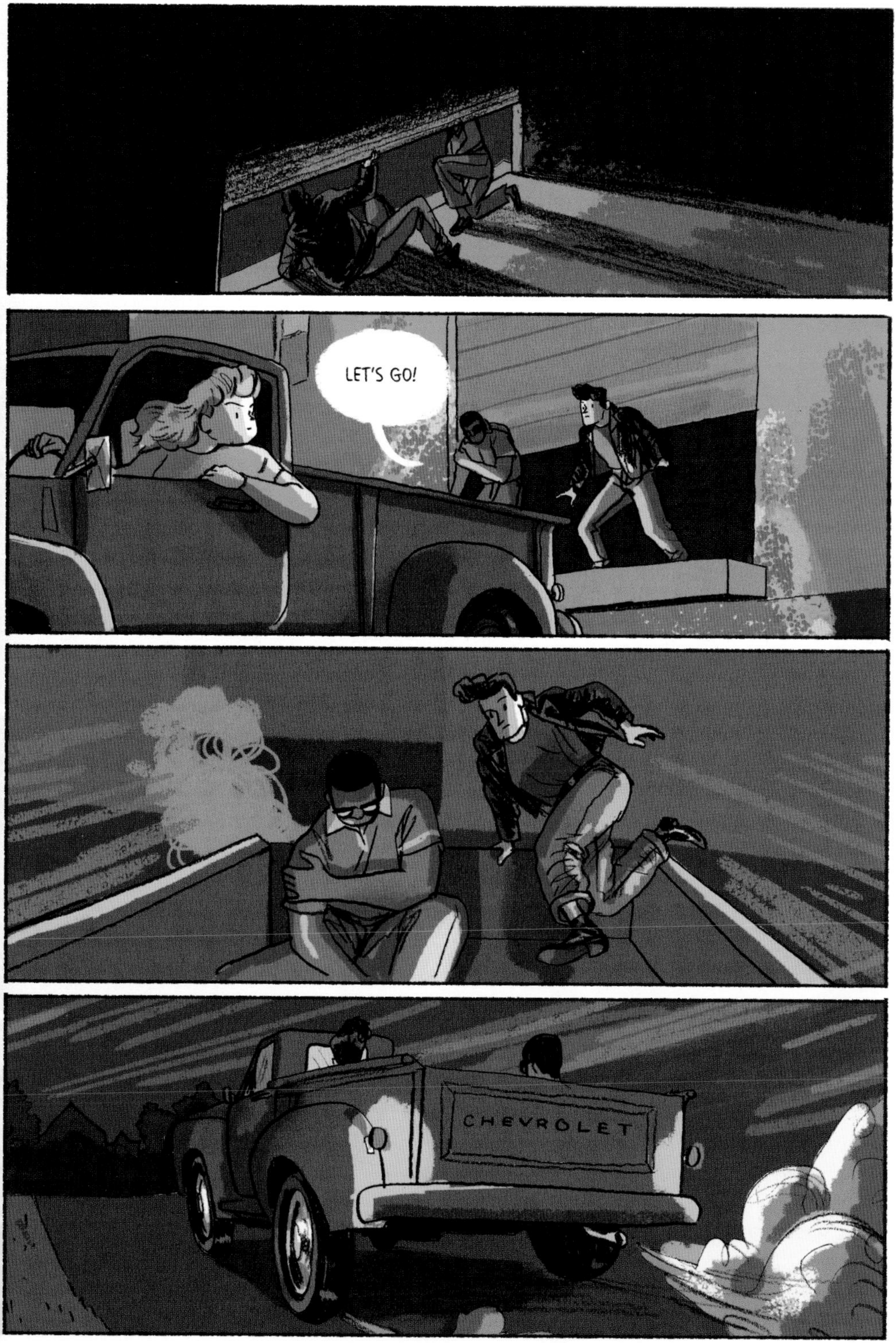
LET'S GO!
CHEVROLET

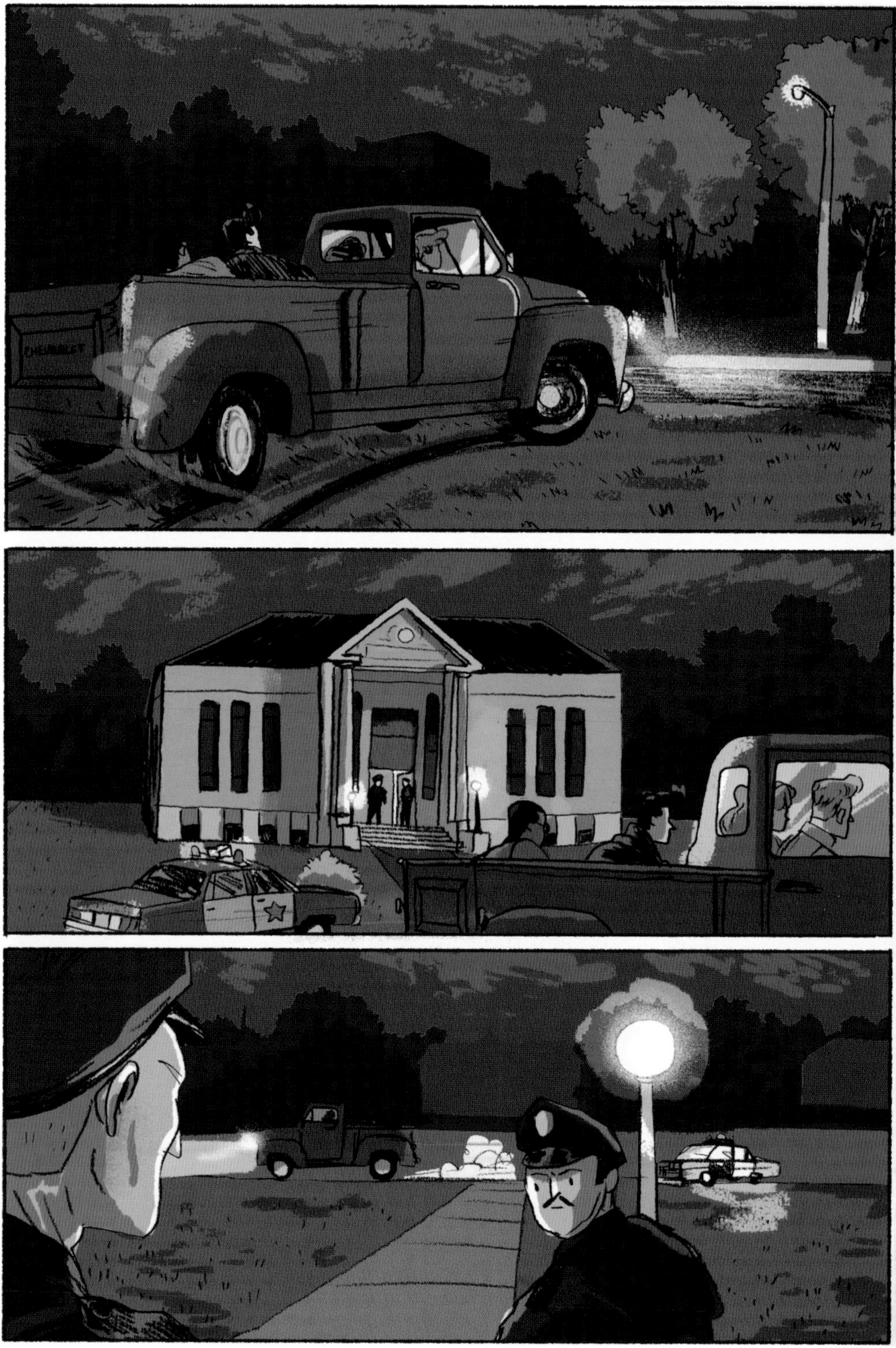

CHAPTER 5

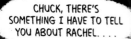

CHUCK, THERE'S SOMETHING I HAVE TO TELL YOU ABOUT RACHEL. . . .

LET ME GUESS. SHE WASN'T "TAKEN" AFTER ALL?

THAT'S A PRETTY INCREDIBLE GUESS.

YOU GUYS WEREN'T THE ONLY ONES WHO FOUND SOMETHING.

I FOUND HER JOURNAL.

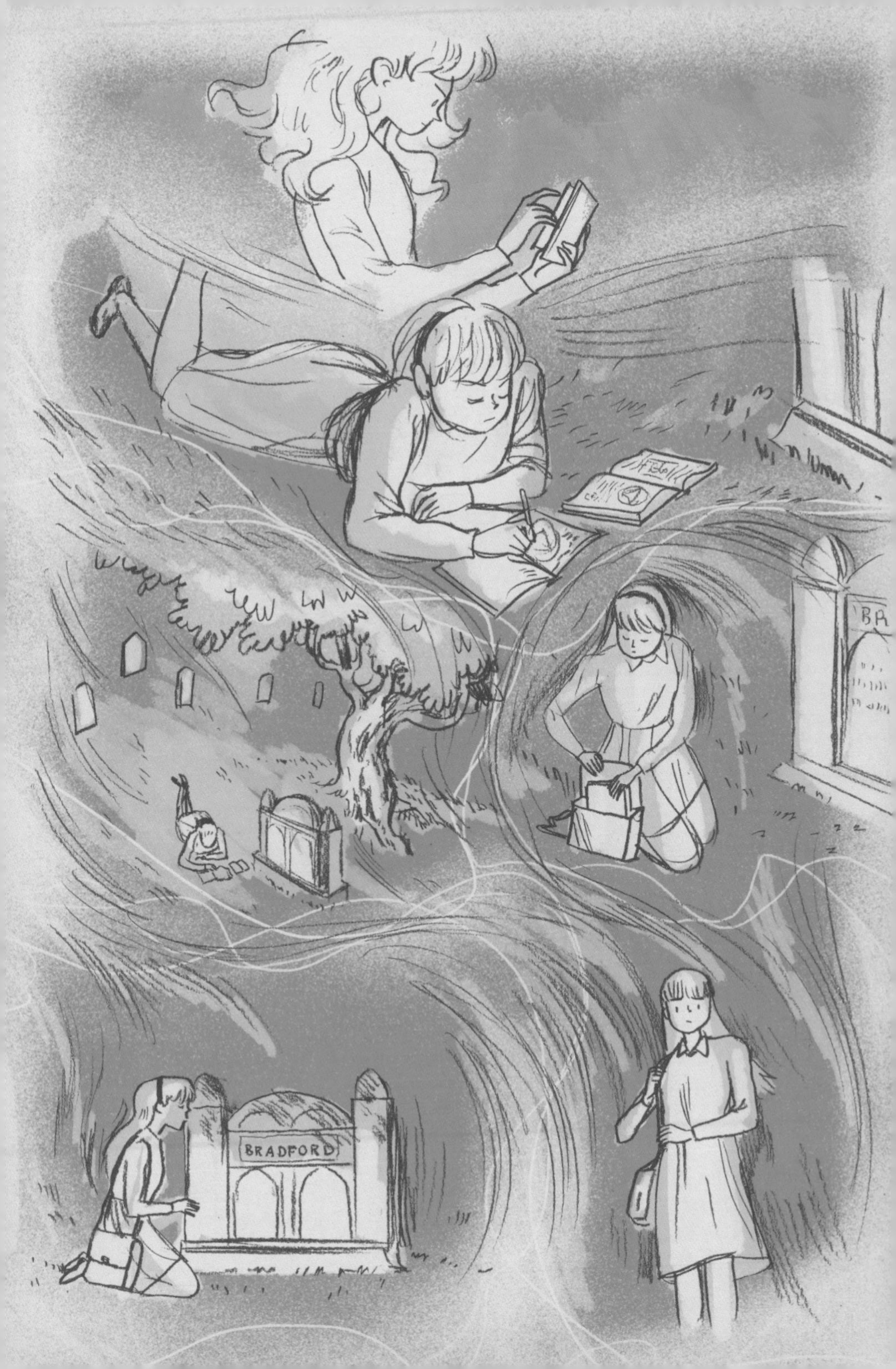
BRADFORD

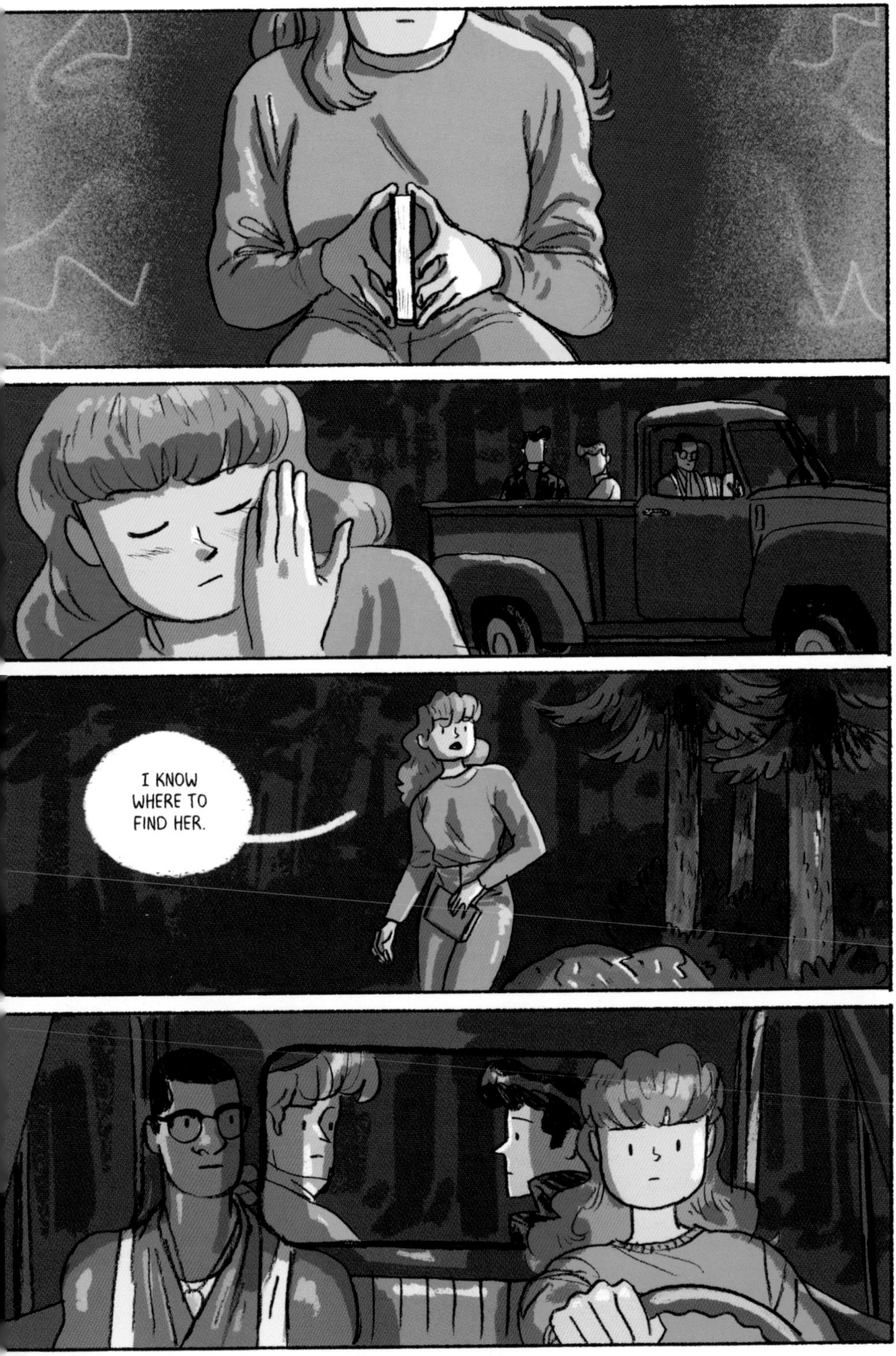
I KNOW WHERE TO FIND HER.

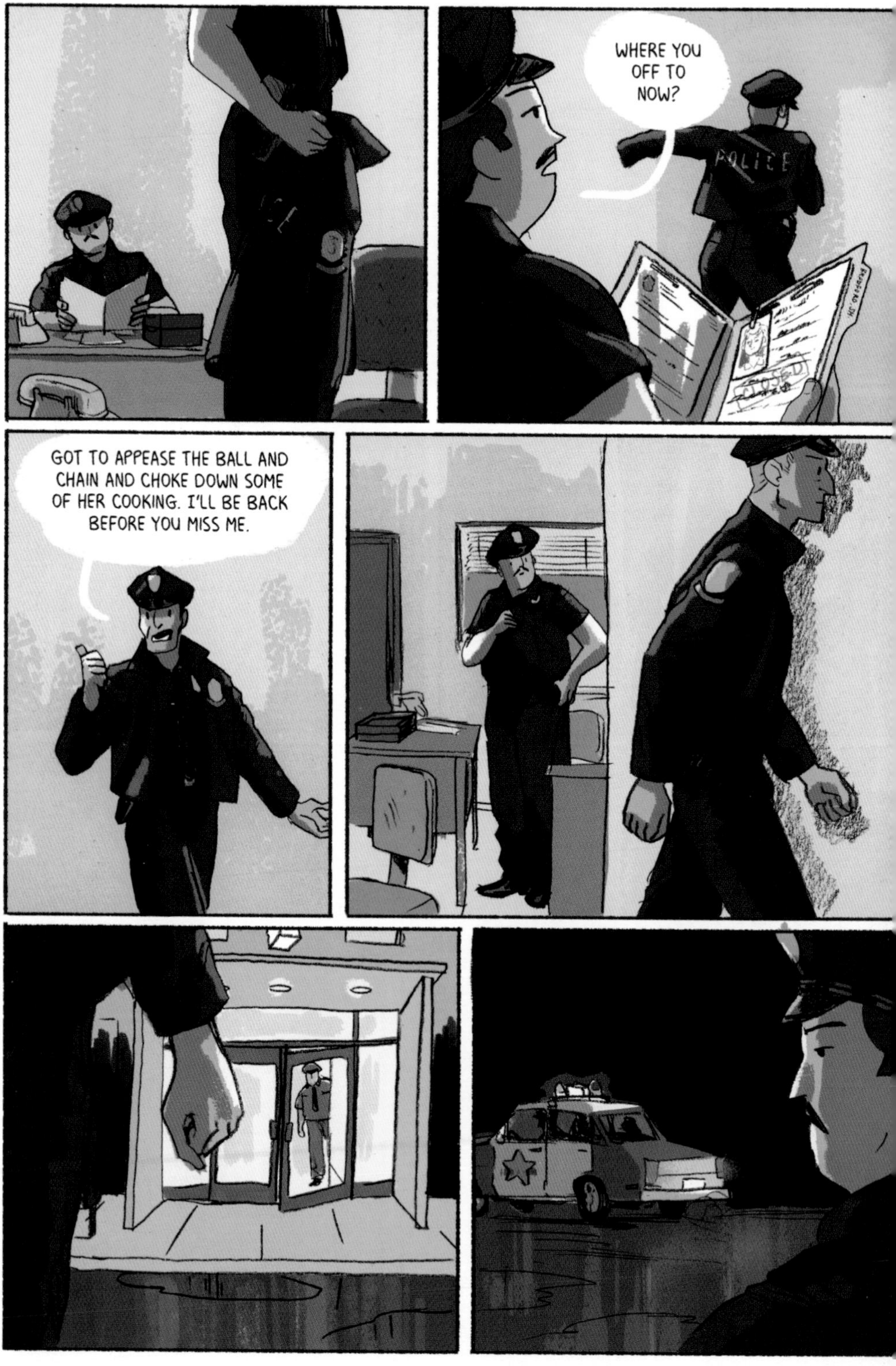
WHERE YOU OFF TO NOW?
POLICE
GOT TO APPEASE THE BALL AND CHAIN AND CHOKE DOWN SOME OF HER COOKING. I'LL BE BACK BEFORE YOU MISS ME.

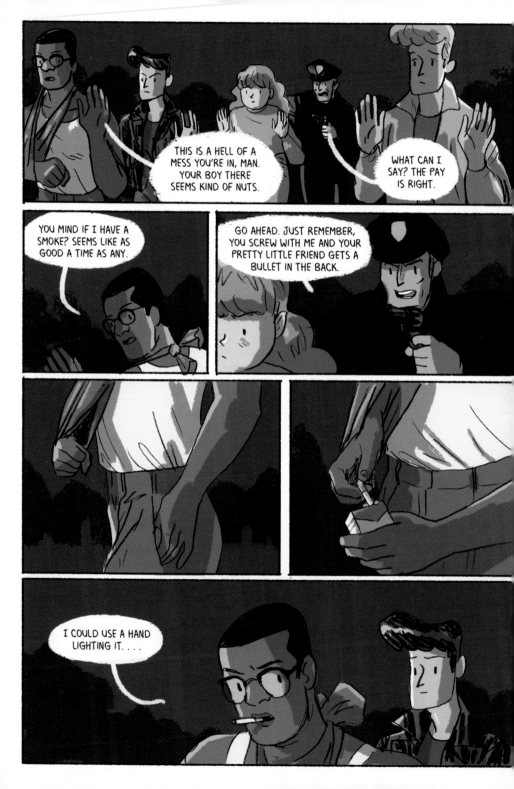

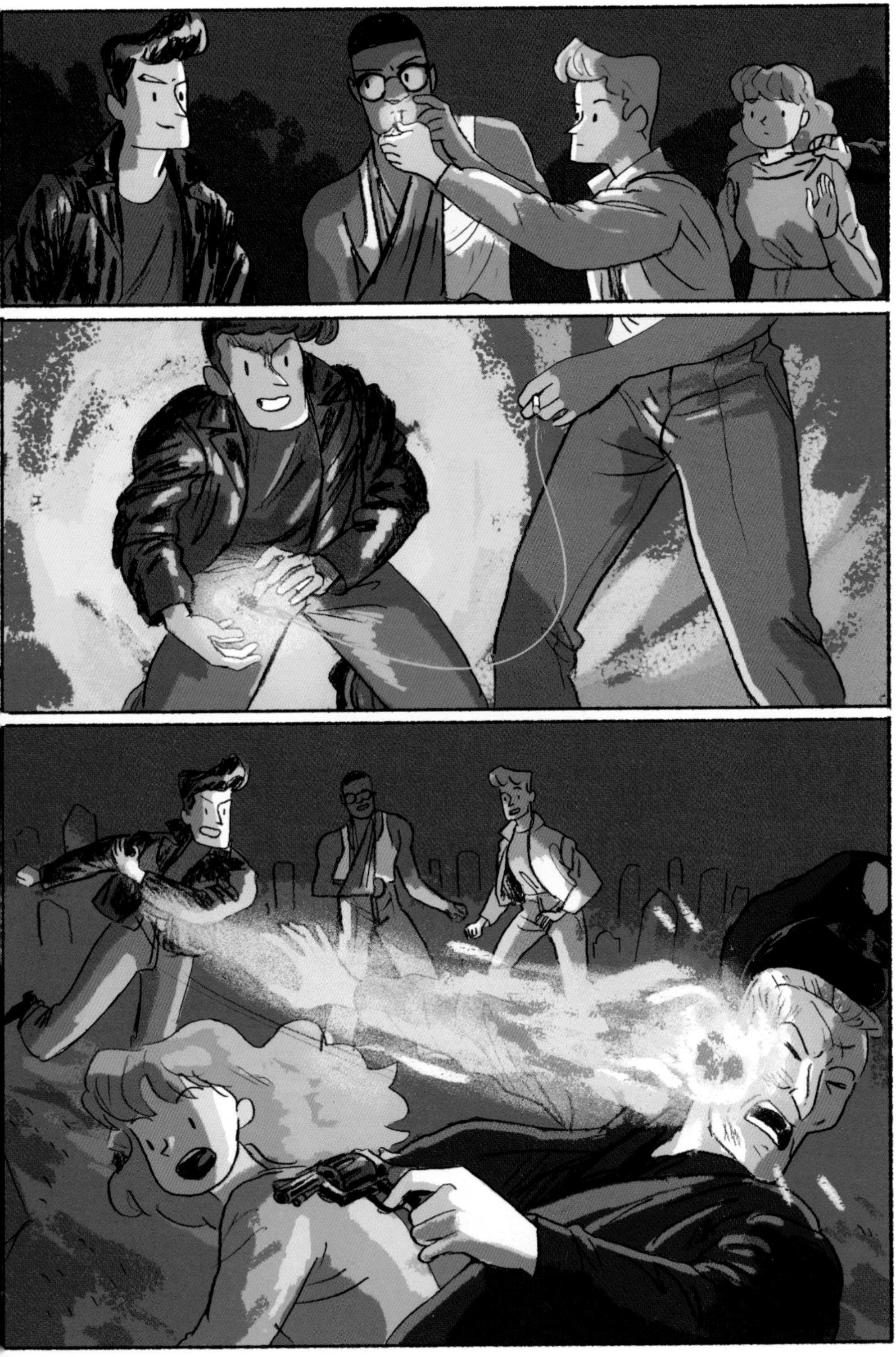

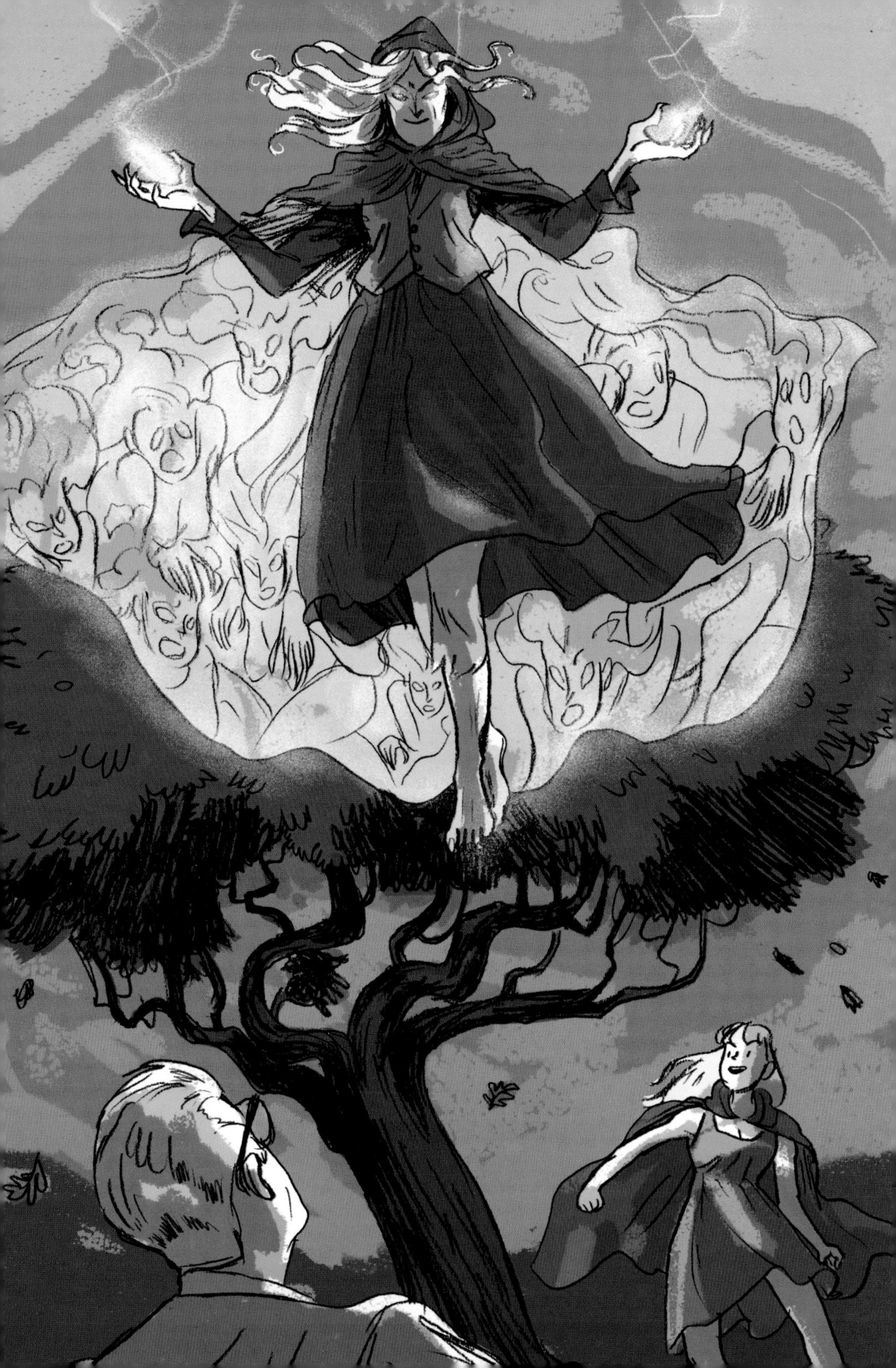

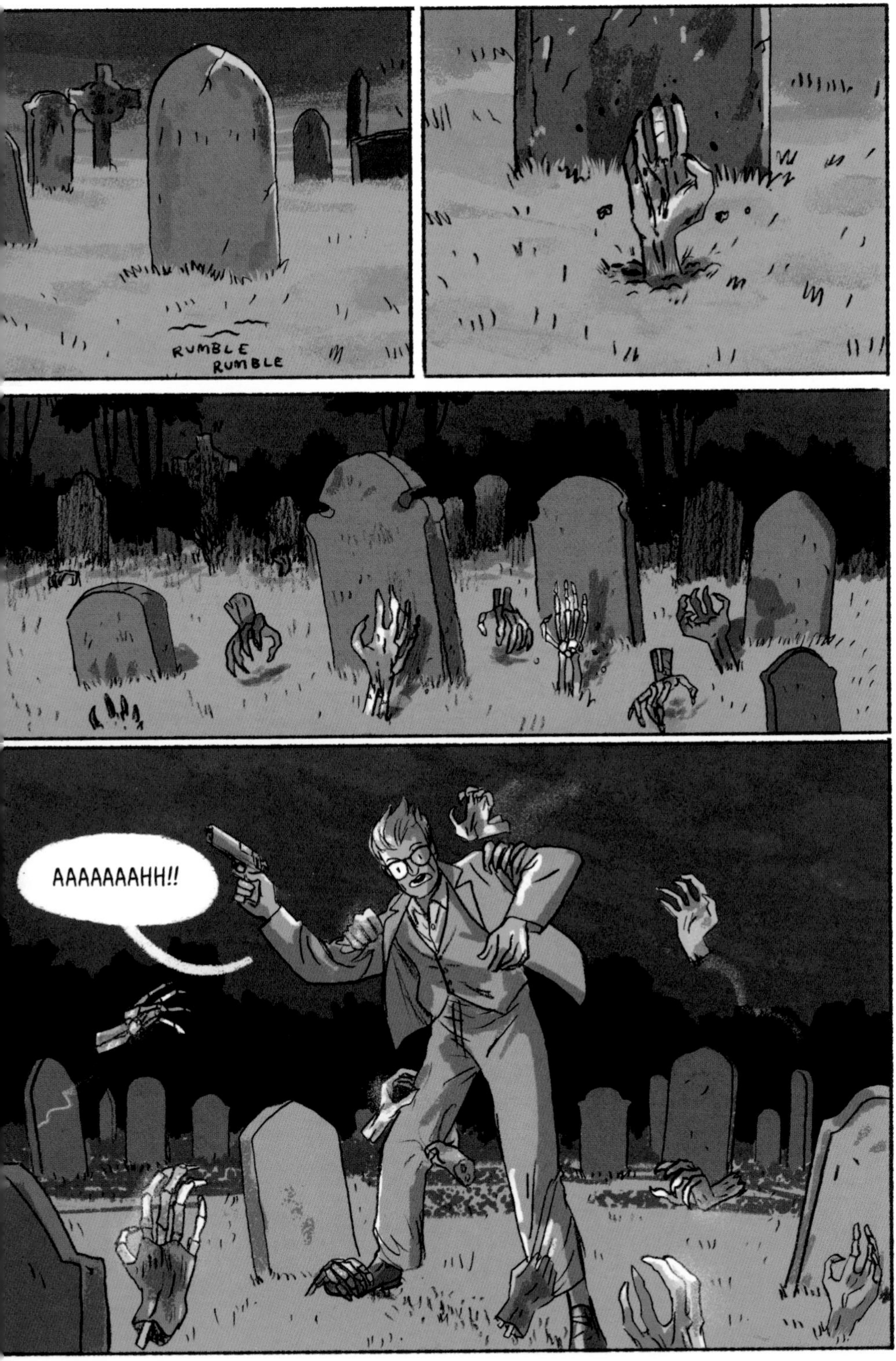
RUMBLE
RUMBLE
AAAAAAAHH!!

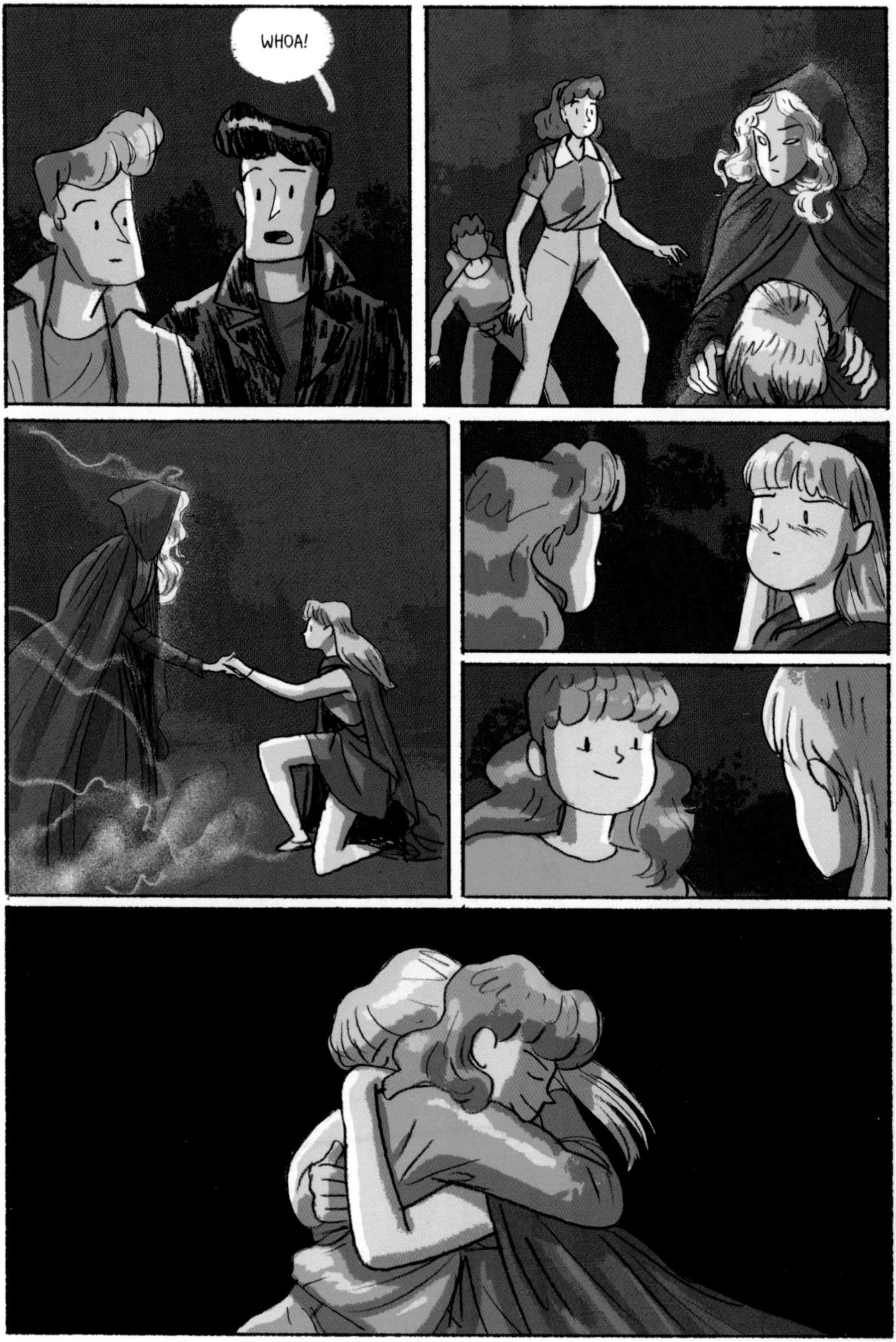
WHOA!

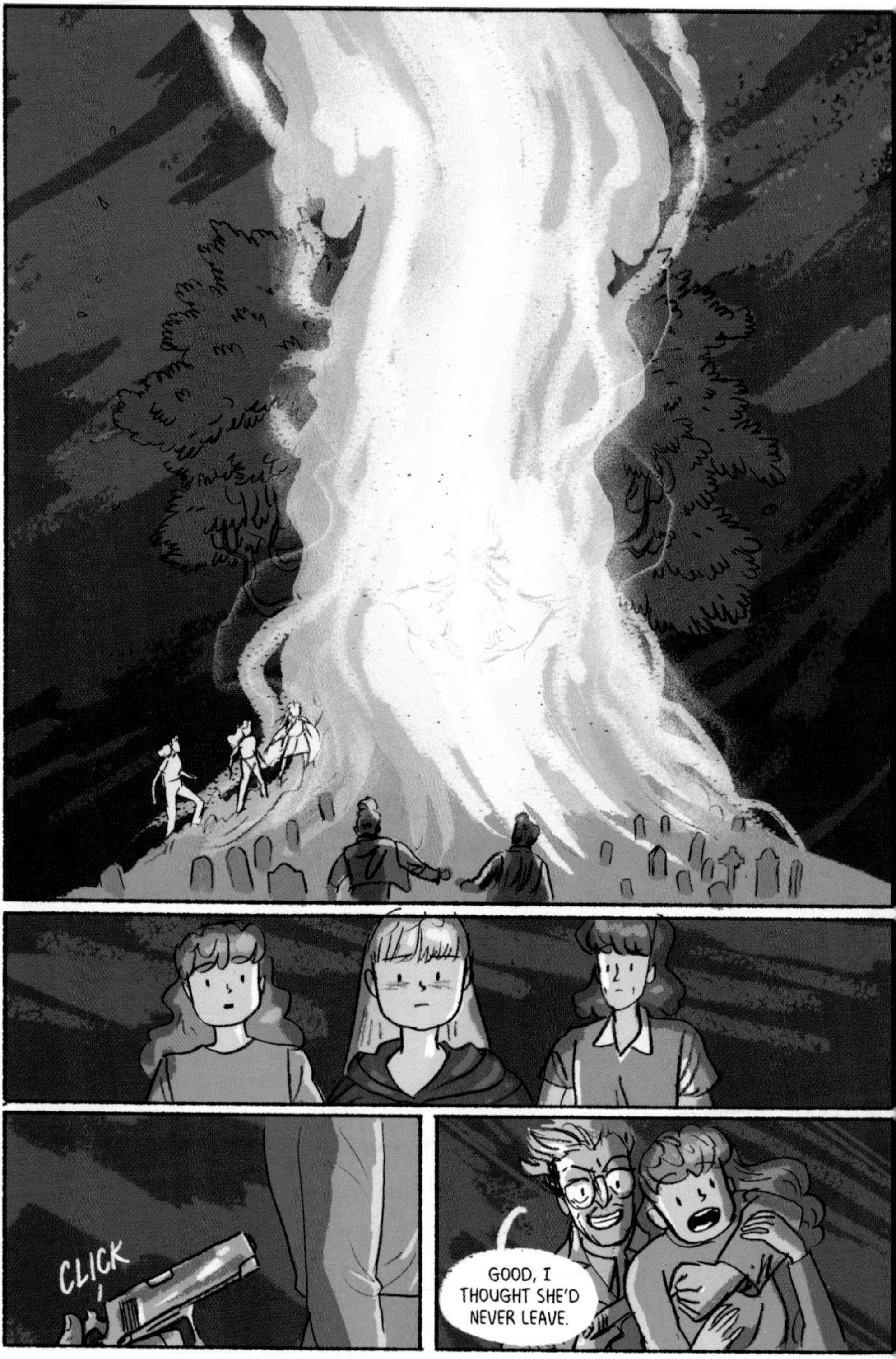
CLICK
GOOD, I THOUGHT SHE'D NEVER LEAVE.

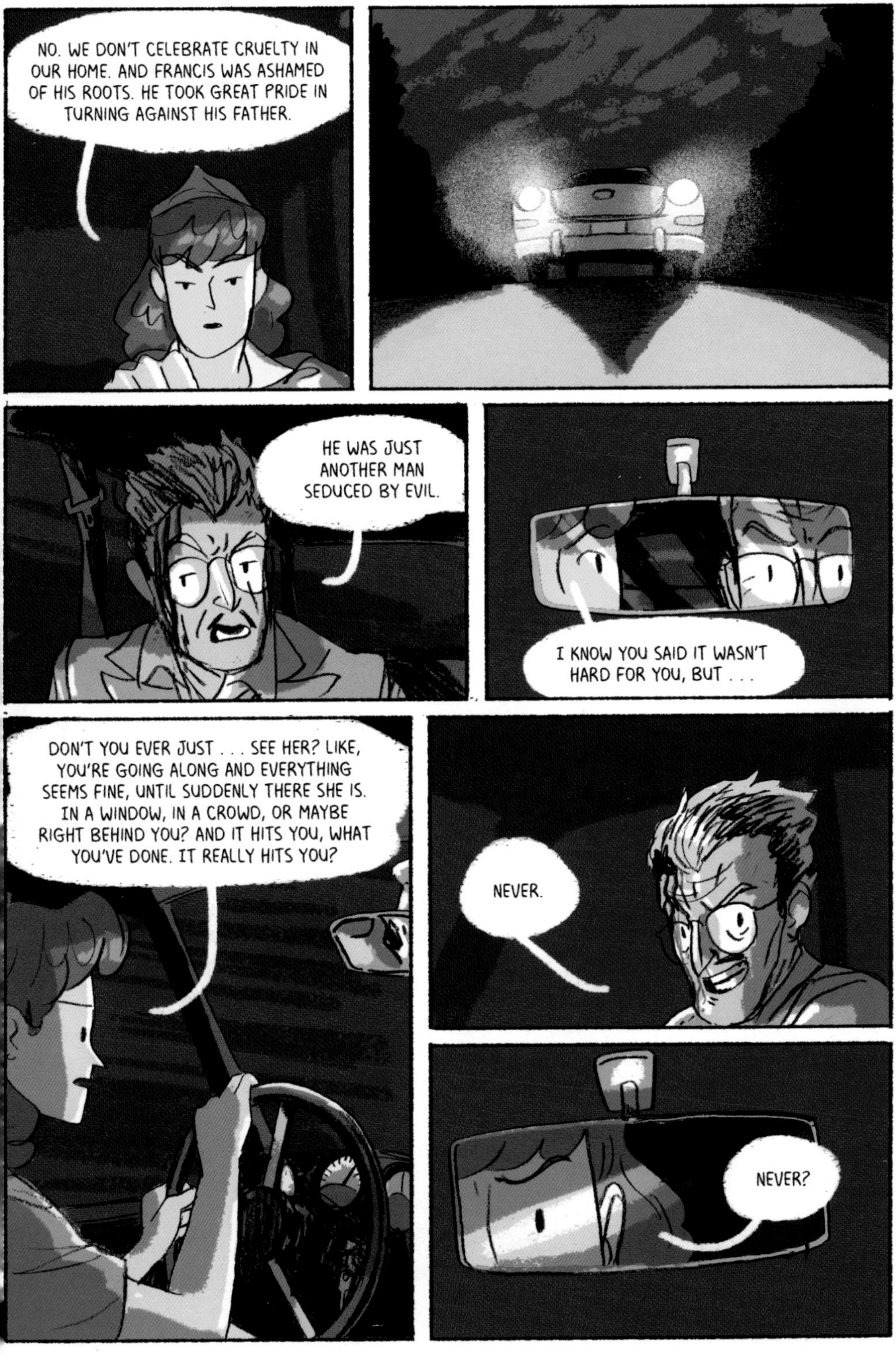
NO. WE DON'T CELEBRATE CRUELTY IN OUR HOME. AND FRANCIS WAS ASHAMED OF HIS ROOTS. HE TOOK GREAT PRIDE IN TURNING AGAINST HIS FATHER.
HE WAS JUST ANOTHER MAN SEDUCED BY EVIL.
I KNOW YOU SAID IT WASN'T HARD FOR YOU, BUT . . .
DON'T YOU EVER JUST . . . SEE HER? LIKE, YOU'RE GOING ALONG AND EVERYTHING SEEMS FINE, UNTIL SUDDENLY THERE SHE IS. IN A WINDOW, IN A CROWD, OR MAYBE RIGHT BEHIND YOU? AND IT HITS YOU, WHAT YOU'VE DONE. IT REALLY HITS YOU?
NEVER.
NEVER?

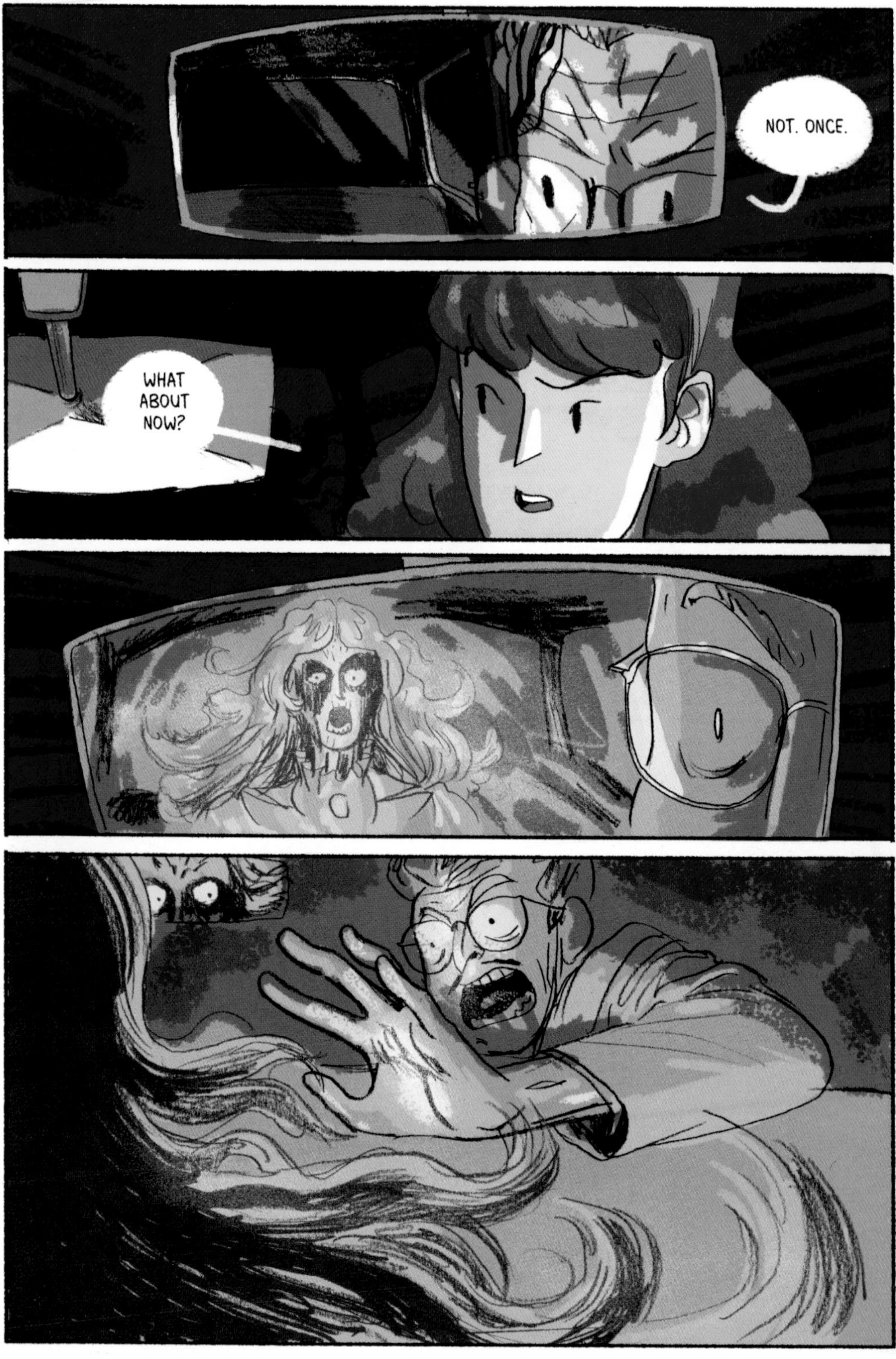
NOT. ONCE.
WHAT ABOUT NOW?

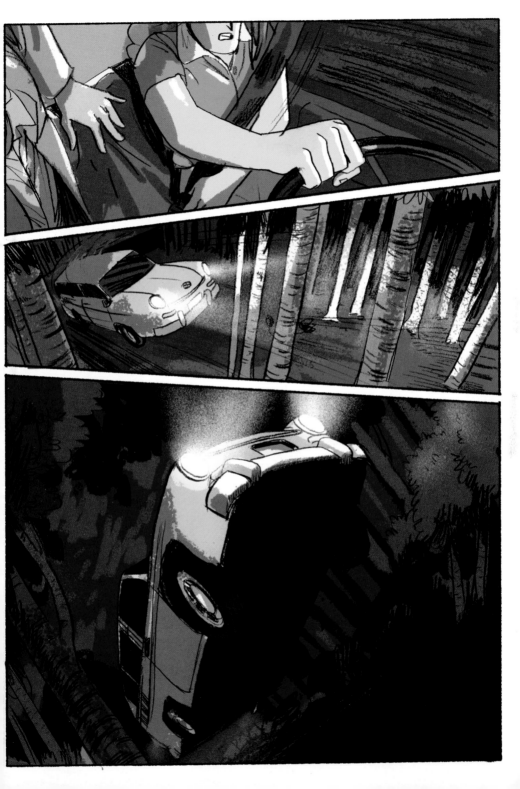

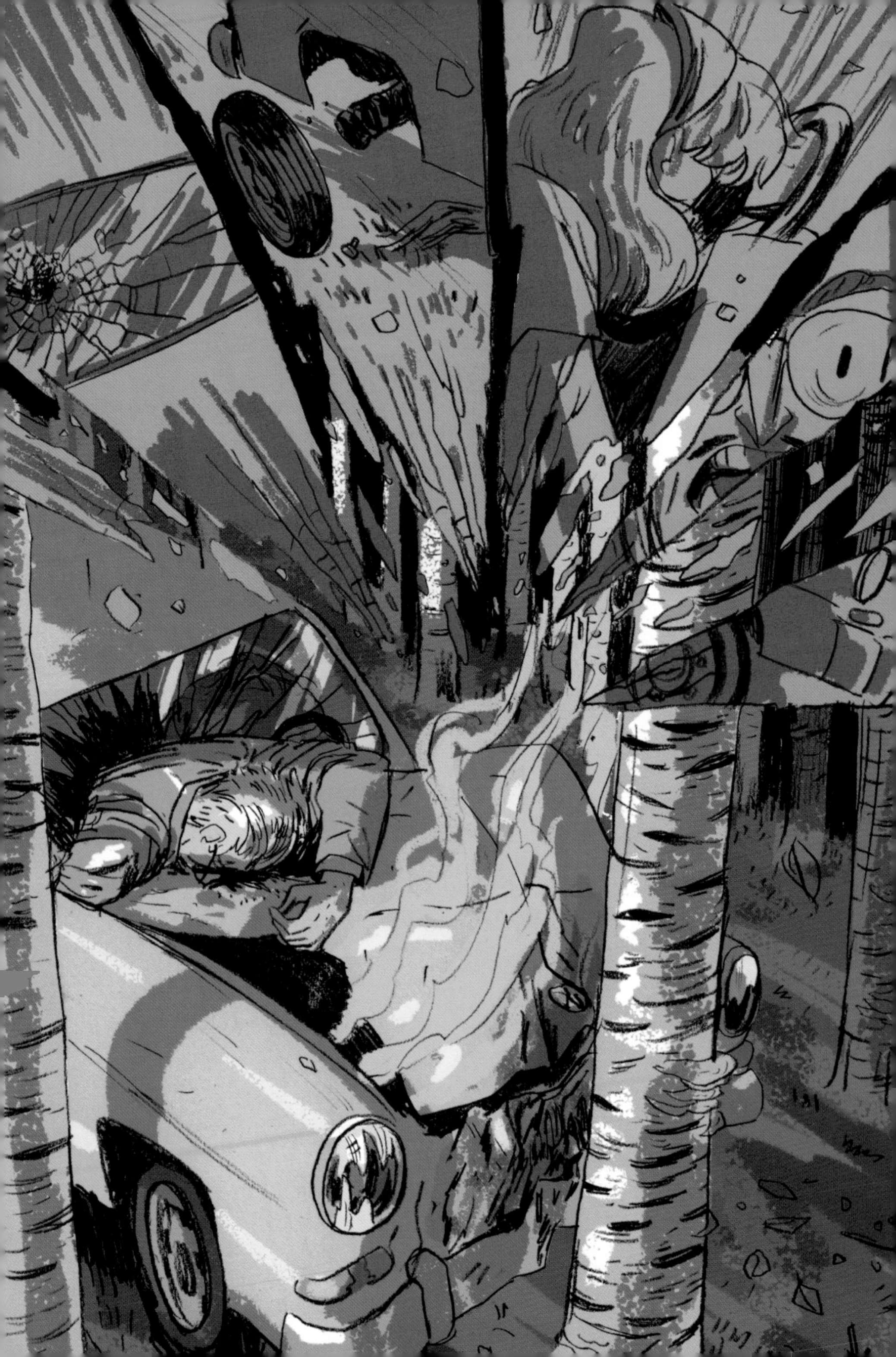

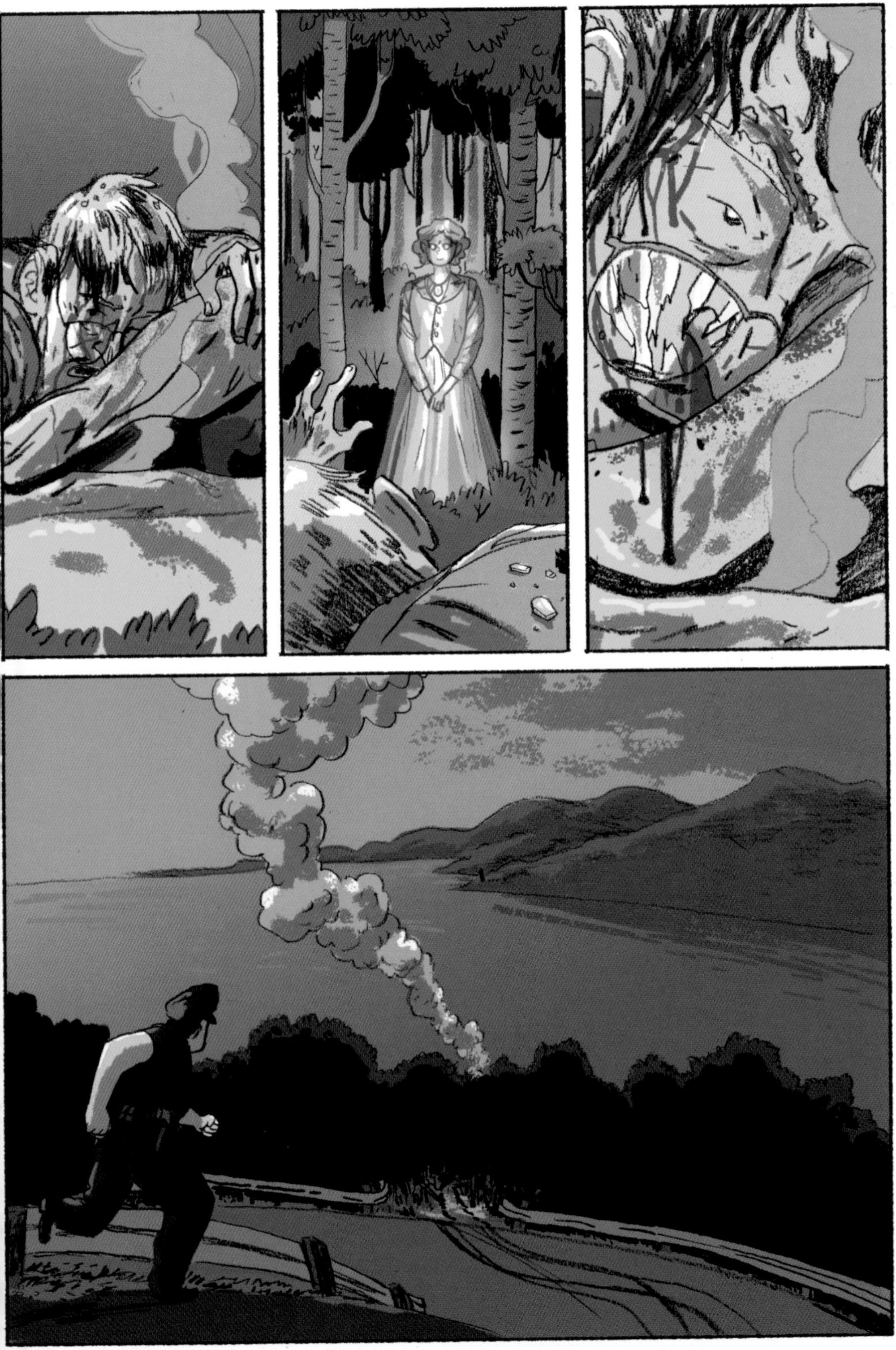

EPILOGUE

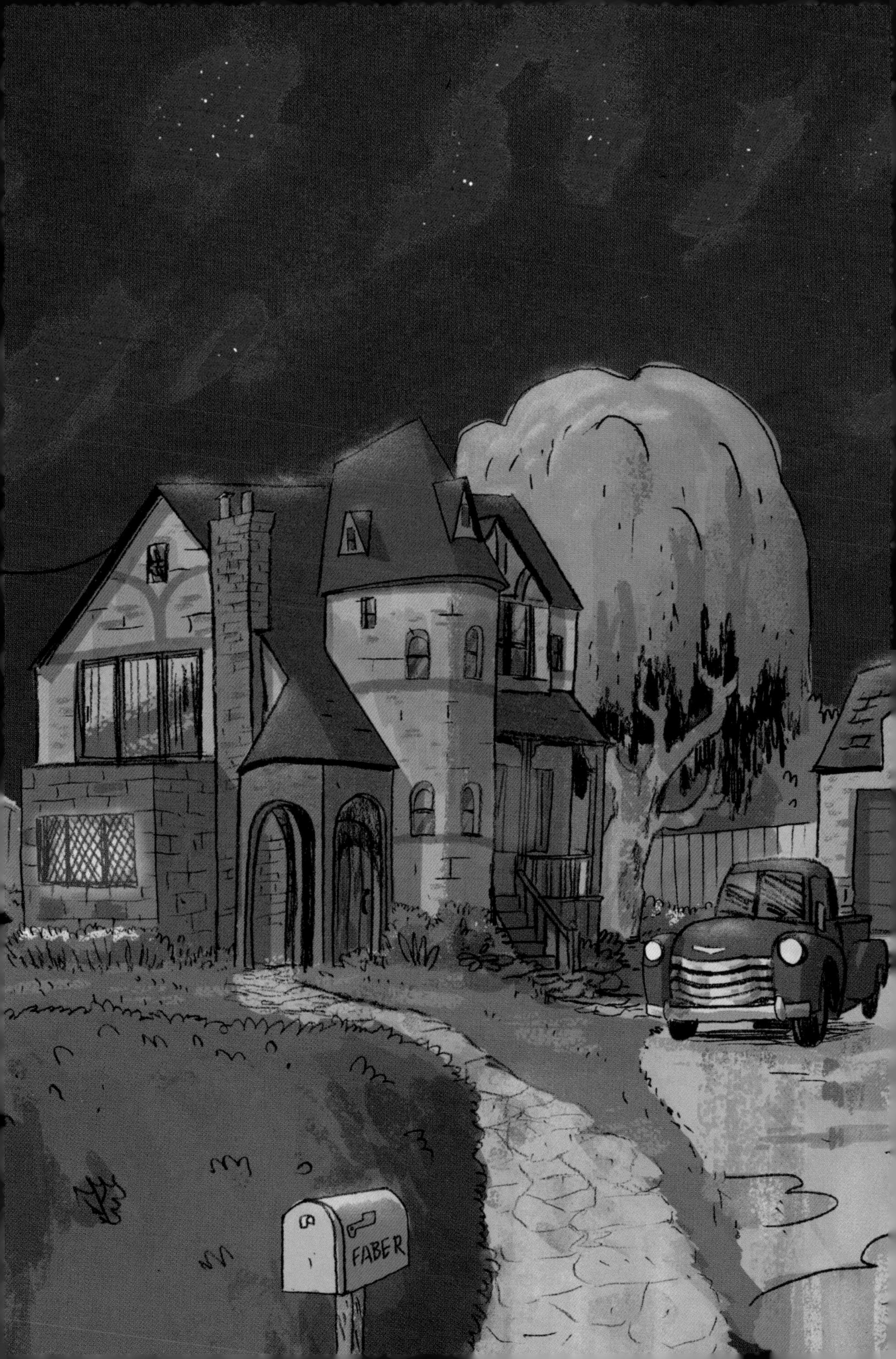
FABER

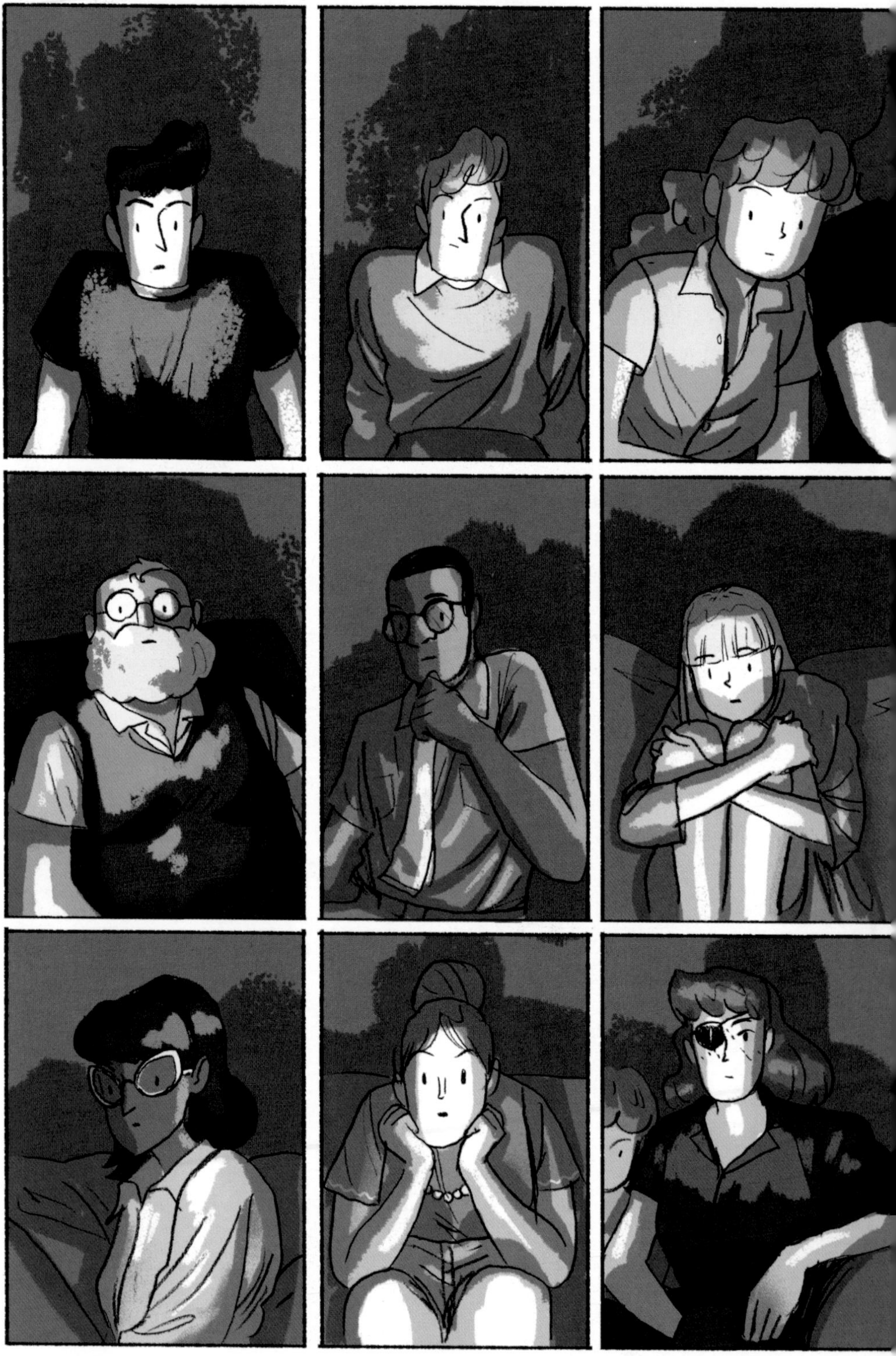

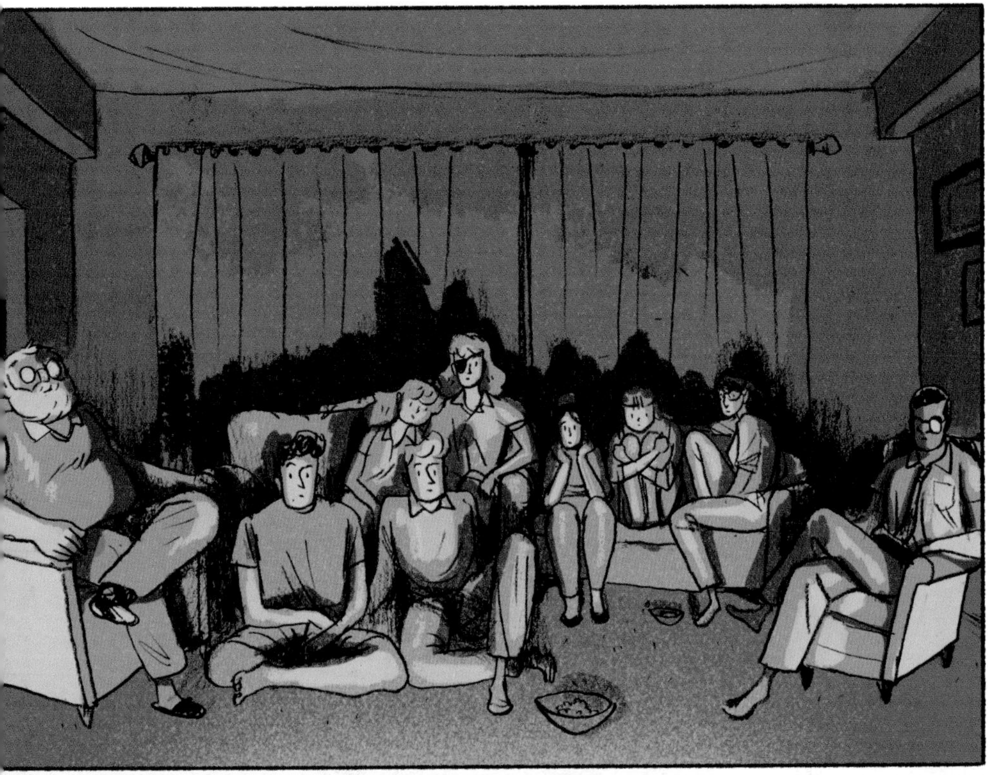

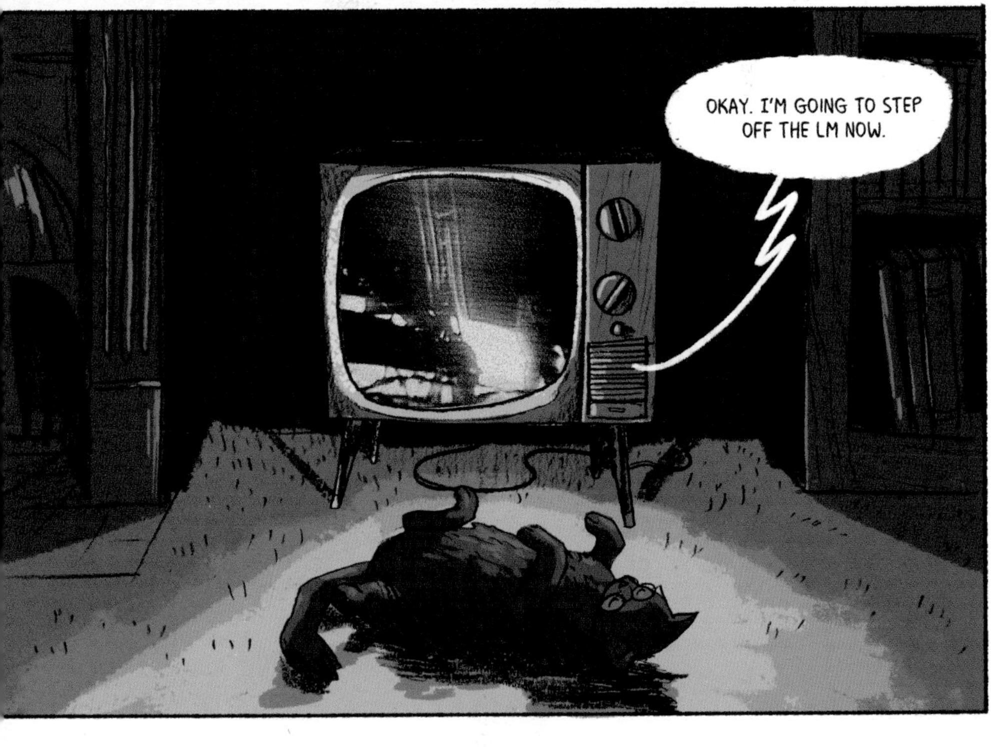
OKAY. I'M GOING TO STEP OFF THE LM NOW.

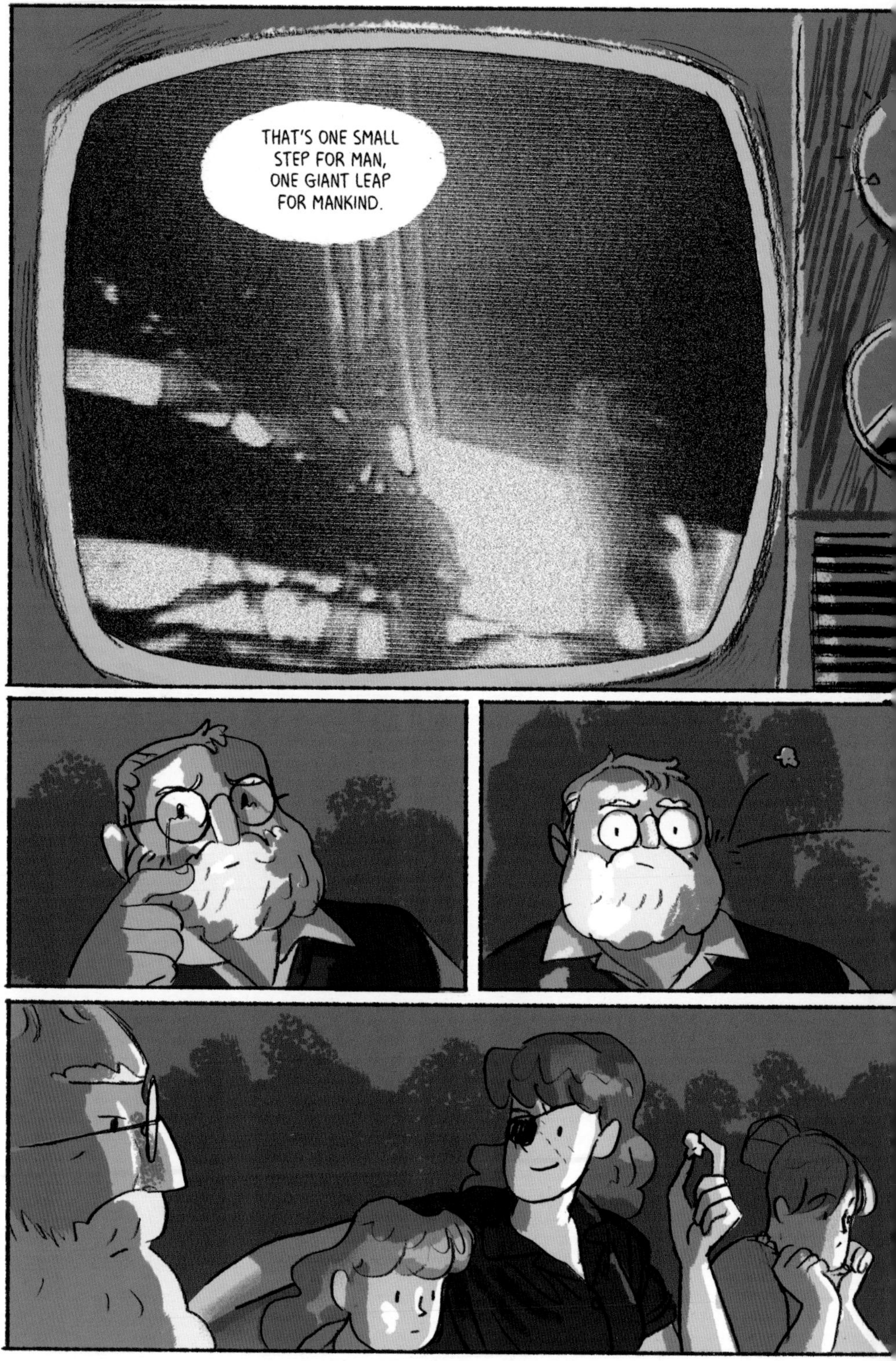
THAT'S ONE SMALL STEP FOR MAN, ONE GIANT LEAP FOR MANKIND.

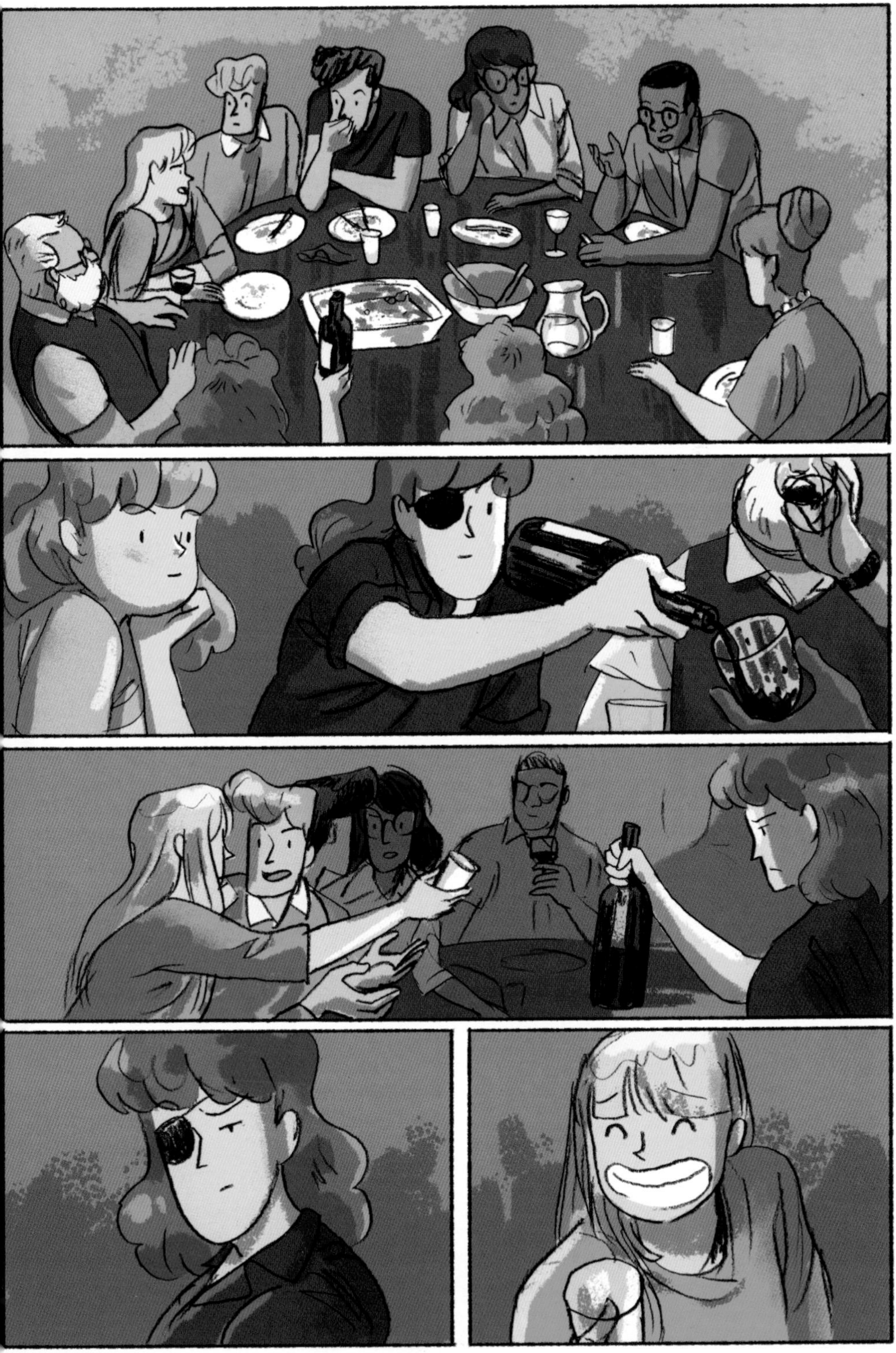

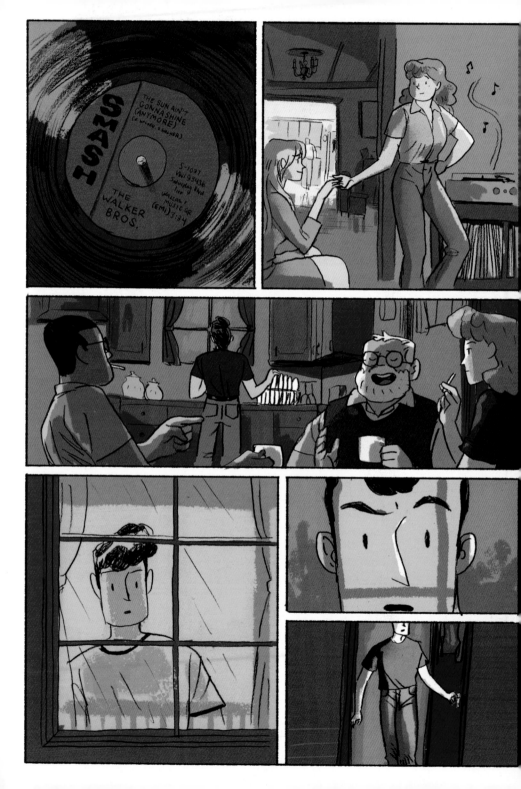

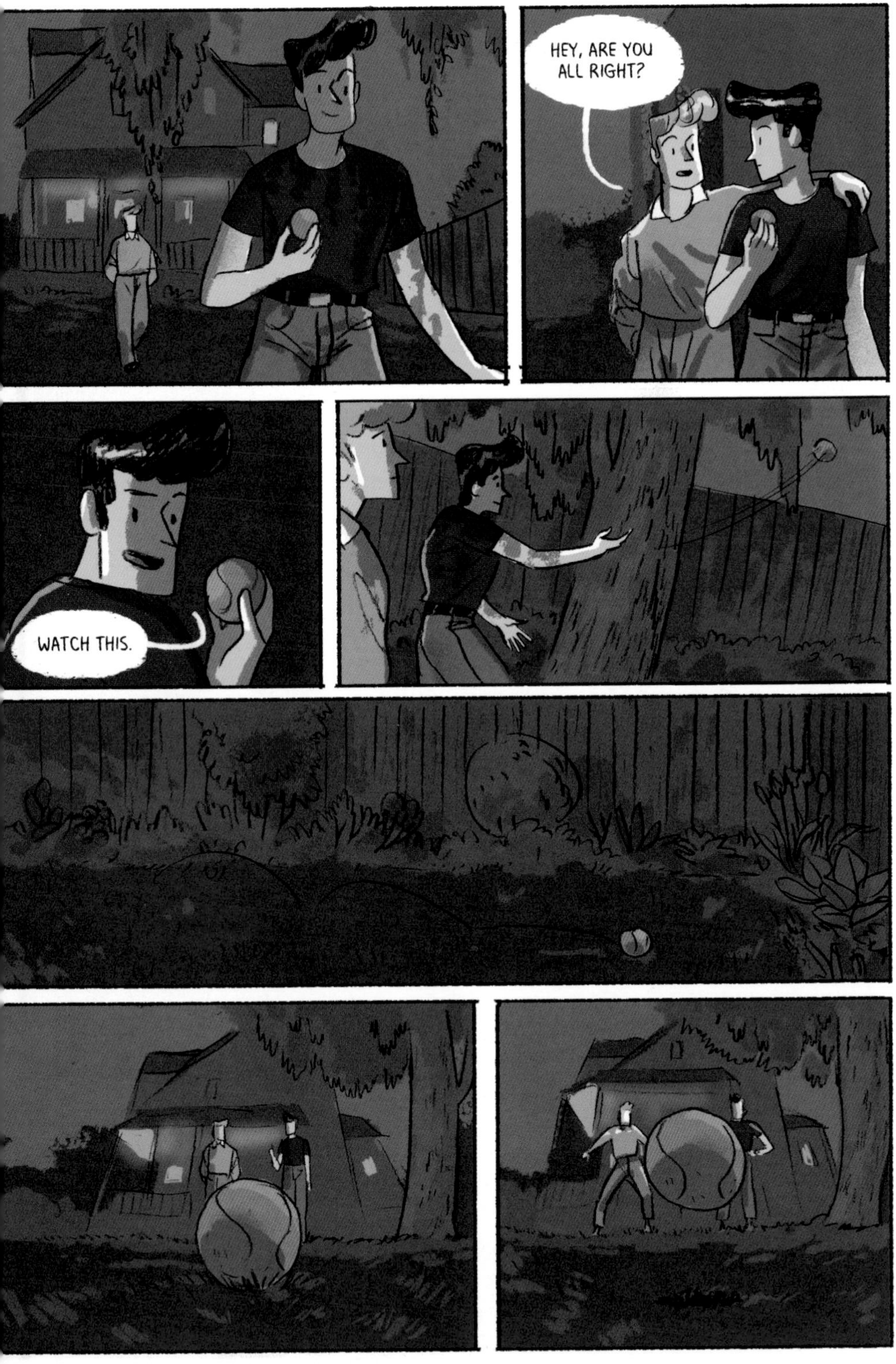
HEY, ARE YOU ALL RIGHT?
WATCH THIS.

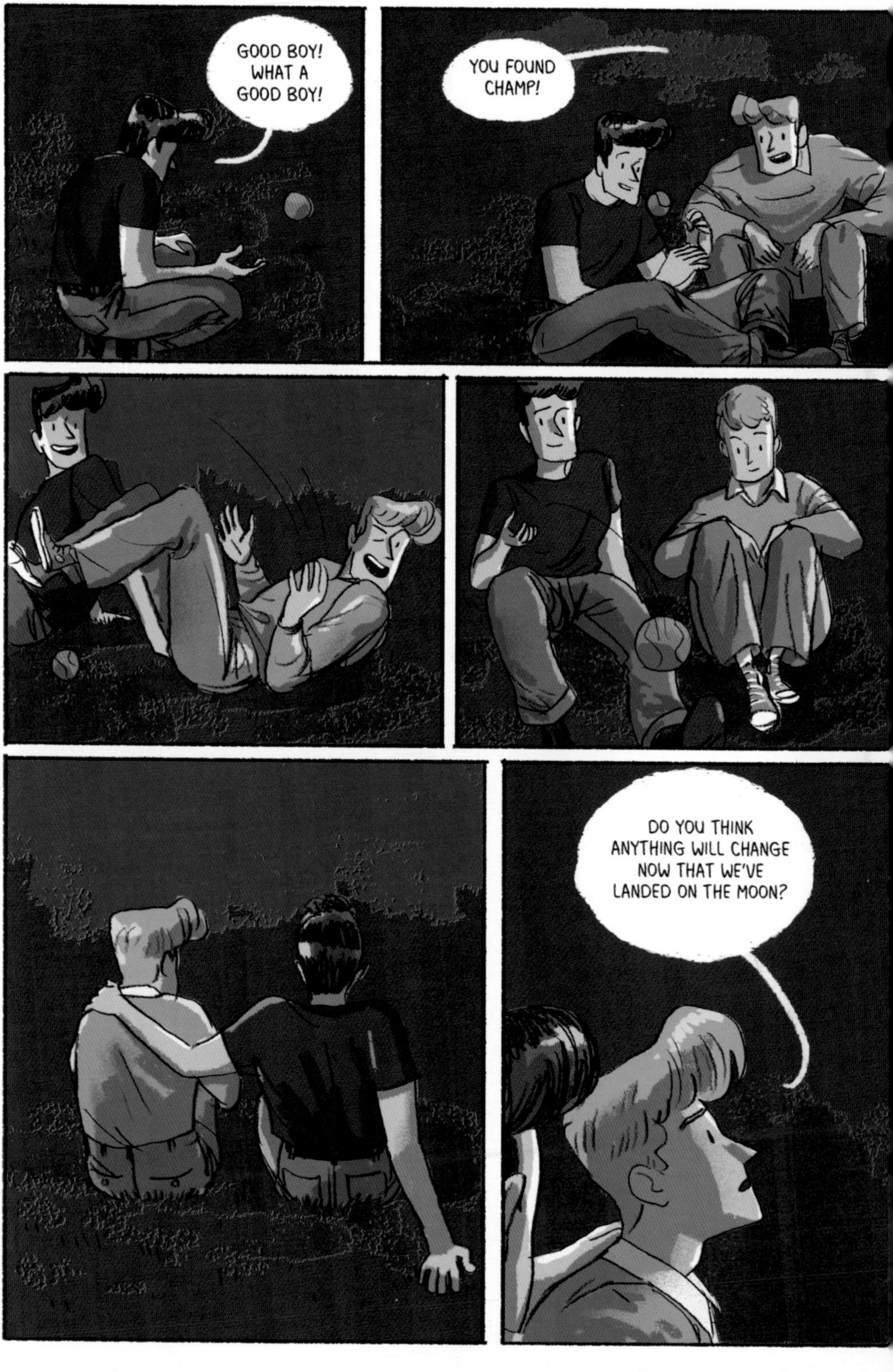
GOOD BOY! WHAT A GOOD BOY!
YOU FOUND CHAMP!
DO YOU THINK ANYTHING WILL CHANGE NOW THAT WE'VE LANDED ON THE MOON?

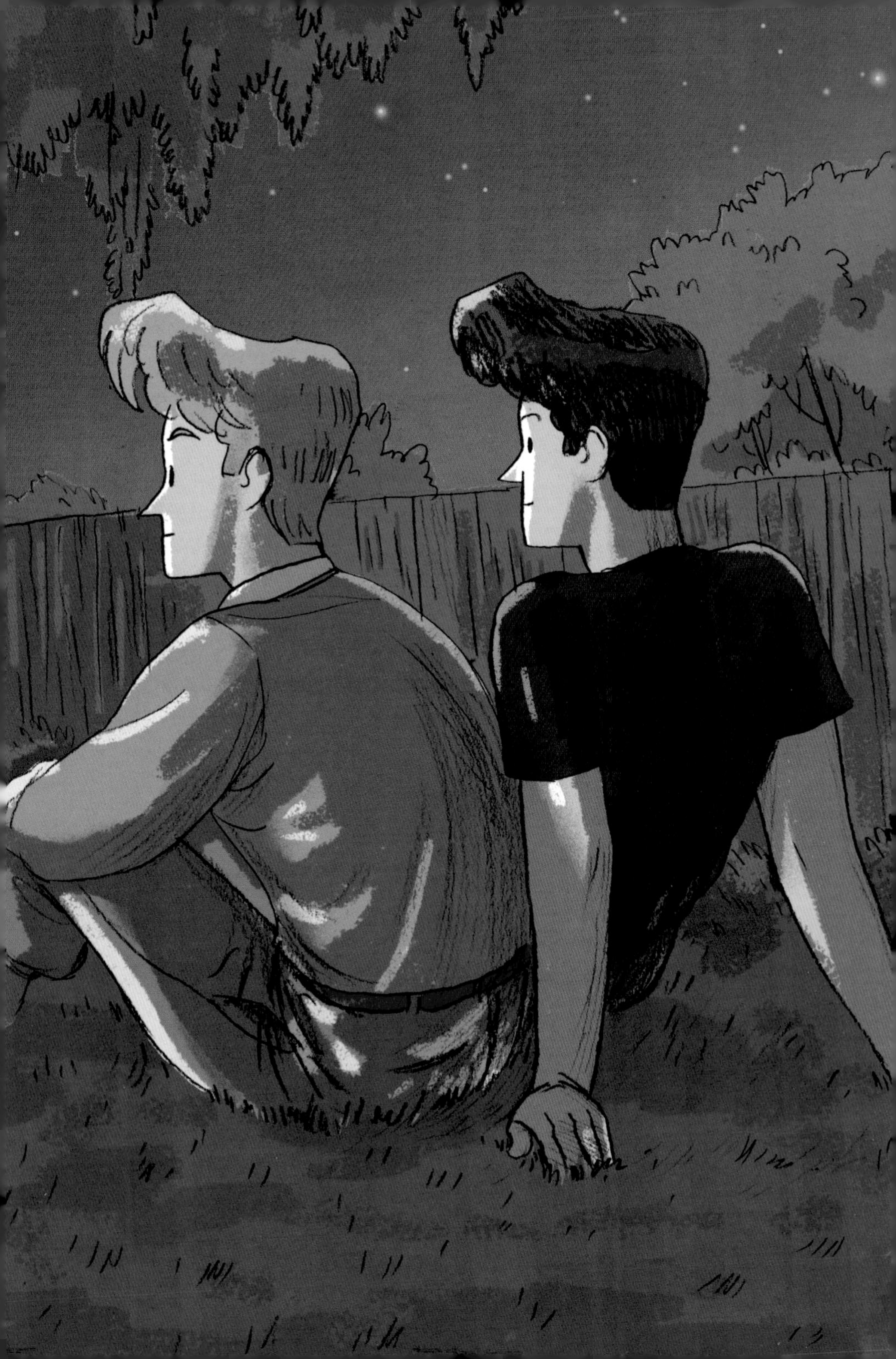

WILL BE BACK!

Look for their next adventure,
coming fall 2021!

_____

Visit **montaguetwins.com**

for news, galleries, playlists, and much more!

These are some of the first sketches of Pete and Al, circa 2012. Their quiffs have gotten decidedly smaller over the years.

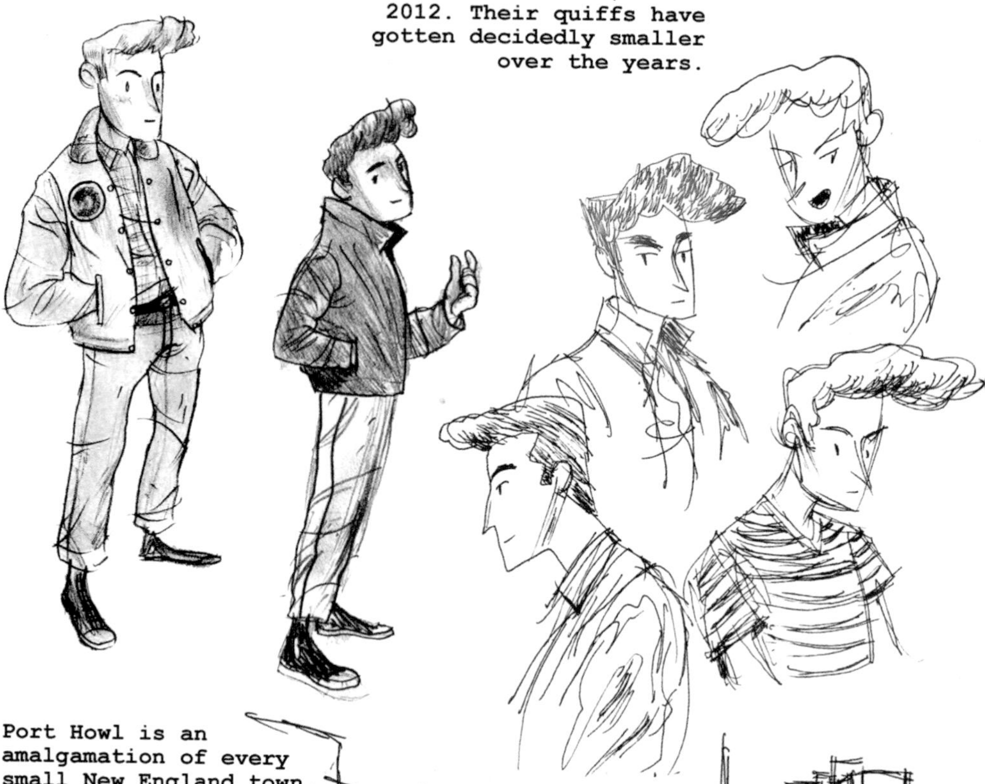

Port Howl is an amalgamation of every small New England town, so of course it's got a Main Street. I forget what town this reference sketch is from...

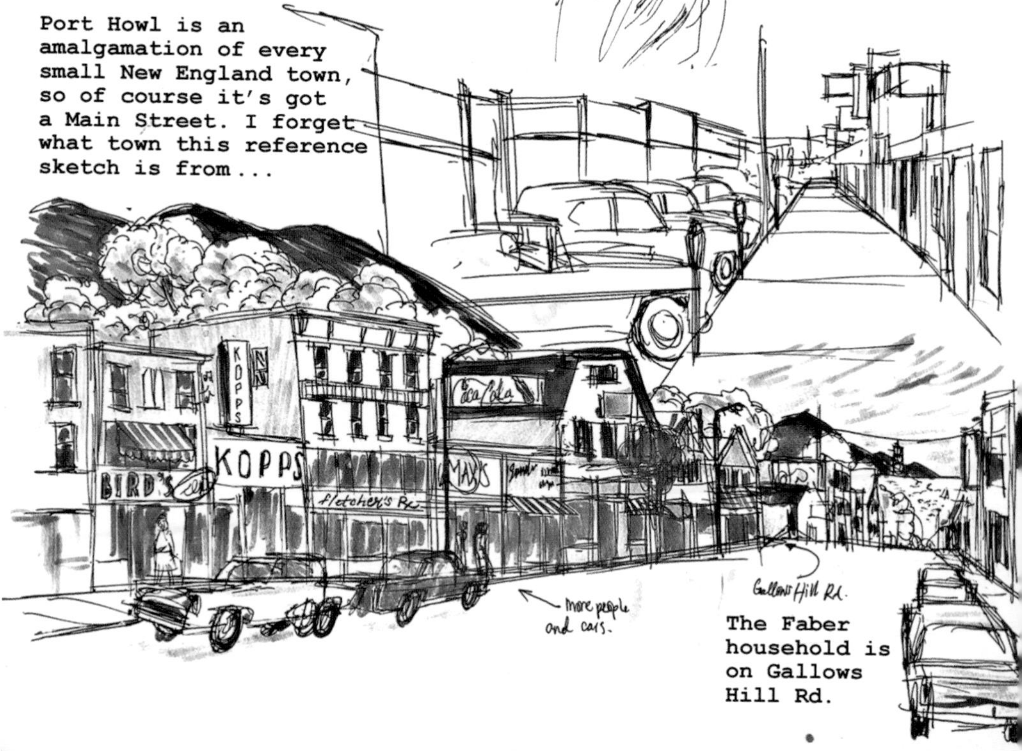
KOPPS
KOPPS
BIRD'S
Fletcher's Rx
MAX'S
Coca-Cola
more people and cars.
Gallows Hill Rd.

The Faber household is on Gallows Hill Rd.

ve always loved reading the original scripts of graphic novels, specifically in the back pages of *Dream Country*, volume three of Neil Gaiman's Sandman collection. This book would never have existed if I hadn't read *Dream Country*. While my writing may pale in comparison to that of a master like Neil, this can give you a sense of what the first step in creating a graphic novel entails. If you're interested in doing it too, I'll get you started:

Page One
Panel One
Go.

Chapter Two
PAGE 53
PANEL 1
Splash.
Exterior shot of resplendent Bradford Manor sitting pristinely apart from the rest of Port Howl. Not so much a house as a modest castle, it looms from atop a solitary hill known simply as Bradford Rock. From its south facing window one can see the entire town and a good bit of the Atlantic spread out before them. A lone gated entrance with a winding drive goes on for a hard mile before arriving at the imposing steps. The grounds are meticulously manicured with monstrous hedges and marble fountains. It is certainly the most beautiful residence in town, possibly the state, but there is something antiseptic about Bradford Manor. One might guess that it was some sort of historic site, that nobody could actually live in a house like this.
The storm that originated on the beach earlier that day has spread throughout the rest of Port Howl. Such a radiant morning devolved into total darkness. The rain is torrential.

PAGE 54
PANEL 1
We are inside Rachel's room. It is lit entirely by candles. There is an incense and cigarette smoke haze that permeates the air. She is lying on an ornate four poster bed. She's got an ashtray beside her. A cigarette is perched between the fingers of her left hand, the stem of a wine glass in her right. Sharing the huge bed, her little spoon, is a record player with the Zombies' *Odessey and Oracle* spinning.

PANEL 2
Realizing her cigarette is down to the filter, Rachel stubs it out.

PANEL 3
She swishes around her nearly empty wineglass. Across from her, in front of a large vanity, are her friends Marnie and Laurel. Marnie is braiding Laurel's hair.

                         RACHEL
              Girls, I'm fading here.
PAGE 55
PANEL 1
Laurel smiles and grabs a bottle off the vanity.

                         LAUREL
                Don't despair, *ma soeur*.
PANEL 2
Marnie gives Laurel's hair a quick tug.

                         MARNIE
                She's got two legs and a heartbeat, she
                can get it herself. Can't you,
                princess?

PANEL 3
Rachel begrudgingly sits up.

                         RACHEL
                You could at least give me plausible
                deniability should my stepmother
                question me about her ever-diminishing
                wine cellar.

                         MARNIE
                Tough love, babe.
PANEL 4
Rachel has gone to the vanity. She dramatically snags the bottle
with jocular severity.

                         RACHEL
                You know how I feel about limits being
                placed on me.
PANEL 5
Rachel takes a cigarette out of the pack with her mouth.

PANEL 6
She looks down at Laurel and smiles. Laurel is shyly looking
away.

                         RACHEL
                You're gorgeous. You both are. Thank
                you so much for coming tonight. I just
                thought it could be like old times, you
                know?

PANEL 7
A smaller panel. Close up of Laurel's hand flicking a lighter
open and the ensuing spark.

Rachel bends down close to Laurel to light her cigarette.

> **LAUREL**
> Anytime, Rach. It's really good to see
> you. To be honest, we weren't sure if
> you were . . . well, if your . . . uh .
> . .

> **MARNIE**
> If your porcelain fingers still knew
> how to operate a telephone.

Laurel's face has gone all hot. Whenever there is tension in a
room, she internalizes it. She knew Marnie wouldn't be able to
resist bringing up Rachel's absence. It was just so nice to be
doing something together after so long, and now it was going to
be ruined by Marnie's big mouth. So Laurel speaks, hoping to
break the tension.

> **LAUREL**
> It looks nice? My hair?

> **MARNIE**
> It looks great, hon. Trust me.

Rachel has turned back toward the comfort of her record player.
She sways a little along the way.

Marnie puts the finishing touches on Laurel's hair.

> **MARNIE**
> Voilà! You can look now.

Laurel turns towards the mirror and looks at herself. She feels
beautiful. Marnie has her hands on Laurel's shoulders.

Rachel is reclined on the bed once more.

> **RACHEL**
> What'd I tell you, Laurel? Gorgeous.

Marnie leans against the vanity, finally able to relax after two rigorous braiding sessions. Laurel is delicately touching the intricate braids.

                    LAUREL
          Thank you. I love it, Marnie.

                    MARNIE
          Well, now what should we do? I'm going
          to go ahead and say the drive-in is a
          bust. Nobody is crazy enough to be out
          in this storm.

PANEL 7
And cue the elements. Lightning strikes nearby.

PAGE 57
PANEL 1
A blast of wind blows open the French doors to Rachel's balcony.
Nearly all of the candles are extinguished.

PANEL 2
Now back inside the room, we are behind Rachel as she throws her
full weight into closing the doors, fighting against the wind.

PANEL 3
She is finally able to slam them shut and immediately sets the
lock.

PANEL 4
Breathing hard, Rachel stares out at the storm. The room behind
her is nearly blacked out now. Her face is brought into
silhouette by another shot of lightning landing nearby.

PANEL 5
Rachel picks up a recently snuffed out candle.

PANEL 6
She discreetly runs her hand over it and in that instant the
candle burns anew.

PANEL 7
She turns toward her friends with a smile twisting at the
corners of her lips. She's holding the candle in her hands,
cradling it.

                    RACHEL
          Who's up for something a little . . .
          sinister?

ACKNOWLEDGMENTS

This book has been in the making for over six years, and we are so blessed to know so many talented and supportive people who have helped shape this project and have participated in the journey. From the depths of our hearts, we would like to thank the following people:

Maria Vicente

Julia Maguire

Joan Lee

Kyle Mowat

Anne Thériault

Irma Kniivila

Hayden Maynard

Erin McPhee

Matt Coe

Sam Maggs

Jeff Lemire

Amanda Lewis

Annie Koyama

Aaron Leighton

Erika Turner

D.C Nchama

Amanda Row

Paul S. Fowler

Sammy Jamison

Rick Ilnycki

Matt and Laura Rushworth

Marc Whittington and his parents

The ATB team

Ajay Fry

Elvis Prusic

Queen Mob's Teahouse

Evan Munday

Ray, Stephanie